Dead Words Publishing is ~~proud~~ mortified to bring you "Uncle Shtunklucus" by SAGAMORE. The author's opinions are his own, and, obnoxious as they may be, represent a work of satire. All characters, places, settings, circumstances, timelines, dates, weather patterns, animals, laws, and other non-entities contained herein are fictional (even if they bear resemblances to, or share common names with, actual real-life persons who might grimace and cough erratically, and proceed to lose their lunch should they ever make the ill-advised effort to actually read any of this garbage). The author himself is also a fiction. Therefore, everything said in these pages is protected under the auspices of fair use! No business or other esteemed organization makes any endorsement of this work, nor should they, because this text is highly antagonistic towards consumerism.

Anyway, the author is about to explain his own legal reasoning about why he is not responsible for anything on the following pages, so if you are still left in doubt after that, please contact your authorized representative in Congress. God willing, they can help you, because we sure as hell won't.

FIRST PRINTING OCTOBER 2022
  First Revision January 2023
  {This revision is dedicated to PATSI, a fellow author who passed away
  yesterday & was the inspiration for one of the "main" characters!}

DEAD WORDS PUBLISHING
ARCATA, CA

[Also, neat fact: this font is called "Bodoni 72" and looks pretty elegant, and cool! It's a serifed font, and it came installed by default with Apple Corp's *Pages* program, for Macintosh.]

Dear Reader,

As I write these words, I am reminded of the social constructs within which we, by whom I mean artists, must conduct ourselves and our work. First and foremost amongst these, is that we may not use the names of others in order to disparage their characters, lest we find ourselves on the receiving end of a lawsuit, which is not the place any of us ever want to be.

But there is at the same time a certain ideal of liberty by which we are promised the freedom to express ourselves, to the point of vulgarity, obscenity, and indeed, slander of public figures. This freedom is often under assault in the highest courts of the land, as well-heeled lawyers swashbuckle their way to verdicts that destroy the livelihoods of those who may cross the line of singling out actual, real people in the pursuit of creative expression, and, indeed, in pursuit of happiness itself.

You may find there to be several, if not many, names of celebrities and other individuals who fancy themselves as being somehow important or relevant to our shared state of existence contained in the following text. This may or may not have been intended to slight the individuals so named. That is the beauty of a name, though: it can't be trademarked per se, as long as there's no specific commercial context given, so therefore, just because a name *seems* similar to the name of a famous person whose feelings are hurt by what is being said about the person in this story with said name, does not mean that use of said name was done with any specific malice, and, most importantly, in no way would it suggest intentional infliction of economic damages.

Now, courts in the UK may see things differently, due to the fact they have no written constitution or guaranteed protection of free speech. So, if you are one of the rich fucks so put off by what you think I've accused you of over the course of the following pages, GO AHEAD AND SUE ME IN GREAT BRITAIN. I HAVE NO INTENTION OF EVER GOING TO THAT SHITTY, DIRTY, STUFFY, PRETENTIOUS LITTLE ISLAND, NOR WILL I BE OPENING ANY BANK ACCOUNTS OR OTHERWISE HOLDING ANY ASSETS THERE. ALSO, I DO NOT RECOGNIZE THE AUTHORITY OF THE CROWN'S COURTS, SINCE QUEEN ELIZABETH II IS NOT THE RIGHTFUL MONARCH. I MET THE TRUE QUEEN OF ENGLAND,

ELIZABETH III. SHE WAS A SCHIZOPHRENIC POET WHO SPENT MOST OF HER LIFE LIVING ON THE STREETS STABBING PEOPLE SHE DIDN'T LIKE. SHE DIED IN A CAR WRECK DRIVING DRUNK IN THE RAIN OUTSIDE OF WEITCHPEC IN 2017. Her two young daughters, Elizabeth IV and Victoria II, were also killed, so the royal lineage is therefore extinct.

The people have spoken; long live the tribe of SAGAMORE.

Arcata
March 2021

Uncle Shtunklucus

A Novel

Chapter I

"OH, LOOK. YOU'VE GOT SOME POOP ON YOUR SHOE." There wasn't enough time to unsee it; the chickens had seen to that.

"It's alright. I have a Mexican maid," Howard offered.

"But won't she be marginalized by having to clean up your disgusting yardbirds' shit?"

"That's what I pay her under the table, substandard wages," Howard said, laughing.

"It's disgusting! Can you call her up and ask her to come over and clean it up, NOW?"

"But babe, I can't stand the sight of her face! I think she's Yucatanese, or something. Honduras," he tried. "They're disgusting. *Planet of the Apes* people. But it's alright, they have chickens. They know what it's about. I just don't think I can keep my dick hard if I have to look at her haggard, brown, bulbous face!"

Howard didn't mean to be racist; he was merely a product of his generation. And Meredith, bless her sluttily-clad heart, she didn't even care that much. "Howard, are you saying you aren't going to be needing me this afternoon?" There was a hopeful upward twinge in her posing the question.

Meredith didn't want Howard to be his weird self. Meredith didn't want Howard to have anything to do with her, come near her naked body, *nothing*, but he was a middle-aged man with money and a wife who couldn't give him an erection anymore. Howard had a kinky fantasy about bringing younger women to the creek in back of his house, and "spying" on them skinny-dipping. When he was a kid, something happened to Howard that caused this strange compulsion, but he never told anyone what exactly it was.

"Poop," Howard continued, "Poop is just a part of life. Everything does it."

"But Howard, it's more than just a little bit of poop." Meredith really wanted to get out of this. She'd come to realizing, the week before, that even as a desperate 22-year-old model/stripper/part-time hooker, she could be doing MUCH better for herself. Howard was, after all, weird.

Howard thought that a $50 bill for no sex required was a more than reasonable deal. And Meredith, having known Howard's daughter since the fourth grade, was playing him as the amateur-hour John that could build her resume. "Just take your clothes off and run down out the back door, don't worry, you probably won't step in any more chicken-dung." Howard was teasing Meredith; of *course* he hoped she would step in a big steaming pile of rooster turds! Oh, but she could even play slip-and-slide and face-plant right next to the rosebushes where the dirty birds always congregated in the hopes of pecking off some sweet rose hips and juicy bumblebees, to get her bosom and her ass all contaminated with mud-shit, like that dirty girl she truly was.

Howard wanted Meredith. He wanted her to get into trouble, naked, with some easily washed-off crap that would just force her to jump into that creek and get herself clean, *so* clean.

"Howard, you don't want me to touch the poop, do you?" Meredith was getting wise to his particularities.

"No, honey, I just want you to run buck-naked out my back door and plunge into that cold, lovely creek!"

"Howard, why do you have chickens, anyway? Do you even like eggs?"

Howard chuckled, his 50-something-year-old gut jiggling like a bowl of his grandmother's jello. "Babe, it's not me, it's Henrietta. She's just obsessed. I can't do anything about it!" It was a half-truth. Howard's wife *did* enjoy the company of chickens.

"Can you get your Mexican over here or not?"

"I told you. I can't stand the look of her face. Even if I had a half gallon of tequila and a sombrero to droop over my eyes!" Howard didn't mean to be racist; he just was.

"Howard, I don't see how I can ever justify dealing with your chickens and your weirdness for only fifty lousy bucks," Meredith said as she slid her panties off. "It's just not worth it anymore. After this, I'm done. I can degrade myself on Fans-Only for five times what I'm making from you, and still not have to deal with chicken shit."

Howard didn't complain; he merely rubbed the backs of his hairy knuckles excitedly, his eyes widening as he fixated on Meredith's well-manicured bush. "Babe, have I ever not paid you *and* given you a ride back to town?"

Meredith didn't bother responding. She just wanted to be though this as fast as possible... her tits mounted a mighty resistance as they pressed against her tight tank top, sent sailing over her head by her ruddy arms, firm and capable from an adolescence spent slinging pots of boiling potatoes to and fro the dungeon-like back of the kitchen at Diane's Diner. She stood in Howard's glass porch, looking every bit the average American woman as depicted on the Pioneer 10 placard, in case some extraterrestrial should ever be curious: a modest bosom, wide hips, a slightly sagging belly, firm thighs, and perfectly *normal* labia.

"OK, are you ready?" Howard had such a goofy look, a five year old boy at the state fair waiting for the cotton candy man to christen his first ride on the tilt-a-whirl, wishing there was still a one-hour photo store in town where he could slip the acne-speckled undergrad an extra five bucks to not report Howard to his youth minister for bringing in a disposable 35mm camera to have nude photos of a random woman in varying degrees of turpitude developed. Howard didn't like digital photography. It wasn't seedy enough to meet his needs; he was an old-school guy who liked old-school dirty girls. *Literally* dirty girls.

"Howard, I fucking swear on your daughter's life, if I end up getting splattered with shit I'm going to tell your wife *everything*."

"Honey, it's fine! Just a little bit of fun, that's all." But really, what would it matter if Henrietta found out? What had Howard actually done that was so bad? He was giving his kid's friend a job, something to get out of the trailer park where her own father would leer after her so bad on some days it seemed like the old sonofabitch might actually sire his own grandson.

The backyard was a mine of swampy ditches, with the fucking chickens roaming around freely throughout; there must have been at least thirty of the goddamned birds; pecking and cawing and crowing and clucking, they hid under low shrubs waiting for an opportunity to lunge at some tasty-looking yet probably inedible item. In the meantime, they busied themselves digging up piles of dirt, spreading said dirt to the four corners of Howard's property lines, and of course, shitting up a storm. Flowing along a 150 foot frontage of lush yet unkept and overgrown lawn, there was the creek, just a stream of water passing by the rear boundary of Howard's sad little spread. It abruptly appeared with no warning and just a muddy, crumbling bank to demarcate itself from the rest of the landscape.

Meredith took a deep breath. She wished she'd gotten high first.

CANDY ANDY WAS ABOUT TO GET the most rude surprise of his life. "EWWWWW, Prashaylata!" he roared. He'd gotten a nasty burn from the chemicals contained within the hybrid car battery he'd been playing with earlier. Now, it hurt. And when Candy Andy hurt, he lost sight of his words. "PRAY-she-la-taaa!"

Candy was stranded, badly. "Luckka-lutty, ash'ta-cutty!" He was going to have to spend the night at the Poop-Sit Motel.

Before we continue, a helpful guide from one Helmut Nuckmiëler would be in order. Helmut is the guy you call when you need something, a set of directions or any other reproduction of information that is best presented in list form, and indeed he even was hired to write one up pertaining to the guest rules and policies of the Poop-Sit Motel:

REGULATIONS AND GUIDELINES OF THE POOP-SIT MOTEL

- You MAY observe other patrons using the toilet in their respective rooms, as long as you're not weird about it. If you ARE being weird about it, Management reserves the right to assess a $25 surcharge, per night, per person being spied upon using the toilet.
- Rolls of toilet tissue are assigned per butt. Each butt gets ONE roll for the entire stay. The rolls are complimentary, but they are also travel-size. If you are a large person who needs to poop a lot and uses a lot of toilet paper to clean up after yourself, you may purchase extras at the Front Desk, between the hours of 12 Noon - 4 PM.
- Proper toilet use is expected of all our guests. If there is a suspicion

that a small child or mentally retarded person is committing an act of toilet abuse, Management will send an instructor to your room in order to educate the offender on the guidelines of acceptable behavior in the bathroom. The instructor may remain in the guest room's bathroom after the lesson to observe corrected usage habits.

- You will notice a barred window overlooking the toilet in your guest room. That barred window leads to a hidden passageway that is exclusively reserved for the use of the Wide-Eyed Man. He is a leftover mutant from the founder's family that stayed behind after they fled to the City. The Wide-Eyed Man is allowed to observe all guests using the toilet at any time, in any room. Period.

- Diapers may not be flushed, but a diaper-cleaning service is available for an additional charge. This does not apply to the mentally retarded. Separate arrangements must be made to deal with their diapers.

- If you suspect your toilet is not functioning optimally, you may request it be tested by the Bean Kid. The Bean Kid is a dedicated vegan who feeds upon soy and legumes in order to consistently produce high-quality, fibrous poop on regular intervals by which a baseline of toilet performance may be established. If the Bean Kid's services are rendered, and testing reveals that your toilet is not sucking down an adequate amount of fecal matter within a reasonable timeframe, you may be entitled to a change of room or partial refund, at the Management's discretion.

- If, however, you do request the services of the Bean Kid, and testing reveals that there is in fact nothing wrong with your toilet, that means you are being a difficult guest. The Bean Kid will then have your implied consent to use an article of your own clothing in lieu of toilet paper.

- Animals are not allowed in guests' bathrooms. Not even the smart, "potty-trained" cats. You may, however, purchase a disposable litter box shaped like a bird's nest from the Front Desk.

- The Pubic Hair Grooming Lady's services are available by

appointment ONLY.

"Belishtenda, BELEESCHTEENDAA!" Candy sung to himself. It was something he did whenever he was *too* worked up, like, he already was prone to fits of outbursts spoken in pure gibberish, but this was something special, when he was escalated to a point past even level eight, when nobody could touch him or get through to him otherwise.

Candy Andy may not have even been qualified to speak. He was old, yes, and he might've had a stroke at some point; nobody was quite sure, as nobody knew him, and nobody really cared.

So it's not too difficult to figure out what happened next: Candy was broken down and needed a place to stay, the Poop-Sit Motel was the closest thing to an actual place that was in any way, shape or form nearby to the desert mountain road he'd been driving upon, and even though in his mind, Candy was still in Texas; but Texas, this was not. He was about to realize it, the hard way.

"Shanna-DEE-shten?" He asked, trepidatiously, as he entered the room he'd been given a key for.

Silence. Darkness. But otherwise, exactly as the brochure had described. There was a bathroom, it did have a barred hole in the wall, the whole decor of the place was really *off*, and somebody had definitely been eating beans.

Candy was maybe functionally mute on the outside, capable of only unintelligible mutterings and exclamations, but the inside of his head still operated in semi-normal English. Without going so far as to gain forced entry into this tiny world in which he found himself continually consumed, try to imagine for yourself what it must be like to be a 75-year-old-man who can somewhat understand what is happening around him, but whom nobody ever would take seriously, *ever* again.

And that would've been it. Candy Andy wasn't going anywhere. He was old, borderline senile and about to drop dead. This would've been the end of the story, except for the fact that the Bean Kid existed, somewhat. The Bean Kid was there, about to make an appearance, and it was going to change *everything*.

THE FIRST THING YOU NEED TO KNOW about the Bean Kid is that he was having a bowel-movement emergency. The shit had backed up to the point of filling out his ass cheeks. Through years of reckless binge-eating and smoking questionable over-the-counter herbal products, he'd perforated his colon in multiple places, and the resulting poop would wind up billowing out to the edges of his *gluteus maximus*. He would contemplate his bowel troubles while squatted over the toilet bowl on many a fateful afternoon, reading the gut-gripping thriller, *One Went Flushy*.

Candy Andy, meanwhile, was wondering what ever happened to grilled hotdog culture. Candy remembered a time, not too long ago it would seem, that a family would gather at their local Diner on a Saturday night to eat a hotdog meal. The wieners were always grilled on the flat-top, Candy recalled, never steamed. Candy had realized, at some point in time when it was probably already too late, that he hadn't had such a hotdog dinner in what seemed to be a very, *very* long time.

He had asked a young kid about where to get a hotdog grilled to perfection on one of his previous roadtrips. Stopping off at a gas station in the middle of the fucking desert, Candy accosted a seven-year-old slurping from a large, decaffeinated "Fappachino" (they had to change the name around to not be the same as that other, similar beverage whose name sounds suspiciously similar to this; and the nimrod who came up with the concept also got all excited and flush with pleasure about the fully intentional reference to masturbation he'd worked into it), demanding that the youngster come clean to him about the last time he'd sat down for a grilled hotdog dinner with his family:

"Boy, don't you know where to get a decent grilled hotdog?" Candy asked, threateningly, and suddenly speaking English.

The child stared back at him, and continued to slurp, loudly. "Boy, when's the last time you sat down for a grilled hotdog dinner with your family?"

The child paused for a moment, and then promptly flipped Candy the bird.

Well, Candy didn't like that at all. What he did like was putting fake honey-flavored syrup on top of his grilled hotdogs. But he also didn't like the fact that he couldn't remember the last time that he had gone into a diner for a hotdog that was grilled the way he liked it, along with some yellow mustard, beans and white bread toast. And also, cigarette vending machines were there.

In fact, Candy Andy had a thing or two to say about the demise of the hotdog family dinner. There should be the entire family gathered together, wife and daughters in floral-print dresses, ankle-length, the men and boys attired in collared shirts with muted, plaid print color patterns.

He was going to try and convert the Bean Kid to this, in fact, if he could ever catch him, which was difficult. The Bean Kid mostly comes when you're asleep. Since you don't know much about him, or what he does, the first thing you need to know is that there's a mole on his ass that expands and contracts, depending on how full of shit he is. You should consider this a warning. If the mole is much larger in diameter than a quarter, he is going to violate the toilet in your room, rest assured. He was, after all, a mutant freak and disowned by his family due to having been born with a leaky colon, exacerbated by recreational drug use, so he had nothing else to do with his days but to lurk around the Poop-Sit Motel, a place nobody ever cared to wind up, but where we are all (and by "we," we mean, "you") are going to wind up to find the meaning of life, and God, and the American Dream. And love, and enlightenment, and the feast of the Seven Fishes and the eight nights of Hanukkah, and the secrets of the Universe (including, but not limited to, Fermi's Paradox, left-handed chirality, dark matter, the Pioneer Anomaly, and quantum gravity), and why Dialectical Materialism was never a sufficient ideology to bring about Marx's ideal communitarian utopia.

But Candy Andy was still hung up on his hotdog fantasy. Nobody, not even the Bean Kid, could understand why he was so fixated. So it goes with those of us who are unfortunate enough to end up old, and confused, and about to be diagnosed with dementia. Plus, he wasn't exclusively talking about Kosher franks; Candy was willing to consider any and all blends of beef *and* pork, which was completely incompatible with, and indeed highly offensive to, a wide range of Abrahamic traditions which were outside of Candy's very narrow mainstream Protestant views.

The Bean Kid, then, intended to teach Candy a lesson, because the Bean Kid was a Reform Jew, and plus, he was a *de facto* resident of the Poop-Sit Motel, while Candy Andy was merely a guest for the evening, not knowing what a giant and impossibly sticky pile of shit he'd just stepped into the midst of, nor did he possess the necessary footwear to successfully navigate said mess.

Therefore, two highly unqualified morons were about to do intellectual battle in order to prove ownership of the moral high ground over the other. If you recall previously, the Wide-Eyed Man was a entity contained within the confines of the Poop-Sit Motel and associated compound, and here we shall witness a demonstration of his raw powers of authority:

The Wide-Eyed Man outranked the Bean Kid, first of all, even though the Bean Kid was allowed to interact with guests, to a certain extent, while the Wide-Eyed Man was relegated to an observer status. This didn't preclude him from issuing orders, however. The Wide-Eyed Man, before he became a permanent resident of the Poop-Sit Motel and general surroundings, was a biologist who had perfected a parasite that could be used for mind-control purposes. This parasite would gain entry to its host via one's anus (which coincidentally, the Bean Kid had to have artificially enlarged in order to compensate for his otherwise fatally defective bowels), so the Wide-Eyed Man conducted a sort of experiment upon his colleague, and the results were that he could manipulate the Bean Kid's every action *while he was pooping*. Which was constantly.

Candy Andy had a plan to get back at the Bean Kid for trying to match wits. They sat down to share a meal, in the most distrusting of ways possible:

"Is this Kosher?" The Bean Kid asked, skeptically. He stabbed a fork into the grilled hotdog in front of him.

"What do you care if it is?" Candy replied, suspiciously.

"Actually, I won't touch this if it's not made from bean paste," the Bean Kid announced, suddenly remembering that he was supposed to be Vegan.

"What are you talking about, bean paste?" Little flecks of desiccated skin and long-forsaken crumbs of cornflakes were carried forth by the dry wind that was Candy's rotten breath. He still couldn't get it out of his mind, how disrespectful the younger generation had gotten, a symptom of the wider dilemma presented by the demise of the Saturday evening hotdog dinner tradition.

Meanwhile, the frozen-sausage song began playing in the Bean Kid's head. It was all about how to properly thaw your sausages so you can cook them and eat them without dying of pig bacteria, or worms. His dad used to sing the song when the Bean Kid was little, and then they'd go to the local gas station in order to eat sausages. Actually, his dad would eat the sausages, while the Bean Kid would go for a hotdog. This was not the wholesome variety of grilled hotdog by which Candy Andy would be satisfied; instead, it was a *steamed* hot dog. The Bean Kid's dad also said he was a wussy little girl for eating hotdogs instead of a truly manly meal, which was a proper sausage (the difference being, it is suspected, that the sausage contains gristle and heterogenous specks of meat remnants, from whatever animal it was that got slaughtered in order to obtain said flesh; it was probably a pig, but *not necessarily*), and for the rest of his life, the Bean Kid's dad would never take him seriously.

Which was so much the better, as it turned out. The Bean Kid was supposed to be a Vegan Jew, and yet here he was, quietly singing songs about thawing sausages under his breath to himself while he was supposed to be debating a senile White Supremacist, who had somehow decided he needed to take up residence in the cheap motel that the Bean Kid was entrusted to occupy, and whose patrons he was obliged to harass.

And the Bean Kid was upset. "Why are you such an angry young man, then, if what you needed wasn't a good, fulfilling, grilled hotdog dinner with a decent family, and perhaps, a bottle of pop?" asked Candy, quizzically.

"My dad promised me the Poop-Pump 2000 for my Bar Mitzvah, and instead, he just got me a N-64," the Bean Kid blurted out, sobbingly. He had in fact never forgiven his father for this perceived slight, and as soon as he'd turned 17, he ran off from the family dirt farm and found his way to the Poop-Sit Motel, where he'd taken up residence and dwelled within its dank and bizarre secret passageways ever since.

"You know, when I was a kid, I read a story in *Reader's Digest* about some young immigrant couple, poor, in New York City, and they had a weekly tradition," Candy explained, proudly brimming with faux-American pride. "They couldn't afford to go out for a grilled hotdog dinner at the local diner, but instead, they would just get a small package of franks from the local discount grocer, and cook them at home. *But*, they would add a little bit of honey-flavored corn syrup to their hotdogs, and that make it a special tradition, that got them through meager times until they were eventually picked up by the flagship of the American Dream, and then they moved on, upstate, where they settled outside of Rochester and started a family, and every Saturday night they could dress up in their second-best, after-church-clothes, because the next day was a Sunday, mind you, but they would gather as a family the night before, and they could have all the grilled hotdogs and beans they could eat, and mustard, too." It was an inappropriate story, but it was quaint. And, it was wholesome. It was an American flag being held indecisively by a mottled child on the Fourth of July. It wasn't offensive, it didn't smell funny, and it might have been old-timey, but wasn't that that the point?

Well, the Bean Kid was actually about to tune Candy Andy out, entirely. He was tired, and his fingers smelled like fish; he had no idea why. He was truly afraid, also, that if he had to continue listening to Candy drone on about his stupid, disgusting hotdog fantasy, he might start talking to the imaginary version of the economist Joseph Schumpeter, who sometimes would take up residence in the Bean Kid's head. And once that got started, things would get very complicated and confusing, and quite dangerous. There would be no discontinuation of the Bean Kid's fantastical conjuring of a long-since deceased Austrian academic who would've been better forgotten by history.

Things were getting so out of hand that the Wide-Eyed Man needed to finally step in and properly enter the scene. But before he did, *somebody* had to have a sudden moment of clarity.

CANDY ANDY CAME TO HIS SENSES, finally; he was greeted in his blank, confused stare by a barren stretch of desert scrub. There was no Poop-Sit

Motel, or any Bean Kid, either, for that matter ("Boy, you can't live off paste," Candy was getting ready to tell the Bean Kid as the opening salvo of a moralizing attack on the strictures of Veganism); there was only a senile old man who'd just spent the last eight hours having a make-believe conversation with derelict figments conjured by degenerative brain disease, and in that time he'd soiled himself, several times over, and he *still* wasn't sure where he was going, or even from where he'd come, so he just sighed and stepped back into his little putt-putt pickup truck and slowly crept away.

"THROW YOUR MOM AWAY," the sign read. Nobody was too sure what it was supposed to mean. But Davey had some ideas.

"If anyone ever asks you if you want to take a poo, you should always, *always* say, 'yes,'" Davey's mom told him once, emphatically. Davey just smiled and listened. He was a little sneak who always got away with stuff. So maybe it was *better* advice for him to completely disregard his mother's wishes, and *not* agree to hold hands with a stranger on his way into a public men's restroom facility.

But Davey had just stuffed his face full of warm, gooey pizza, and now he really had to poop, badly.

"Do you remember when MICHAELPAN came out to play with the Micropans?" His Auntie asked Davey, dreamily. Davey couldn't remember, because he had probably been pooping at the time; also, he didn't really care, because he was a priggish little squirt of a spoiled, miserable child. His Auntie, however, was fondly reminiscing about what had happened on that particular occasion:

MICHAELPAN, freed from all of his erstwhile political responsibilities as a nominal candidate for President of the United States, incorporated, at the time, was just having another off-day basking in his own misery and low self-esteem. He'd consulted a coterie of leading self-help authors about his dilemma; having rented several cheap, older limousines, several of which lacked air conditioning or toilets (he had always been led to believe, as a young man, that every limousine would have a fold-up seat revealing a portable latrine, in case any of the well-to-do clientele had to make a little dookie while in transit to their destination, and had been dismayed to find out that indeed, those limousines that he *could* afford for his half-hearted book-tour-cum-grassroots-campaign did not have such fanciful technology, and he and his staff were compelled to take turns using the comically large top hat worn by one of the drivers, who was an acid casualty of the end stages of the Grateful Dead, as a chamberpot of sorts while struggling through some acrid stretch of swampland, dying in the 100 degree July heat), he was now bereft of any firm grasp of his own identity or value to society. So when he'd come upon a fresh lot of Micropans being attended to by Davey's auntie while Davey was probably, but not definitely, making BM in the secret basement bathroom he'd constructed, because he was dodgy and weird like that, MICHAELPAN was momentarily freed from his despair and collapsing-weight-of-the-world-on-his-shoulders complex.

"MICHAELPAN played with those Micropans all afternoon," Davey's Auntie proclaimed, triumphantly. What she failed to mention was that *none* of the Micropans present that day answered to the name, "Marneshta."

"HEY BUDDY!" SHUPPEL UPTION EXCLAIMED, earnestly. "Your dog is walking sidewards! Hey! Hey buddy!"

The man continued walking his dog, which was, actually, walking sideways (the dog was defective, but it was okay, since it had a decent insurance policy). He had a personal policy of not engaging with the sort of people that Shuppel mostly resembled: slacker, useless college students who thought that they were smart, or something.

And, true to form, Shuppel was being a particularly poor excuse for a waste of an existence on the day in question. He was drinking something that "wasn't water" from a glass bottle concealed within a brown paper bag.

Outside, it was warm, and green. And, it was bright. It was, essentially, the least challenging environment a human being could ever find themselves in. So it was that Shuppel Uption was loitering on a well-to-do person's front lawn, who felt it their civic duty as a dyed-in-the-wool liberal to tolerate such shenanigans. And surely, Shuppel was full of those.

There were several other things of particular interest to nobody at all that Shuppel happened to observe while he was lingering about, being completely unproductive during a perfectly normal workday:

- At least five cars came to a halt at an imaginary stop sign. They were confused, and scared. And high on marijuana. And stupid. As clear as the weather conditions were, and as completely straight as that stretch of street was designed, these petrified morons were so incapable of successfully operating a motor vehicle while stoned that they perceived every flapping leaf and screaming squirrel as an immediate collision danger, and rode their brake pedals accordingly, until, as Shuppel saw firsthand, they brought their sorry parade of minivans and SUV-crossover-type vehicles to a standstill, just staring off down the roadway, wide-eyed with panic.

- Gene Simmons was crudely operating a cheap, electric set of hedge-clippers while wagging his tongue at unassuming members of the public. Nobody was ever quite sure *why* Gene Simmons did this with his tongue, which is, as most people are well aware, better kept contained to the inside of one's mouth in order to assist with vocalizing words and directing food towards the proper teeth for chewing or gnawing, as would be appropriate. Anyway, his band was no longer popular since most of their fans from their 70s heyday were now stricken with diabetes and confined to wheelchairs. So, Gene became a landscaper, and not a very good one at that. He struggled to keep an even line across the tops of even the most basic of hedgerows.

- Some men in hi-vis apparel were plotting something. Ostensibly, they were municipal workers, orchestrating some minor act of infrastructure improvement, but Shuppel knew better than to take them at their word. In reality, they were employees of the *true* non-governmental organization which masquerades as the UN but actually exerts global domination vis-a-vis weather manipulation and mind control. They were installing test devices into the sewer that could direct microwave energy beams filled with disinformation and cancer-causing frequencies directly into peoples' buttholes.

- A Sheikh man was standing in front of his convenience store, arms crossed, glaring disapprovingly at the entire world before him. Some white supremacist eco-warrior kids had accosted him the week before for having an overflowing dumpster that was spilling garbage out upon the vacant lot next to his shop. They demanded he clean it up and remediate the dirt that had become contaminated, or else they were going to descend upon his business with chains and metal pipes, and kick him repeatedly with their Doc Martens. This was not the American Dream® he'd been promised.

Shuppel then emitted a loud belch which released a toxic cloud of brewer's yeast spores, the byproduct of a contaminated batch of high-gravity malt liquor that had failed to be filtered from the bloom of microorganisms within. These little buggers were now free to land on anyone and anything within the blast radius of Shuppel's burping. The spores found their way into follicles and crevices, and even someone's foreskin, where they took up residence and multiplied, leading several months later to a diagnosis of phimosis, which is what happens a foreskin can no longer be retracted from the glans of the penis, resulting in "ballooning" during urination and a general "stuck" feeling; it was the same condition suspected to have influenced Hitler's megalomaniacal ambitions, as his frustration from being unable to pee and ejaculate properly led to him logically blaming the Jews for the whole ordeal (since they ritualistically sacrifice the foreskins of their baby boys in order to appease their bloodthirsty tyrant of a god).

MICHAELPAN, HOWEVER, WASN'T AROUND or listening to their pathetic little complaints or concerns. There were more pressing matters at hand. MICHAELPAN's dad, God, had just disinherited him from the throne of the kingdom of heaven. Then, God died.

MICHAELPAN was most upset when he found out that he wouldn't become the next all-being of creation. His best friend, Satan, dressed up to take him out to a bar to commiserate in misery over a shared bottle of fine Scotch.

Satan was actually possessed of an ulterior motive: true to his deceitful nature, he wanted to play a sex-fantasy game wherein he took the form a statuesque blonde, and had MICHAELPAN roleplay as Cupid. [The real Cupid was a heroin junkie, and even though he had the body of Adonis (who was, in reality, a fat asexual curmudgeon who made sculptures of himself to look like his ideal lust-worthy mind's image of the body type that would be most desired by the swinging, bisexual "in" crowd of ancient Greece), and just the most amazing mop of messy blonde hair that screamed freak in the sheets, he was impotent due to his opiate habit, and actually quite boring and uninspired even when sober.]

Satan spent all day having his minions fit him for a bright, red cocktail dress, apply layers of Venetian ceruse, cherry lipstick and a penciled-in beauty spot, just so he could end up at a nondescript local tavern with MICHAELPAN, who came dressed up as a lame excuse for a Robin Hood joke, failing to grasp how special of an occasion this was for his best pal, Satan, who, beside his sheer joy at the death of God, really wanted to get fucked, *hard*, by Cupid.

MICHAELPAN was too angry at his dad to be of any use. He neglected to let Cupid out of his cage so he could go have a date with Satan, and try to scrounge up 50 bucks so he could go cop a fix of heroin, which was going to be laced with fentanyl, obviously, so that then MICHAELPAN would have to scramble to try and resurrect Cupid, which he couldn't do unless he asked his dad, God, for intervention. God was tired of playing drug counselor, and also, he was dead now, so that wasn't even an option; now every time Cupid OD'ed, he also died a little bit, *for real*. And slowly, he began to look more like a zombie than a love-fairy.

Satan looked down his golden horn-rimmed glasses at MICHAELPAN, disappointedly, as MICHAELPAN proceeded to fume and rant about his station in life.

"Like, I get it," he slobbered, the booze quickly catching up to his sad rhetoric. "My dad, was, he was, he just got raised to be a petulant little, RUNT, he always was *bitching* and *moaning* about his brothers, and how they would, like, be better at sports and getting pecked at by Ravens. But! He wanted to play hardball with me, sometimes it was baseball, and he, he would *hit* me with the ball, because He. Told. Me. That. Was. Going. To. Make. Me. A. Man. But, dad, I am *not* a man!"

Satan sighed. He didn't know why he even bothered to think this was going to be a halfways decent idea. He wasn't getting laid, no matter how drunk and horny MICHAELPAN was and leering at what he started to think *might* actually be a real woman. Satan shuddered at the thought.

"You're not an all-being, either," Satan said, coyly. He'd rather be having cocktails with a goat.

"And that's another thing!" MICHAELPAN continued, waving his arm recklessly around the bar, knocking over two drinks in the process.

"Hey!" one of the fellow patrons yelped as his single-malt Scotch went flying.

Someone had drawn some crude shit on the wall of one of the bathrooms, which had commanded the Bartender's attention, since he had a mild form of obsessive-compulsive disorder, and just couldn't let it go. He was seething every second as he'd been pouring drinks for these sorry sods that were congregated in his establishment on this particular evening. After he'd made that last neat pour, he made up his mind that he *absolutely* had to deal with the situation. In the Bartender's vivid imagination, a n'er-do-well by the name of Charles had scrawled a lewd depiction of himself fornicating with the mother of this guy who, he felt, hated his guts. Even though, in reality, the questionable spot on the toilet stall's wall had been scrubbed at least a dozen times since the actual crime had been committed, which was a rather mediocre statement about how the only time this person felt like scrolling through the gay hookup-app "Grindr" was while they were having a bowel movement, the Bartender was convinced that the ink would come blotting back through the steel-wool-scoured paneling and reveal some heinous truth about the actual intentions of his imaginary friend, Charles.

So, when MICHAELPAN went and made a mess out of at least two persons' evenings, the Bartender was busy growling and grunting and searching high and low through the cleaning closet for any exceptionally mean, fast-acting corrosive agent. The best thing he could find was a jar of lye, which he stuck his hand directly into, and began rubbing the toilet stall's wall frantically, as his skin began to disintegrate and leave smears of blood and dissolved tissue all over his work area.

"Sorry, buddy," MICHAELPAN said, nonchalantly. "Lemme buy ya another. Bartend!" MICHAELPAN's dark, beady eyes scanned the room frantically. There was nobody immediately present to fix the poor man's ruined drink, so MICHAELPAN took matters into his own hands. He catapulted himself over the bar, haphazardly, creating an even bigger mess out of the situation, and then began sorting through the bottles of liquor in a most deranged fashion. Casting aside multiple bottles of perfectly fine vodkas and rums, he eventually found the motherlode of Scotch, lifted the fullest bottle, ripped the nozzle off, titled it back, and began swigging intently.

SOMEBODY WAS ABOUT to attempt to write some poetry. Like all the rest, this poem began the very same way:

These are the names of monsters.

Then, the poem kinda stumbled around, trying and subsequently failing to find itself:

Stalled out, engine stall—

Aerodynamic stall;

I am stalled out.

The Poet scrunched his face up and stared hard at these words through his crooked spectacles. "I don't like it," he mumbled, indecipherably.

"Did you put out cheese for Mitt Romney?" His wife asked, demandingly.

"What... why? Whatever for? You mean, like, cut-up cheese?"

"You know what happens if you don't put cheese out for Mitt Romney," his wife continued, uncertainly.

"Nothing. Nothing at all happens if we don't put out cheese," the Poet proclaimed, indignantly. He was correct; and that was the most terrifying thing of all. *Nothing.* Nothing had no form or shape, and could not be confined to even the darkest reaches of the Human psyche. Nothing was implicitly scary, and every person who ever lived spent their entire lives fighting against its inevitability. Nothing was the thing waiting at the end of all days.

So, cheese must be put out for Mitt Romney, so that nothing doesn't happen. Let's try this again:

"I am so sorry, dear wife. I will slice up some various cheeses and place them on a small platter, and put them out, just like Mitt Romney likes."

"That's better. Thank you, dear."

"You're welcome, dear."

"Don't get caught like a deer in the headlights, dear," the wife continued, like an ambient tone-poem comprised of discordant sounds. It sent a shudder right down the poet's spine to hear her say such a menacing thing.

Mitt Romney was the name of their cat, who was a minor monster, but cheese is actually not very good for cats. They can have a little bit of it, once in awhile, but it can wreak havoc upon their obligate-carnivorous digestive tracts otherwise. The myth got started by some random rumor that Mitt Romney liked to eat little chunks of cheese as a meal.

Mitt Romney wasn't a cat, however. He was a man, and a semi-successful politician, and the namesake of this random, weird, otherwise useless aging couple's cat. But none of those predicates made the feeding of cheese to the cat an appropriate action.

Dopamine, propane, the Poet continued, aimlessly. He put the cheese out for the cat anyway, because the cat was sort of a pompous jerk for the most part, and the Poet didn't really care if it ate too much cheese and got constipated as a result. He wasn't going to pay for any more veterinary care for the stupid thing; his wife made more money than he did, since she still had a job, at Wal-Mart.

He stopped, and thought a little bit more about the situation; then, he doubled back, and confronted his bitch of a wife. "I don't think it's fair that you should be so mean to me about everything. You know I haven't had a satisfying dump in months now," he said, regretfully.

"Just have some of these. Here!" His wife shoved a box of Poopwells'® patented digestive cookies in the poet's direction. They were guaranteed to make you poop better. They were mushy chocolate cakes that tasted like baking soda, coated with a fake-candy shell that had imitation sugar in it. They looked like what Richard T. "Dick" Doobler, founder and creator of the Poopwells'® brand, thought that every turd should look like. It was *fresh*. For old people.

And that was the fatal flaw in Doobler's erstwhile multi-level-marketing scheme: he didn't plan on the elderly suffering from bowel obstruction often enough to be useful as consumers. "They're like Devil's food cake," he would say to the hip young people who he thought would like his special, disgusting cookies, "if the Devil were made out of poop!" And, Doobler was probably at least semi-retarded (like, not bad enough to have to spend the rest of his life in adult daycare facilities and getting all giddy and sloppy when the special-needs assistants would strap them all down into the shortbus seats and take them for a field trip to the duck farm, where they could pet the birds and a few of them got hissed at by the geese, which led to them screaming and crying and attempting to bash their heads against the wooden fenceposts, and soiling their adult undergarments; no, Doobler was a more garden-variety sort of mental invalid , like the numbnuts who can't remember to close their gas flap door on their giant monstrosity of a gas-guzzling SUV before driving off, probably with a long sheet of toilet paper trailing their left shoe after having had explosive diarrhea in the gas-station bathroom where they *had* to spend at least $5 on gas that they really didn't need in order to get the key from the disinterested man reading the lifestyles section of a hardcore pornography magazine who was tasked with running the otherwise derelict minimart, because normally they go to the generically exclusive wholesaler's club down on the other end of town, where they could save 10 cents per gallon if they purchased two bakers' trays worth of white-bread muffins that week), so it's not like many people took his poop cookies, or indeed, any of his other companies, too literally, at all.

Doobler's first invention, in fact, was called the ULTRA-fuck Deluxe, which wasn't sure if it was supposed to be a kitchen gadget, a sex toy, or a discreet listening device intended for espionage, both business and romantic. So nobody was surprised that he couldn't sell his patented line of Poopwells'® digestive biscuits. First of all, they were absolutely disgusting to anyone except for maybe some old people who were too far gone down the lonesome road of senile dementia to know or care about the taste, but Doobler got told that he *shouldn't* target senior citizens, because it could be construed as being discriminatory. Black and gay people who were still of working age should also be considered for marketing eligibility, since both groups also occupied privileged status for being handicapped, and might also have issues with pooping regularly. Black people eat too much fried chicken, naturally, and that would always lead to spending up to 50% more time on the toilet than is absolutely necessary (John Witherspoon, in the groundbreaking 1995 docudrama *Friday*, illustrated this point in excruciating detail). And the gays have a nasty and juvenile habit of shoving things up their butts that don't belong there, so clearly they need some help getting all of that impacted fecal matter dislodged.

None of this really mattered to the Poet, who was working on a new equation, in order to solve the creative mysteries of the Universe with one succinct refrain that would echo across the nooks and crannies of all timespace, for eternity:

Michael FRAKEY-la,

Michael FRAKEYLA;

Shandra LOOMMIS!

Now, the deeper meaning implied by the Poet's writing of these nonsense words was unclear. It was purposely vague by design, intended to leave people pondering the big five questions: Who?/What?/Where?/When?/Why? And then, never to provide any definitive answers.

But in the absence of authoritative opinion, idiots will make assumptions; and so, idiots did. First, there was rampant speculation that MICHAELPAN may be somehow involved. His media representatives denied this; yet still, the rumors persisted.

And then there was Shandra Loommis, which sounded suspiciously like a senator from Wyoming. Actually, it was a replicant of that senator, which was supposed to help the robot army take over and win the war of attrition against water, and all the rust it created. They desired a perfectly dry planet, devoid of oxygen and replete with rare minerals. Shandra Loommis was going to be their spokesperson, manipulating the masses into engaging in small acts of self-sabotage, like not eating enough leafy greens, in order to hopefully, eventually, bring about armageddon.

A ROVING GANG OF IDIOTS was out to cause trouble, and possibly break the law. They were:

- Smiles. He'd be properly introduced later on, possibly.
- Dial. He thought that he was Irish. But in Ireland, it is actually known as the *Dáil*, and Dial was not a member of it, nor did he have any Irish ancestry. But it was fun for him to pretend like he did.
- The Grandfather of Poop. He called himself this because he was the oldest of the group, but nobody really expected that he was *anyone's* grandfather. That would've meant that, at some point in the perhaps distant past, he had gotten a woman pregnant, which was entirely unlikely. He had the personality of a dead raccoon, and all the charm to match. Women would rather make uncomfortable small talk with a socially awkward, overweight dwarf who worked in IT than go on a date with this guy.
- The dog who kind of looked like that dog from that one ad. You know, the one where he drools a lot and tries to speak. And gets mocked for it.

They had gotten bored while binge-watching that show, *Farting Around with the Cuppertons*, which was some absolutely pretentious slop of a period-piece about an aristocratic and classy English society that never actually existed that was streaming on some cut-rate internet service provider's in-house competitor to broadcast television.

They were supposed to have gone to the Denver Donkey Show, but their minder, a leotard-wearing woman with a puffy labia that stood out all silhouetted against the crotch of her signature garment, making people think that it was really just a man trying to tuck his wee-willie-winkie between his legs so he could *pretend* like he was a woman wearing a leotard, had a mental breakdown because of this, and couldn't attend to her charges that particular day. [The state government had sponsored a program to pay willing individuals a sub-minimum-wage stipend in order to look after the "differently abled," as the government literature referred to these mental midgets. The Leotard-

Wearing Woman was bereft of opportunities otherwise, as she'd been rejected by the US Olympic committee when she'd tried to sign up as a gymnast, because she was wearing a leotard, and because they had that doctor who touched a bunch of other young women in a non-medically-relevant manner, it was determined that the women on the gymnastics team would have to be wearing *unitards* instead, so that they didn't tempt other male doctors to perform unnecessary medical examinations. And because the Leotard-Wearing Woman refused to change her outfit, since it was an integral part of her core identity, they rejected her; and she didn't have any other viable career paths. That's when she saw a billboard advertising a need for adult foster care services, to be performed as an independent contractor, with no benefits.]

Anyway, before they set out on their adventure, they were coached by their virtual aide, in whose care they were left as a substitute for the Leotard-Wearing Woman, as to what to do should there be any sort of funny business afoot, as they went and explored the great wilderness that was the general public:

"And what do you do if someone offers you a poop popsicle?"

"Smile!" said Smiles, innocently.

"Die," commented Dial, pugnaciously.

Grandpa spun around in circles, trying to recite the Gettysburg Address. The Dog proceeded to lick its asshole, in case its flavor had changed in the last five minutes, which was the last time he'd checked down there.

Grandpa was also upset, because he felt that dark-skinned people were making his life difficult. He had been watching Fox News again, and they did absolutely nothing to dissuade him from maintaining this biased and incredibly *rude* belief. It wasn't their job to provide education; their mission was to deliver entertainment and confirmation of prejudices deeply-held by older people, so that they could joyously reminisce about days long gone by, which never existed in the first place, just so they could forget to change their adult diapers, because that is an embarrassment that any of us would rather suppress, deep into our subconsciousness.

So the team was going out for a stroll. "Sounds like a bunch of jerks, if you ask me," commented a random passerby, of whose opinion nobody had asked. Dial wanted to stab the guy. Smiles just grinned at him, mercilessly, as the parade commenced.

The Denver Donkey Show was off-limits to this wayward group of degenerates, obviously. Tickets had been purchased, and subsequently scalped, in the names of these three (the dog was omitted from the get-go, since everyone assumed he'd just eat the ticket, and then shit it out, and *then* make someone pick up the poop and sift through it in order to delicately piece the torn, ragged and stained shreds of paper back into a negotiable instrument. There were people at the larger banks, in fact, who provided this service on a daily basis to their more well-heeled clientele, who owned expensive and highly defective canines that would commit such atrocities against extremely valuable pieces of paper. These poor saps would spend most of their working hours picking through dogshit in order to recover their customers' high-stakes assets, and that is why the International Bank Shit-Pickers Union eventually went on strike, because the health benefits were not adequate to protect against repeated incursions of dog diseases, such as heartworms, which would cross the species barrier and infect these unassuming hourly wage-slaves and take up residence inside their guts, and require multiple rounds of treatment, surgery, and even unnecessary chemotherapy in order to get their bodies back into a condition where they could preform at a baseline level in their lowly occupation, that being professional dogshit picker, and otherwise be completely unable to muster enough energy to pursue out-of-work pastimes, like attending their inner-city schoolchildren's soccer games held within abandoned warehouses, played with soccer balls stitched together from rat hides. So the union went on strike, and all the pickers lost their jobs immediately, because management-level corporate types do not tolerate dissent amongst the ranks of their peons. And the asset classes then found out about NFTs, and promptly dumped all of their wealth into those, instead, which dogs could *not* eat, unless they stored their digital assets on a thumb drive and left it carelessly out somewhere that a small animal would mistake it for a tasty peanut bar, or, in the case of most dogs, a lovely pile of cat turds. Then, they would have to call up a technical support representative, who would lovingly and caringly walk the rich asshole through the necessary steps to untangle their USB storage device from whatever fecal matter was entombing it) so the machinations of global capitalism were protected, which was the most important consideration to make in any given situation. It was therefore a net gain for the entire economy that the minder of the gang had such an existential crisis.

It was detrimental for the gang, however. The Denver Donkey Show was quite a spectacle to behold, and, if these morons had actually been able to attend, they may have come out of the experience acting a little bit *less* like the jerks that one guy thought that they were.

The Denver Donkey Show started off with a parade of beautiful burros that were directly imported from Mexico, led by a naked Cowboy (except he still had on a cowboy hat and spurs). Then he would hand off the lead to his burro train to an assistant, probably a little creep they liked to call "Mortimer," and head over towards the other side of the stage, where there was a naked Cowgirl with perfect, tight blond braids and a voluptuous ass that was toned and conditioned from many years of experienced horseback riding. Then, they would have sex. A Japanese midget wearing an octopus costume would emerge from the shadows, proceeding to molest the couple with bright, purple tentacles while the Cowboy was secretly trying to overcome his same-sex attractions in order to maintain a suitable erection for the cock-hungry Cowgirl, who was also a reigning mechanical-bull-riding champion at multiple local bars. Being molested by a midget in cephalopod apparel really wasn't doing the trick for the lonesome cowboy, but still, he was getting paid a certain amount of money to perform what was otherwise a boringly straightforward and mundane act of staged intimacy, in public. The tentacles tickled his balls and asshole, and while he tried his damnedest to remain aroused, none of this was really *doing* it for him, and at that moment, he would shudder and quickly develop an advanced state of dick-panic. He remembered the other boys in the locker room when he was younger, teasing him and calling him "Floppy Do-Right," since he would neglect to continuously stroke himself to impress his peers, like all the rest of them did; he instead let his flaccid penis dangle down, crookedly, to the right. He would start crying into the Cowgirl's tits, and she would sigh, and roll up a cigarette with one hand while the other was buried, deep up inside the Cowboy's rectum, trying to coax him into finishing off the job he'd been hired to do. The Cowboy would convulse and spasm, as he was conditioned to do every time he had a nervous breakdown, and urinate a bit into the Cowgirl's ripe twat. [Cowhands don't bathe regularly, so there were antifungal agents offered contractually to the performers.] She would then toss him to the side and stomp off the stage in extreme frustration. The audience loved it.

What else did they have going on at the Denver Donkey Show? Oh yeah, there is this one part when a morbidly obese man clad only in dirty tighty-whities makes obscene gestures towards the audience, and then demands that a well-kept middle aged woman offer up her toy poodle, which she's allowed to keep with her in public spaces because it's been certified as an "emotional support animal;" and, shocked and unwilling to risk the ire of the audience for committing a grotesque act of non-compliance, she reluctantly hands her dog over to the man. He grabs it by the neck, and proceeds to the center of the stage, where a toilet that is specially equipped to support the girth of the fat man has been strategically placed. Holding onto the clueless canine with one chubby hand, the guy proceeds to have a very noisy and extremely public bowel movement. He then grabs the poor poodle, the fur of which is always pure white and immaculately groomed, and uses it in lieu of toilet paper, and, once he's finished, he releases the dog, screaming and yelping and covered in shit, by flinging it towards the best-dressed member of the audience.

Critics loved it. The Denver Donkey Show won multiple awards over back-to-back years, although they were just pointless local awards, chamber-of-commerce style commendations, so it didn't really matter that much.

It certainly didn't impress Dial. "They should fucking die, all of them," he growled, menacingly.

"Smile!" Smiles admonished him, commandingly. Grandpa grunted, and the Dog lifted his leg to pee on the nearest object.

The gang continued their walk. Suddenly, Smiles seized up, jaw agape, gesturing wildly towards some bushes. "There's a boy peeing in the yard!" And indeed, someone's child had been released into the wild, to compete with the Dog to see who would become the reigning neighborhood urination champion. The kid was on a roll, and he *might* have actually beaten the Dog, who was suffering from early-stage renal failure, had it not been for Uncle Michael, who emerged from out of absolutely nowhere and beat the boy over the head with a shovel, because he didn't like it when youngsters would whip out their little pee-pees and piss all over everything, because he was jealous.

UNCLE COLOCHLUCUS

A NOVEL

CHAPTER I

IT IS TRUE THAT COCKATIEL BREEDING is an odd habit mostly practiced by small-town types hopelessly bored with mundane rituals. One time, an escaped specimen of this particularly cruel and unnecessary species found its way through an open window and into the offices of a little radio station that occupied the second floor of a medium-sized office building in a minor, outlying city. The bird landed on the chest of a surprised host about to conduct an interview, and promptly took a shit all over the man's sweater-vest. It proceeded to squawk, abrasively, and then fluttered away to harass some other unsuspecting employees.

The radio host didn't let the sudden appearance of birdshit down the front of his pretentious dresswear interrupt his task at hand. And it was completely appropriate that the interviewer would in fact be wearing fecal matter upon his attire. For this was an episode of NPR's "Tiny Desk" that had as its special guest stars (and we do mean "special"), the band POOP. If you're not familiar, it's comprised of these two brothers. One of them is mentally retarded. The transcript went something like this:

NPR Dick: So nice of you to join us today.

Retard Brother: Hi. Hi! Hi!

Normal Brother: Thanks for having us.

NPR: Not at all. So, tell us something about your band, since you're here, we might as well waste everyone else's time.

NB: It's not much of a story. Like, nobody's ever going to pay me to tell it. There won't be a movie being made about our lives. We're pretty ordinary, except Paul's mentally challenged.

RB: Special!

NB: Yeah, you're special, bud. So anyway, the first thing people want to know about us, is why do we call ourselves POOP? It's childish, right? Well, you try living with a retard and see how easy it is.

NPRD: We don't like to use the word "Retard" around here.

RB: Special!

NB: Look, you've got him triggered now. He's going to want to hear the "Special People" song, and since that's not one of our original songs, we're going to get sued. I guarantee it. I start singing the Special People...

RB: Special! Special!

NB: ...The Special People song, on here, on your little radio show or whatever, and the lawyers are going to come crawling out of the woodwork in your "tiny desk" and sue my ass for infringement. They're such a bigger band than we are. I can't even say their name, I don't think I'm supposed to—

RB: Special!

NB: Yeah, and now look, he's so worked up he's banging his head on the stupid little desk, what do you want me to do? What can I say instead?

NPRD: You can say, "retreaded."

NB: "Retreaded?" That's retarded.

RB: Special! Yay!

NPRD: I think you were telling us about your poop.

NB: Not my poop.

NPRD: Somebody's poop.

NB: Yeah, right. So actually, it was my Dad's. He hated having a son that wasn't all there mentally, so he used to antagonize Paul. He took his retardation—

NPRD: Retread-ation

NB: Whatever. He would get in Paul's face, first thing in the morning. We'd be eating breakfast, and like cheap cornflakes and government milk, and Dad would come in and he'd look like shit, probably hungover.

NPRD: You do realize there's a link between substance abuse and developmental disability.

NB: What's your point?

NPRD: Didn't realize I needed to have one.

NB: Stop interrupting.

RB: Be nice lady!

NB: Dad would come in and get in Paul's face, he'd snap his fingers and do like a Frankenstein style impersonation, really not accurate at all, Paul's just autistic spectral with Down's tendencies, but Dad didn't know, or he didn't care, I'm not sure which. He'd get like two inches from Paul's face, and that was getting him really worked up, spilling cornflake-and-milk mush out of the sides of his mouth, he'd be rocking back and forth and trying not to grin.

RB: I like it when lady's nice.

NB: Dad would get so close to Paul's face, and then he'd holler, "MAKE WAY FOR POOP!" And to be fair, my Dad's bowel movements were always in the mornings, and they sounded pretty painful, so I understand that on a certain level there was some anger he had–

NPRD: Pretty unreasonable anger.

NB: Right, 'cause you're some kind of vegan with a puckered asshole I'm sure. So, Paul wouldn't actually be in my Dad's way. I don't know why Dad had to make such a big deal about it. But Paul thought it was hysterical.

NPRD: Can you hurry this up, please? I'm going on a latte-date in fifteen.

NB: Bite me. But that's what you have with POOP, you have two guys, with a dad who didn't give a damn, one of them's retarded–

NPRD: eh-EM

NB: Retreaded.

RB: I like tire track! Truck track! Vroom-VROOM!

NB: So it's like a reflection of low self opinion. You dad thinks the best thing he can do for his special needs son is make fun of him, when he's just a bitter alcoholic who has constipation issues, and after he died and we were alone and even more broke than we had ever been, my buddy Jaden had a fifteen dollar amp and a guitar he built out of a milk carton, we were down to our last ten bucks after paying the storage unit bill we were living out of, and we start fucking around and come up with this real repetitive sound. I thought it would be a good way to lull Paul to sleep, since it's easier to pass the time that way when you're retar– retreaded. But no. Paul sits up, and he's all excited, and he just starts yelling–

RB: MAKE WAY FOR POOP!

NPRD: There. Perfect. We're done. That's the story.

NB: No, hold on there, butt-cheeks. We get to sing our song first before you kick us out.

NPRD: But it's not even really a song.

RB: MAKE WAY FOR POOP!

NB: Too late. He's singing it.

RB: MAKE WAY FOR POOP!

NPRD: I don't know how you guys made it out of the storage unit, honestly.

RB: MAKE WAY FOR POOP!

NPRD: Did you have an instrument to play with this nonsense? Not that I expect it would make it any easier on us.

NB: I'll pound a rhythm on your skull.

NPRD: (sigh). This is NPR, National Public—

RB: MAKE WAY FOR POOP!

ROBIN WAS THINKING ABOUT IT. He had that special tingling sensation, originating in his groin and going up the fat of his back, all the way into his fully dysfunctional brain, or the excuse for thereof. He was stroking himself, up and down his flabby gut, reaching, with effort, all the way to his short, stubby, ugly little penis. [His mother always told him to check his wee-wee before he left the house for the day, a tradition that ensued up to this present moment; he fondled himself when he was angry, scared, confused, or bored. He'd grab his nuts and squeeze them, ever so slightly, until he started to feel pain, then he'd suddenly yank his hand way, catching his foreskin with the edge of one of his fingernails during the hasty retreat, feeling the hot sting of flesh tearing away as he sliced across a blood vessel. He'd be highly agitated about this compulsive behavior, having not realized he was groping himself until it was too late. Then, he would sniff his fingers.]

This was a new low, even for him. His kids would never understand, let alone be able to forgive him, as adults, in a therapy session:

"Bobby, what happened when you were a boy?"

"I don' wanna talk about it."

"Bobby, you're in a safe place now. He can't hurt you anymore."

"He touched it."

"Bobby, what did he touch?"

"The Elf." Yes, the Elf on the Shelf was the new target of Robin Bradley's affections. Not in a good, wholesome, Santa-drunk-on-eggnog way, like when Mrs. Claus would come out to the Reindeer stalls and find the old bastard with his bright red trunks drooped around his ankles, balls deep into Rudolph; she'd written to an advice columnist about this behavior, who informed her that Mrs. Claus should just carry on as normal and think nothing of it, but, if she was continually burdened by the thought of sharing a bed with a serial Reindeer-fucker, then the advice columnist snidely suggested that Mrs. Claus take up drinking, herself.

Robin didn't care about any of that. He was just inexplicably drawn to what appeared to be a doll of an adolescent boy with pointy ears and a blank stare, this pointless toy that his annoying kids and fat wife would always insist on placing strategically around the house during the holiday season. The spirit of festive naughtiness was high, and Robin felt entitled to take advantage of this useless object. It was just a relic of some braindead slob's marketing scheme to get parents to buy more bullshit for children in celebration of an antiquated tradition wherein a portly Germanic man would try and entice youngsters to follow him home in an old snow sled, to a place where the old man would keep a meat locker and his butcher knives sharp as a tack, ready to carve up some nice, tender, supple flesh.

Robin was planning on fucking the elf, of course, but nobody had ever thought to put a hole in the damned thing, so it was going to require some creativity. He had to position the opening in such a way that nobody would be wise to what he was doing, so he could bask in the cheap pleasure of seeing his spouse and children gently and lovingly cradle a thing he'd effectively made his masturbation vessel.

"Bobby, it's alright. He can't hurt the Elf anymore." The therapist herself was not so convinced. This man, Robin or "Rob" as he preferred to be called, since he thought the name "Robin" was gay, was still out there, somewhere; he had maybe attended some court-ordered psychological testing sessions, but was in no way rehabilitated. She was concerned for the safety and wellbeing of her client.

"Bobby, how long ago did this happen?"

"Uhm, two years," Bobby said, proud that he could remember. He was 35.

"Was it a German man?" Bobby couldn't remember. He didn't know what they were even talking about. He wanted a Happy Meal, and he wanted it *right* now, or else he was going to have a screaming shit-fit in the ice cream aisle.

Robin was still getting inside his brain, though. All these years later, after he'd ruined Christmas for at least the *seventh* time with his selfish sexual shenanigans, Robin Bradley was tormenting Bobby in every waking moment; each interaction throughout the day was as soiled and stained with shame as that elf.

THEY WERE GOING TO MAKE a "Slaptathon" to benefit all the kids who got killed over at SHIT CAMP, INC. this year. The hosts were pledging to slap the ever-loving silly shit out of whoever, for a pledge of only $100.

Public Access Television was the main facilitator of such operations. They got most of their revenue from cribbing off these bullshit charity fundraising scams.

The whole scheme was produced and underwritten by a roving gang of Uncles. They were, in no particular order:

- Uncle Michael. Uncle Michael was a drunk, an angry man who lived in Cherry Hill, New Jersey and had no children. He would often terrorize high school girls by rubbing their legs "for good luck" while giving them driving lessons, which was one of his part-time teaching gigs. He belonged to a discount country club, where everyone hated his guts, because he couldn't play golf worth a damn and spent most his time getting loaded in the clubhouse. One time his wife forgot to pick him up after a "round" and he tripped over his untied shoelaces on the frozen walkway leading down to the driveway where he'd requested a cab (the driver of which he fully intended on stiffing once he got back home, by falsely claiming that his wallet was stolen). This led to a skull fracture, and while they had him at the ER on a slow night, they also diagnosed him with cancer. It was the treatable kind, unfortunately.

- Uncle Lauri. He was also a drunk, but he hid out in the woods of north-central Arkansas and set pieces of wood on fire. Sometimes it was intentional, in that he would write confusing poetry into valuable slabs of hardwood with a heated metal rod. Sometimes he would make a bonfire and throw old televisions and dead motorcycle batteries onto it, which would invariably explode and send shrapnel into his arms. He'd chuckle, and shrug it off in a typical, southern "aw-shucks" manner. He also passed out, rolled over, and barbecued the right side of his face in the fire on occasion. When he wasn't burning things, he would be listening to conspiratorial rightwing talk radio, and plotting to assassinate Hillary Clinton. He ended up dying of being a drunk, and also, not having air conditioning.

- Uncle Joe. Uncle Joe was a former wannabe-alcoholic, who thought he was sneaky by sequestering himself in the attic of the house he shared with his wife (who wouldn't allow him to sleep with her because she didn't want to risk getting pregnant again; he was Catholic, and the kind that *still* won't use a condom) with a case of Bud Light and proceed to drink it all in one night, and subsequently get caught for it, because he hardly ever drank at all, but being caught just meant a few sideways glances from his family, which, at that point, didn't really care. He had the face and personality of a rat, or other medium-sized rodent. After nobody else seemed to notice or be bothered too much by his intermittent low-calorie beer binges, he checked himself into a support group and basked in the attention he subsequently received.

- Uncle Ronnie. Uncle Ronnie drank beer, but it didn't ever seem to do too much, not since he'd retired from being a trucker who'd been caught for DUI on multiple occasions, and beaten up by cops. It wouldn't matter even if he *was* truly drunk, as he'd not been actively engaged in any manner of work in some years. He had the constitution of a string bean. His main pleasure in life was to chain-smoke cigarettes, from first awakening at 5:45 every morning, sitting around his living room in silence, then migrating outside to his porch as the day warmed, staring blankly at the Sun as it arched overhead. On the rare occasion he would speak, it would be perfect Alabamian, and incomprehensible to anyone who was not well versed.

Anyway, so: "The League of Lunch," Uncle Lauri said, philosophically. "That's what we'll call ourselves. Huh heh-heh hoo-ha."

"Shut up, that's stupid!" shouted Uncle Michael, defiantly. He always looked up to Spanky from *Our Gang* when he was just a little guy, so naturally, he would need to be in charge.

Uncle Ronnie nodded, more concerned with the dwindling life left in his off-brand cigarette, ash drooping precariously close to the butt; in one smooth action, he withdrew the next cigarette from the pack, propped it strategically between his lips as he simultaneously ejected the spent one, quickly positioning its cherry-red ember up against the fresh end of its replacement, and taking a deep drag as it exploded into combustive joy.

But Uncle Joe wanted to go back to what Uncle Lauri had said earlier, about lunch. Uncle Joe's ratlike tendencies necessitated that he regularly feed his ego with a snack of assorted pieces of cheese. He rubbed his hands together excitedly and made a weaselly cackle in eager anticipation of being fed. He had been getting distracted lately, by a book he'd been reading about a man who was ill-mannered, unkempt and generally a dirty sort of fellow, who nonetheless refused to leave his bathtub because he was all paranoid and convinced that he was going to be stabbed to death inside of it, like had happened to some French guy a long time ago. The bathwater stank of raw onions and garlic, yet the main character of the story was unwilling to ever empty it out and refill the tub, let alone clean it out ever. Uncle Joe almost forgot that he was supposed to munch on some cut-up cubes of cheddar, lest he show up at home at the end of the day and need to cook a meal to satisfy his wife, who was a professional tinkerer and expected that he would perform household duties at least 25% of the time, so she could tend to her various nonsensical projects. He was starting to lose sight of himself, because his cheese time wasn't happening frequently enough.

Uncle Lauri was about to say something else that he fancied as being clever about his demented "League of Lunch" concept, when they were interrupted by a serious problem:

"UNCLE! UNCLE!" a small child was wailing, inconsiderately. "He, the man, played with somebody else's poop!" Breathless as he was, the child was sorely mistaken, though. What had actually happened was, somebody had pooped *on* Micropan Marneshta.

The Uncles didn't realize this, nor were they in any way equipped to deal with such a "shit-uation." Most of them were distracted; Uncle Ronnie, for one, was transfixed by a poster advertising that movie everyone was talking about, *The Peeing Poodle*. "How'd bout a damn ol' dog been pissin' 'round be makin' into a movie, now?" Uncle Ronnie wondered to himself. He couldn't understand why someone would make a feature-length film about such a mundane act as canine urination. Yet, he was enthralled, because he reckoned that he knew a thing or two about dog piss, having multiple stray mutts lounging around his cabin, deep in the woods of the Ozarks. He was also secretly delighted that such a pointless thing as this was attracting mainstream attention (the film had even gotten James Franco to star as the dog's owner, a role that he enthusiastically accepted, *un*-ironically), making him feel like his daily habit of chain-smoking and staring straight into the Sun was, suddenly, not so freakishly antisocial after all.

Uncle Michael, meanwhile, was attempting to hatch a plan. He first had to take his pinky finger and stick it up inside of his butthole, rolling it around too and fro for good luck, just like his great Uncle Arnold had done before every bowling game (or, as he pronounced it, "boweling"), when Uncle Michael was just a lad and not yet anyone else's Uncle.

"My dick itches/ it itches, SOMETIMES/ my dick, my little dicky/ itches so bad!" a street busker howled, discordantly, in the background. Uncle Michael got angry that he was being distracted by anything so meaningless as a dirty stranger singing a sad tale of sexually infectious woe.

Uncle Joe was slightly upset. He really, badly, wanted to go to see *The Phantom of the Anus* which was having its worldwide off-broadway premier that weekend. But, when he mentioned it to Uncle Michael, he did not get a positive reaction. "Shutup! That's stupid!" Uncle Michael shouted, and then scampered off to grab a middle-aged lady's goiter. He was totally over-stimulated by all the commotion and borderline interactions.

The whole reason they were there in the first place, in the mall or some similarly shopping-themed area, was because Uncle Michael was somehow under the impression they had an Auntie Fanny's kiosk there. Auntie Fanny's, if you weren't already aware, specialized in the "poop pretzel," which was a twisted ring of compressed, dehydrated feces from various animals: cats, rats, birds, orangutans, etc., which was then dusted in a generous coating of sugar and hydrogenated fats. It made Uncle Michael nostalgic for his childhood, when he had grown up down the street from the widow of Bruno Hauptmann.

[Hauptmann was the guy who got zapped for stealing and murdering Charles Lindbergh Jr.'s baby, even though he probably didn't do it, because the only evidence anyone really had against Hauptmann was that he was German, and the US was about to go to war against Germany.

"Do germs come from Germany?" a dumb child just tried to ask, and we will not answer that absurd and stupid question, because it would distract from the story that we are trying to tell, and nothing should come between the storyteller and the story-tell-ed. This is just the kind of inane bullshit we were taught to avoid in writing a narrative, along with other such nonsense as, "Does coffee make you cough?" Which, of course, it *can*, like after a night of heavy drinking, when your sternum is sunk down into your esophagus, your head hurts, everything is spinning and all the water you thought you were smart for chasing down your booze with before you passed out that night was about to come gushing back up, right through your pie-hole along with all the coffee and chunks of rare bacon you thought might help get yourself back to Normaltown this morning.

Anyway, Hauptmann couldn't have killed little Lindbergh just because he was German and angry about the impending war, because the Lindberghs *were* in fact themselves German, and Charles Jr. was even a born-again Nazi sympathizer. But, they needed someone to step up to the plate that secured the electric chair to the floor at the New Jersey State Prison, and Hauptmann served in that particular role heroically. But, he left behind a wife.]

Mrs. Hauptmann took a special liking to Uncle Michael from an early age. Maybe it was because she never had children of her own, and maybe that was the real reason that her husband, who was probably *not* guilty of kidnapping and killing the Lindbergh child, actually *did* steal it so that his wife would have something small upon which to dote. But, since he was a man, and kind of rough around the edges from the looks of his mugshot, like he could have been a hitman for a bootlegger syndicate in the Roaring Twenties, and maybe his wife *was* psychotic enough to want to raise someone else's stupid baby, then it's *slightly* possible that he inadvertently stepped on little Lindbergh, or slapped him too hard to stop him from crying, or committed some other act of slapstick numbskullery that led to the infant's demise. But, most likely not. Mrs. Hauptmann was probably just sort of sad and lonely and wanted a young boy to fatten up.

So, she did. She called Uncle Michael her "spretzel little boy," which was a term of endearment scavenged from a portmanteau of "special" and "pretzel," as she was German and pretzels had a special place in her heart, and a special place in Uncle Michael's increasingly rotund little belly, as well. She wanted him to be her perfect sausage boy, in fact. She fed him bratwurst and liverwurst and knockwurst, and taught him many patriotic German songs and fantasized about spirting him away to join the ranks of the Fourth Reich, and their reformulated Hitler Youth, in Argentina.

Now, it wasn't that Mrs. Hauptmann was a racist, or particularly bad for the Jews in any way. She just resented the country that had slaughtered her husband on account of politics. And, in fact, Uncle Michael wasn't a ripe candidate for the job at all.

You understand what is intended by assessing the "ripeness" of a male child, right? In the unlikely event that you do not know, well, it is the point at which a Catholic priest has determined the boy to be ready for statutory rape. His penis must be larger than that of the priest's, because the priest basks in the humiliating dissatisfaction of having a dick shorter than that of a juvenile;

yet his ass must be hairless, as the priest should be able to imagine it as the the shaved vulva of a woman (for tax purposes, you understand, since Jesus is always watching, and taking account of goings-on; if he suspects that the priest has *not* deluded himself into thinking that the orifice into which he stuck his pecker was that of a girl, then he could get fined and sanctioned on account of homosexuality, which is sinful conduct and requires stiff penalties). Which, the priest wasn't supposed to be doing, either, in the first place, even if it *was* an actual woman with which he was contemplating sex.

Uncle Ronnie didn't care for this explanation at all. He was an unreliable Southern Baptist who was taught that queers should be stoned, and Catholics could not be trusted. Uncle Joe was an alter boy who *did not* get diddled by a member of the clergy, even though he desperately wanted to be, so that he could, later in life, capitalize on the experience by being a guest on some Oprah-knockoff daytime TV show. Uncle Lauri knew full well that the Catholics were trafficking children as sex slaves in order to satisfy the perverse desires of the Clinton family, because he listened to Alex Jones, and he took notes. This left Uncle Michael, the only one to have ever successfully been raped, to lead the plot forward.

Suddenly, everything got just a little bit sticky. Uncle Lauri quaffed, and Ronnie got a disgusted look on his face as he proceeded to light cigarette number 87 of the morning. Uncle Joe wrinkled his nose. "Hey, do you think this is going to be safe, for cats?" Joe's wife wanted him to *always* ask this question first and foremost whenever he was confronted by an unfamiliar situation. She liked to rescue stray animals and her son's heroin junkie ex-friends, and became very distraught when she found out that, sometimes, people like to shoot feral cats with crossbows (also feral humans, but she wasn't as worried about that). In her view, the exorbitant reproduction rate of cats was outweighed by their relatively short lifespans, and therefore, they were deserving of her protection at all times.

Uncle Michael howled in anger. "Shut up, Joe! Stupid!" He started smacking Uncle Joe over the head, repeatedly. It wasn't enough that the little pervert wanted to go see something as schlocky and gay as *The Phantom of the Anus*, which was written by a consortium of extreme homosexuals from the

44

Village. Even though Joe was straight enough that he stayed married to his wife (with whom he hardly ever had actual sex, but did so out of an obligation begot of pure Catholic guilt), in Michael's view, Joe was just a simpleton who had no valid motivating factors in his sad, pathetic life.

Uncle Lauri was getting worried. He feared that he wasn't drunk enough. Normally, he'd have on hand a case of whatever the cheapest ice beer that could be had from a discount grocery store, strategically positioned within a yellowed and dirt-smeared 20-year-old cooler. But someone told him this was a fancy museum that they were going to as part of their musical-cum-crimefighting mission, as outlined in the general bylaws proposed by their attorneys for the formation of *The League of Lunch*, and so, out of a misplaced sense of obligation, he'd put on his least-paint-stained jorts and the only wifebeater he owned that didn't have a crude caricature of Bill Clinton committing lewd acts with a Mexican child.

Michael was also getting concerned. He knew what Lauri was capable of when he got drunk enough, that is, those times when he felt like the cheep beer wasn't getting him to where he needed to be, and switched to hard liquor. Then, people would get shot. Michael was still trying to uphold some level of family-friendliness in their caper, even though he despised children; but Michael was the sort of drunk who was just a bump on a log in a bar somewhere, not a *real* threat.

There was a *real* threat, however, and it was coming closer to Uncle Michael. It was a gaunt creature, its eyes deeply sunken into hollow sockets; the lips of its small mouth pulled tight against its jawbone, in an awful grimace. Its skin was an off-shade of yellow with dark undertones. "What the fuck is that?" Michael screamed, horrifiedly.

"That's Elliver," Uncle Lauri stated, matter-of-factly. "It used to be Ellen Page. It played Mr. Lahey's daughter on *Trailer Park Boys*. It became a man, and then, it had its identity stolen."

"What's it doing?" Michael hollered, as Elliver crept up to him on its knees, a hunting knife tucked between its teeth, groaning and grunting and gesturing frantically towards Michael's abdomen.

"It... wants... your... Liver!" Uncle Joe stammered, rubbing his hands together and grinning excitedly. Since he wasn't allowed to see *The Phantom of the Anus*, watching the legendary Elliver try to steal Uncle Michael's liver was the next best thing.

"They... *told* us about it, in AA," Uncle Joe continued, proudly reciting a speech he always hoped he'd have the chance to deliver. "It got real drunk once it had its identity stolen, and felt sorry for itself. It didn't have any support networks, because nobody wanted to associate with it, since it didn't have an identity anymore. It started drinking even more heavily, and all the bartenders and convenience store clerks took pity on it, and didn't even ask for its ID. All the safety checks went out the window. All the residual checks from its acting career got cashed at payday lenders, which took high fees. It had enough money each week to get wasted in a cheap hotel room. It got serious liver damage after awhile, and the doctors told it that it was dying. But they wouldn't do anything to save its liver, because it didn't have any health insurance. So, someone told it that the only way it could stay alive is if it stole healthy peoples' livers, and ate them."

"Michael ain't got no liver's worth takin'," Ronny stated, bluntly.

"Oh, I remember when you were a real girl. You smelled nice," said a trendy mall girl passing by, repugnantly, towards Elliver.

"Aww, I always thought you looked like you would smell nice," said another cool girl, cluelessly.

"Shut up! This is my story!" shouted Uncle Michael, incoherently.

"You look like a murdered crouton now!" the first girl screamed at Elliver. It was so true. Girls could be *really* mean to each other, except Elliver was no longer a girl. Elliver was no longer even a human, and this one fat bitch that was making fun of it was plump, and had a *very* inviting abdomen, so Elliver lunged and, with one imperceptibly quick stoke of its katana, had the chubby girl flayed open, liver now held up in the air triumphantly, viscera and tendrils dripping and drooping off of the doomed organ.

"Mister," the child from earlier continued, earnestly. "I heard that someone said that Micropan Marneshta licked the President's toes, and he giggled!" The boy was so excited, his lips began smacking together, involuntarily. He imagined himself being so fortunate as to be able to lick the

President's feet, at least once, on a field trip to the museum that is our national capitol. He tugged at Uncle Michael's sleeve for emphasis.

Michael was completely aghast about all these goings-on. Whose kid was this? Did he think that Michael was *his* uncle? And who were these other clown-shoes who were associating themselves with him, as leader of the so-called "League of Lunch"? Didn't someone have their underpants on backwards in this entire equation? And where was his wife?

Michael's wife, Aunt Piggy, was off on vacation in the desert, secretly testing chemical weapons for the government. He wasn't going to ever see her again, probably, unless it was some kind of a government-funded drone that poorly imitated his wife's mannerisms. Michael wouldn't care at all, at that point; for he would be far, *far,* too drunk.

So, he punched the kid in the face, and sent him sliding on his ass across the floor, bleeding profusely from the mouth and screaming at the top of his lungs, that high-pitched wail that effeminate little boys who grow up to become full-blown queers do, a piercing screech that would make any regular man stop and think twice about his abusive conduct. But Michael was no regular man; he was the leader of these Uncles, that were here, gathered around in a mall or some such shit place, doing absolutely nothing as they tussled and procrastinated, and wallowed around in their own gross insecurities.

It was the perfect setup for a major motion picture. Someone should quickly show up with a medicine bag full of money and purchase the rights to the story.

It wasn't done just yet, though. Because one of the girls who was making fun of Elliver (poor Elliver!) now decided she didn't like how Michael was handling the situation with the boy, and she proceeded to put him into a headlock. His fat, ruddy face immediately started turning beet red, as he tried to shout, and flung his fists around wildly, succeeding in hitting absolutely nothing.

"Joe, you sniveling little creep!" Michael gasped, desperately. "Come help me!"

Uncle Joe was reminded, though, of the whole thing with the Catholic priest, and how *he* wanted to be the one to have "special sacred time" with the Father. Father, though, had preferred Michael, since he told Joe that he was kind of a scrawny little twerp, and how instead of coming to confirmation class, he should just go collect stamps or look at dead worms under a microscope or something. So, Joe just hung back for a minute, smirking smugly, and waited to see how this thing would play out.

Meanwhile, someone was about to start some shit with Lauri. "Listen, I don't care if you touched someone, bud," a random guy said after listening to Lauri (who was decently drunk by this time) rant about how the girl on the television newscast was just a dirty slut in desperate need of a good dickdown.

"Nice fuckin' shoes, man," Lauri responded, unequivocally. He said it unevenly, as well, since he couldn't stand up straight any longer, due to being as drunk as he was.

Michael bristled with great fear and agitation. He knew what Lauri was like when he was good and drunk, and he knew that this was going to be some awful distraction that he really didn't need, want, or deserve. He was so upset, he actually pooped a little bit. And also, he was still getting choked out by some fat girl, since none of the other Uncles wanted to come to his aid.

"FREE PILE OF SHIT," THE CRAIGSLIST POST read, literally. There was a photo of a mound of poop. "Pick up at your mom's backdoor."

And then there was an ad. "Can Micropan Marneshta help you realize your goals?" it asked, cryptically. At this point, things began getting a bit out-of-focus. Someone swallowed a blood pressure medication that led to machine elves dancing on top of refrigerators, air conditioners, dehumidifiers and other similar appliances. A small girl went door-to-door selling knives, but not of the quality kind. Oh no, these had rusty, bent and dull blades that she'd fished out of the slough down the street from her family's shack. Some of them still had encrusted blood blending seamlessly into the corroded metal.

A centipede crawled out from the decaying woodwork of a support pillar for a derelict billboard. "Have a Jolly Jaunt at Johnny's Juicy Jam Junction," it read, although half of the letters were faded and torn. It required decisive action from the county's planning commision, to either coerce the absentee owner to recondition the sad, leaning structure through sanctions, or just make the bold maneuver to seize it under eminent domain law and auction it off to the highest bidder. Such action was not forthcoming, however, because the Board was evenly split between aesthetic liberals who wanted to restore the natural weeds and noxious molds that inhabited the swampland within which the billboard was located, and radical free-enterprise conservatives who screeched the gospel of property rights and conveniently overlooked the fact that the reason the billboard's owner was not located anywhere nearby in order to do something with his overgrown disaster was because he'd fled an impending indictment for tampering with child pornography, which was one of the five leading local enterprises. The billboard's owner had donated to the board members in question, though, so they were completely remiss to bite the hand that fed them.

The Centipede didn't know about any of this, and proceeded to bite the arms off a grasshopper. He was just living his life in the only home he'd ever known, blissfully unaware of the greater forces at play in his reality.

Then, things got completely shaken up. An earthquake measuring magnitude 7.7 on the Richter Scale struck, leveling what was left of the billboard and kind of making a moot point about all of this.

Which leads into how things got so far off-topic to begin with. You see, once Uncle Michael started fighting with the fat girl, their resident bartender, "Longe" Licraposa (who makes an *amazing* mimosa, if you weren't already aware) decided to cut off the entire League of Lunch from any further alcohol consumption on that particular day.

It was already too late for Uncle Lauri. He was too drunk to go back, but needed to keep the insanity-juice flowing. Having to abruptly discontinue drinking at that moment led to a catastrophic rip in the fabric of spacetime. It completely disrupted the entire plot of the story, about the League of Lunch.

Lauri didn't care. He was still obsessed with the Man's shoes. "I had a nephew once, who took my shoes, and he said he was going to use them, and I said it was going to be okay! But, he *didn't* wear them, and then he said that he was going to send them back, to me, and I told him not to worry about it!" The Man was paralyzed with a combined feeling of disgust, contempt, and hatred towards this drunkard for wasting his time with these nonsensical rantings, words flowing forth like so much effluent from a broken sewage pipe.

The Centipede, sensing the imminent danger of being stepped on in all the commotion and discussion of footwear (he was taking remedial English classes in order to gain an overseas job in telemarketing, which paid the American equivalent of forty-five cents per hour, which was really more than a Centipede needed, since they don't really spend any money, ever, on anything; but the Centipede wanted to make his father, whom he'd never met, because he was hatched from a large cluster of insect eggs, proud that his son had accomplished some upward mobility in his short, leggy life), quickly departed from the situation, seeking refuge in the fine oak grain of a nearby pickle barrel.

Uncle Michael, meanwhile, was getting arrested by a mall security guard for fighting with the fat girl, even though the Security Guard was not empowered to enforce civil law; he didn't care, because he'd seen that movie, with Seth Rogan in it, and that made him believe in himself enough to overstep his bounds and assume powers that he did not legally possess.

Uncle Joe was getting antsy, because he was still wearing his wife's panties that he'd pilfered the night before, because he thought it might make him aroused enough to actually enjoy having sex again. But, he was Catholic, so he was only allowed to have sex with his wife, and even then, it was supposed to be of the baby-making variety. So, it probably wasn't ever going to happen for him, ever again.

Uncle Ronnie was getting anxious as well. He was down to his last two packs of cigarettes, which would barely be enough to get him through the next hour. The mall cop was yelling in his general direction as he struggled with Uncle Michael, who was a 275-pound tub of lard that would challenge any moderately fit man engaged in a grappling match with him. Mall cop was grunting and grumbling something about how this was a NO SMOKING mall, and that also implied that there would not be any convenient news-stand style stores that also sold tobacco.

Uncle Lauri coughed up a bit of beer-and-vodka flavored phlegm, and some of it landed on the Man's shoes. They were pure leather loafers that the

Man had just purchased from an overpriced footwear outlet for several hundred dollars. The Man shrieked, and kicked off the shoes hastily, sending them flying in the general direction of a nearby trash can. They missed. One of them, however, caught the Security Guard in the middle of his forehead, and landed some of Lauri's spit into his eyes, temporarily blinding him. Uncle Michael broke away from the Security Guard's grasp, squealing his head off, and then sucker-punched the Man and dashed off in a sad attempt at a sprint that saw him getting winded after making it twenty feet down the mallway.

It was alright, though, because he spotted a generic sports-bar that was *not* owned and operated by one "Longe" Licraposa, so he would be allowed to drink, or so he thought. Nobody else felt like sticking around, since they no longer had any vague clue as to what their purpose was or why they were even fighting and smoking and drinking and talking about dog piss in the middle of a mall during a workday in the first place.

And, that was pretty much the story of the League of Lunch. They never accomplished anything, and the TV special that was supposed to air had to go on without their continuing support. The rest of the Uncles broke off and went their own separate ways, probably never to be heard from again. It was a very bleak and pointless story, after all.

ELIZABETH CHICKEN WAS GETTING HARASSED by her slightly racist owner, who kept referring to Elizabeth (or "Liddy" for short) and the rest of her flock as a bunch of "Chins." It was funny, because it was said in a disparagingly Chinese-y way, such as follows:

"Chin-chins! Chin-chin the chicken!" the man would call out in greeting to the hens every morning, as they jostled and squawked for front position at the door to their coop. The man did genuinely believe that their eggs went good in some fried rice, which sometimes also had chicken breast meat in it; but he didn't actually slaughter his own birds, because he enjoyed just having eggs, and also, there had been one time when he saw someone cut a chicken's head off and left its body racing around the fenced-in pool area, jettisoning blood all over an immaculately clean, white, concrete deck, which then had to be throughly disinfected, because chickens do carry a bunch of germs and various diseases, which cannot, under federal law, be preemptively treated with vaccines, unlike in Europe where that is allowed.

The Chicken-Man wanted to continue mocking his birds, but Nasty Scatterson and some guy named Loureschten wanted the Chicken-Man to go out hunting for cigarette butts instead, so they could collect a bag full and then spend the rest of the afternoon delicately picking them apart, separating out the filters and the charred ends, and carefully re-packaging the tobacco into hand-rolled cigarettes that they could then smoke, and sell the rest of to schoolchildren.

The problem was, the well-to-do liberal community within which they resided had recently implemented an outdoor smoking ban. Ostensibly, this was to protect children; however, at least three of the city councillors had accepted donations from an anti-smoking pyramid scheme, which promised to help its clients quit tobacco for good, by occupying their spare time with the frantic drive for recruitment of further victims. Once thirty people had been lassoed into the scheme, the client's status was upgraded, and they earned a merit badge.

"Participation trophies, if you ask me," huffed Nasty, inconsiderately. Unfortunately, nobody had actually asked Nasty Scatterson for his opinion, so it was entirely disregarded by the very people who probably should have been paying attention.

Elizabeth Chicken was having none of it. After finishing her breakfast of indiscriminate peckings around the yard, she was ready to make a quick exit. With a heroic leap and frantic fluttering of her underpowered wings, Elizabeth bounded over the fence, and quickly encountered the secret dumping spot for the neighbor's car's ashtray.

The Chicken-Man was keen to this. He came running breathlessly up to Nasty and Loureschten (because he was a heavy smoker, and also, the reconstituted cigarettes that he smoked often had clumps of grass, star-thistle, and shit rolled up in them, so his lungs were under a continuous assault from irritation), doing his best impression of a Chicken, clucking, arms folded under his shoulders, pacing back and forth, thrusting his head out with every step. "Chin-chins got it!" He exclaimed, emphatically.

Loureschten drooled and gurgled, lazily. There wasn't much in life that motivated him anymore. He relied upon others to provide him with cigarettes, except on the rare occasion that his greatly compromised eyesight allowed him to spot a mostly-unsmoked cigarette that had been carelessly discarded on some brightly-lit sidewalk.

Nasty shrugged. He wasn't sure that they were going to have much success in this plot, actually. The anti-smoking multilevel marking ploy was owned and operated by the Shramlicore Corporation, and nobody got to fuck with them and live to tell the story. Nasty was far more content to just quietly die a death of despair, as it is said by the politicians these days.

For tax purposes, they were calling their enterprise "Beloved Butts Recycled Cigarettes." One of their best customers went by the name, "Noodle Boy," who was balls-deep into a valium habit and didn't have enough money to support both his pill-popping and smoking habits. Thankfully, through the kindly and charitable efforts of Nasty and Loureschten, and to a lesser extent, the Chicken-Man, they were able to bring a product to market that would ease the financial burden of degenerate drug addicts having to choose between their addictions.

Noodle Boy would stumble himself over to the pre-fabricated Rubbermaid brand garden shed from which the cigarette business was operating, and roll his head around, vaguely grinning, and telling them all about how he was planning a trip to Maine (because its motto is "Vacationland," and since Noodle Boy had never really travelled anywhere, that was the first and only destination that came to mind, since he'd seen a few advertisements on television, which, in his opinion, made him a quasi-expert), and he'd be needing to save up his pennies and dollar coins in order to afford the plane fare and the cost of room and board at an oceanfront lodge.

Nasty and Loureschten couldn't stand Noodle Boy. But he was their best, and usually only, customer, so they couldn't exactly beat him merciless and leave him by the side of the highway. Nasty only had one other job, which was stupid and boring and in a small, dingy office. Loureschten didn't have any other gainful means of employment, except for those times when he could qualify for temporary disability benefits from the Government, because he'd forgotten how to see things and make his eyeballs function properly.

Meanwhile, Elizabeth Chicken was getting increasingly pissed off. She blamed the Jewish media for having led the Chicken-Man to make such nonsensically racist comments about her perceived Asian heritage. She was absolutely sick of getting accused of being oriental on a daily basis. Also, an opossum named Erstwhile Davenport had been stalking her as she tried to sleep at night. Erstwhile was a behemoth, a total fatass who had bullied his way to the top of the local food chain and now thought he could steal chickens at his leisure.

The Chicken-Man had been so distracted by his stupid startup enterprise that he'd not been living up to his title, nor the obligations that accompanied it. Elizabeth Chicken was having to go around and plan for her own security, a thing she really shouldn't be having to do, since the name *Elizabeth* was the same as the Queen, and royalty would never have to do such a self-effacing thing like protect themselves or their own interests from adversarial forces.

Elizabeth did have a soft spot for Noodle Boy, however. He'd told her that, after he returned from his fantasy trip to Maine, he was going to bring her some leftover Lobster shells and viscera to peck through. Elizabeth approved of this, since Lobster was a fancy food, and suitable for royalty (even though it was often suspected that any crustaceans could pose the risk of food-borne illness, which presented a severe moral hazard to those operatives who were tasked with delicately coordinating every waking minute of a monarch's day, since one bad batch of seafood could cause an incident of public vomiting, just like what happened that one time with Daddy Bush and the Prime Minister of Japan, although it might not have been from eating fish, the exact cause remaining a highly classified state secret; still, it went against well-established protocol to let any high profile person run the risk of having something so stupid and common happen in front of international media), and Elizabeth trusted Noodle Boy to live up to his promise.

The Chicken-Man was oblivious to the fact that Noodle Boy was openly flirting with his most prized hen. He had a much bigger problem simmering on the back burner of the stove that was his failed existence, which was that he had both maliciously and unwittingly violated numerous health codes as a chicken-keeper (because, let's face it, chickens are kinda filthy animals, they shit wherever they stand, they cock and bob their heads back-and-forth as they walk, they make weird sounds sometimes and they bathe in dirt), and now he was the subject of a multiagency investigation.

"So you mean to tell me," asked a detective, quizzically, "that there was a man who had stockpiled a collection of used aluminum foil, with bits of food stuck to it, inside every single one of his kitchen cabinets?"

"Yessir," the Chicken-Man responded, confidently. He'd seen this done on TV once, where a guy who was about to be in some very serious legal trouble was able to convince the proper authorities that what he was doing really wasn't that bad, and that, in fact, there was someone else doing something far worse. He was able to provide ample anecdotal evidence, and the investigation was dropped.

Well, but Chicken-Man was also a certified moron, and he wasn't able to fool the Detective at all. Even though he felt very smart about himself, and began preening and strutting, like a true cock, around the yard where he was being questioned, having already decided that he'd won this fight and was about to move on to bigger and better things, like Beloved Butts.

The Detective, though, had other plans. He whipped out his handcuffs and moved swiftly to arrest the Chicken-Man, on charges of operating an unlicensed Chickenry, aiding and abetting bacteriological contagion, slander, public indecency (the Chicken-Man often didn't bother to wear pants while he was tending to his flock, which was conveniently located adjacent to a school bus stop, with no fence or other dividing barrier present, since the Chicken-Man thought it was funny and cool to get the kids to feed his birds leftover crusts of bread and dried-up boogers, and also, it would save him the cost of having to purchase chicken feed on a regular basis), illegal manipulation of weights and measures, fraud, impersonating an elected official, disobeying a lawful order, racketeering, hate crimes, and arson.

"But, wait! Wait, sir!" The Chicken-Man hollered belligerently as the Detective was attempting to read him his Miranda Rights. "I got proof there's worse fuckery going on here!" He then proceeded to tell the Detective about

Beloved Butts, and how they were about to execute an international, multi-billion-dollar confidence scheme.

"So, this other dude's name is Nasty?" the Detective asked, chuckling.

"Yes! Nasty Scatterson."

"Yeah. Sure, I believe that," the Detective replied, shaking his head, furiously. It angered him greatly whenever simpletons would try to lie to him.

"Tell me one thing, sir," Chicken-Man continued, plaintively. "Have you ever had splatteria?" The Detective thought that he had not, but he wasn't entirely sure what this pathetic nimrod was talking about. So, we asked Elizabeth Chicken her opinion on the matter; but, she just clucked, and scratched and pecked around at something on the ground.

Splatteria was diarrhea that splattered. It was a very basic concept, and also, it was considered to be a borderline "spanglish" term, except no self-respecting Mexican would ever *say* such a thing. Of course, the guy who coined the phrase was white. He didn't look white, but he was.

It didn't matter. Chicken-Man was still getting taken into custody, but what he didn't realize was that it was *protective* custody, meaning that he would end up in a group home with a bunch of other intellectually deficient adults who couldn't care for themselves. They'd be looked after by a kindly, greedy old woman who was hooked on pain pills and horse tranquilizers, who used to be a nursemaid but now collected a hefty check from the government every month so she could feed peanut butter to these fully-grown rapscallion wards of the court.

And Chicken-Man would eventually be convicted, of being generally disgusting, which meant that he'd have to spend at least the next fifteen months in the care of Mother Miserly, which was the name of the LLC that the derelict woman had established, in order to provide legal immunity should anyone come accusing her of neglect. That was something that would never happen, though, since developmentally challenged adults were at the bottom of the basement of priority lists for any politician, local, state, or federal, to advocate for, so Mother Miserly knew full well that she could probably get away with murder, and be okay.

Released from all repercussions that would normally be imposed for doing so, Elizabeth Chicken was now free to roam around her territory, solidifying her position as reigning monarch of the neighborhood. Which really meant that she was becoming a bloodthirsty tyrant. Small birds were rounded up and placed into internment cages, to be tagged and categorized and cataloged based upon their worth to the nation. And it was all going perfectly, according to Elizabeth's master plan, until Nourfren Kinka showed up.

Nourfren Kinka was some type of alien, both illegal and extraterrestrial in origin. It didn't have a valid interstellar passport, nor did it have so much as a temporary work visa. Still, though, it was horny.

Chicken-Man had tried to warn the Detective about it, but, of course, he was just laughed at and mocked, hideously, for having the audacity to claim that he'd been intercepting secret radio transmissions for weeks now that outlined Nourfren's plans of getting laid. Also, Nourfren wanted to pick up some cheap repurposed cigarettes, and it had heard from some of its spacefaring buddies that Beloved Butts had some of the best prices in this part of the Galaxy, and, also, Earth was one of the very few planets that had not yet imposed the death penalty for possessing tobacco.

Nourfren had not bothered spending the time to learn the intricacies and expectations of Human society, however, since he was a lazy bastard and had flunked out of alien dental college. So, upon landing his decrepit flying saucer (which looked like something out of a bad sci-fi joke from the 50s) in the field adjacent to where Chicken Man had tried, and failed, to raise a successful flock of laying hens, he immediately bounded over to the first person he thought he saw, which was Elizabeth Chicken.

"Mmmmurrgh, cigarette!" Nourfren growled, gleefully. Elizabeth looked him over, from three heads to slimy webbed toes, and decided she didn't approve of what she was looking at, so she initiated the chicken-emergency-screech, which sounded like anyone's impression of a dying animal.

Chicken-Man heard her cries and tried vainly to escape the grasp of the evil Detective, so he could go and see what was bothering his most prized hen. Chicken-Man doted on Elizabeth, which was how she came to have such a superiority complex. He would pick dandelions and scatter the petals before her, wherever she strutted, making for a great show of pomp and circumstance that Elizabeth swooned over.

Well, Nourfren Kinka was not so good-mannered, and it kind of ruined his one shot at proving to the remaining staff at Beloved Butts that he was cool, and deserved to be able to buy secondhand cigarettes without being charged the necessary taxes, which was totally illegal, and if the Detective was at all competent, he would've *done* something about it, once Chicken Man spilled his guts, but, since he was a useful idiot to the powers that be, the Detective shrugged it off, assuming that was a matter best left to the ATF.

Nourfren wasn't about to give up on his great ambition to smoke himself retarded. So, after getting the brush-off from Nasty and Loureschten, he tried to go legit, and half-hopped, half-rolled, and half-ambled to the nearest gas station (Nourfren's strange and highly uncoordinated appendages did not lend themselves to mobility in anything even approximating a dignified manner), thinking that he could just grimace and drool at the cashier, and walk off with multiple cartons of different brands and flavor profiles.

It didn't work. The cashier, a morbidly obese 19-year-old with a severe video game dependency, just assumed that Nourfren was trying out a shoddy and wholly unconvincing Halloween costume way early (the Cashier thought it was July, even though it actually *was* the end of October, but he had no clue, since he spent all his off-work time sequestered away in his room, with the lights out, and hundreds of used kleenexes crusty with jism and the residue of frozen pizza and fried chicken scattered around unceremoniously), and just did what he was told to do, under threat of hefty fine and termination, and asked Nourfren for his identification.

"Aye... dee?" Nourfren stammered, confusedly. On his planet, the government was run by libertarians, and they had banned any and all forms of official documentation.

"Look, dude, just give me twenty bucks. I mean, you're cool, right?" Well, Nourfren always wanted to be cool, even though he wasn't, and also, he didn't know how American money worked, so he just winged it, unhinged his massive jaw, and swallowed the cashier's head, whole.

UNCLE PROCHLUCUS

A NOVEL

CHAPTER I

AND NOW COME BEFORE YOU, we have one Robin "Rob" Hoover who was most excited. It was the third Saturday of the month, which meant it was almost time for Mr. Sucky. Mr. Sucky was a stupid blowjob game that his wife would let him play. She was tired of it, but Rob was such a depressingly little man, a complete nothing of a person, that she allowed him this simple pleasure of chasing her around the house while she was clad in trashy lingerie.

These were the rules for Mr. Sucky: Rob had to hide for at least five minutes. If Wife Hoover could get out of the house and disappear quickly enough, she would win, but then Rob could "phone a friend," by which it was implied that Rob would call one of *Wife's* friends, because Rob was such a contemptible excuse for a human being that he had no actual friends of his own. Usually one of Wife's friends would be willing to suck Rob's dick in order to exact passive-aggressive vengeance against her husband.

Otherwise, Rob could not use the actual vacuum cleaner. Wife had forbade it at the very start of this stampede of nonsense. Rob could also not brag to the neighbors about having received fellatio by taking a sample of his semen, rubbing it on a cocktail napkin, and sticking it on the neighbor's front window, car door handle, or other prominent place. While he was coming, Rob could not shout out the name of a local politician, minor celebrity, or imaginary friend, because it was really just too weird.

And this was a contentious point between Rob's understanding of Mr. Sucky, and everyone else's. Rob felt very much like he was entitled to shout whatever name came first to mind when he was climaxing in some rotund housewife's mouth. To him, that was one of the critical core aspects to Mr. Sucky. How else could a score be reasonably counted? Although nobody had ever volunteered for the job, Rob imagined that, at some point in the unforeseeable future, a referee could be enlisted to count Rob's victories against all the mouths of all the women who had ever said something critical about him, which he had then subsequently conquered with semen. Having a name to put to every successful goal he accomplished with his penis was crucial to the mainstream success of Mr. Sucky.

Unfortunately, nobody felt comfortable with Rob using their names for such an occasion; not even any of his imaginary friends would tolerate this shit. Rob was also forbidden from masturbating should he not find a willing accomplice for his sad, confusing and smarmy hobby. All in all, these conditions attached to Mr. Sucky meant that, in actuality, Rob would only manage to orgasm once or twice a year.

"YOU'VE GOT IDEAS. MAYBE THEY'RE GOOD Ones," the Librarian sighed. "But think about who you're talking to."

"Who am I talking to?"

"You're talking to a middle-aged librarian working at some crummy small liberal arts school in a little New England town. You're talking about wireless internet technology, but the year is 1989. To me, at least."

And then you're stuck. Not just a little bit stuck— it's a long Thanksgiving weekend, 1989. What do you do? Cable TV barely even exists anywhere. Certainly not where you're at.

There's a video store open in the town plaza, usually closing at 7 PM but there's a snowstorm, the first big one of the season, so they may be closing sooner. You do have a color, 13" Zenith TV set but no VCR. The video store will rent you one; it's $25 a week, with a $50 deposit.

You hurry your ass over there, the shop in question appropriately named, "Cabin Fever." You know it's the kind of place with a secret-passphrase-accessible backroom deal, a small stock of low-budget porn that can be had for only four times the normal rental fee. You smile, wink and nod at the big-hair headbanger sarcastic-looking dude at the counter and he waves you on through, and then you find yourself holding a fresh copy of "Fantasy Flings 5," wondering just how bad this thing could actually be.

You hate the Librarian for trapping you here. But your failure was in underestimating the coercive powers of words. Librarians have a sinister agenda in pursuing their chosen occupations. You had gone and offended this one in particular; now, you were bereft of all the modern conveniences you'd ever taken for granted, and find yourself stuck in a time and place so basic and uninspired, a revolutionary act of blowing your brains out with a .38 snub nose packed full of hollow points would rise to the occasion of fine art.

You pick one of the pornographic VHS cassettes at random and pay the counterman for the privilege. You also rent an overpriced and underpowered machine to play it back, cursing yourself for having years ago chucked out your last four-head dual-deck Magnavox.

In your cold, barren room, you spend at least 45 minutes trying to remember how to route the coax connections between the machine and the TV, fumbling around with the loose dial switch until, you think and hope like hell, it has been properly adjusted to channel 3.

The cassette gets sucked in noisily by the machine. It whirs up the reels and begins to play.

On the screen, a man named Rob, or "Robin," is being interrogated in a very plain room.

"WHAT'S THE BEST WAY to have your time wasted?" David asked.

"Doing the Shit Camp chant, of course."

"I don't think I know it."

"It's easy, it goes: SHIT... CAMP! SHIT... CAMP!"

It wasn't quite *that* easy. You needed to get the dogs going as part of the ritual. Especially Shitta, the Shit Camp™ mascot dog. She was a half-Husky, half-German Shepherd cross that Sprightly Bob had the wise idea of just terming "North American Shithound," as a more succinct nomenclature. We love you, Sprightly!

Shitta would need to get stirred up. Grabbing her by her stubby little tail until she began to growl and nip at your hand was a tried and true technique. Any other dogs in the area would need to be similarly stimulated. The dirtiest kids in your group then need to start wrestling on the ground, kicking up enough dust to get everyone thoroughly coated in anticipation of actually *arriving* at Shit Camp™.

Eating a hearty meal of beans or other fibrous matter well in advance of departing was also essential. You would need to resist any and all temptation to have a bowel movement on the road during the several hours' drive to get to Shit Camp™. The special "humanure" patented trash-can-filled-with-dung-and-TP was awaiting! The Shit Camp™ chant was mostly about squirming around in your drawers, trying like hell to prevent any uninvited guests from bailing out the ol' back door before your buttcheeks were properly positioned on the raised platform built especially for this purpose– then it was fire at will!

Beer helped too: nasty, shitty, warm iced beer that would be cheap anywhere else but cost a filipino child's ransom at the corner market closest to Shit Camp™. The beer would need to be mostly drunk along the final fifty mile stretch of winding road, challenging one to quick and efficient pre-game drinking, to the point of being drunk enough to be allowed to enter Shit Camp™. Nazi Mark would make sure of it. If you weren't drunk enough for him, there was no way in hell you were getting through the gate– and that motherfucker was inhaling JD in front of his trailer all goddamned day. So, the Shit Camp™ chant was *also* a drunken dance ritual to convince an actual, full-blood Nazi, who was quite drunk, that you were also drunk.

"ARE THOSE REAL BIRDS?"

"Paul, don't shout."

"Uh, yes, those are real birds." She had to wonder; did this guy actually know what things *were?*

"Don't mind him, he's retarded."

"Uh-OHHHH!"

"Paul!"

"It's... okay." Really, it *wasn't* okay. She didn't know any retards, and if she did, then she would immediately take the necessary steps to *un*-know them.

"You're a pretty lady!" Paul was really better with compliments than his brother was. His brother just wanted to know how fast he could find a kid sister or other worthless acquaintance to pawn Paul off on for a couple of hours while he got to know this girl better.

And this girl really was worth knowing. Even though he'd met her just the night before after another doldrum set of playing backdrop beats while Paul vehemently shouted incoherent lyrics and called it a musical act, Paul's Brother was sure that he wanted to spend the rest of his life with her. She was extremely average-looking, two steps away from a dumpy classical hourglass figure, pale, with light-brown hair of the poorest quality. The girl had traveled the world, doing meth, but stopped in her early twenties when her rich grandma paid to put her up in rehab, or else she'd be cut off forever from the family fortune. The girl was counting on that money in order to finance a fake career as an artist.

Paul's Brother didn't know this, of course, and even if he did, he wouldn't have cared. He was completely and totally in love, like the love his father had for their mother before they both dropped dead, a love of obligation, of feeling blessed by the stars for having something resembling a relationship to cling to in an otherwise pointless existence.

"Do you have a nice toilet?"

"Ehhhh…" the girl was quickly re-evaluating the situation. Sure, her friends had all pressured her to go out with a guy who was a *something*, instead of a *nothing*, for a change, but what exactly was the nature of his music, and why did he have this, this *retard* following him around?

"Paul's just happy he met a nice person like you," Paul's Brother gushed, slobbering. "He's sure a nice lady like you would have a pretty, quiet little bathroom that Paul would never, ever, *ever* think about defiling." He turned to his brother, with a threatening, maniacal glint in his eye. "Isn't that right, Paul?"

Paul's Brother was completely serious that he would disown Paul, maybe even execute him, if he fucked up this one last chance at finding true fake happiness. Really, what *was* the point anymore? He was dragging his special needs brother (who really belonged in some institution for the mentally handicapped where he could rot away the rest of his natural life and be forgotten) from one cheap nightclub to the next. Paul's Brother would be so much more like an *average* idiot if it weren't for this terrible, horrible burden.

What was there, really, that Paul brought to the table? How many times would Paul's Brother have to sacrifice his time in the service of pressing "play" on some uninspired, pre-recorded beat to use as the supporting orchestration for his brother to start ranting about poop? Who was *truly* being exploited in the situation?

"More like a shit-uation."

"Huh?"

"Nothing. Do you want to go out my back door so we can mount the bald knob behind my special house? We might be able to see butterflies, but probably just killer bees," the girl said, dejectedly. She already knew her grandmother would force her hand in marriage to this sad clown of a man, six weeks hence. The whole sob story about him caring for his retarded brother would be more than enough for the wretched witch to point her wrinkled, arthritic, curled index finger one more time at the girl and curse her with unreasonable demands and expectations of what was quickly shaping up to be a decidedly *non*-artistic life.

"WHEEEEP?"

"Paul!"

"No, I think that was a bird. They're cockatiels," the girl added.

Indeed. They were cockatiels, after all.

ANYWAY, STABBY WAS SINGING TO himself, or maybe it was actually Stubby. It was the song that goes,

In a shmikes-maree

In a SHMIKEMAREE!

Abul-eh-yah!

Stabby/Stubby wasn't sure what it meant, because his mom had always sung it to him when he was so small, and back in those times everyone immediately suspected there was something gone bad wrong inside his head. He couldn't speak right, he always smelled just a little bit off, no matter how many sponge-baths his poor mother would diligently give him; it was just never enough to make people think he smelled *normal*.

"In a SHMIKESMAREE!" he continued shouting, like nobody cared. Just about everyone did, and was bothered by it. Stabby/Stubby didn't mind it so much; he had more pressing things going on in that special mind of his, like how his mom would always interrogate him whenever he announced he had to go to the bathroom:

"Do you need to pee, or poop?"

Stabby/Stubby didn't understand why his mother needed to know this. He was at least eight, ten, probably as many as fifteen years old (fingers AND toes!) when she would still be bugging him, adamant about gaining knowledge of exactly what he was planning on doing once he got into the bathroom and had successfully (hopefully) shut the door.

Stabby/Stubby's mom never bothered to follow him into the toilet. She never offered to help out, either, which he thought was incredibly rude as he got older; still, it bugged him immensely, the fact that she always needed to know his business, when in reality that should be privileged information between the man using the toilet, and the Roto-Rooter guy sent out to unclog it. There was an unspoken bond between toileteer and plumber; the muck-suckers got paid handsomely not to report crimes of sewer abuse. Nobody ever *caught* Stabby/Stubby in the act, but in his time he'd put probably 250 used condoms (from jerking off in front of his roommate's door at three in the morning, using protection so he wouldn't leave a sticky mess and get caught and kicked out, which is what eventually happened anyway; he got sloppy), seven dead hamsters, the contents of a factory-defective bag of Flamin' Hot Cheetos that had all gotten clumped together like a rat-king, a decent-sized chunk of his ex-girlfriend's scalp with long greasy black hair still attached (don't ask), and a small pipe bomb down the drains into the public sewer and storm runoff drainage system. This is why the Mr. Rooter man would get paid in stained, crumpled $20 bills that Stabby/Stubby had laboriously earned over multiple nights of slinging counterfeit meth.

Stabby/Stubby's mom was a fussy, obsessive woman who went to her grave still expecting her son to come clean to her about what he was planning on having for lunch, how many minutes' drive-time it took for him to get to the hospital where she was dying of cancer (Stabby/Stubby rode a street bicycle with a bent front rim, so a lot longer than a functioning car would've taken), and if he'd been eating candy again (he was ONLY eating candy in those days, because the meth and the heroin would cause his body to spasm and contort so hard it would break his back if he tried eating any solid foods of substance). He assured her that he was pooping every day, which was all she really wanted to know.

Relaxed, the woman closed her eyes and nodded off, contentedly, forever.

THEY WANTED BOBBY TRASHTION (pronounced "TRAY-shtun," not "trash-tion") to star in this new movie they wanted to make, called "The Peeing Poodle." It wasn't actually going to be a film of any noteworthy accomplishment. Nobody was going to nominate it for an Academy Award or any other manner of esteemed recognition by High Society ®. It was going to be a cult film, a cut-up abstract abomination that would be just about guaranteed to be unwatchable.

It wasn't the producers' fault; they would never have promised millions to back this foolish project, had the director not been the retarded half-son of Sir Charles Exemplary, who was himself pretty goddamned eccentric; but nobody dared to say that to his face unless he wanted them to, for he was the heir to some title of nobility, everyone assumed. He spoke with a proper air, a vaguely British or perhaps Mid-Atlantic accent; regardless, it was intimidating. And he had a half-son who always wanted to make a movie about a dog taking a piss. So, if Charles Exemplary said something had to happen, there were always a bunch of dick-riders ready to pony up their pocket change, which was more than most people had in their retirement accounts at that time, which may have been recently, or possibly 20 years ago.

Bobby Trashtion was already beside himself with guilt for having allowed himself to have been portrayed as an invalid chasing obese women away from the ice-cream-freezer section at a grocery store, in some ill-fated attempt to remake a short film that originally had no dialogue, just nothing but a bunch of slapping, so everyone assumed it was a foreign flick where the people who made it were just too dumb and poor to have learnt any English, and therefore, the film *must* be completely redone in order to make it suitable for American audiences. Bobby thought this was completely silly, lacking of any and all merit, and, for once, he was correct. That didn't stop him from cashing the studio's check, however, so he just swallowed his pride and assumed that this would be the low point of his career, the one thing that every social media influencer now and into the next few decades would deride him for, mercilessly. He was wrong.

"The Peeing Poodle" maybe could have worked as one of those weird little acts of microcinema that sometimes get made and shown as a lead-in to an actual movie. Instead, an entire 90 minutes were devoted to following this stupid fucking dog around the tree-lined suburbs of some nameless midwestern city, as it proceeds to piss on every single last stick and branch protruding from the ground, its owner forced to engage in small-talk level banter with passersby while stumbling into a number of yawningly predictable happenstance scenarios. The main character falls in love, gets engaged, and is ready to wed, just to have the marriage called off at the last second, all within a matter of fifteen minutes and two blocks' worth of trees and shrubs upon which the dog had urinated.

The retarded half-son of Charles Exemplary thought he was a genius, of course. And nobody called him out on it! Because of who his half-daddy was, he could take a shit in a flower pot and everyone would applaud it. Disgusting.

Bobby Trashtion was not impressed, but then again, he wasn't being paid to be impressed. Actors are like hookers, in reality. They just get paid to perform and do as they're told. If they suck, or don't suck good enough, they get replaced. Bobby Trashtion was always in fear for his livelihood for this reason. He couldn't go back to the life he used to have, with his obesity, and his schizophrenic father, and girls making fun of him. It was *worth* playing this idiot who allowed his dog to haphazardly piss all over everything for entire film. He just had to keep telling himself it was necessary, and, after awhile, it didn't hurt so much.

THERE WAS A PILE OF POOP over there. This one person noticed it. "That's poop," they said, plainly.

Some other people were around as well. "You need to find someone else to play your stupid games with," one of them said.

It was a very basic setting. There were no houses or trees, and very little to eat or drink; that's why everyone was mildly surprised to just see a pile of poop sitting, right over there. There were no toilets, either, so it wasn't really *that* surprising.

Still, the sense of the situation was that something ought to be done about the poop. It couldn't just be left right there, not with all these people milling about. People deserve some baseline level of respect and courtesy, after all. Having to see, and inhale the stench, of poop was not a very polite way to pass the time.

Nobody was really that amused by it, either. Sometimes, people find poop to be funny. This was not one of those times. But, one of these people must have put it there. There was nobody else around.

None of the people there were really all that special or even sure as to how to tell one another apart. They all went by "they," and they were all wearing nondescript clothing and had very plain faces that showed no emotions, ever. They didn't talk that much, and didn't ever bother to get to know one another, at all. So, there was a serious lack of consensus-building, for one thing, and that was impeding their ability to collectively problem-solve the troubling predicament of what to do with this big, steaming, pile of poop.

"It's not funny, or cool," one of them said, horribly. "It's poop."

"Well, maybe Messel Pringitt did it," another one said.

"Shhh. No proper nouns, remember?" But the one who said it *did* have a point. Messel Pringitt certainly had a tendency to leave fecal matter strewn around.

"This isn't about what did or did not create the pile of poop," said another one of them, who was probably the smartest one there (but not by much). "The pile of poop is there, and we are here, and this is *almost* a situation in which us, and the poop, are occupying the same space." It was close enough to make for a bad smell, that was for sure.

And the poop wasn't getting any younger, either. As it aged, it was quickly approaching peak ripeness. That is the point at which flies would be flocking to it (if, indeed, there were any flies left; nobody had seen a single one for days now) to lay their eggs inside of the poop so their maggots would have a nice, warm home, heated from the decaying fecal matter, stocked full of scatological nutrition upon which they would feed, and grow into big strong healthy adult flies, ready to take flight and make poop homes for families of their own.

It was very touching, the fly's circle of life; but the people in this scene weren't impressed at all. All they knew was that there was some poop, and someone or something had left the poop there; and it didn't seem like whatever had created the poop in the first place was going to be coming back to clean it up.

Nobody knew what to do, though, about the poop. So, they just did nothing.

"And doing nothing is a very exhausting thing, actually. Lots of people say they'd love to do nothing, but have you, personally, ever tried it for any extended period of time? It's actually very exhausting. It gets really tiresome. It's an extremely uncomfortable position for any cognizant being to occupy for very long. Your dopamine reward system shuts down quickly. Without any external stimuli, your thoughts rapidly turn to mush. You find yourself unable to form complete sentences in your mind. Dogs start sniffing around, waiting to take a thick bite out of your corpse. There's a general sense of unease that pervades all corners of your ever-shrinking sense of reality. You can't hide from it, it's not anything identifiably bad; but, you don't like the way it makes you feel. You start sweating out ingrown hair follicles and reciting avant-garde poetry, backwards. You breath stinks constantly like stale Doritos even when you haven't eaten in days.

"You understand, now, that doing nothing really isn't a solution to anything. *Not* doing some specific thing that you should have done isn't the same thing as doing nothing, but then again, if you had a better thing to be doing than the thing that you're not currently doing, but which you *should* be doing, then you would be doing that thing, and not nothing."

The procrastinators amongst them realized this was a valid point, and took it upon themselves to educate the rest of the assembled denziens of this barely-a-place about the reality of the situation, just so that they wouldn't have to, later. So, in desperation, and realizing that they wouldn't be able to survive much more nothingness, the people there did something. They came up with a name. Dosringgit Spataphingit. It wasn't very good, and not a practical name at all (except maybe for some Italian-Malaysian hybrid person), but it was *something*, not just more of nothing. Poor ol' Spataphingit (or *Spat* as he was more commonly known by those deplorables who couldn't ever be bothered to consider how to pronounce a name that wasn't "Bud" or "Buck" or "Brad") was now the one to blame for the poop.

Luckily for Spat, he didn't live over there. Over there is not a good place to live, nor is it fun, nor is it much of anything; Spat wouldn't ever have to deal with the poop, or the people who had duly accused him of leaving such a large pile of said poop, and wouldn't ever even have the slightest clue that somewhere, in an that was just barely a place, some nondescript persons were thinking that he must have pooped over there, in their general vicinity, where they would have to deal with it, *at some point*. The people in the place over there, however, had their work cut out for them now; because, since Spat was never going to *go* there, they would have to clean the poop up, which was a type of activity, it could be assumed. It would need to be scraped up and disposed of in some manner. These were definitive things that would need to tangibly occur. Those people over there were beside themselves with shock; having grown so accustomed to doing nothing, they weren't sure how to take the first step, towards doing *something*.

They would need to figure it out, on their own.

THERE WAS A MOMENT WHEN, it could be said, there was no longer any humor in the scatological references being bandied about with reckless abandon; now, then, it had become more a morbid curiosity of an outsider looking in through the wicked windows of a shameful basement, located somewhere in the vast indeterminable expanse of Middle America, beholden still to the intellectual curiosity of a higher lifeform observing the imminent demise of a certain specimen, and learning all there was to know in order to satisfy that insatiable itch of knowledge: that being, the ritual of the morning bowel movement.

Schlafly, as he was known, had a reputation for only pooping within the first hour of waking up. It was ordinarily a dry, boring affair, as desolate as the desert of the great American Southwest, and as vapid as a weekday-morning television talk show. Schlafly aspired to be more than just a byproduct of his own disgusting bodily functions; he sought a greater sense of purpose in his habitual endeavors. Therefore, he closely inspected the poop he'd left in the confines of the toilet bowl each time it happened, searching for any signs of discoloration or deficiencies in its consistency.

As he had a fairly regular diet and no drug habits of which to speak, Schlafly was usually satisfied by his leavings. Then he would move diligently onward, into phase two of his routine: he would begin laughing, uproariously, pointing and screaming in sheer hysterics at the pile of shit that was now sitting in the toilet, stinking all to high hell, and otherwise leaving the facilities in complete ruination for his wife and two-and-a-half children to stumble upon later on (Schlafly was insistent, as a good upstanding male denizen of these United States, that he have first position upon the communal bathroom in their unremarkable ranch house, since, in his view, he worked a job that paid more than minimum wage but otherwise required absolutely no talent or special skills, and was therefore able to barely meet the cost of living; yet he felt entitled by merit of the fact that he *did* possess a job, while his wife, who was formerly a man, had no inclination to work, or do any basic chores or maintenance around the house, and instead made her contribution through reliance upon the government assistance checks provided on behalf of the two-and-a-half children, who were after all foster kids and placed in the home as a result of the government's anti-discrimination policies, theirs being one of the more socially liberal states of that disgusting expanse called the Midwest, where it would be acceptable for a couple of whom one half was a woman with a penis who had no biological capacity to bear children of her own to instead be assigned the care of high-risk youth by a well-meaning, but poorly managed, agency), and it was absolutely the funniest friggin' thing that he could imagine to begin yet another in a long-running chain of completely pointless days. He pointed and howled with unimaginable amusement at his own poop.

Schlafly viewed every turd he squeezed out of his sorry asshole as a masterpiece, a marvelous contribution to the upper echelons of society, high art at its greatest and most contrived level. He saw it as a blatant act of social commentary, something to do with his prostate, and how his exceptionally poor diet was continuously imperiling that absolutely pointless gland in his body, which would ultimately lead to some catastrophic health scenario wherein he might very well perish. It was shit that would kill him, he'd long ago decided; and what better a response to this otherwise reasonable sense of mortality than to laugh in the face of death, the very thing that was, one day, eventually, going to lead him to an untimely demise?

The poop would sit there, bored to shit, looking back at him as much as it could be said that any pile of dung ever did such a thing. It was in the process of being drowned, constantly, and knew full well that it was a most unwelcome presence in the existence of its creator. Bestowed with this lacking sense of self-worth, the poop was willing to accede to its lower ranking in the hierarchy of bodily functions, but couldn't help but question *why* it was that its primary benefactor was continually attempting to drown it in a shallow pool of water. Couldn't there be another option? Say, for instance, disposal in a steaming pit that would quickly cook it down into the consistency of manure? The poop was aware, at least, that some other forms of dung were relatively prized for their value as a nutritive aid for plant life, or indeed, even as fuel for cooking. The poop wanted to be self-perpetuating, as any reasonable entity ever could hope to be, and contribute its material worth towards the pursuit of bringing into existence more biomass that could be subsequently consumed and digested and then shat out through some animal's anus, or organ serving the essential functions thereof, thereby fulfilling its role in the never-ending cycle of feast-to-feces.

Schlafly had no comparable respect or philosophical awareness when viewing his own poop. He merely thought it was hilarious whenever he would have a really satisfying bowel movement over the old porcelain throne. He had been given a "squatty potty" at the company Christmas party about four years ago, which he was curious about, but had never attempted to use, mostly because he was so familiar with the regular sitting regimen that had for so long delivered a great sense of colonic satisfaction every morning (unless he'd been drinking excessively, or eaten an absurdly large serving of steak the night before, situations which invariably led to constipation, diarrhea, or some other disruption in his regular schedule and posture), and in order to proclaim the overall sense of accomplishment he experienced at the conclusion of each shitting, promptly after pulling up his drawers and as he was washing his hands, he had to cackle uproariously while pointing at his poop.

The poop was not impressed.

HELMUT NUCKMIËLER WAS WORKING ON HIS latest masterpiece, a list of random questions that had been commissioned for the Google-branded "search engine" to contemplate and attempt to formulate answers to:

- Why do Asians have dry earwax?
- What's a good dessert soup recipe for a cat?
- Are oranges God's testicles?
- Is it safer to fart when sitting down?
- Does Dagny Taggart ever get penis? I don't want to actually read the book.
- How many dead people live in Florida?
- Is it sinful to speak to fat folks?
- How many different ways can I go to the airport?
- Is it bad luck to put out matches in a birthday cake?
- How do I teach my birds the meaning of Largie Gripbvens day?
- Do you know what happens when a small boy gets run over by a very large truck?

Well, since you asked, little Tommy would know something about getting run over, because that was the very same thing that happened to have gotten him killed one summer at SHIT CAMP, INC. He was being an obtuse child, naturally, and playing in the middle of the road with one of his Micropan toys (it was not, however, Micropan Marneshta, since that was too expensive for the likes of little Tommy's family) and not paying attention at all to the refrigerated cargo truck that was delivering a shipment of poop popsicles to all the hot kids at the summer camp there.

He was splattered more or less instantaneously. Little bits of boy meat ended up strewn across the roadway, his baby teeth all mixed up together with the few adult teeth that had managed to grow into his imbecile jaw having become stuck in the truck's radiator, and his eyeballs popped like jello shots chucked by drunk, naked, horny chicks at the truck's headlights. His spleen and liver landed fairly intact on the grassy shoulder of the street, and were immediately set upon by a wayward flock of California Condors. [Incidentally, California Condors' nutritional requirements are best met by the entrails of adolescent humans.] The birds got competitive and began squawking and lunging at one another, pieces of Timmy's viscera flying through the air as the scavengers engaged in the most savage combat. They ended up having to be shot to death by a Game Warden in order to protect themselves *from* themselves, since California Condors are still considered to be critically endangered as a species, and the Game Wardens are empowered to execute any living thing that would potentially compromise the life of one of the rare, pristine birds.

And of course, there were some escaped badgers and carnivorous parrots and feral huskies who intended to get in on the feasting as well. You see, little Tommy had been *butt*-killed, which meant that the impact of the truck made its way first through his rectum, before liquefying the rest of his body, a process that occurs in mere fractions of a second, yet leaves the most succulent and desirable carrion residue that any beast within scent-range will immediately set upon. It was a true gourmet opportunity that would only occur once that entire Summer for all the creatures, large and small, that inhabited the delicate ecological niche surrounding SHIT CAMP, INC.

Shrumpy Dielshit, as it turned out, had something to say about the whole sordid affair:

Actually, first of all, his name was *Stumpy* Dielshit. And he was having some severe intellectual problems. The professionals who'd examined him previously suspected it to be some form of "Cluster A" personality disorder, like Schizotypal. He was having great difficulty in organizing his thoughts, and he suspected that he knew exactly why: he really had to poop, but there was a large man in the bathroom, fiddling around with some kind of electrical wiring security box. Stumpy was terrified.

His mom had tried to help him, when he was younger, to feel more comfortable while defecating. She told him to first take all of his clothes off before using the toilet. That way, the poop-germs wouldn't get on them.

But she *didn't* tell him what to do if there was a large person in the bathroom ahead of him. Stumpy shuddered with revulsion. This man was diddling around in there, doing who-knows-what, and there was no way that Stumpy could do anything to interrupt him, because this other man was bigger than he was, and that wouldn't be appropriate. Big people needed to be left alone, so they would eventually just leave of their own volition, like a bear. Confronting one would never end well.

Still, Stumpy really needed to poop. If there was a Waffle House in the area, he would just go there, since that was a nice place to poop sometimes; but, there wasn't. He decided that he would try his luck, and go over to the gas station down the street from his workplace.

Once he got there, there was a disturbance. Apparently, Smorsevol Delouchticant was starting some shit.

Everybody hated Smorsevol Delouchticant, and for good reason. First of all, they would rather be dealing with a Delouchti*can* than a Delouchti*can't*. It set a bad precedent and introduction to any particular sequence of events, like the one that ensued on this fateful day. Smorsevol had gone to the store because he figured he needed some more milk and cigarettes. He grabbed a half gallon jug of the cheapest, nearly-curdled 2% milk he could find in the deep recesses of the store's back cooler, and opened it up and took a nice big gulp, right there in the aisle, before he'd even paid for it. If they had cigarettes merchandised openly, out on the shelves like they probably used to do before everyone got all paranoid and illegal about such things, he would've pulled one out and lit it up on the spot. It's not that he was a thief; he was just extremely lazy, and an asshole to boot.

And what a complete and total asshole Smorsevol *was*. Instead of smoking, he chewed on a thick wad of gum as he guzzled his disgusting cow-tit-juice, and tried to blow a bubble. It quickly inflated with the milk froth, until it exploded all over the braids of someone's nine year old daughter in front of him. The girl screamed, and clawed at her hair as if someone had just fed five-hour energy shots to fire ants and strategically placed their nest in the middle of her scalp. The girl's parent figure turned around, saw Smorsevol and the mess that he'd created, and began giving him a stern lecture about not being able to do two things at once, because, like President Johnson once said (in not so many words), if he wasn't smart enough to be able to chew gum and do something else at the same time without fucking something up, like a child's impeccable hair, then he really should stop doing multiple things and instead focus on trying to do just one thing successfully.

Smorsevol didn't appreciate being talked to like that, the first thing in what (for him) was still the morning, since he hadn't yet had all of his milk mixed with cheap coffee-flavored syrup, and smoked through at least half a pack of cigarettes, so he proceeded to let the girl's parental figure know as much by splitting the person's glasses right in two, along the bridge of their nose, with his fist.

"You tetrasexual freakazoid," the parent, who was nonbinary, said to him, disparagingly. Smorsevol didn't seem to mind very much, since it was true; and it certainly didn't make him any more qualified, in the view of the state and local governments, to reward him with the holy grail of all welfare cheats, the golden EBT card, which would allow Smorsevol to purchase liquor *and* cigarettes, as well as toilet paper, shaving cream, and novelty sex toys.

There was a small commotion when Smorsevol decided to take exception to being called out for being an ugly, little coward. "I've seen this sort of thing before," he announced, confidently.

Nobody was quite sure what, exactly, he was referring to; but it was probably this one time that a guy by the name of Dumb Icicle was being harassed by either another small child, or a midget with a poor attitude. Smorsevol loved to tell the story anytime he felt like it was relevant, which was never. People would groan in protest, those who knew him at least, because they were fully aware that precious minutes of their time were about to be wasted.

The story went something like this: Dumb Icicle was walking down a frosty street, minding his own business, on a cold morning in a minor outlying city surrounding Boston. He was about to hop over to the local Donut Shack, because it was 11:14 AM and the morning crew was about to be throwing away all of the unsold glazed donuts, because if they didn't, the donuts might get salmonella from cheap eggs, because the maniac who ran the kitchen at night, known only as the "Donut Master," refused to sterilize or cook the eggs at all; he would just brush the donuts down with raw, nasty egg wash *after* they had already been baked. [Some people took exception to the idea of a baked donut. Aren't donuts supposed to be fried, by nature? Rolled out and dipped in hot grease until fully saturated and brown on the outside? No, said the Scientific Community, which secretly harbored a compulsion to become grotesquely obese. There were better ways to stack what was once a mundane breakfast snack with countless more calories, puffing and filling the dough up with sugar and other highly refined ingredients, as well as a consortium of artificial flavors, ensuring that the end result was not just some shriveled-up ring, but a large, glorious pastry that barely even continued to meet the working definition of a donut. To add extra weight to the item, they contrived an alternative spelling, *Doughnut*, which contained three extra and wholly unnecessary letters. Icings and creams became ever more extravagant, and *then* some dickwad even had the overfed notion to create what was christened the "Cronut," which had more of a croissant consistency, but still formulated into a round shape with plenty of extra sugary, buttery nonsense that just invited immediate weight gain. Personal trainers around the country threw up their arms in despair and quit their jobs en masse. Science had won, and people were getting even fatter, faster than before, just like the accelerating expansion of the Universe.] The Donut Master refused to conform to what he considered to be completely arbitrary and oppressive health standards enforced by the city government. He thought that raw egg belonged on donuts by birthright, and the revolutionary traditions of 1775. After a prolonged court battle, the Donut Master won the right to continue making donuts in his own weird and unsanitary fashion, provided that he made sure to throw them all away no more than twelve hours after he'd dipped them in the rancid egg preparation.

The problem was, nobody wanted to actually *eat* any of the nasty things. The management, along with the rest of the employees, decided it would be safer to just set up a cart selling actually edible donuts across the street from the Donut Shack, since they feared that the Donut Master would put something strange in their ears, and maybe disable the brake systems on their cars when they weren't looking, out of spite for having dared to question his technique.

Dumb Icicle didn't know or care about any of this. For reasons that don't need to be explained, he was legally retarded. But, he was the nice kind of retard, so it was okay. Coincidentally, he had a bulletproof gut, and could eat three-week-old dog shit that had been scavenged from an abandoned rat's nest underneath a dumpster outside a dirty little Chinese restaurant in Brockton, and still be fine and walking around like a normal, healthy, and non-demented person.

So he waited, with great anticipation and glee, for the clock to edge up against the legally imposed deadline for disposing of the dripping, sulfur-reeking, deformed sorry excuses for donuts that were sitting out in trays lining the store's main counter, attracting flies. The Donut Master realized that Dumb Icicle was his best (and only) customer, and took pity on him, since the Donut Master himself probably wouldn't want to eat the crap that he was trying to shove in the faces of innocent members of the public. He made Dumb Icicle a deal on the first morning that he stumbled into the Donut Shack: buy at least a dozen, and he could pay only a dime a donut.

Dumb Icicle, being a retard, didn't have much earning potential in life; yet he continually failed to live up to even the very low expectations that society had set out for people like him. So, he had to pick up random strands of hair off the streets and out of trash cans (sometimes, he'd tried suavely pilfering hair off the floor of the neighborhood barbershop, but the Barber had quickly caught on and chased him out with a broom, shouting at the top of his lungs in a foreign tongue that Dumb Icicle couldn't identify, because he was retarded) and take them down to the group of Tarot-card readers and other grifters that would congregate in the town square, and sell the hair to some Voodoo Priestess. It wasn't much of a hustle, but it made him a few dollars regularly, so he could restock on his sordid donut supply the following morning, which, indeed, was all he had to eat throughout every waking day.

So Dumb Icicle was getting ready to enter the Donut Shack, like he did every morning around this time, when the small person confronted him. "Damistacle, Damistacle!" it crowed, hideously.

What had happened was, Dumb Icicle had earned an unwanted reputation for being the only guy stupid enough to eat the Donut Master's nasty concoctions. It earned him certified freak status amongst all the locals. People were telling their co-workers, families, maids, bartenders, baristas, flight attendants, stockbrokers, lawyers, associates serving five to seven years in federal penitentiaries for fraud and embezzlement, mistresses, lunchladies, trapeze performers, and even a few minor rock stars, about what they witnessed Dumb Icicle doing *every single morning*.

This one little thing, kid or dwarf or whatever it was, had heard about Dumb Icicle from multiple sources, and was quite enthralled and even a bit aroused by the notion that some poor idiot would actually want to eat the kind of crap that the Donut Master would bake. However, this small person also had a severe speech impediment, owing to an easily preventable birth defect, and couldn't articulate the two words, *Dumb Icicle*.

"And Dumb Icicle got so upset, and embarrassed, and he couldn't even speak, he started stuttering, and pulled out his last shitty donut, and...." Smorsevol was breaking down with laugher. No matter how many times he told the story, it never grew old. At least not for him.

"Hey bud, why don't you take all the facts in that little story of yours, right, and stick them between two pieces of white bread. Then you can shove it up your asshole like a reverse shit sandwich!" yelled the person who Smorsevol had originally offended. They were getting all bent out of shape because they were a trend-follower, a particularly braindead variant of your generic, average moron, who had just completed "Sober October" and was well on their way into "No-Nut November," and greatly anticipating "Dirty December," which was a time when a bunch of Incel-types and other various troglodytes would refuse to bathe for the full 31 days in the calendar month, much to the chagrin, humiliation and disgust of their family members and close associates, all the while growing antsy from being sober and horny. And, they were about to stink up the place all to high hell, too.

Smorsevol couldn't remember what they were all standing around in line for. Was this a small convenience store, or was it some kind of post office? His mom had warned him about trying to go to the post office on his own when he was little. He always got frightened by the fascistic eagle logo hanging over the entrances to most of these sorts of places. It looked like a distorted head of a crude, angry puppet, about to swoop down and bite some child's head off.

Also, the place stank like sweet, rotting garbage. You know how the sugars and remnant fats from discarded meat scraps like to drip, and get fermented, and visited by flies so they can lay their eggs and hatch their maggots to squirm around and eat some nice, juicy, rotting shit? That's the smell they were experiencing.

Smorsevol was about to launch into another long-winded and highly pointless fable about this time that some guy managed to collect eighty-seven gallons of similarly constituted trash juice in order to shower his neighbor's convertible with it, when the person who had originally taken exception to Smorsevol's disheveled appearance and antisocial manner punched him squarely in the face, heading off any further opportunities for Smorsevol to accost these genteel folk with further nonsensical ramblings.

"The end," stated a small, mousy, midwestern woman, matter-of-factly.

"IT'S NOT MY FAULT I'M A WORTHLESS DRUG ADDICT!" Jordan Peterson screamed, unemotionally. "It's everybody else's fault that they're drug addicts, but it's not mine! I got addicted to drugs by telling people about how addictions were their own faults, and, it was so stressful, that it led me to start abusing prescription medications."

"And you don't believe that your substance abuse issues stem from the fact that you are a liar and a charlatan?" Doctor asked, condescendingly.

"No, because Americans are disgusting and obsolete," Peterson replied, defiantly. Since he was Canadian, this statement ostensibly didn't apply to him (even though Canada is, by all definitions, part and parcel of the continental landmass that is North America, along with Mexico, it was commonly understood that the term *American* referred exclusively to those residing in the United States, since they had such grandiose chips on their shoulders, and felt entitled to claim ownership over the entirety of the landmass by extension, so it was permitted to make this argument, and it was also considered to be highly uncool to point out the obvious contradiction implicit in making such a broad generalization in the first place), which satisfied Peterson's ego. He did not like to make any criticism that could possibly be directed at himself.

"Hmmm. Well, Mr. Peterson, it seems to me that you suffer from an advanced case of constipation," Doctor replied. And this was true, physiologically, since all the drugs that Peterson had been scarfing down with reckless abandon *did* effectively shut down his lower gastrointestinal tract.

But it was *more* true that Peterson suffered from constipation of the mind. He was fixated on old-timey crap, boiled hotdog dinners and hockey games, teacup-sized wives and non-erotic male-on-male wrestling. In his vivid imagination, Peterson conjured up a make-believe era of back-and-white logic, a place where toilet paper was always in great abundance and juvenile delinquents were locked away in maximum-security facilities to be looked after by certified sociopathic guards.

As Peterson silently sat and indulged his inner fantasies, unbeknownst to the parties physically present, he had attracted the attention, and indeed, seething ire of William S. Burroughs and H.P. Lovecraft as they ambled about in the Afterlife.

Peterson, Burroughs argued, was guilty of "Committing nameless and insensitive acts of poetry. This is the sort of man who most likely feels filthy at the climax of every bowel movement. He leaps into the shower with desperate hopes of scrubbing himself clean, like a wet toad burrowing under so many rotten leaves."

"He suffers from historic myopia," concurred Lovecraft. "He continuously harkens to a past that never existed. Let us disabuse him of his perceptions." So, the two dead authors devised a plan to drive Peterson insane. Burroughs, as the Patron Saint of addiction, and Lovecraft, the intellectual godfather of ostracization, created an ingenious pattern of hallucinations with which to bewitch Peterson.

It began as Peterson left Doctor's office, after having been told that his insurance policy had been cancelled for nonpayment as he had spent the prior few months at an in-patient rehab center. As he was walking out into the dimly lit and crowded hallway, a small man approached him. "Hey buddy, what's your sickness?" the Dwarf inquired, calmly.

"It is not my sickness; it is modern society that is demented," Peterson responded, confidently.

The small man pulled out a satchel and whipped it open with great flourish. Inside, there were five dimebags of scag, a slightly-tarnished silver spoon, and an antique glass syringe. The needle wasn't empty, however. The tip squirmed and drooped like a trouser snake, and inside swam a hoard of glowing, tentacled orbs. "Wanna try? First taste's free," the little guy offered Peterson.

Peterson scoffed. "Just like so many other young men these days. Don't you ever bother to think that your growth impediment was due to such reckless behavior? I doubt you even made your bed this morning."

The Dwarf tilted his head back and began laughing uproariously. A dark green cloud of noxious gas began emanating from his throat as he guffawed, drifting slowly up to the ceiling like a plume of smoke from a graveyard cigarette. It gradually coalesced and took the form of a specter, lacking much detail except for two large, empty vortices where its eyes should've been.

Peterson swallowed. He'd always had an issue with haunted houses. When he was six years old, his mother had taken him to a Halloween carnival (because she was single at the time, and wanted to get boned by as many of the freakshow performers as she could manage in one night, to set a new neighborhood record for which she could boast to all the housewives on the block, maligned and unsatisfied as they were), and abandoned him at the "Ghostly Gallows" attraction. Naive and incompetent a child as he was, Peterson skipped through the entrance curtain, just to be immediately confronted by a very poorly rendered figure of a ghoul, constructed mostly out of asbestos. Peterson froze, and promptly emptied his bladder into his brand-new school pants.

These were unpleasant and highly defective memories, Peterson decided, promptly dismissing the Dwarf and his smoke-friend as he shuffled down the hall. "Goulash!" the cloudy figure growled after him.

Well, that was also a problem. Back when he was a teenager, Peterson had once been hungry after a pickup game of squash, and found his way to a Hungarian diner on the outskirts of Edmonton. The weird, dark hairy man behind the counter glared at him when he asked for a hamburger. "No burger!" the man shouted, hoarsely.

"What would be your pleasure, then?" the innocent young Peterson asked, inquisitively.

Without any further conversation, the man slammed a bowl down on the counter in front of the lad, deftly drawing a greasy spoon from the front pouch of his stained apron as he did so, handing it to Peterson while pantomiming the act of eating, in a desperate and highly sloppy manner.

Peterson stared down at the bowl. It had chunks of unidentifiable meat and a few wilted vegetables floating around in a generous pool of oil. *Some of these things were once alive*, Peterson thought to himself, astounded. The chef stood, silently, smoking a harsh, unfiltered cigarette as he stared Peterson down. The whole scene was unsavory.

"He put your pee-pee from that night long ago into your bowl of soup," whispered an accordion-shaped being with eyestalks that was currently harassing Peterson in the present moment. Suddenly, it all made sense. Peterson had never felt right about eating that slop that he later found out was supposed to be a form of Goulash, the Hungarian national dish. He had choked it down as the dirty man suppressed great glee and delight at defiling the insides of a future monster. Which is what Peterson was.

He was still in denial about this fact, though. Lampshades were splitting open and transforming into giant, bloodsucking moths; a person with a dark complexion was lunging towards him with a switchblade held between his teeth, one leg trailing the other badly like it had been run over by a long-ago street trolley, and a conspicuous unibrow gracing his forehead; all the while, the man was muttering something about the industry and wisdom behind the act of getting high. Peterson failed to appreciate that this was being done for his benefit.

He retreated further into his distant and distorted memories. One time, his father had smacked away his hand as he attempted to tune in a station on their car's AM radio dial, and little Peterson had a crying fit. His father, self-conscious about being a divorced dad, immediately felt sorry for his little turd progeny, and they promptly went to a Tim Horton's so the small asshole could get a doughnut and forget all about his dad's obsessive-compulsive act of violence, which was instigated by the fact that only *he* should be able to touch the car radio dial, which he did, thirty-seven times each day, or every time a traffic light flickered.

Peterson was suddenly afraid. Why were all of these dark thoughts suddenly troubling his conscious mind? He reached into his jacket pocket, where he normally kept his stash of high-powered benzodiazepines, just to find a gaping cavity. Doctor, that motherfucker. He'd manipulated Peterson into going on one of his tangential rants, and had probably hired that Dwarf, who was now stalking him down the hallway that was beginning to melt into another realm entirely, to crawl underneath Peterson's suit and cut out the pocket which held his drugs, so then Doctor could end the session early with that bullshit excuse about health insurance, and take off for a long weekend of partying with whores and high-stakes gambling!

And this was the thing that Peterson feared most: that he would be exposed as another worthless excuse for a man, undone by his hubris about personal responsibility, having spent so much time criticizing everyone else that he never stopped to look in the mirror at the smug, disheveled and droopy prick staring back at him. He shuddered and dropped to the floor, convulsing and crying and writhing about, feeling pathetic and ultimately doomed. Also, he pooped his drawers.

Burroughs and Lovecraft cheered and toasted at having accomplished their mission.

UNCLE KRONKLUCUS

A NOVEL

CHAPTER I

"OH, BUT IT'S SUCH A CUTE LITTLE PIECE of poop!" Jackie Bopper, the highly inappropriate children's camp counselor for kids, had a rather unique way of looking at things. She would strut around, with an impossibly manic smile on her face, 24/7, even in those rare moments when she would pass out involuntarily for a few moments from physical exhaustion, her face would be paralyzed in this toothy grimace. It was disturbing, and rubbed pretty much everyone the wrong way.

But she was cheap. She'd get the job done for next to nothing, and that is what the upper management of SHIT CAMP, INC. expected. She doubled as a backup for their insurance policy. Like one time, when little Tommy got intentionally run over by a Dodge V8 driven by some reckless Christians from Clean Camp (their competition), Jackie had to play funeral host to hundreds of mourners who may well have otherwise opted to sue.

[Note: SHIT CAMP, INC. binds all of its clients by contract to arbitration. Meaning, something goes wrong, and you try to sue them; it goes to court, and the judge dismisses it once the opposing counsel rips his fancy sport-suit-coat-jacket off and howls to the rafters, "ARBITRATION!" You then end up in a mind-numbing loop of mandatory deposit fees, and you meet with a mustachioed man wearing a sweater vest in an abandoned bank vault that has been converted to low-cost office housing. This man explains to you in a very indelicate manner that he's already made up his mind that you are wrong and SHIT CAMP, INC. is right. He's not at all interested in hearing your side of the story. You paid him, so he can impartially tell you in no uncertain terms how very wrong, wrong, WRONG you are. You were stupid for having ever had the audacity to file a lawsuit in the first place. You should have just taken the candy. Then, at least, you'd have something to mask the leftover shit-taste in your mouth after having undergone this pointless and trivializing experience. Instead, no candy for you.]

Jackie had the best idea: a fire-truck themed funeral! Just like a birthday party, because Jackie could never be sad, so she rolled out balloons and a cake. A clown read the eulogy, punctuated at the end by a kazoo solo. The clown was paid in cocaine, and Jackie then proceeded to share her own memories of little Tommy:

"Tommy was a small boy who loved big trucks and fast cars," she started, bright white teeth gleaming under her spray-tan wrinkled emaciated cheekbones, dirty blonde bangs hanging low and thick, saturated with grease.

Tommy's father looked up from his sobbing, tears welling in his eyes, his mouth contorted with pain. "Why?" he moan-cried.

Jackie nodded approvingly in his direction. "Sometimes, when little boys have uh-ohs, it can seem really scary and sad. But it's okay! We have sparkles, and light, and lots of fun ahead of us!"

"But he's dead, you bitch!" Tommy's mom wailed out.

"Yay!" Jackie clapped in response. "We can all be loud and call out names! Tommy would be so happy right now, he loved shouting!"

Back up: Tommy was sent to SHIT CAMP, INC. due to a severe case of Tourette's Syndrome. Like all the other campers, he had some special needs which required adult supervision, and not by his normal caregivers. Caregivers are often burdened, even by "neurotypical" kids. They never get a break; the small bastards constantly demand money, attention, and cigarettes, and feel entitled to make sarcastic, smartass demeaning remarks when their grownup has been at work all day just trying to provide the best they can for their families, while eating all the shit their bosses make them shovel.

So Tommy wasn't a regular kid, and didn't deserve a regular kid's funeral. Jackie made sure of that.

"I want us all to hold hands while we sing the next song," she said, picking up her acoustic guitar. All gathered mourners proceeded to moan loudly.

"It's a really big step / To start walking away / From all of our friends / The journey starts today / But I've got a pal / To help me on my way / His name is Satan / And here's what he's got to say...."

"Completely inappropriate!" exclaimed one of Tommy's aunts, the rich pretentious cheapskate one.

WENDY WAS STUMBLING AROUND TOWN AGAIN, putting up fliers for her lost dog. A man stopped to inquire.

"What's his name?"

"Iggy Pops," said Wendy. She'd been crying.

"When's the last time you saw Iggy?" The man wasn't sure why he'd even bothered asking. It was clear he was dealing with yet another drug casualty, the woman worn out by street life under the California Sun, her brain cooked for too long to be salvageable.

"Last yesterday, at my friend's tent. The one who, okay, he likes to dress up in women's clothing."

The man had had enough. What kind of loser names their dog "Iggy Pop?"

But Wendy had *not* had enough yet. She would do this two, maybe three times a year. "Rainy Wendy" they would call her, for no apparent reason; "they" were the collective cohort of bums roaming around the general vicinity of coastal California.

"My sister married a Nigerian scammer," she continued, matter-of-factly. "And that's why I couldn't be seen with the transvestite, okay? Because the FBI is going to get confused if they think the same person is actually a man AND a woman! Or at least, he pretends to be a woman! He thinks that, if he spends a lot of money on clothes and makeup, and plays dress-up around the trailer park,"that his mother would then accept him as her own. It would never happen. His mother was a corporate type, a real Phyllis Schlafly sort of cunt. She did, in fact, chase him out of San Francisco before they passed a law *against* chasing out crossdressers, and he'd been hiding out in a thirty foot camper trailer ever since, playing dress-up.

"Improbable," the man who Wendy had initially asked to help find Iggy Pop said. "Of all the stupid sorry sob-stories out there, that is indeed the very worst I've ever held my ears open for. And by 'worst,' I don't intend to convey any sorrow or condolences on behalf of you, your crossdresser or your sister. Rather, I wish to express my absolute contempt and disdain for the very fact you'd see fit to waste my precious, precious time with such nonsensical blabbering. Do not ever speak to me again."

A dirty man pushing a shopping cart full of his belongings careened into the scene just as the helpful gentleman was inspecting the bottoms of his shoes for any indication of "Iggy Pop" residue, and blurted out, "GRANCH OBSBLEF ON AN D'GOTTA."

Wendy started crying again. Poor little girl.

ROBIN "ROB" BLEDSOE WAS A SERIAL paint-huffer. He did so discreetly, so his wife did not know this about him, and he intended to keep it that way. She was already irritated enough by his obsession with this made-up, stupid blowjob game he kept trying to convince her to play with him. So in the meantime, he would get all kinds of fucked up off of tiny little sample jars of model toy paints. Into the paper bag they would go, every time, while the hobby shop was trying to convince teenagers to stop playing fucking video games and start dressing appropriately, building little boats in their spare times outside of school, NOT CUSSING, saying their prayers, and keeping their peckers in their pants, which should not be too loose *nor* too tight-fitting.

Rob was one of the "good guys," the old man who owned the store figured. In his fantasies, Rob would be taking those little tubes and jars of paint out to confront troubled youth; after severely beating them with his belt, Rob would then introduce the wayward children of God to the ways of model-crafting. There would be no drugs, no vulgar "hip-hop" sort of singing and dancing, the black kids would always sit in the back, young women would not be coming home with semen dripping from their tender parts, and all would be right with the world. Sweaters and tobacco pipes and John Wayne films. Sweaters and tobacco pipes and John Wayne films. Sweaters and tobacco pipes and John Wayne—

"Sciclopans?" Rob jolted up from a huff, thinking he had heard something.

But it wasn't Sciclopans, or anything really of the sort. It was Micropan Marneshta, and wanna know a secret?

MICROPAN MARNESHTA WASN'T SUCH A BIG DEAL after all. Many normal-folk types have mocked and dismissed any possible relevance that Marneshta, or indeed any Micropan, may have to their nominal existences. And this is ostensibly true; Micropan Marneshta was a fringe character playing in a niche movement, and probably not worth otherwise explaining, but for this: it was a dog, originally. Just a plain old run-of-the-mill, Australian Shepherd she-dog. A bitch, if you would.

"OK, so, he was the star of that *Birdseedfood* commercial, right? The booger who would let all the birds violently peck seeds that were glued to the sides of his head and his face and groin and be all 'ohhh!' and 'owwww!' and shit. Literal shit, birdshit, they would shit all over him, matter of fact. Nobody ever wanted to talk about THAT during the post-production!" This guy took a triumphant swig of coffee, knowing not why anyone was even listening to him. "The point being, I was keen to this act before it became such a cause célèbre. And it wasn't all everybody though it was going to be, or ever was before or after the fact. Nothing.

"Micropan Marneshta, I was at the shoot for the first one. It was indeed just a dog, and that wasn't even that important at the time. The picture was called, 'Small Dick's Hot Lunch,' and in a snapshot, it tells the story of a clown, or at least a man dressed as a clown, the audience has no idea if he ever completed clown college, who owns a lunch-cart van and drives around empty parking lots, looking for dogs to feed. He finds one dog at first and lets her eat a pack of cheap, raw hotdogs. The dog gets so carried away, as dogs do, that she scarfs the whole thing down and then backs up a way to go off and puke in the corner.

"Then, some other dogs in the neighborhood get wind of what's going down. and come galloping in, a good four or five, and they just start a big ol' dogfight over who gets to eat up the pile of vomit the other dog just chucked up! And the whole time, 'Small Dick,' or at least that's what we are led to believe his name is, the clown, he just stands by with a pre-recorded high-pitched laugh track, playing over stock circus music."

This description doesn't do justice to the short film's stunning visual aspects: the haphazard, yet coldly calculated manner in which the lunch wagon is driven into the shot, zigging and zagging dramatically around the cordons of the empty lot, Small Dick then emerging and doing a horizontal skid across the field of vision, smooth and graceful, laying out his equipment in a complete mockery of culinary preparation work, knives and boilers being completely and wholly unnecessary to the ultimate objective of serving raw wieners to hungry, deformed dogs.

And then the star of the flick, Micropan Marneshta as she came to be known, comes gliding across the vast expanse separating her from the object of her greatest desires, this rancid hot-dog stand run by a mischievous and unqualified clown, her tangled, matted fur dragging behind her in a desperate, existentially-driven scramble to devour the dull pink franks before some unseen competitor beats her to it; she skids into position at the very last second, chomping a massive hunk of processed meat product and inhaling it in one courageous gulp.

The regurgitation sequence is the stuff of awards-show legend. We know what's going to happen before it does, there's an unspoken sense of inevitability, even for those who hadn't before watched the film or lived with a dog previously. The torrent of yakking offers a quick succession of suggestions on what this particular canine specimen had been previously subsisting upon: roach legs, mangled fur, a cat's necklace, and half a lid from a steel can of refried beans all make cameo appearances in this quick yet poignant sequence.

After this, it was impossible for any of the critics to see this masterpiece as being anything but a career-launching vessel for one Micropan Marneshta. Small Dick was, understandably, severely disappointed by this unexpected turn of events. He killed himself shortly thereafter.

THEY WERE GONNA DO A slaptication (a slappy adaptation, where the dialogue and action of a story is entirely replaced by slapping) of *Grandy Duloch gets Contaminated*, but there was a problem. More of a controversy, really. The one character, Spoils McGurshtin, is cruising the grocery store aisles at the local scratch-and-dent discount retail outlet for foodstuff-related products, when he spontaneously breaks into song:

"All the fat girls

Get out of the ice cream aisle!"

And he really gets in their fat faces about it, too. Fat girls *do* need to stay away from the ice cream section, but they never do. And Spoils, in the book version of *Grandy Duloch*, knows about this, and he tells them and everyone else. It was a very bold statement to make. The ice cream industry executives' mouths were frothing, screaming and crying and carrying on about how unfair it was to say that ice cream is the root cause of all obesity-related illness, and moreover, that being fat is a "lifestyle choice" which people can make if they want to. [It is NOT a crippling disease, like alcoholism, where the mangy scumbags can just be washed out of society like shit from off the bottom of your shoe; nor is it like being gay, which is a genetic illness just as bad as being a dope fiend. Being fat is simply a reprehensible character flaw, a habit borne of sheer laziness, and something that fully deserves mockery just like any other instance of poor behavior.]

The ice cream lobby wasn't having any of it. They petitioned the Congress to slap (no pun intended) sanctions on the book, *Grandy Duloch gets Contaminated*, because of the offensive message just described. And congress did acquiesce, and Spoils was banned as a character, both from the serial and from syndication. That's when the studio that had bought the rights to the novel (the author, who shall remain nameless because he's a pathetic slob, was compensated with beer) decided to make it a slaptication. That way, nobody had to know *for sure* that Spoils was still very much a character in the feature, and that, instead of talking to the morbidly obese women who pissed him off every time he walked through the frozen foods section at the cheap, horrible grocery store he'd frequent, he could just slap the ice cream right out of their hands, and be done with it.

Depictions of physical violence against women were, of course, *completely* acceptable, and in fact, tacitly encouraged.

YOUR BOYFRIEND, MONSTREESHEN, was calling again.

"A little bitty-ditty peenie-weenie dip-dop hoobey," Monstreeshen said. Nobody else wanted to take responsibility, so you do, don't you? For your boyfriend, Monstreeshen, was tripping about all wingnutted out and directionless; you must own this debacle!

Monstreeshen had, somehow or another, gotten a hold of a cellular telephone. He was dialing at random, speaking with strangers, data harvesters, Indian call-center people, penguins, and upper-level staff at the Vatican. "Beep a doyle?" Monstreeshen asked, to anyone who would listen. Nobody did. That's why you need to attend to your boyfriend's misbehaviors, not now, but *right* now!

Stully Braeshtion knew. Stully was the *only* one that knew. Monstreeshen was in no way complex; he was simple folk, one who was possessed of a false sense of self-importance. There was something about his manner that invariably rubbed people the wrong way, of which he had no awareness whatsoever. He thought his name sounded like royalty; so, in this vague way, he justified a near sociopathic existence, hugged from cradle to grave by this air of entitlement, this absolute sense of—

"MAMA, tell me a story," the fat, ugly child said, inarticulately.

Well, here's one, Momma replied:

Once there was the story of, "M'Brashtion." It was based on actual, true events! It seems like this one time, there was a cute little blonde reporter girl, lithe and young, just like they like them, and she was telling a tale of something pointless; but it was something *she* believed in, some story that seemed juicy and tasteful enough for the crowd of bloated, bored working stiffs at home who still bothered to watch the stupid little local news channel.

So one day, our ditzy heroine was out on assignment to duly report on meaningless happenings, and in the course of her drivel, something remarkable occurred: she began to speak in *actual* gibberish! At first, she caught herself, surprised that she would flub some basic English vocabulary that most people at home probably weren't even paying that much attention to. She uses the word, "Bertaishton." It sounds like it could actually be a real word, does it not?

What nobody realized at the time was, this was a stroke. The little girl reporter was having a stroke, live on camera, oh, wasn't it wonderful? What a fun time for all! Well, maybe not for the reporter, but she tried her hardest to keep reporting the completely useless story! The words quickly broke down into ever-more-garbled vocalizations, "lasta-cayesh-belasty-lokinstuf," until she was frantically nodding her head up and down, her eyes pleading for help. A blood vessel had just exploded in her brain.

"Mama, will I ever get to have s—stroke?"

"Of course you can, if you just believe in yourself," Mommy replied.

And Stully Braeshtion took this advice fully to heart, having listened intently during the preceding passage, just to come away disappointed when he learned that the stroke reporter had said, *Bertaishton*, instead of *Braeshtion*, which Stully had been eagerly waiting for, hoping he could at long last find out the true meaning of his birth-name, and not just keep believing the made-up story that his parents would tell about it. After all, these were the same dastardly folks who told him the Poop Fairy was real!

Stully had been cheated by the media once before. When that almost-planecrash happened in New York City, the pilot's name was "Sully," and Stully thought there might be a connection there. But, there wasn't. Sully was a hero; Stully was a dull-wit and not at all creative. He kept looking in secret places for some sort of an easy solution to the existence-problem. [That is the space that every person of borderline intellect and personality will try and claim as their own, as if they've been recruited by some academic overlord in order to establish definitive and lasting credentials, and validate their presence and involvement in any of a number of high-society functions. These poor fools try to suss out "meaning" from their lives; grasping at straws, they usually fall far short of convincing *anyone*, save fellow morons, that they've ever figured anything out. They are good at posturing, though, at putting on the act and trying to solicit support for their bullshit quests. They start playing around with numbers, for instance (this is a most popular pastime of the lazy and ill-informed), thinking that if they string together enough digits and perform a sufficient number of arithmetical functions, they can proof out the meaning of life. They browse the internet for weird and unexplained accounts of others' hallucinatory experiences so they can vaguely craft a sensible framework for their own existences. All of it amounts to this endless ambition to derive a short sentence or two that can sum up the entirety of who they are, what they are thinking at any given time, where they've landed in the context of the greater Universe, and the ultimate fate of everyone and everything inside of it, including time itself.]

"I TOUCHED A GIRL'S BUTT!"

Paul was at it again. With his guitar out, making random fidgety strumming sounds that would soothe his tortured, twisted mind, he tried to write a song about this one time, when a girl let him touch her. He was one half of that band, POOP, along with his brother.

But there was some competition. Two fat black girls on youtube going by the names "Pee" and "Poop" were blowing up the spot that had been so carefully carved out in the independent-rock scene by the members of the band, POOP, which was comprised of Paul and his brother.

Paul didn't mind. He wasn't able to operate a computer on his own, and relied upon what could be delicately described as his "special helpers" to manipulate buttons, clicks, and keystrokes in order to pull up his favorite cartoons and other media fit for a simpleton.

But the producers of the band, POOP, very much *did* mind. This band was a money-maker, not in a prominent or excessive way, but enough to do more than just keep the lights on in an abandoned warehouse, somewhere on the outskirts of Detroit, or perhaps Milwaukee or Pittsburgh. The producers, who were obviously *very* Jewish, wanted to make sure they were earning a reasonable return on their investment; naturally, they tried to trademark the name, "POOP."

The guy at the patent office wasn't sure about this one at all. "What the fuck is this?" he asked aloud of nobody in particular one dismal December afternoon. The remnants of his greasy paper bag lunch lay crumpled up alongside half-completed applications for products such as stool softener for dogs and devices like an upside-down time-out chair for toddlers; the man was accustomed to having to review the tedious and ridiculous machinations of overly-imaginative people. This one, however, was breaching the heights of newfound stupidity, and also carried some political intrigue.

You see, the girls who went by the youtube monikers "Pee" and

"Poop" were also steadfast supporters of President Dump. In reality, these girls were two big, fat, black pieces of shit. This confounded thinking members of the public to no end.

"Surely he's done nothing to further the causes of the blacks, or the fats, or the womens," the detractors of the President would begin to muse, cautiously. "I can't for the life of my chiropractor begin to imagine what his appeal to these otherwise fine young ladies would be." And for sure, nobody else could quite understand *their* appeal to the United States at large. It was, most likely, a black thing.

That didn't stop them from proclaiming their unyielding love and undying support for the President, however. And just because they had chosen the most banal of bathroom references as pseudonyms for the characters portrayed on their internet video channel, didn't mean that President Dump *wasn't* a big fan and follower. In fact, whenever the rest of the network television "news" correspondents would begin to huff and puff and make critical, and sometimes even bordering on defamatory, remarks about Mr. President, he would instead usher his minions to pull up the Pee & Poop Channel and watch them rattle off a list of things that bothered them, and also, the President, so he could clap and shout and laugh and scream along with them.

This was no longer the "era of good feelings" that was the early-2000s. In those times, who could forget such hits as the Fox News production of "A Present for the President?" Taking place just after the 2004 election, the special starred George W. in his jammies one morning near Christmas. He was eating a bowl of cereal (with only minimal amounts of sweeteners added, and a whole heaping loving spoonful of fortified vitamins) at the little table in the breakfast nook of the White House's Children's playpen, and he had slurped down all of his milk afterwards and even put the empty bowl in the sink and rinsed it out just like the big boy that he was, when his nanny showed up and told him, "Georgie, we're going for a walk!"

Well, ol' Dubya got so excited, boy, if he had a tail it surely would've wagged that empty ol' cereal bowl clean off the dish rack and sent it smashing to the floor in a thousand shattered ol' pieces that Belem, the illegal Mexican housekeeper, would diligently sweep up and then disinfect. They bundled him up to keep him safe from the cold, and then whisked him away in his armored car while Uncle Dick held down the fort back at home.

"Where we goin'?" Georgie asked, excitedly.

"You'll find out when we get there," his nanny replied, assuredly. "I can tell you there's going to be a lot of happy people with smiling faces who are going to be very, very excited to see you!" And sure enough, there was. It was the Fox News Studio Headquarters, in New York City!

Chris Wallace met them at the entrance. "You must be big Georgie! I've heard so much about you!"

"I'm this many," Georgie replied, flashing his full-five finger digit hands in rapid succession, until enough years had been counted that his nanny nodded to him that, yes, Georgie, that's enough fingers to count how many years you are.

And then inside the studio building, just like Nanny had promised, there were a lot of rosy-cheeked middle-aged white men who were applauding and cheering with bulbous faces, squinting through narrowed, porcine eyes at the boy wonder who had made their dreams for the entire decade come true. They hoisted Georgie up on their shoulders and led him to the TV anchor desk, where Chris Wallace presented Georgie with a big box wrapped up with bright, sparkly paper, a ribbon neatly tied around the sides, an extravagant bow on top.

Georgie was so excited, he began hyperventilating, but his nanny patted him on his wee-wee and that settled him down enough to proceed with tearing the delicately packaged parcel into shreds, just to reveal the greatest prize of all:

A Diebold voting machine.

PEE AND POOP WERE ON the warpath. Even though they acted like they had no idea what anyone was talking about whenever the controversy would arise in the course of an interview, they secretly *were* jealous of the indie band, POOP. They were so upset, they scheduled lunch with that rapper, Butt-Fuckie.

Butt-Fuckie had momentary fame in the early nineties before he got overwhelmed by the bang-BANG Boys, the little dark-skinned children who just looked like they needed a good meal, but instead, spent all of their daddy's dollar bills on cheap guns and ammunition, and proceeded to shoot at one another, rob liquor stores, and, overall, be a real drag on society. Butt-Fuckie didn't condone that; Butt-Fuckie only condoned fucking butts.

That, actually, was his most successful song, the one where he describes anal sex in great and hilarious detail (about all the myriad ways it can go horribly wrong and ruin everybody's evening by forcibly ejecting fecal matter around the general vicinity wherein said acts of sodomy were occurring), and then finishes it out with that addicting riff, "Fuckin' butts!"

Butt-Fuckie actually *had* been awkward in High School. The original title of the song was, *Fuckin' Buts*, which was a direct reference to how he used to get all nervous and weird whenever he'd smoke pot with the other teenagers, and, instead of stammering when he was supposed to say something, but didn't know *what* exactly to say, he'd instead buy himself a few seconds by starting each sentence with the interjection, "But, fuckin'...." And all the other kids would laugh hysterically:

"*Butt* fuckin? HAhahahahahaha!"

So, Butt-Fuckie was born. He wanted to OWN the idea of being into anal sex (even though he wasn't, because it was gross; but, one of the cool kids had been telling the entire senior class that he broke up with his girlfriend at the time because she demanded that he make love to her through the back door, and he adamantly refused, because, from his perspective, that would be "gay"), so he even started rapping about sticking his finger/penis/other objects up inside of other peoples' poopers. It was a hit, even for a weird boy like him.

His downfall came suddenly. He had started getting louder, and louder, every time he performed his signature single, until there came a time when he was shouting at the top of his lungs: "FUCKIN' BUTTS!" And then everyone realized it wasn't funny anymore; they were being *yelled at*, and modern people really don't care for that at all.

Immediately, there were stories all over the media and peoples' social networks, going on and on about how that rapper Butt-Fuckie, who everybody had used to think was so cool, was actually just intoxicated, or mentally challenged, or otherwise age-inappropriate. He wasn't really that bad, he had just smoked some weed a few times and been awkward around people because of it. But that wasn't a good enough excuse for the general public anymore. So, they stopped listening to him, which was okay, since he didn't have any new material after that one song he made, about fucking butts.

Pee and Poop, however, didn't care. They figured that, as a washed-up has-been, Butt-Fuckie would be sympathetic to their message, about how very much they loved their mister President. Losers and droolers were united in common cause for the re-election campaign, and Pee and Poop were about to make a very generous offer to one Mr. Butt-Fuckie, former rap star, in order to validate their scheme to convince enough other morons to vote for Donald Trump.

Just as they had entered the restaurant and were about to be shown to the VIP table where Butt-Fuckie was awaiting their arrival, getting drunk because he knew that he wouldn't be the one paying the check, since he knew Pee and Poop well enough (he didn't actually know them, but he did know the *internet* version of them, which he was studying vociferously and vainly trying to replicate their no-talent-having degree of success in media exposure, and also, maybe *exposing* himself to some select young female members of the audience; he knew enough to know they were richer than him, which wasn't that much of a challenge these days, since most of the time he had a negative net worth from being drained for child support from this one time, when he was drunk, and he thought he was sticking his penis inside of a girl's butthole, but it was actually her vagina, and he got her pregnant), he was fairly confident he could show up to the table a good hour early and convince the waiter to start plying him with Moscow Mules until his lunch-dates arrived.

Suddenly, the two fat girls were distracted by a terrible screeching sound, and what sounded like the frantic flapping of a small-to-medium sized bird's wings...

SUBCHAPTER 1.A
"THE COCKATIEL PLOT"

Shabeenul L'Brashtion was a beautiful sulphur-crested cockatoo. His owner cooed at him daily, and gave him expensive toys like he was a human child. He trilled and shimmied and learned to imitate many of the mannerisms and cadences of the well-to-do people who frequented his house. He got to eat organic, fair trade mangoes and jackfruit and kiwis and persimmons that were flown in fresh from around the world every morning. He had his own pet aviary, in fact, where he could watch lesser birds while chewing on the finest green Kona coffee beans. He was, by every account, a spoiled creature.

He was targeted, though, by these ugly little gray cocka*tiels*, who were known amongst themselves as:

Largie Gripbvens (pronounced GRIP-b-PIV-ens), the leader. He was a nasty little bird who was continually scheming and screaming, and also, he had a terrible addiction to chips.

Squarmie Bolshton (no relation): he was Largie's lieutenant, and not much of one, at that. But, then again, Largie wasn't that much of a bird, either. If he had held a mid-level leadership post at an anonymous medium-sized city's law enforcement agency, he would've lost his job about six months into his tenure. He tried calling himself a private bird detective, but not many people bought it. Actually, *nobody* bought it, because the sort of people who would be duped into hiring a cockatiel to perform investigative work wouldn't have any money in the first place. So, Squarmie was an even lesser-ranked entity than that.

They wouldn't have even been such terrible birds, and certainly not so jealous of Shabeenul, if Largie hadn't blown their seed budget for the month on hiring some woman to record the opening lines of what he felt like was about to be a major YouTube (or some other, non-affiliated video streaming service available exclusively through the internet) project: *The Failure Rate of Birds,* it was going to be called.

Largie had, this one time, flown into a bar where a guy who claimed to be a movie producer was getting drunk during the day. Largie explained his business plan for opening up the detective agency (which, let's face it, wasn't really so much of a business plan as it was a few empty sunflower seed husks), and the guy immediately saw potential in the plot.

Helmut Nuckmëiler was, in fact, hired to compose a non-linear list of concepts and devices to employ in the pilot episode of the show:

- Largie and Squarmie bill themselves as legitimate, crime-solving professionals, but, they're birds; and not even good birds, they're *cockatiels*. But, they can also talk, or rather, they can mimic human words closely enough as to suggest the idea of talking; so it would kind of work, on a certain level, to entertain the kinds of people who liked to watch stupid things on the internet while drunk and/or high.

- However, talking birds didn't do much of anything about the problem of entertaining the Deaf. The Deaf are their own challenge, and research is still being conducted on how best to reach them so that the rest of us can pretend like they're people, too.

- Largie also wants to be a tee-shirt designer. He comes up with a design that he spends an entire episode perfecting, that he calls the "COCKATILE," which is a mashup of a crocodile rising up from a swamp, but with a cockatiel's head that is the size of a crocodile's, and just as intimidating. The beak is open, and menacingly directed towards some innocent white kids lingering along the shore of the swamp. The image itself was actually pretty well done. However, the time that Largie was wasting while creating his tee-shirt design was time they were *supposed* to have spent solving the abduction and murder of a high-school sweetheart named "Brandy" who had a golden retriever who loved her very much; her dad had paid the birds $10,000 to catch the psychopath who had buried her alive, or drowned her in a big aquarium tank, *or* ripped her head open with a timer-activated reverse bear trap. Regardless, the girl died.

- Largie is abusive towards Squarmie, both physically and emotionally.

Basically, they were thieves, totally self-absorbed, and one of them

(Squarmie) was borderline retarded as well. The target audience, Middle America, was rapt with wonder and joy, expecting nothing but the most mediocre and juvenile jokes and easily predictable situations to arise. As the series proceeded with its first installment, where the two fake bird-detectives are asked by their artificial-assistant minder (kind of like an Alexa, but with less of a vocabulary, a penchant for repetition, and a terrible habit of ending each sentence with an upward inflection; for instance, the majority of the lines performed by said voicebox, which had a nondescript woman's voice with an indeterminable accent, would come at the open of each episode:

"Largie?

Largie Gripbvens?

Squarmie?

Squarmie Bolshton?") to take on a new case, this one being the disappearance of Shabeenul L'Brashtion, which they themselves had orchestrated, because they were jealous, ugly little birds.

Largie was distracted at first with his doodling on a tablet that some grateful former client of theirs had been stupid enough to gift them. His rendition of a crocodile with a cockatiel's head was rudimentary, at best; it was of the quality that some parents would be heaping praise upon, if the bird were actually a mentally deficient four-year-old. He chattered and chortled as he worked.

Squarmie waddled over to inspect his colleague's efforts. "I dunno, Largie," he said, hesitantly. "It looks like a scab that someone picked off and flung on top of a pile of cheap spaghetti."

"Shut up, Squarmie! This will work!" Largie screeched indignantly. Satisfied with the drawing, he then logged into the tablet's eFax account and dialed up his T-shirt publisher.

Secretly, however, Largie was willing to concede Squarmie's criticism of his doodling, since he'd been distracted throughout the entire creative process that went into the design. It was far from his best work, but that was fine, since Largie was actually about to write a remake of the popular film, *The Peeing Poodle*, called, instead, *The Pooping Poodle*. You see, Largie Gripbvens hated dogs. He thought they were stupid, and they frightened him badly whenever they would bark and lunge at his cage. He would slick down his headcrest feathers and spread his wings out and hiss and lunge back at the canine menace, but it never seemed to accomplish the intended effect.

However, if he was ever going to get serious about his career in abstract creativity, first little Largie Gripbvens would have to stop being a degenerate bird, which he was being presently, by forcibly fucking a miniature merry-go-round toy that someone had strung up from the top of his cage. Cockatiels, by nature, are chronic masturbators.

"But what are we going to do with Shabeenul?" Squarmie whined, abrasively.

Largie stopped violating his plaything for a second and looked up, confusedly. He hadn't really thought his plot all the way through, so he just stared off into space, like a fourteen-year-old who just railed three lines of pure MDMA.

Then, he thought of something. There was a news story on the TV that had always been left on in the background, since the cockatiels' human owner was absent most of the time, and it had shown one of those obnoxious, irrelevant lifestyle segments about some cockatoos in Australia that had been teaching each other to open up trash cans and steal the rotting garbage inside.

"We're going to teach him to eat shit, Squarmie!" And Largie started cackling with a riotous shriek, like cockatiels do when they get over-stimulated.

First, though, they were going to have to figure out how to capture Shabeenul L'Brashtion. He was a much larger bird, and would probably kill the little cockatiels if they got too close to him. Cockatoos can be very ill-mannered, and hostile towards other living things, if they don't trust that they're going to earn food out of the deal.

It was starting to seem like an awfully large amount of work. As much as he recognized his obligation to drive the subplot forward, as a minor protagonist, Largie Gripbvens just wasn't up for the job. So he resigned, and flew out an open door, probably not to be seen much from ever again.

Squarmie wasn't confident enough in his ability to take over the storyline from there, and so he, too, gave up and went and hid in a dark corner of his cage, hoping like all hell that nobody would ever notice him.

...But, Butt-Fuckie was also under duress. As an expected guest of the lunch party being orchestrated by ones Missus Pee and Missus Poop, he was obligated to order all of his consumables just like the favored Mr. President would have done, if he still cared about his little Post Office diner business, which, actually, he *didn't*, because he was now living in Florida. Still, Butt-Fuckie was made to order a dried-out, nasty, flavorless piece of meat with little independent bottles of catsup surrounding the plate, sentries protecting the meal from any invasion of taste or class.

He was also getting quite frustrated, and impatient, on waiting on Pee and Poop to get done with their business and join him at the fancy restaurant. While he was sadly gulping down iced water, because it was free, the table next to his got into a commotion when the former Ellen Page pulled out a steak knife, sliced open another diner's abdomen, and stole his liver, grabbing and slamming it down on its plate and munching away contentedly with still-warm human blood dribbling down its face and neck, scarfing up the frightened and dying victim's organ like it was somehow socially acceptable (it wasn't; at least, not *yet*).

And, Butt-Fuckie actually ended up dying at that stupid restaurant waiting on Pee and Poop to be shown to the table. He'd had diabetes, and lymphoma, and all of that put together, along with experiencing anxiety that *his* liver might get eaten next, was too much for his poor heart to bear, so it failed in a spectacular manner, as the big guy lurched and heaved to and fro, clutching his chest and gasping horrifically, coughing desperately on the maitre'd who was scampering around like a rabid fox, trying to prevent Butt-Fuckie from falling on top of one of the other diners.

After he was officially dead, Butt-Fuckie's bowels released themselves all over the carpeted floor. It was fancy carpet, from some middle-European country. Everyone else in the place was so disgusted, they threw down their cloth napkins in unison and proceeded to march out the front door, promising to leave the Restaurant negative reviews on social media.

Meanwhile, Pee and Poop had just burst in the door, and were quite agitated that the Maitre'd couldn't have kept Butt-Fuckie alive for long enough for them to have a meeting, and strategize about how they were going to sabotage and ultimately defeat that band, POOP. Pee rushed to the site of Butt-Fuckie's untimely demise, and she was carrying a bouquet of cheap, plastic flowers that she'd inherited from her Auntie, and she thrust the bundle of frayed, fake petunias skyward and let out a monstrous roar, something between a soul-crushing yell of pure hatred, and the loudest belch that had yet been heard in the tri-state area.

Poop confronted the staff at the restaurant, who were hurrying to throw Butt-Fuckie's corpse into the dumpster. "Couldn't you've just propped his little butt up and let him be dead here for another thirty minutes? Is that too much to ask?" Well, it *was* too much to ask, according to the county's Office of the Coroner and Health Inspector. They told Poop, in no uncertain terms, that she and her sister would have to leave the scene at once; but maybe, at some point, they could get revenge.

"Revenge isn't a dish... it's a dessert!" cried Pee, alarmingly. They swaddled one another with their rolls of fat in a sweaty embrace; then, they left for the nearest grocery store ice cream aisle.

"WHEN WILL THIS CRAP STOP?" read the sign of a man who was protesting. What it was, exactly, that he was protesting was unclear. He was strategically positioned in front of a dying, nondescript DVD rental store that was averaging about nine customers a day. It was definitely *not* Blockbuster, though, because if it were, there would have been a hundred gangly morons congregated around, being sloppily nostalgic and adamantly defending the store's integrity from the invisible bulldozers of progress that they imagined it was about to be demolished by, if anyone cared. Nobody did, so there was no protest in front of the last remaining Blockbuster store, and this guy didn't have a backup plan.

What happened was, somebody had gotten touched. They tried to report it to the police, but the detective who responded didn't like people who would just allow themselves to be molested, and not do some damned thing about it. "You could've shot him," the Detective said, remorsefully. "Was he black?" No, he was some white dude, and he couldn't find a child to rape, so instead, he grabbed someone's butt who was old enough to know that it was wrong, and tried to do something about it, legally, and was refused by the police department on the basis that, as the victim was a transvestite, it must enjoy the attention it was receiving (albeit unwanted), and should be grateful for the opportunity.

What opportunity? Well, it appeared that the city had taken some strong steps towards affirmative action, which by implication meant that sexual harassment of deviants could no longer be considered a crime, because naturally, that was what they *wanted* to happen. They knew full well before they left their homes that fateful morning, or late afternoon as it were in this particular case, that they would be subjected to certain rituals of humiliation and degradation. They were expected to fully enjoy such demeaning treatment, and when this specific crossdresser did *not* enjoy the rape-y sort of vibe they were eliciting from members of the unassuming public, it left the city government feeling confused, embarrassed, and slightly exploited. Why wouldn't someone that fit this description be a willing participant in an activity that used to be considered a crime, before the city council got hip to the times and decided that, if anything, they should *encourage* this sort of behavior?

So, the man with the sign felt that it should still be a crime to sexually harass transvestites. He had a cousin that was one, once, one time when they all got drunk and dared one another to do stupid shit. The man with the sign had put a living, but drugged, rat inside of his mouth and walked around like that for a half hour, until the rodent sobered up and tried to desperately claw its way to freedom by attacking the back of the sign-guy's throat. And his cousin dressed up like a woman.

Or was it a man? The guy couldn't remember, except that, his cousin was born one way and wanted to play dress-up as the other, *for fun*. On a dare.

I AM SHLURPIS DERMIT. I am Shlurpis Dermit, I am Shlurpis Dermit.
    "What did you do?"
    "I'm not sure, but Shitbag Shilston told me to."
    "No, that's not how it goes at all!"

"What do you mean? You have some better idea? Why don't you just come out and say it, then, instead of just asking stupid questions repeatedly!"

"I meant, you have to do the catchphrase."

"It's not a catchphrase."

"Yes, it is."

"No. It's just a stupid thing that he says whenever he's getting some dumb idea that's just going to end up getting him in trouble, once he starts doing the stuff that he was thinking about."

An example: he was walking past a pig farm, and stopped, and sniffed the air ever-so-slightly. It was a warm spring day and the hogs were wallowing around in a freshly uprooted patch of daisies, which had been growing in a recent pile of composted garbage from the dirty Chinese restaurant down the street. Then, the imaginary-thought-lightbulb blew up over his head, and one of the various shards of glass that went flying down managed to lodge itself right in his frontal cortex. Sticking his left index finger first into his mouth, and rolling it around his tongue for a good twenty seconds, Shlurpis then thrust that same finger high into the air, and proclaimed:

"I'm gonna go roll around in that pigpen and get myself infected with a swine virus, because I'm Shlurpis Dermit!" And that's exactly what would happen.

There wouldn't have been a cure, either, if it were not for the kindly folks at the Oscar Meyer corporation who developed a vaccine. Most of their customers refused to take it, even though it was required if you wanted to continue eating hot dogs, since they'd recently switched over to an asian variety of pigs that were truly nasty critters, and ate their own young, which, in turn, had been fattened by eating human shit. The circle of life, and all. Anyway, the implied contract when purchasing a package of weenies was that you were supposed to have a "Doctor" employed by the company arrive at your doorstep between the hours of 8AM and 5PM, and they would give you a special "hot beef injection." [Which wasn't really hot at all, and it certainly wasn't made of beef. What it actually was, was a hot dog that was only slightly toxic, with a far more mild version of the virus infused within it, and the medical professional who was administering the vaccine would tenderly pull out a nitrile glove (since some people were allergic to latex these days, and it had become fashionable to be unnecessarily allergic to common things that didn't used to affect anyone negatively, until some popular people started claiming that they were so afflicted, and so all the pedantic morons who followed their social media channels *also* believed they were sensitive to things like latex, and since they were desperately seeking attention, conjured up a sense of inflammation in order to break out into a rash through psychosomatic means), and they would gesture for the patient to remove their pants and undergarments, and then proceed to remove the vaccine-hotdog from a sterile package, and carefully and delicately the "Doctor" would proceed to shove the wiener up the person's rectum, where it would need to remain until it dissolved.]

They thought that this approach would cure Shlurpis, and all his foolish friends; but it didn't work, because they were stupid.

Part of the problem was that "Shlurpis Dermit" wasn't much of a name, at all. Oscar Meyer decided they were going to fire him from the position of guinea-pig spokesmodel, and execute him for cause. Then, they set out and found a more suitable substitute: Shempis Gomblit. Shempis was a cool, fake skateboarder, and far more successful at being a dipshit than Shlurpis ever was. He was also kind of fat. It was an amazing opportunity for the company.

"I'm gonna bust my gnads on this pig's nose, because I'm Shempis Gomblit!" he would shout, and then proceed to smear the crotch of his dirty, baggy shorts with peanut butter, and begin thrusting provocatively towards a group of angry sows. One of them charged him, slamming its snout right between Shempis's legs as intended, but then, in a surprising show of raw force, tossed him up in the air a few feet and quickly distended its jaw, opening its pig's mouth in a wide, gaping, toothy demonstration of sheer horror. Shempis, initially gleeful that he'd managed to do yet another completely and totally dumb thing, was in mid-air when he happened to glimpse down and see what was about to happen. It all unfolded in slow-motion; he knew that, in a matter of a second and a half, his testicles would be pulverized and quickly emulsified with pig-saliva, but he didn't have the agility to contort his way out of *this* particular situation. He started screaming, and the pig started grunting, his legs flailed out from under his now-falling body, the pig lunged, and it was all over. Shempis Gomblit had been castrated.

Oscar Meyer tried to keep him on for another stunt, but after he lost his balls, Shempis Gomblit was pretty much worthless. Gone was his aptitude for reckless behavior. He now preferred to eat bean sprout sandwiches on ancient grain bread, drink weak tea and listen to recitations of lesbian poetry. Mr. Meyer shook his head sadly, and sent his henchmen out to remove Shempis's penis, as well. Then, they fed the penis to a *different* pig, and once the pig had had a chance to digest the penis, they slaughtered the pig, and made it into an extra-special line of "specially spiced" hot dogs. The packs were then given out as Christmas gifts to the employees for the following holiday season.

And this is what most people don't realize about the corporate ecosystem: it is a beautiful act of perfect balance, weighing and considering the needs of all involved stakeholders in the process. Corporations are not evil, and they are not *just* legal persons, either; they are better than people. They were invented by white people, for the benefit of other white people, *disgusting* white people, who do stupid things.

It was a corporation, for instance, that managed to get the famous imposter Mega Sex Wrestle out of jail for being a deviant. It was a corporation that sponsored all of Firefighter Bob's spaghetti dinners, and it was a corporation that paid for the basic experimental conditions that allowed for deeply insightful philosophical simulations using fecal matter as metaphors to be successfully conducted, leading to existential awakenings for most of the individuals who bore witness.

THE BUTTSUCKS CORPORATION WAS IN THE MIDST of an emerging disaster. One of their main shipping routes was getting plugged, like, anally. The only person who was in charge who was supposed to be able to do anything to stop it, Nasty Scatterson, was eating lunch. His lunch was a dead chicken, whole, white and un-plucked, since he was a strict adherent to the raw foods movement. It took a lot of effort, though, so he was thoroughly distracted while his erstwhile employer was facing a catastrophe the likes of which had never been seen, in the entire history of industry.

Nasty was chewing on his chicken; actually, he was kind of disappointed, because the only thing he was allowed to have in his weird diet (besides raw meat) was seasoning, and he had to choose between lemon-lollipop-cajun dressing and mushroom-compost flavored dust. He thought that the lemon one might have some sort of refined sugar in it, even though that was the one he was absolutely *dying* to try, he was frightened that it might violate his sacred diet, and that his diet-sponsor would find out and expose him to the whole raw foods movement. So, he went with his less preferred option, mushroom-compost. He was hopeful that it might actually taste somewhat OK, but as expected, it sucked.

Nasty was somewhat cheered by the antics of this boy named Soup who had shown up, mysteriously, to entertain Nasty while he had his dead-chicken lunch. Soup did kind of a mime routine, where he would strut around in his coverall-shortpants outfit and spit and pantomime cursewords, and slick his hair back with shoe polish while grinning. [Actually, Soup was a midget, but it didn't matter, because by now, midgets were considered to be actual, whole people, and had the right to cast votes as such. At least in this country. In certain other places, like maybe Malaysia or somewhere, that might not be the case. The rights of small people in international settings has not yet been fully investigated. Rest assured, at such time as it should be, a properly-formatted report will be issued by the responsible NGO, for full consideration of whichever UN agency deals with dwarves.] Nasty found it to be hilarious, like something that his father would've watched on TV back in the 1950s, which made him feel good, and mushy, and warm inside. He wanted to take Soup back to his house and introduce him to his flock of pet chickens, which were actually his main source of food, as well. And, in just a small way, Nasty fantasized a bit about having Soup for lunch. And not like, the broth-based dish that is commonly referred to as, "soup," which certain people can't stand, because it was all they had to eat for like three months during this one winter when their depressed mother refused to leave the couch, because she was overeducated and overmedicated, so the strategic stockpile of Campbell's chicken noodle that they had inherited from their grandmother, who was a serial food hoarder, was the only thing that this person who doesn't now like soup had to eat, when they were little. No, Nasty wanted to eat the *midget*, who was posing as a young boy, who was known as Soup.

Soup was a total distraction, though. He had been contracted by Natchen Industries to sabotage Buttsucks, commercially. You see, Buttsucks was handling the transit of a new shipment of both Micropan-brand offical toys, and the knockoff Sciclopan line, which was produced in Saipan, so there was a lot of money and general commerce hanging in the balance. Nasty was supposed to make a phone call, every half hour, and sexually harass a woman in an office that was dedicated to blocking international shipping lanes. She would get so distraught, that once she hung the phone up, sobbing all over her abnormally small breasts, she could barely compose herself enough to properly perform the functions of her job, which was to misdirect large shipping vessels and make them run aground in strategically sensitive areas, which would block any further freighters from being able to make passage through certain vital channels.

After thirty minutes, she would've calmed down enough to carry on with her objective, which is when the phone would ring again, Nasty would go on about how her anus wasn't even clean or wide enough for him to dip his testicles into, and then she would start screaming and crying like a sixth-grader, all over again.

But this time, Nasty was late for his call. Soup pulled out a clump of tailfeathers he'd stolen off a rooster, and began shredding them to bits. He scattered the pieces of plumage into the air, allowing it to drift down, like confetti. Nasty was completely mesmerized.

Soup's employers were getting excited. The woman was now on the radio to the captain of a large vessel known as the *Dickwad*, and convinced him to steer just a little bit hard into the embankment of one particularly narrow stretch of the Suez Canal. The upper management at Natchen Industries were beside themselves with joy. Now, they would be able to make *another* line of counterfeit Micropans, and completely take over the market for dumb-sounding toys.

Nasty was happy, though, since Soup was still there, doing his thing. Soup was thrilled that he would goon get to stab Nasty. And the woman was relieved that she wasn't getting sexually harassed anymore.

Oh yeah, the woman's name was Betty Ann Barbecue.

UNCLE LURCHLUCUS

A NOVEL

CHAPTER I

HOWARD STAIN WAS JUST A SMALL MAN in spirit. He coyly posed as a campground host during summertimes at a state forest two hours north of his home in Stiflington so he could spy on women at the local nudist beach. It was worth having to scrub shit from out of the toilet bowls so often abused by discount vacationeers hauling their illegitimate children to and fro as they got drunk on cheap, high gravity malt liquors. Up at three in the morning, these kids would inhale neon orange spraypaint fumes and wretch their little guts out all over the complimentary indoor shower stalls. Stray dogs would congregate, fighting one another for the privilege of scarfing down the barf. The toxic child-vomit would irritate the mongrels' lower digestive tracts, until they too would be piling the entrance to the communal bathrooms with fetid feces.

The adults, once awakened from their fitful slumbers, would themselves inevitably be nauseated from the fresh, clean air that was so anathema to their accustomed urban existences, and join in the kid-puke-dogshit-pile party with bits of their own viscera regurgitated vis-a-vis chain reaction instigated by low-quality beer.

Howard would tend to the mess, of course, slopping up the muck with his trusty mop and bucket. Shoved into the back of his truck at the start of each season, along with every other tool and trick of his trade, Howard's implements of destruction were always at attention. With a sigh, he would lustfully envision the bare-naked asses of traveling mothers and local dirty women, sunning their pale flabs on the hard river rocks during lulls in the constant showers of summer rain. Howard's impure desires helped distract his attention from the otherwise abysmal state of his existence.

His wife, Meredith, didn't see what was so worthwhile. Sure, it was a free getaway to a slightly cooler, slightly less crowded environment; but there was nothing much to *do* in the forest. Chase black bears out of the dumpster every night, man the entrance station and collect fees from the wayward campers while the park rangers snuck off to fuck in the back of the old fire truck, watch her husband make a drunken fool of himself trying to challenge every twenty year old football lifeguard college dude to feats of strength in front of the campfire. It was all about Howard, Howard, Howard; but, if Meredith was herself an-ever-so-slightly more interesting person, maybe she'd just leave him and become a drag king in Reno.

Howard did like to get drunk, however. It was usually leftover cases of Miller or Coors, abandoned by city-dwelling scumbags he'd chase out of the forest or smugly confiscate from high schoolers. Howard didn't like paying for alcohol. He felt entitled, just like privileged himself to steal off in the rangers' golf cart with his dollar-store binoculars and park just above the bend in the river where all the homely women would loiter, topless and bare-assed.

"Shit," he said.

"Did you poop?" his wife asked. She knew that one of these years, with all the beer-drinking and the gutbusting feats of hamburger devouring contests Howard would undertake in order to prove his manliness to the twentysomething lifeguards, coupled with a sudden spasm of excitement if he should catch glimpse of an average-looking girl he fantasized about doing dirty things with, that Howard's sphincter would give out entirely and he'd be confined to wearing adult diapers for the rest of his days.

"LONGE" LICRAPOSA MAKES THAT AMAZING Mimosa; you know about it, right? No, you don't know about it. You *will* know about it.

But: the guy was making faces again. "Don't mind him, he's just been getting more isolated and weird lately," someone said.

It was OK, though. Nobody was really too concerned about this criticism of Longe and his famous Mimosas, because that's not what we were all gathered here for; what we *were* gathered here for, was to welcome an author who was about to be interviewed:

"Hi. So you're a writer?"

"Yes, that's correct."

"And what drove you to write?"

"I would have to say, because my friends never let me hang out with them in Elementary School. And then Middle School. And High School."

"I see. And how long, would you say, has Cynicism been the main organizing principle of your life philosophy?"

"Hard to say. A long time; it was a gradual process. The late nineties. I was always a fan of Dave Barry when I was a kid."

"Do you feel like you've grown as an artist since then?" That was a loaded question. It was hardly even fair. If this had been a political event, and a candidate was asked by a reporter some kind of nonsensical derivative of gotcha-style interrogation inquiry such as this, a throng of aides, assistants, concierges and consultants would whisk the victim away, briskly. Journalists made it their business to be adversarial by nature, and that's why nobody liked them or felt sympathetic towards them whenever they would end up the target of some act of mass violence. They'd beg and plead, at that point, when their lives were in jeopardy; and you could be forgiven for feeling sorry for them, when they're about to get their fucking heads sliced off by some jihadist that they flew illegally into some third-world sandbox country to interview, confrontational as always; but then, you have to remember that reporters invite this kind of abuse, by merit of their given occupation.

"Yes. No. Difficult to say," the author said, trepidatiously. "I've had a lot of ideas over the years, but none of them ever stuck. I always wrote these zany stories with highly defective characters placed into grandiose, marginally-adult-centric situations, and all the other kids loved it. The Principal hated it. I almost got expelled."

"Do you believe in free speech?"

"I used to, until recently. Now, I think it is a privilege that has been taken for granted and abused to excess. It's become an excuse to justify absolutely contemptible behavior. Now, I must take advantage of it, in order to *show* everyone how bad it's gotten. You know about that, right?"

"About what?"

"Didn't your English teacher ever say that you need to *show* more than you *tell* when you're writing a story?" No, the interviewer's English teacher never did teach him about that. That's why he went into Journalism.

"No, my English teacher never taught me that. I'm a journalist."

"Obviously. May I ask you some questions?"

"No."

"Alright. When did you decide you wanted to spend the rest of your life asking pointed questions against people who never did anything wrong to you, whatsoever?"

"What are you talking about?"

"You're a reporter, and you don't have anything more than a minimally technical grasp of the English language. You possess no sense of literature whatsoever. You are sullen and uninspired."

"Sir, I have a job to do, thank you very much."

"You're no artist! You don't have it in you to present anything interesting about the world that your audience couldn't behold with anything beyond the power of their own eyes and ten fingers. You reduce the joy and wonder of living to a series of facts, dissociated from objective reality."

"But you do admit that you're a cynic?"

"Yes. No. Maybe. Does it matter? Maybe it's a good thing, after all. Maybe all the people who get bothered by that need a brutal dose of honesty. They can't all be a bunch of tightwads and pricks like yourself." But, sadly, they *were* a bunch of tightwads and pricks. Every. Single. Last. One. Of. Them. What do you do now?

"But, by the time I got to College, it didn't matter anymore."

"Huh?"

"I tried to have friends, but not really. I didn't care too much. I just smuggled pot into the dormitories and got high with some of the cool rich kids until I got caught. They didn't want anything to do with me after that."

"Why are you so angry?"

"But I did manage to write something, complete, a major work, for the first time in my life. It was a movie."

"But you're not a screenwriter."

"I know. I got screwed by the studio system. I wrote a beautiful script about two friends who have to travel down the Eastern Seaboard to escape prosecution for intentionally igniting a wildfire in northern New Hampshire, unwittingly giving a ride to a couple of cannibals along the way who wind up eating the President, just to almost get caught by the border patrol in southern Texas before they launch their Ford Mustang off a ramp conveniently provided by a mutant, 40-foot-tall Armadillo that was expanded to gargantuan proportions by the radioactive fallout resulting from South Africa launching a nuclear attack on the states of the former Confederacy, and landing over the Rio Grande in Mexico."

"Did you write any other movies?"

The author gritted his teeth, menacingly. "I wrote a *bunch* of movies. In my mind."

"That doesn't count!"

"Why do you sound giddy about that?"

BUCKWALTER SNEEZEBORD HAD DECIDED THAT, on this particular morning, he was going to actually try and be nice, and do good things for people, and not do bad things that other people detested and found completely reprehensible. He hired the services of one Helmut Nuckmëiler, master craftsman of listmaking, to prepare a guide of sorts, because Buckwalter was an insecure and a highly incompetent man; and, as useless as he was, he had somehow managed to earn enough money through some menial process in which he sold his efforts to the highest bidder in some manner of a "free-market" economy, and could therefore afford to pay for a Germanic man who billed himself as an expert in list-making to compile a personalized regimen by which Buckwalter felt he would be better justified in living his life:

WAYS IN WHICH BUCKWALTER CAN BE A MORE DECENT PERSON

1. I will wake up every morning without a debilitating hangover. It is difficult to resist drinking to excess on some evenings, but the satisfaction of being able to slumber the whole night through with no interruptions, save for perhaps the occasional night sweat and existential fear of dying alone, is a worthy goal unto itself. If I get scared, there are meditative approaches that can help to assuage

any apprehension of REM sleep cycles.

2. I will say "Hi" if I should see Micropan Marneshta, or any other Micropan, *or* any other lower lifeform in general. It is understood that the author of this list was sired in a region that was previously occupied by certain political forces that possessed deeply-held beliefs regarding the Jewish question (problem). It was ultimately decided that it is better if we say "Hi" not just to people that are similar in appearance and disposition to ourselves, but indeed, even those who look like they had spilled Swiss Miss © hot chocolate formula all over their faces and hind-quarters. [It was disgusting really, that such chocolate-contaminated people were permitted within the borders of the snowy white Alps; yet, this was the modern reality within which we all were expected to function normally.]

3. I will NOT seek out and proceed to masturbate to images of children being tortured and sodomized on internet websites only accessible through the "dark web." It is morally contemptible, first of all; also, it is welcoming a criminal investigation from the authorities who are continuously monitoring traffic to such dens of sin on the information superhighway. It doesn't matter if this is a deep-seated obsession cultivated through a lifetime of repressed memories of being systematically raped as a child.

4. I won't bother people by going on long-winded tangents about make-up characters with bizarre names, like "Shebuleshta" and "Constraghston." Random strangers have a legal right to not be bothered by me and my irregular and highly inappropriate antics.

"Take your sick fuck down to the dog park for a walk!" A disheveled woman screamed at him, menacingly.

"Suck a shitty-fuckin'-hee," Buckwalter responded, dreamily. It was a song that was to be sung on those occasions of great joy and satisfaction, like ejaculating successfully or making a bunch of money in the Stock Market. It was also applicable to occasions of severe frustration and sorrow, like when a used transmission salvaged from a vehicle built for the Japanese domestic market revealed itself to be ever-so-slightly unlike the American-built model it was supposed to replace (and Dr. Dirty David would know a thing or two about that, if we should ever meet him again!).

The song was sung with the opening like delivered more like, "Suck–a–SHITTY–fuckin'-heeeee," with emphasis on the "shitty," culminating in a long, low, nearly-growled, drawn out "heeeee." And actually, the song didn't have any further verses or lyrical content. It was merely a repetitive refrain, by merit of its design and intended purpose as giving the mentally retarded a way of expressing emotion without becoming frantically violent.

Buckwalter himself wasn't necessarily retarded, but more of a generic spazoid and person of all-around low-quality character. He would flick boogers on fresh produce at the grocery store. He'd leave half-empty styrofoam coffee cups on the floors of public restrooms. He would pick up cigarette butts off the ground and continue smoking them.

SOMEONE NAMED "MITCH" WAS FUCKING AROUND with the telephone again. He was plotting some combination of wire fraud and sexual harassment, for he was not a particularly creative lout, but merely a by-product of his times: a small man with a dysfunctional penis who sought meaning through casting vulgar and violent innuendos at unsuspecting, random women.

The Dial Tone wasn't having that, however. It had more enjoyable things to be doing with itself. The Dial Tone once was something approximating a human consciousness, but it had been long since disregarded, forgotten by a society that had sold out to the convenience of cellular telephone technology, that for whatever reason had never an inclination to incorporate an audible standby-signal to reassure its users.

The Dial Tone's options were, thereby, somewhat limited by the reach of the landline telephone infrastructure, existing as it still did for reasons unknown. It fled Mitch's slovenly apartment and cast about for more meaningful conversations. An IRS agent was patiently explaining to his wife that he was working late at the office and would be unable to attend their regularly scheduled dinner program, even though he'd promised her that he would show up on time. It was a longstanding arrangement, unique to their relationship: he would, once a month, agree to promptly arrive home, change into a ghastly "French Maid" sexual roleplaying costume, complete with frilly panties, and proceed to cook his wife dinner, and afterwards, give her a pedicure. Then, once he was finished, if he'd performed satisfactorily, he was entitled to a foot-job. [He was lying to his wife that he was working all night; although it was tax season, being early April, he was instead conspiring to join up with what could best be described as a "roving gang of Uncles," in order to cause some manner of drunken mischief.] The Dial Tone could pick up on his gross insincerity; once upon a time, circa 1960-1985, it would have proceeded to redial the number after the IRS man had hung up, and doing its best, gravelly impression of a Human voice (and it had preformed such, to great comedic effect to many naive telephone owners, by pretending to be a dead relative buried in a graveyard where a telephone wire had recently been blown down in a storm) and warn the wife that, indeed, her husband was full of shit and he was totally up to no good.

Then, there's a guy who used to be a middle school science teacher. "I've got a solution to everything!" he says, plainly, drinking from a half-gallon of cheap wine. He doesn't trust cellular technology. "Those signals emit radiation," he explains, to nobody at all. He has become somewhat *unhinged* in the years since his retirement, and since his wife left him. He tried statutory rape, but it just wasn't the same. So, he ended up hobnobbing with a bunch of HAM radio goons. They would gather on an irregular basis to try and sell outdated technology to one another, to very little profit. But, they would commiserate over stale donuts, watery coffee and cheap cigarettes, and reach a consensus about what the government was up to (hint: nothing good), and speak in hushed tones about birther-ism and improvised explosive devices. Needless to say, science teacher dude still has a conventional telephone in his residence. The Dial Tone took advantage of this little scheme to sell its services to the very government that the former science teacher was convinced was out to "get" him, by assisting in the wiretapping of all of his conversations with likeminded acolytes of the pseudo-white-supremacist movement of the mid-2010's. The government, naturally, paid the Dial Tone a pre-negotiated rate to conduct such espionage.

The merits of serving one's country were not lost on the Dial Tone, even though it was a just a mechanically generated pair of signals that produced a noise audible to the human ear. It had a common patriotic sense of duty that was similarly possessed by every young man with a buzz-cut who left High School in order to join the ranks of the military, or the police. Yet, the Dial Tone, being a mostly abstract entity, couldn't physically wield weapons of mass destruction, to its never-ending despair. So, it did what it could do, which was to listen in and report upon many an unseemly citizen's private conversations in order to better appraise the various intelligence agencies that *actually* run this country of any and all threats against their continued hegemony.

But the Dial Tone, being so otherwise disregarded by modern society, had ultimately decided to pause its moral crusading, and learn to relax and enjoy its niche existence with few, if any, responsibilities. The men it was surveilling for the government were ugly, hairy, short little degenerates with sexual problems who never actually intended to follow through on any of their vague threats, and the Dial Tone was disgusted by their bizarre proclivities, and, ultimately, by their lack of testicular fortitude. *I'm an inanimate non-object, and even I have more balls than these pussies*, it thought to itself, smugly. The Dial Tone had determined that its efforts would be better expended elsewhere. It was expanding its horizons, pursuing new opportunities and indulging its creative side for a change.

For instance, it had briefly been a member of the Crystal Method, performing 90 hertz pulse during a few of their live sets, when they were being sloppy, all strung out on stimulants as they were, and allowing the computers to do most of the beat-matching work. The Dial Tone didn't mind. It was an easy gig, none of the mind-numbing stress that accompanied the regular deluge of New York stockbroker offices frantically calling in trading options, and Hollywood executives berating overpaid character actors for blowing off the set for the weekend in favor of a bender outside Cancun.

The Dial Tone appreciated the fact that it was now in the sunset years of its life, but at the same time, felt doubtful that it was being adequately replaced at its job. As custom ringtones gave way to the silenced-call-settings that many people employed by default, the Dial Tone was slightly perturbed that its unglamorous life spent in dedicated service of telecommunications was going to be tangled up and disposed of by the copper wires of history.

That was about it, though. After that one time at Burning Man, nobody ever remembered or thought of the Dial Tone, ever again.

DAVEY AND HIS MOM WERE GOING to go buy her a trailer, so that it could get parked next to Davey's trailer in the cheap RV park in which he lived, and she could spend the last years of her wretched life tending to her son's special needs, licking his ego every morning like a caring mammalian mother only ever could. Also, she meant to keep an eye on him, because he was a little sneak, even at the age of 66.

She glared at him as they drove. He'd been munching on a piece of pizza, secretly grinning to himself as they meandered down through the hillways and drives of the mountain country. She absolutely *hated* how self-satisfied he'd get whenever he'd be fed pizza. It was like watching the Cheshire Cat mock and torture Alice, psychologically.

What Davey's mom *didn't* know was that he'd been secretly feeding her poop pudding for about the last six months. She thought that it was off-brand *Ensure* and that her vitality would become reinvigorated by drinking the sludge on a daily basis. In fact, consuming poop *did* actually help her have more regular bowel movements, so there was that. But, Davey was smug as always about how he'd done something so sneaky and horrible, to his own *mother*, no less. [He also had sponsored a peep-show for all of his neighborhood chums when he was littler, where they would gawk at his mom as she would proceed to shower and listen to that song by Petula Clark, the one that the guy who blew up his own RV played before he set off the bomb, which was appropriate later on, when both of them, Davey and his mom (not the guy who tied to blow up Nashville, he was dead by then) were about to be living in the same RV trailer park, which was less than even an actual trailer park with fixed-in-place modular homes.]

Mrs. Davey's Mom wasn't feeling particularly good after having drank three poop pudding milkshakes that morning before they went off on their little drive to buy her a nice little trailer. She got her stomach turned all inside out by the shaking, wobbly truck her son had chosen to drive down the mountain roads with poor brakes, and demanded that Davey stop at one of the turnouts so that she could proceed to wretch. She also demanded that he hold her hair, which he acted like he was *about* to do, but instead he grabbed a small satchel from the backseat that was stuffed full of her panties, opened it, and chucked it at her while she was hunched over the side of the road, vomiting. He started laughing, and then tried to do a sick burnout with the truck, which slipped in second gear and stalled out; he made it about fifty yards down the road before Mrs. Davey's Mom was back in the truck, hollering and clobbering him over the head with her dirty panties bag.

Davey's mom wasn't proud that she had raised such a little sneak, but since Davey's wife wasn't part of the picture anymore, and couldn't help calm him down whenever he started lashing out like this, Mrs. Davey's Mom decided that it was up to her to do what no other woman possibly could, which was to take her lit cigarette and put it out in the little turd's ear.

"OWWWWW! Momma, why did you do that?" Davey yelled, uncomprehendingly.

"You're a sneak and I don't trust you," she replied, coyly.

"Mamma, you need to say what you actually *mean*," Davey said, exasperatedly. Davey's mom had been spending a lot of time alone, minding her business, and hadn't bothered to be nag or a nuisance. Davey expected that she was trying to re-establish a bond with him, as her only son, before she dropped dead of emphysema. As her health had begun to fail, he first considered donating her to a wildlife refuge in Nevada, so she could be properly put out to pasture with all the wild horses and feral donkeys that she'd spent her life not caring about at all in the slightest bit. But, he also felt somewhat guilty that he wasn't being sneaky enough, divorcing his mother from his life just like he'd divorced his alcoholic wife, once he'd run out of money for her to steal. No, there were plenty of pranks left to be played on an eighties-something woman.

And the biggest prank of all was about to go down. You see, what

Davey and Mrs. Davey's Mom didn't realize was that they had agreed to see about a trailer that was being sold by a hipster who had actually built a "tiny house" on wheels, which was actually a converted dumpster. His name was Schneider Dupree, and he was a flim-flam conman of the highest degree of snobbery when it came to dumpsters.

He'd begun his illustrious career as a Berkeley dropout, frequenting refuse bins all up and down San Pablo Ave. His favorite one was at the Indian restaurant, which he would linger around the back door of, every weekday afternoon at 3:25 promptly. He'd have scavenged at least a dozen empty potato chip bags, ready to package, conceal and ride away on his rickety street bike with the fruits of his caper: the remnants of the Indian restaurant's lunch buffet. They would dump multiple steam-table bins of various curries, masalas and pakoras, along with plenty of rice and naan bread, in quick succession directly into the improperly secured dumpster. Then, they would go back inside, to smoke opium or some shit, before the dinner service started that evening.

Schneider would become giddy with delight, and also, from starvation from having not eaten anything at all up to that point in the day (especially if it was a Monday after a weekend-long drought of used Indian dumpster goodness), and he'd shovel handfuls of chicken tikka masala commingled with dirty napkins, snot rags, and perhaps a diaper or two, for good measure. Curried eggs and used condom residue would dribble down Schneider's chin as he moaned with pleasure in what could only be described as an ecclesiastical orgasm.

This went on for way too long a part of Schneider's life (given that it was cut short when he was executed by a member of the Vegas motorcycle club for failing to deliver the precursor ingredients for methamphetamine production, as had been stipulated by the contract that he'd signed with the gang, so he *knew* what the consequences were, and he still opted to take "no" for an answer when, having procrastinated until the very last weekend before the due-date for the term project in the class of introductory chemistry at the school of hard knocks was due, he stumbled into a CVS pharmacy and demanded three dozen boxes of generic, unbranded pseudoephedrine, to which the pharmacist laughed and told Schneider that if he did a little "something special" in order to prove his worthiness, he could indeed be entrusted with a criminally negligent amount of what used to be a common decongestant drug.

So, Schneider was directed towards the waiting area for the diabetes patients. "Just saunter over to that little old lady who's here for a blood glucose test, and dance the Charleston for her!" the Pharmacist instructed Schneider, impishly. Schneider wasn't sure that he even remembered the first two steps of the Charleston, since it had really been that long since he busted out ragtime routines with his best friend from fourth grade, but he gave it a go, and wouldn't you know it, but that old bag promptly keeled over, dead from a heart attack!

The Pharmacist came out from behind his bulletproof-glass-encased counter, and pointed and laughed and even shrieked with delight at the old woman's corpse all contorted and twisted on the floor, because he was *that* happy that he wouldn't ever have to draw her blood for any reason, ever again, because she stank like cat food: greasy, sloppy, third-hand factory remnant, processed-animal-scrap canned *cat food*. The Pharmacist hated cats.

But, once Schneider busted out grinning, and very politely asked for his shopping bag full of fake Sudafed, the Pharmacist scampered back into his safe zone, behind multiple locked doors and away from all the weird, smelly customers, feeling secure and content in the company of all of his wonderful pills. He reneged on the deal, because pharmacists are terrible people and can never be trusted.

It was also Schneider's fault for waiting until the last minute to try and fill his order, though, so he kind of deserved to get a .44 magnum through his skull by some amped-up biker), and eventually he began to realize there was some true untapped potential in all the dumpsters within which he'd spent most of his existence, rummaging for barely edible items that he felt compelled to consume. He felt so happy and satiated whenever he'd crawl into one of the things, and it slowly dawned upon him that other people might feel the same way; in fact, they might want to spend *most of their own lives* inside a cozy dumpster!

It was actually Schneider's first attempt at making a dumpster-house that had attracted Davey's and his mom's attentions. He felt slightly self-conscious about calling them "dumpsters," so he instead said, "trailer," in the advertisement.

Davey might not have known the difference, even if it had been expressly spelled out for him. After all, as Mrs. Davey's Mommy knew all too well, this was the same guy who expected her to organize, begrudgingly, his regular "Potty Parties" well into his fifties. What would happen was, Davey would want to have some friends together, but he wouldn't want his mom lingering around to make sure he didn't accidentally poop his pants, *or* intentionally try and talk one of the other kids into pooping *his* pants, because Davey thought that was hilarious, because he was a little pizza-eating sneak. So, she would rent out one of those campground-style bathrooms, where all the toilets are lined up in a neat row inside the same room, so then she could park Davey and all of his friends with their asses squarely over the toilet bowls, to ensure no accidents would happen, and then allow them to smoke cigarettes and complain about all of their ulcers and cysts and intestinal polyps, and otherwise swap war stories about the very real and serious health consequences of their poor dietary habits.

One thing of particular note, too, about Davey's Potty Parties, was that there would always be an invitation extended to a younger man, so that he might piss in front of all the old timers, and remind them of what having a functional urinary tract looked, felt, and smelt like. They would make cheap beer freely available to the targeted specimen of peak health and fitness, and sit back, and "Oooh" and "Aaah" in delight at the demonstration of a functional urethra. Davey and his friends, at their advanced age, would often huddle over the many toilet bowls and standing urinals of public restrooms, straining to pee and cussing and scrunching their faces up so hard, that it nearly caused a burst blood vessel, all to deliver the tiniest little trickle of piss that might come spurting out from their diseased and weathered penises.

So, they were quite jealous of younger men with working bladders, and their jealously was only overcome by the faint memory of when it was so simple a task to relieve themselves, when they were younger, *if* they could even remember when or where that might have been. One guy though, Jackwold, liked to make fun of the older men who couldn't pee too well anymore. Jackwold was an asshole, and he ruined one of Davey's potty parties. It was pitiful.

THEY WERE PLANNING ON STOPPING somewhere and pooping for the night. "Why not stay at the Poop-Sit Motel?" suggested a stranger, unhelpfully. Davey didn't think that that would be prudent.

"No, my mommy's got a rash!" he cried, disdainfully. In fact, his mother *did* have a rash, but it was because of all the poop pudding that Davey had been secretly feeding to her.

What he really should have done, instead, was to feed his mother *butt* pudding. That was a proper nutritional meal, all unto itself, because even though it had the taste and texture of rancid diarrhea, it had the added benefit of asscrack sweat, mucous, and some live yeast cultures that love to live down there, in the bottom region. Butt pudding was sloppier and greasier than poop pudding, and all around, it was better. It was also the name of a living person.

Butt Pudding (which he'd changed his name to when he was 18, from Buttwald Puddington, which he felt to be overly pretentious-sounding, and it would often get him beaten by the other children on the playground, who assumed that his father was rich, because Butt had such a name; in fact, Butt's father was a minor pervert who was generally disregarded by society, so he could lurk at middle school girls' softball games and stroke himself through his stained white briefs discreetly, and the other people in attendance would just assume he was one of the girls' fathers, or, at least, maybe an uncle, but Butt's father didn't make a lot of money, or indeed, hardly any money at all– the Puddington family got welfare checks from the government for living in a brokedown travel trailer, ironically, of the same make and model that Davey was supposed to be buying for his mommy) didn't have that much to do with people making the questionably poor decision to literally eat shit. Instead, he thought of himself as a grifter. In his mind, he knew how to play poker, even though the rules weren't anything like any card game ever invented. Each player starting from the primary position would have nine cards, less one, for each successive player would automatically forfeit their excess cards and leave them laying on the table, face up, for everyone else to see. Then, everyone would get to guess real hard about whose hand was probably the winner, by having the most valuable cards. Screaming was permitted, and indeed, slightly encouraged as a distraction tactic.

Davey tried to play Butt's game with his mom one time, but she grew extremely agitated and cursed Davey out, and spat on him, and then stomped off to go play chess at some coffee shop, instead.

That sort of reminded him of when he grew up in this one neighborhood, with a wheelchair person who was part of it (*Handicapped-American*, to be correct) who also happened to hate one of the other neighbors with a passion.

What happened was, one morning, Davey woke up to some loud grunting across the street and peeped out through his blinds to witness the wheelchair-man (the kids called him "Legs") pooping in the neighbor who he hated's yard. And it truly was a spectacle: Legs was toppled out of his wheelchair, dragging his naked ass backwards across the grass, crying and yelling and cursing as his arms grabbed one clump of rich soil after the other. The poop was coming out in a slow smear, since it was morning and the grass was still wet with dew, so a lively brown stain was quickly growing in length across the yard as Legs proceeded about with his business. The property owner was also watching this, and grinding his teeth, uncertain of how best to approach the situation. It occurred to him to roll up one of the unnecessary newspapers that he kept around for starting fires and smack Legs repeatedly, like a dog. In the view of the neighbor who Legs hated, Legs was a subhuman scoundrel and deserved nothing better.

Or, this man figured, he could call the cops and report harassment and illegal dumping of biohazardous material. He wasn't sure who the cops would make fun of more, though, when they did respond: Legs, for being a cripple and dragging his shit literally behind him, or the neighbor, for allowing this all to happen in the first place. How difficult can it be to keep a handicapped person off one's lawn?

Well, in this instance, it was quite difficult. Legs wasn't only angry; he was also extremely drunk. He'd spent all night on the telephone arguing with his ex-wife, who finally suggested that he do exactly what he was now doing, just to get him to stop ranting at her about how much he really, *really* hated this neighbor of his. Legs' wife didn't like that neighbor either, but she did fuck him once, because she was pissed off at Legs, but didn't tell Legs anything about it after the fact, nor did anyone else, because wheelchair people are the last ones to know about anything. It's not safe for them to; also, they don't deserve it. This is the way that our society functions.

"MY PENIS ITCHES!" CRIED OUT someone, inconsolably. "It burns, oooohh! Owwwww!"

"And, sweetheart, what is your favorite lunch?" A nice lady asked him, cooingly.

"Boiled eggs and poop!" Because Dr. Seuss was a racist, at heart, and deserved nothing better than having his precious memory besmirched by this ruffian, now come before you, that is demanding you serve him up a plate of... *what did he just say?*

"Boiled eggs and poop!" He declared, more confidently. It wasn't the best thing to have for lunch, but, then again, lunch wasn't much of a meal in the first place. It certainly wasn't necessary. Starving people around the world skip out on lunch every day, and they do plenty well for themselves. Have you ever seen a fat starving person? [Well, like a person who is *actually* starving, not just saying that because you didn't stop at Subway to buy them four footlongs with cheese on toasted honey-oat rolls.]

And Simpy Shemplet, the food ethicist, agreed that a meal of boiled eggs and poop would be completely moral and proper fare for a person to consume. Simpy's justification of this otherwise questionable behavior was based upon the philosophical works of Kant. According to Kant, eating poop of any variety demonstrated superior virtue, as the person eating the poop could not have possibly ever done so willingly, if presented with any other viable option. No, people who ate poop were sucking hard at life, which meant they had never learned the basic skills of exploiting others. Kant loved failure; he fetishized the pain and suffering that he expected Jesus to have experienced being strung up on the crucifix and such, never stopping to realize that Jesus was an old Japanese dude, ジロ氏, who had just happened to have been unfortunate enough to be caught practicing some ancient form of eastern mysticism in the general vicinity of the Roman/Hebrew empire, around that time. But he escaped from the circus and returned to Japan, where he lived to be 126 and spent the last half of his life trying to create the world's first pyramid scheme by promoting the supposed life-extending benefits of natto beans (there actually were none; they were just soybeans contaminated with some weird, mucous-like bacteria) and never claimed to be related to any of the Israelites.

Kant thought that eating poop was just about the most amazing thing that any human being could ever do for another human being. Bonus points were awarded to those generous enough to eat *someone else's* poop, instead of just sticking with their own. Most of the post-reformation Catholic popes were known to engage in this particular subset of coprophagia: consuming the fecal matter of the poor, the destitute, and the mentally ill (many of which, ironically, also had sex with animals; and some of the animal scat had gotten into *their* bloodstreams, parasitic worms and such, and it just so happened that the peasants who had the good fortune to shit into the mouths of these esteemed Bishops of Rome happened to contribute to the untimely demise of no less than six of them), in order to demonstrate their complete and utter subservience to their god, and also, so they could continue taking sexual liberties with small children, without being apprehended.

Now, Uncle Lauri (who really should've been someone's hero) actually had a theory about all of this. He believed that these people were living amongst us, plain as day. "Shiteaters," he'd growl, menacingly. He was convinced that they were hiding right out in the open, just like that movie with the wrestler guy and the magic sunglasses. The shiteaters would plot and prowl until, right when they thought nobody was paying attention, they would pounce, and grab some actually important or valuable shit, and carry it back to their caverns and sewers in order to consume said shit, in secret.

This was the kind of thing that would be outlawed, if these were regular folk. Lauri reckoned that, once someone became a millionaire, they were able to avoid prosecution for the act of eating shit, and could instead convince their lawyers to blame it on the Blacks. Not that Lauri completely disagreed with this; he was a southerner, by relocation, and nominally racist as such.

But Lauri was also able to see through that ever-loving screen of bullshit that had been erected by the people who were actually eating shit, and doing bad things as a result. In spite of what Kant fantasized, the consumption of feces does not actually make a person more trustworthy, or even more relatable. Kids would make fun of those fat children in the lunchroom who would show up with severe halitosis, and mock them using falsetto psychotic voices (like what they imagined these kids with the smelly breaths would be experiencing as auditory hallucinations), saying they *loved to eat shit*, and also trying to sabotage any chance that these losers might ever think that they may stand to construct and successfully execute the act of masturbating via a peephole looking into the girls' locker room, at groin-level.

None of this was inimical to the story of the boy who cried poop-and-eggs; it was just nice to have on background. But the boy was insistent that the stupid, make-believe item that he thought he read about in one of Theodor Geisel's nonsensical books was something that could actually be served, for lunch, at a real restaurant. He'd even tried having his auntie take him to the swamps of southern Louisiana in search of this particular "delicacy," to no avail. He just got crawfish shells thrown at him.

So, he was pretty much useless. But the food ethicist, he was much more of a problem. He was a jerk, and he held some kind of relevance to the modern condition in which we all find ourselves. Where did we get the idea that this was even a job? "Food ethicist?" The very act of eating something means that thing had to have died, unless one were to try to live off of pure minerals, which would likely lead to death by acute toxicity. It's actually not a bad idea to, instead, pursue the "vulture" diet, where you buy up meat that is about to go bad, for cheap, and just eat that. You save money, and, if you're smart, you probably won't get sick.

If you're dumb, though, you should continue eating poop. And eggs. And sometimes, the chicken poop gets on the eggs, just to make it easier for you.

THEY DID HAVE GIRLS IN CHEERLEADER OUTFITS trying to sell edible forms of poop, though. The thinking was, people liked girls, and they loved to stuff their fat faces with random crap, and they thought that poop was funny. It sounded like a winning proposition, so some of the leading players in the industry tried it on for size.

McDonalds developed a patty made out of pig shit that they were attempting to market to the "conscious" crowd at the mid-entry price point of $7.95. The Jews hated it; they doubly would be cursed if they ever let such a wretched thing even exist in the same room, so they went to war against the company. The Jews were awarded $4.1 billion in damages, because they had all the lawyers. All the good lawyers, at least.

Burger King tried to compete with a sandwich made of *pure, 100%, cow dung*. It was served on a bun made from Cheetos, which were, in turn, fabricated from dehydrated cat urine. [At least the mascot was more or less accurate.]

Wendy's attempted something different; they force-fed a fat girl cheap, aftermarket animal gristle formed into fake Happy Meals, and then collected all of her stool and tried to make that into some kind of burger monstrosity. Squared. It didn't work so great, so instead, they brought back their salad bar, which was 65% *more* likely to cause severe food poisoning. Salmonella or better, or your money back!

Jack in the Box didn't even need to adjust their strategy. They had been successfully serving up pure, unadulterated shit to morons up and down the West Coast for over fifty years. Carl's Jr couldn't make up its mind if it even wanted to do poopburgers, or instead pivot to the up-and-coming hispanic market with a full selection of diarrhea burritos.

Chick-fil-A got crafty and made a deep fried secret recipe based off of poultry manure as their competitive offering. In-n-Out went with some small, flavorless pucks of horse shit (wrapped in packaging that contained cryptic bible references, of course), while Fuddruckers, desperate to remain relevant in the new, edgy market, had the audacity to collect fecal matter from the toilets in their restaurants and sell it back to their own customers as a condiment, in a crude, real-life rendition of a MC Escher drawing.

The overall marketing strategy was a failure. "Oh, but that was Dan Glimmerman's department," they said, inconsiderately. It didn't matter. The sales targets were far off.

"I dabble in smoking," he replied, remorsefully.

"So. There was this perfect piece of poop, sitting there, and, and, somebody *stole* it!" The patient was getting long-winded, and Dan sighed, unassuredly, since he wasn't making enough with his fast-food consulting gig. He had to pick up part-time work as a therapist.

"I am very sorry they stole the poop," he told the patient. This still didn't address the issue that Dan was smoking again, goddamnit. He had been trying his best to hold the addictive beast at bay; he was buying those used cigarettes they'd been advertising, but it didn't work. He more than dabbled in smoking. He was a tobacco *aficionado*.

"There was actually this guy," he continued, irreverently, "and he was an immigrant." It was at a bar called The Stockroom, a little toilet-supply style closet well off the main promenade of town, which was small, and probably midwestern. Dan came from such a wholesome place, naturally.

Anyway, once they found out there was an alien in their midst (a *legal* alien, mind you; this is not that kind of a set-up that would permit for some undocumented person to have such an integral and consequential role in the development of the narrative being put forth in such an unconventional manner as Dan Glimmerman currently was), everyone's jaws hit the floor. Slack-eyed yokels from all the surrounding hills descended immediately to cast their amazed gazes and gawk at the man.

One well-intentioned fake cowboy wrapped his arm around the foreigner's shoulders. "In America, you find a shit job, and make yourself unhappy with it," he explained to the stranger, diligently. "But first, you should find a barber and do something about that armpit hair. Well," he continued, gulping down his last shot of cheap Canadian whiskey (which was an abomination and total crime against nature by anyone's accounting, since there was a plethora of similarly-priced bourbons of which the counterfeit cowboy could avail himself), "Time to go settle up with the toilet, partner."

"So this man *did* so graciously take the time and effort, in the end, to simply give away the spoils of his bowel movement, which was a highly successful one, I might add," Dan continued, smugly.

"Are— are you saying that— that I'm over-valuing *poop?*"the Patient asked, incredulously.

"I'm not saying that you aren't *not* over-valuing the poop." Therapists had to be very cautious when using words in complete sentences with utter morons and imbeciles like this one patient obviously was. It is in their training manual, the DSM-V, that they must talk their way around direct conclusions and always refrain from offering concrete advice. Double- and even triple-negative conjunctions were some of the most commonly employed rhetorical tools at their disposal.

Dan lit up another cigarette, which was his fifty-fourth of the day. As the idiot whom he was attempting to counsel about not being sad over lost poop sat and pondered his worldview, Dan's phone vibrated with a text message alert. Apparently, White Castle had just come out with a slider that claimed to be 177% *shittier* than any of its competitors. This was a major marketing disaster, as there had been no agreements, gentlemanly or otherwise, before the new round of turd-sandwich wars had escalated.

Congress was threatening an investigation. An oversight board would need to be appointed. Scientific consensus over the proper metrics by which to measure the amount and quality of shit that was contained within each serving of fast-food was nonexistent.

Sometimes, and this was certainly one of those times, Dan wished he was still a baby, and that his mother was a stripper with giant fake tits which he could suck on for hours and receive no nourishment, save for some dribbles of silicon residue, since Dan's imaginary mother had gone to Mexico for her faulty implants, since there plastic surgery was offered on-demand and at a steep discount compared to clinics in the US.

"But, then, what *should* I value?" the Patient asked, quizzically, after having taken five minutes too long to contemplate his life choices.

"I don't know. What do *you* think you should value?" Dan's heart really wasn't in this therapy hustle. He would much rather have made just one profitable ad campaign in his otherwise lackluster career as an over-glorified garbage salesman, and then he could retire on the residuals and not be bothered by these bastardly simpletons who had too much time to worry about pointless and irrelevant matters.

"It sounds like, you know, that poem, *These are the Names of Monsters*."

"Now, Billy, I wouldn't go equivocating like that."

"But, but, but you said that we weren't allowed to use real names!" Billy the patient said, emphatically.

"I'm sorry. 'Patient X,' I meant to say." Dan Glimmerman wasn't *really* sorry, though. He'd never been sorry once in his life, actually. "So, when did you first notice that this poop was stolen?

"I dunno," Patient X replied, despondently. "I was just, you know, currying my eyeballs, and I couldn't see too good, but my naturopath says it's important that I do it at least three times a day. The turmeric, it's good for stopping tumors, and I might have some growing on the insides of my eyesockets. But I think I saw this creepy guy, Solorgnum, lurking around, right before I rinsed away, it was burning, and I have this saline solution that I keep in my sock drawer, open, so it can grow helpful bacteria and fungi. And as soon as I could see okay again, it was gone. The poop, I mean."

"Are you mad?"

"No!" Patient X proclaimed, defiantly. "I have never been angry in my entire life. My daddy wouldn't allow me to be, because it was not christlike, and we were raised better than to raise our thoughts in anger!" He was reduced to shouting, flailing his arms around like a rubber puppet, stashed away and forgotten in some spoiled, fat child's back closet, left for months without lubrication.

"That's not the kind of madness I was referring to. Does it make you upset to think about getting mad?"

"No. Yes, I mean, well, I *would* if I *could*. But, I can't!"

"I see. And your values, are they tangible or abstract?"

"I— I never believed in anything I wasn't told about," Patient X offered, unhelpfully.

"You seem to have a lot of confidence in words. What was that poem you were referring to, earlier?"

"Oh, the one about the monsters! It was never finished, you see, and, and, the author had never even put his or her name on it, I can't say *theirs* because that would imply some non-gendered weirdness, and Jesus wouldn't allow that. But it was a great story, about how someone never finished what they got started, and never even remembered to put their name on it! Do you remember, when we were children, and the teachers would tell us, 'You get five points for writing your name at the top of the quiz'? It's really hard for teachers to grade, I think, if they don't know whose work they are grading."

"Do you feel like you sometimes doubt authorities?"

"Oh, no, I, I would *never* question someone with authority! But then again, it seems kind of confusing that there would be this poet, who never bothered to claim or even finish writing what he'd gotten started on, and that's not a very authoritative thing to do, if you ask me."

"Did anyone ask you?"

"Oh, no. Thankfully, because I don't know that I could even have an opinion about something like that."

"But you do have an opinion about poop. And somehow, you have an interest in this poem that was never written."

"It was written! Just not by the person who wrote it. It got found, later on, by a couple of *other* poets, who then did write some more, poetry I mean, and gave it a title and proper attribution."

"Do you ever get tired of thinking about these things?"

"Never." And Patient X was telling the truth, for once in his pathetic little life. Actually, he always told the truth; but often, the truth didn't make any sense, and Patient X began to suspect that he was lying. Lying to himself, and to his cousins, and his co-workers, and the guy who coached his daughter's volleyball team.

That was when he became infatuated with poop. Poop was warm, at least when it was fresh, and it was squishy, and it felt nice on his fingers, he could play with it and roll it around in tiny balls that he could stack up neatly in the palm of his hand. And sometimes, he could paint a false mustache on his face with the poop, but certainly *not* in the fashion similar to that sported by one Adolf Hitler, who was a monster, by most accounts, contemporary *and* historical. No, Patient X would much rather prefer a Wyatt Earp style imitation of facial hair.

"Is you mind wandering again?" Dan asked, disinterestedly.

"I'm sorry, I just can't help it. I, I need to know if the poop is okay, if it's being looked after tenderly, and if the person who took it has any knowledge about the care and responsibility that comes along with poop ownership."

"I am going to ask you a question, now, Patient X, and I know it's going to be difficult for you to answer." Dan put both of his hands on Patient X's thighs and began rubbing them, aggressively. "Do you think that the person who stole your poop is a monster, and that's why you have so many mental problems?"

Patient X shuddered and quickly reached for his smartphone. He began frantically scrolling through his news feed on whichever social media app had been pulled up prior to his therapy session, and spoke to himself in a small voice that always helped overcome his fears by saying nasty things, about Jesus and mommies and encouraging the commission of lewd acts with cantaloupes. These were terrible notions for any upstanding citizen like Patient X to be even so much as contemplating, so the voice took great pains to translate its words into an unrecognizable form of gibberish.

Dan wasn't sure what to do next. He'd not had much, if any, formal training in the diagnosis and treatment of severe mental disorders. Most of the time, he was paid to listen to fat people moan and gripe about how unfairly the world treated them, and how average-sized persons should learn to get out of the way of their mobility scooters, and drone on about how much of a scam diet culture was.

"I think you should consider talking to someone," Dan suggested, morbidly.

"But I am talking," Patient X said, his voice taking on a new and unsettling hollowness. He slowly looked up from his phone and locked eyes with Dan, as a grin wider than his mouth grew menacingly across the corners of his jawbones. "Do you think it's possible that I am the monster?"

"I can't say anything about that," Dan replied, worriedly. He was getting anxious about how angry the corporate executives at all the mass-production eateries he'd defrauded with his stupid marketing strategy were going to be when they found out that, maybe, just *maybe*, people weren't always content to be eating shit, regardless of how pure the advertisements claimed it was.

Dan looked around, hurriedly, and fumbled with his notes. "Now, um, Patient X, did you ever take any of the poop in your mouth? I mean, uh, did you ever eat or gargle or otherwise try to ingest it?" Dan had heard about some obscure study that was conducted to evaluate the effects of humans repeatedly being fed excrement. The results were shocking. Every subject had, over the course of a few weeks, devolved into a primordial, psychotic state, convulsing and uttering nonsensical phrases, and planning grandiose political campaigns. Several of them attempted to run for public office, and one of them was even elected as a member of the state House of Representatives. Which state, Dan wasn't sure, but it must be in these notes, *somewhere*.

Patient X was growing more somber and unpredictable. "These are the names of monsters," he began to recite, inconspicuously. "The gentler they sound, the meaner and more wretched their souls. They cannot eat themselves. They grow angrier with each passing stranger. The menace which is life no longer distracts them, for they are the beasts that grow inside!"

The phone rang. Any phone. It didn't matter at this point. Dan jumped up out of his chair with the power of a six-hundred-volt third-rail. A clap of thunder sounded in the distance. Ravens squawked and made failed attempts to mimic human speech. The Queen of England held a parade in her honor, with acrobats and fire-dancers marching down the street, single-file and respectfully; but gin was still flowing freely. It was a British invasion the likes of which hadn't been seen in centuries, or at least, not since the Beatles. History was collapsing in on itself, like a prolapsed rectum.

In the bathroom of his office, Dan's toilet began overflowing.

Uncle D'Lonchlucus

A Novel

Chapter I

THERE WAS A PROBLEM IN PROPERLY EXPLAINING Micropan Marneshta.

A helpful guide, first, from the creator and originator of the fine art of professional listmaking, Helmut Nuckmëiler:

WHAT TO DO IF SOMEBODY COMES BY ASKING ABOUT MICROPAN MARNESHTA

- **Do not attempt to reason with them.** We all know that Marneshta is the craziest, fastest and most unpredictable Micropan. Talking sense to this person is just going to wind up screwing with your sense of logic.
- **Try engaging with them about one of the other Micropans.** If this person is interested in Marneshta, it's safe to assume they are ONLY interested in Marneshta. But still, if there's even the slightest chance you can steer them toward any other Micropan at all, please do so.
- **Whatever you do, DO NOT start singing the song with them.** You know the song we're talking about here. The "Micro! Micro! Micropan! Micro-Pan-Marneshta!" song. See if you can get them to sing the "All the little Micropans, all the way to France!" song instead. That way, you're not being specific about Marneshta.
- **See if they know where their parents are.** Although we realize that Micropans are mostly for mentally disturbed adults, sometimes they might have a parent or guardian nearby who can (hopefully) handle the situation.
- **Ask if they've heard about any of our affiliate programs.** This is a great opportunity to give a hard sell on the Abrony Shixtacoula vocal detraining summer camp initiative, for example!
- **Recommend they take a shower and have a beer.** Standard

medical advice that most doctors give when dealing with an onset of Marneshta-obsession is to immerse in hot water, and rapidly consume alcohol.

- **Remind them that playing with any Micropan comes with a lot of responsibility.** Micropans need to be fed, clipped, defenestrated, masturbated and paraded on national television if they're going to be maintained in collectible condition. It's a lot of work for anyone, so see if this person wouldn't rather just take a nap and forget about all this nonsense.

- **Tell them to write it all down in a letter to the President.** Often, deranged people like the sort that would be interested in Marneshta are seeking attention from authority. Encouraging them to redirect their freakish energy towards this meaningless task also comes with the added benefit of letting professionals deal with the situation, should it escalate to the point of mail-bombs.

- **Finally, if nothing else works, let them meet Marneshta for themselves.** It's a desperate last resort, but sometimes this person will realize the error of their ways if they just get a chance to see, smell, touch and hear Marneshta for themselves. Unlikely as it may be, once in a great while, people who are touched in the head enough to think they're interested in Marneshta will end up being completely disgusted by it once they have a chance to meet her. Again, ONLY do this if nothing else works, because as you're fully aware, we want to have as little interactions with Marneshta as possible!

Micropan Marneshta, what is it? It's a state of mind, yes; and it is one particular attribute of the tortured psyche of one Dermetia Miller, an entity of unknown sexual definition or prowess, who spies on people in the shower and recites tortured names, but does so politely.

Dermetia was inspired by the prophets of Ragnar, the Instigator, and Cloellen, in particular. Dermetia loved the way Cloellen would appear, like a beautiful man dressed in drag, with perky tits that looked almost real, the brightest shade of cherry apple GMO red lipstick, a finely penciled-in beauty spot, impossibly lush blonde curls; Dermetia was jealous, all right.

Cloellen was a fundamentalist when it came to its belief in Ragnar. Ragnar, the Instigator, was given unto the world to fight against the weak, the pitiful and the meaningless. Ragnar, according to Cloellen, always commands us to destroy our enemies. Cloellen never stuck around to contend with the aftermath; it was always just this endless coaching, *go and fight in the name of RAGNAR, THE INSTIGATOR!*

This was attempted on a couple of unsuspecting Mormons. Elder Scott Attlebrough and Elder Rormesus Clayston were canvassing the street, looking for converts, when they happened upon a narrow single-family dwelling which had just been indoctrinated by the Ragnar people. [Their neighbor had a "Ragnar" sticker on the back of his Saturn Vue (since discontinued, for good reason) and that was probably all that was meant by it.]

The Elders knocked. Jason answered the door, sized them up without saying anything, and just immediately knew. As they pulled out their Mormon Jesus playing cards and began to force them into Jason's face, Elder Clayston got ready to drop his tightie-whitie long john Mormon secret special magic underwear bottoms around his ankles, his dick dripping and throbbing from years of celibacy, and he was about to fuck Jason's chubby ass in the name of Jesus, when suddenly, Jason's kid started screaming,

"MORMONS!"

Jason had to remind his kid that wasn't technically politically correct, that they preferred the name "Latter Day Saints," but he also didn't want kid to worry. Dad Jason had a plan to deal with these tortured, blue-balled suckers.

"We follow Ragnar, the Instigator in this house."

"Oh, uh, I'm not familiar with him," said Elder Attlebrough. It was a disarming technique Jason had learned in the Dipshit Army.

"Ragnar commands us to destroy our enemies. Does your guy do that?" Jason didn't wait long enough for a response; he knew there wasn't going to be one. The Elders looked at him, and at each other, in a state of confusion and mild discomfort. Elder Clayston began pulling his drawers up. Obviously, there was no fucking for Jesus to be done at this house. He didn't know what exactly had just happened, or who Ragnar, the Instigator, truly was;

but he had a nasty feeling he was about to find out.

And that's where Cloellen can help out. For, at the very least, it is effective at spreading the gospel word of Ragnar, the Instigator. And Dermetia was jealous, so *very* jealous, that it made her already-bloodshot eyes clot up.

"Fucking snobs! I hate their fucking guts! Die!" And with that, she stabbed a dainty pair of scissors into the eyes of all the ugly, horrible vintage dolls her auntie had left to her.

SOME FLAPPING STARTED AT THE WINDOW. It was cockatiels.

"Disgusting birds! Australian pigeons!" Garly snarled. He didn't really believe what he was seeing; yet, again, this was a trashy part of the country, full of goons and fools who lived in decrepit apartments overlooking gray rivers and dead trees, huddling by outdated and inefficient portable propane heaters, staring dejectedly off into space for hours on an end, stinking like stale cigarettes and cheap, spilled beer— the Cockatiel breeder crowd.

"WHEEP wheep-wheep! Ahhhurr-ehhp!" The birds screamed. Garly attempted to shoo them away; but, being stuck in a wheelchair like the retarded loser that he was, he could only flail his arms around stubbornly, pathetic to all who were watching.

Only one person *was* watching. "Garly, dear, you need to calm down and un-stuck yourself." Garly was trapped between boxes of expired newspapers he was holding onto for, as he would describe it to acquaintances, archival research purposes. Garly *did* fully intend to, eventually, plumb the depths of two decades' worth of local-news drivel and poorly written sports columns to formulate a decisive oral history of the entire United States. This was *not* another episode of "Hoarders," as some of his colleagues would suggest under their breaths, not daring to actually make their criticisms of Garly known forthrightly, out of fear that they would be cut off from his at-home governmental disability support funding, the proceeds of which they would help themselves to on a monthly basis, filing false claims of having changed Garly's adult diapers, when, in reality, Garly had the means to acquire a high-end fat-person-style toilet that was fully capable of, to put it in the crude vernacular, *sucking the shit right out of his asshole.*

Garly was not a man incapable of self-sufficiency; he just liked to have people around to get drunk with. Those people, of course, similarly liked to drink, but they also did other drugs, and, if they'd known half of what Garly's assets were, he'd have ended up dead at the bottom of the Gray River long before he ever was bothered by Cockatiels on that fateful morning.

"When you were a kid, did you ever use *Starmitchlication-69?" he asked, blankly.

She immediately got a bad feeling. She actually *had*. It wasn't something she ever wanted to talk about, but, since it was brought up, here it goes:

*Starmitchlication-69 (and here there should likely be a trademark logo, or a rights reserved "®" icon, to avoid being sued, but since this report is being offered up anonymously, it will probably be fine; the publisher shall be some manner of limited liability company, if only they because they haven't yet made a NO liability corporation— it will be coming, soon, though, legal folk take notice and read the sheets) was made by a guy named Mitch who was pissed off in the middle of the night one time, way back in the early nineties, when he wanted to commit an act of drunk-dialing but was informed by his long distance carrier that he'd exceeded his credit limit for his phone bill that month, and he couldn't make calls outside the local calling area until he paid the $700 bill, which was a lot of money back then, and still is, for that matter.

Mitch wanted to find a different way to approach the telephone business. He also wanted a convenient and foolproof way to mask his own personal landline number from any emergent caller ID technologies that may well have been coming onto the market at that time, circa 1992-1994. He enjoyed saying dirty things to plump, middle-aged women who he didn't actually know. After he'd exhausted all suitable contacts in his rolodex he stole off the last office job from which he'd been fired, Mitch would start dialing random numbers. This was, coincidentally, roughly the same time period when women actually started expecting real rights, not just a bunch of talk; they went and got pants-suits and shoulder pads and law degrees, and started prosecuting men like Mitch who would mumble things about licking tit-sweat and masturbating into his daughter-in-laws' pantyhose when they'd come visit the house over the holidays (Mitch's wife had left him for a Cro-Magnon looking motherfucker from Belize who worked on the gay cruise ships encircling Jamaica, or else she'd immediately notice and inform Rebecca, the daughter-in-law, what her husband was up to, because women *always knew* these things and would glibly share the scandalous details amongst themselves, like hens clucking over a handful of cracked corn).

Mitch wasn't the kind of guy qualified to own a telephone in the modern, trendy, colorful first half of the 1990's. He had violated many edicts of the contemporary standards of society, and would've lost his phone privileges a dozen times over, if anyone had the means or desire to track creeps like him. But alas, he persisted in making harassing calls in the middle of the night to realtors and manicurists who just wanted to relax from an exhausting day at their respective home offices, crack open a light beer or two, and maybe fart a bit; but, whatever they did, they did NOT expect or want a tipsy Mitch babbling about how his mother didn't breastfeed him long enough when he was little.

So, Mitch was really at a crossroads. He couldn't afford to keep calling out-of-state semi-professional women who had made the lethal mistake of making newspaper advertisements highlighting a phone number which they shared between their semi-legitimate "businesses" and their domiciles, as their husbands would inevitably foot the bill for their dalliances and explorations into "careers." In all honesty, the best hustle women had at that point in history was the proliferation of divorce attorneys who could suck wealth out of the unwitting husbands' bank accounts faster than the Filipina mermaid of cock death could suck the foreskin off a sailor. But they couldn't seek the satisfaction of having a newspaper promote such a financial endeavor, so they had to settle on selling floral arrangements and catering for their girlfriends' life events.

Mitch wanted to feel some kind of a connection, no matter how sad and strange it may be, to these middle-class hussies with average tits and sub-par skin, so he subsisted on his regimen of hitting up small, women-owned businesses under the cover of darkness, until one lucky ring brought a real life female-bodied person onto the receiver of the other end, about to have her night ruined. Yet the phone company, those greedy, slovenly bastards, they wanted to tax him to death in order to satisfy his peculiar urges.

Mitch, the next week, got together for doughnuts and cheap coffee with his high-school friend who now worked as a lineman for the phone system at the nearby state college. Over starch, caffeine, sugar, and anger, Mitch and his friend came up with a plan to re-route long distance traffic through the phone closet at the college, something that could be triggered by any clod who pressed the star key, and then smashed the keypad and mumbled/shouted anything closely approximating "STARMITCHLICATION", and followed it up by pressing "69." [That part was an obvious innuendo.]

It worked, for a couple of years and a few hundred horny bastards who wanted to not pay their phone bills, and also not have their numbers traced so that they could harass women faster, cheaper and better. Then cell phones started and it was all forgotten to history.

But not to Cindy, or Shramlica, or whoever Garly's friend was that was having to suddenly think of all this antiquated nonsense. Just having this avalanche of bullshit triggered in her mind made her quickly decide that her time would be best spent elsewhere. That worthless cripple, Garly, was done in her life. Never another midnight-stoned-junk-food-snack-run phone call would ever be answered again. Ever.

"I'M DOING GOOD!" SMARNACH SAID, with great gusto and confidence. "I'm not smoking. I'm saying 'Hi' to Micropan Marneshta, everyday." Smarnach didn't really have much of a reputation left, so everyone knew this was as well as could be expected out've him. He used to follow the punk rock scene before he started huffing glue so bad, and his friends all became straight-edge.

He'd lost his good Christian name in a game of puff, the magic paper bag. Some other decrepit loser had tricked him into getting more high than he'd ever gotten before, and he was even willing to, as he put it, "stake my name on it." What "it" was defined as, is a mystery to anyone outside of Smarnach's head; but let it be known that, at one time, he *did* have a set of parents who had given him some sort of normal sounding name. He thought he'd be lucky, and maybe even recklessly fortunate, and get a taste of sweet intoxicating solvent without having to pay the hobby-store man. Arts and crafts people, however, are known for being deceitful.

So there he was, this now nameless bum all reeling and pooling what was left of his brain over the rain-drenched moldy sidewalk of an anonymous town, probably in the midwest. The police wanted to know: what do you call this sort of a thing? Surely a "John Doe" label would only hold up so far in court. John Doe was a wanted fugitive with a rap sheet so long that no reasonable judge would ever be stupid enough to try and hold him to answer for his many, many crimes. They just don't pay officers of the court what they must if they expect *that* level of justice to be doled out.

Smarnach was stuck, then, with just another gibberish label by which he would thenceforth be known. Dottie Blanker was the one who so endowed him with his new name. She was a likewise disaffected individual who couldn't make it in society; the heiress to a hot-dog fortune, she had whittled away an entire mansion's worth of decent existence burning candles from both ends while trying to please and appease all manner of riffraff she'd pull in off the broken alleyways and from dirty campgrounds.

So Smarnach wasn't really doing that good, not like his momma and his daddy would've thought "good" would represent for their son. He was lying, as usual. He probably was still getting high, even if the part about saying "Hi" to Micropan Marneshta was true (or any of the other Micropans, for that matter; he probably didn't have fuck-all to do with Marneshta herself, since any other Micropan is more hygienic and easy to approach than Marneshta).

Plus, talking to Micropans in of itself is a presentation of some underlying psychotic symptoms. People have been manifesting imaginary friends for themselves for hundreds, thousands of years; and many times those figments aren't even *remotely* bearing the resemblance of an actual human person. Marneshta, and all other stupid, ugly little Micropans, really represent an intellectual, and indeed, even a moral failing on behalf of those who rant and preach about their supposed existence.

We can establish, then, that Smarnach hadn't owned up to his responsibilities as a man, and Dottie Blanker could do nothing to defend his existence before the court; so, once it was determined that he would be charged as "Smarnach," and not as the un-prosecutable John Doe, it really wasn't as if Dottie had done him any favors in the first place. She could call him whatever fanciful, make-believe pet name she wanted, but she couldn't protect him any longer from that long, hairy arm of justice. Smarnach did NOT do good, he did NOT make his parents proud, and whatever it was he was up to now, it was just a matter of time before they caught up with him and hauled him away to a place, far beyond the desert, where he wouldn't bother anyone ever again.

"I WANNA MARNESHTA BRING ME A HOTDOG!" The baboon child cried. He was black. Nobody had ever taken the time or trouble to teach him about eating real food. It wasn't his fault; but it wasn't anyone else's, either.

He had maybe seen that stupid youtube short with the deranged clown who thinks it's funny to feed cheap, raw hotdogs to actual dogs. The monkey-boy would be so easily amused, even after everyone else in the streaming community down-voted that flaming dumpster of a video. He didn't care what civilized people thought; he was just lost in a world of his own.

It kind of reminded Rob of that time when he was in his early twenties and he got hired to fuck spoiled fat rich dogs up the ass. You see, it was during a time when colonics was all the craze; some people took it a step further, to suggest that their pets would benefit from having a tube shoved through their rectal cavity and irrigated with warm water for up to an hour afterwards. And some people took it even further than *that*, suggesting that, as the sterile plastic tubing was far from natural, a more suitable alternative would be to recruit some fat loser to use an actual human penis to inject semen into the lower intestines of their pet.

Robin "Rob" Biden was not well in the head, in the first place. He thought he'd seen a newspaper ad for this job, but it was really just a hallucination. At first, he tried to convince himself that, okay, maybe the original solicitation *was* a figment of his imagination, but that was only because he needed to challenge himself to pursue a new career in an emerging field. This could be it: bestiality, but for hire, so therefore it was no longer such a sinful thing, since someone else was *paying* for it. Why would someone pay someone else to have sex with an animal? It didn't make any sense, but Rob wasn't one to question it.

Well, maybe he should have. Nobody was actually going to pay someone to have sex with their fancy pet dog, and Rob's brain was already known to be highly defective, so it shouldn't surprise anyone that he was immediately charged, criminally, for trying to make a career out of this. Turns out, these rich people thought they were just hiring him to *dog-sit*, not have anal sex with their pooch.

Rob, though, swore in front of the judge that he had watched multiple instructional videos and successfully passed a 20 hour course that taught him that, indeed, contrary to legal opinion, sodomizing inbred pedigreed dogs *was* beneficial to their health.

Everyone in the court let their jaw hit the floor simultaneously, with a nauseating sound of dentures coming loose within the gums, just multiplied by a hundred. As bad as that was, everyone present was much more bothered by the fact that this rotund little man, the one with the glasses and the receding hairline and the sad, thin mustache, was gleefully confessing to having non-consensual intercourse with a dog, with the expectation that he was going to be paid, and specifically *because*, in his mind, he was qualified to do these things with an exacting level of professionalism.

Baboon kid didn't care. All of this was really just drivel to him, at his level of awareness. He was an overgrown lad of 14, about 270 pounds, and as retarded as they come. Of course, he was only still alive because his disposition was marginally *nice;* if he had been any bit meaner style of mental defective, it would've equalled trouble, and they would have made sure to put him down.

He wanted to pet Marneshta, if the clown man would just feed them both cheap hot-dogs on a sunny afternoon in the parking lot of the abandoned warehouse discount store, over there in Plain Meadows. No harm in that.

WHAT DID ROB DO, EXACTLY, THOUGH, that got him in so much trouble?

Well, there was a witness who saw it all go down. It was Christmastime at the Mall. The Poop-Pump 5000 had dropped, and it was a cutting edge work of sheer innovative genius that had been released just in time for the holiday shopping ritual. Working class scumbags and other lowbrow acolytes were lining up in droves to beat down the doors of the nefarious retail giants anchoring each wing of the Plain Meadows Concourse, drooling at the opportunity to fistfight, scream, yell, holler, whoop some ass, and rip each others' hair from out their scalps. It was a rowdy bunch, and they'd had their regimen of pain pills cut back recently, by a consortium of tightfisted insurance executives and moralizing puritans in Congress. It was a recipe for sheer bedlam.

The Poop Pump 5000, though, was pretty amazing. It was a gaming console, and an interface, *and* it had a rectal probe that would insert itself into one's anus at the beginning of each session. The designers of the device, through years of painstaking research, had determined that the most effective way to manipulate the body's reward system was by irrigating the lower bowels with a saline-and-mineral solution administered in varying amounts at slightly above room temperature. [In reality, this was just another ploy by the Colonics industry. They had failed at their latest attempt of masterminding a multilevel marketing scheme to further sow chaos in the at-home healthcare industry, and make an obscene amount of money by offering impossible promises to morons who thought they themselves would be getting rich by pushing this crap, which actually *did* literally push crap out of peoples' intestines, but not in a very safe or sanitary manner. They manufactured a test run of the devices at Mr. Chin's factory in China, before he was executed for making a pass at a Communist Party leader's daughter who had already been promised to a high-ranking comrade. The contraptions just barely functioned; several of them caught on fire as soon as they were plugged into a wall outlet. The orchestrators of the scheme realized, dejectedly, that this plot wasn't going to advance very far; still, they were determined to at least instigate a MLM chain in order to see how far they could get away with some stupid shit like this, just out of curiosity.] So, once a gamer got a shot of the secret, patented formula straight up their butt, it was said to boost performance by at least 25%.

But the *really* exciting feature of the Poop Pump 5000 was that the nozzle you were supposed to stick up your asshole was fully reversible! That meaning, it would suck the shit out of your lower intestinal area, and then hold said fecal matter in reserve for later use. Use for what, you may ask? It is well known amongst those who partake in video gaming culture that it is a highly competitive pastime, and that losing a match is an invitation to ridicule and humiliation, and thereby, revenge on behalf of the losing party. That's where the shit reservoir becomes *extraordinarily* useful. The reversible flow out of the Poop Pump 5000's patented anal nozzle means that you can blast your opponent with BM from a distance of up to 100 feet! Biohazard regulations be damned; the Poop Pump 5000 does it all, and that is why you need to run your un-nozzled ass down to the local community shopping mall at once. Drop everything you are currently doing and head right over there, Bucko, because there's at least a hundred other angry idiots ready to beat you to death in order to obtain one of these things. Gladiator match time, bitch. Free market edition.

That's why Rob, all giddy and defective like normal, decided he, too, would head on down to the Plain Meadows Concourse And Novelty Shops Plaza. Rob had no interest in the Poop Pump 5000, but he did have an interest in Santa Claus and his little helpers. An *unhealthy* interest. And he had a plan. It went something like this:

1. Eat a very large meal, at a cheap Mexican restaurant. Lots of beans and hot sauce. And pork. Request that the pork be undercooked (it probably would be, but he had to be sure).

2. Find out when the Santa shift was changing, so that the maximum number of people employed by the mall to portray jolly ol' Saint Nick and his elves would be present.

3. Very sneakily gain access to their wardrobe/costuming/locker room area, just before anyone actually went in there to change.

4. Quickly pull his pants off.

5. Gather up all of the performers' underwear.

6. In rapid succession, slide up all of the boxers, briefs, jocks and bikinis that he could locate, up as far over his butt as he could get them (Rob was about 50 pounds fatter than any elf would legally

allowed to be).

7. Take a little dump in each one of the undergarments. Not so much as to run out of poop prematurely, but certainly, enough to be noticeable.

By the time he was caught, Rob had soiled 62 separate pairs of britches.

In the aftermath of the disaster, some people suspected it was all a very elaborate scheme to steal the last remaining Poop Pump 5000 units off the stockroom shelves, while everyone was distracted by the foul-smelling odor that was emanating from the cordoned-off section of the foot court lovingly referred to as "Santa's Workshop." And indeed, not enough of the costumed morons had brought a fresh change of underwear, even though they were supposed to in case some mentally-handicapped child happened to pee when he or she was sitting on Santa's lap (and would then quickly be passed off to one of the elves to address the situation, because there can be only one true Santa Claus, and he was far too busy dealing with non-retarded kids to have to put up with that shit, or piss, as it were). So, some of them had to continue on expressing sentiments of Merry Christmas to unsuspecting members of the public, while wearing their shitty drawers.

So, Rob was on trial now, for several charges, including: (1) public indecency, (2) lewd conduct, (3) moral corruption of a minor (one of the "elves" was underage), (4) creating a public nuisance, (5) disruption of lawful commerce, (6) disobeying the direct order of a law enforcement officer (when he was caught, Rob was in the act of actively pooping in someone else's underpants, and the cop who accosted him saw what he was up to, and instructed him to cease immediately; but then the cop had to lean his head over his right arm and puke profusely, since the locker room area stank like feces and sweat to all high hell, so Rob acted like everything was still OK and continued his act of defecation), and (7) impersonating a public figure (he happened to be crapping in Santa's drawers when he was finally tackled and taken down by five other cops with stronger stomachs, but, since it was Santa's candy-pinstripe boxers, *specifically*, it was argued by the prosecution that he could've been mistaken for the big, fat jolly man himself by some unsuspecting minors. They were size XXL boxers, after all, and pre-stained with old man jism and bowel drizzle).

Anyhow, there were a bunch of people, foreigners, who had been arraigned on multiple counts of committing frog that had to appear in front of the Judge before Rob's testimony would be heard. They were dirty people, from filthy little countries (communist) with unpronounceable names, and they were in BIG trouble for having accosted good, hardworking white people on the telephone with frivolous sales pitches and outlandish claims. They were interrupting Trailervision® time for a good number of these folks, these fine upstanding American individuals who just wanted to cook up some homebrewed methamphetamine derivatives in their bathtubs using time-honored recipes handed down from multiple generations since passed. They worked in peace, mostly, unless there was a need for violence, which was frequently. Most people found violence distasteful, but not as much as deviant expressions of human sexuality; and, that is precisely what one Mr. Robin "Rob" Biden was suspected and stood accused of, here in this court of highest esteem and greatest regard.

"How does the defendant plead?"

"I am not guilty!" Rob proclaimed, frantically.

"Your Honor, we request bail set at $50,000. Obviously, this man is of corrupted morals and has a bizarre sexual fixation on scat, and the Santa Claus mythology," the Prosecutor said, contentedly.

"I didn't do this because of sex!" Rob hollered, indignantly. "I just did it because it was funny! I was bored, it was just for fun! Why can't a man poop in another man's underwear and get away with it? I just wanted to have some fun! I thought it would be a funny thing, because, you understand, it's like, who would ever expect that someone would go and do such a thing? I know it's strange, but I never once got a woody!"

"Excuse me?" the Judge interjected, confusedly. "*Woody*? Would you care to explain this term?"

"A hard-on, an erection!"

"Oh." The Judge wasn't sure how to respond. He thought that maybe Rob had been talking about Woody Harrelson, or maybe even Woody Allen.

This seemed like the kind of sick shenanigans that bastard would be sneaking around and trying to instigate. He was a funny man, though, that little Jew. The Judge chuckled to himself. He always wanted to be an extra in one of Allen's pointless, narcissistic films. The dry humor and obscure social interactions that defined Allen's work appealed to the imaginary sense of culture our esteemed Judge thought he himself possessed. The Judge daydreamed, and imagined that he was a wealthy New York person, flitting around department stores and flirting with frumpy, middle-aged women.

"I didn't do it for the sex," Rob continued, cautiously. He was afraid that one of his children might seize the opportunity to lodge some false complaints about molestation to get out of having to do their chores for this week. "You see, my wife, she means well, but we have an arrangement about playing 'Mr. Sucky' at least once a month, or more if I've been a good boy. Well, I *was* a good boy, they even said so at my job, but she didn't want to play with me! And nobody else did either. Not the neighbor's niece, not the Taco Bell girl– nobody."

"Your Honor, I don't see the relevance in this," the Prosecutor sighed.

"Mr. Biden, you are here because you allegedly pooped in someone else's underpants," the Judge said, authoritatively. "That is what the court intends to hold you to answer for. Any further discussions of any dialogues of a prurient nature that you may have held in confidence with your spouse are irrelevant to the matter at hand. Furthermore, if you persist in your digressions, I shall be forced to hold you in contempt!"

It was at this moment that Rob's attorney proceeded to make a motion on his behalf. "Your Honor, I'd like to take this opportunity to instruct the jury that they may, in fact, find my client to be non-restrunchtable in this matter."

The Judge began coughing hysterically, losing his breath as he began to turn beet-red, like an erect pecker that had been rubbed and stroked all afternoon without being able to fully release its built-up mass of ejaculate. He was caught entirely off-guard by the defense's request. He had heard the term, *somewhere*, before, but couldn't remember what all exactly was entailed by it.

And he couldn't just bring himself to admit that he was clueless in the moment; that would reveal the Judge to be the complete and utterly incompetent moron that he, in fact, was. Before being appointed to the Bench, he had been what is known, charitably, as a "country lawyer." He'd never been sufficiently privileged to attend law school, so he instead gave blowjobs to a transvestite personal injury attorney who, in turn, took the Judge on as his apprentice, allowing him to then, eventually, stand for the bar exam, which he just barely passed. Then, he had an affair with the wife of the chairman of the County Board of Supervisors, who was into the "cuckold" lifestyle, and was then successfully blackmailed (actually, it was fully consensual; indeed, the Supervisor was fully encouraging of the whole manufactured shakedown, blushing and biting his lip to stop from smiling a cum-guzzling grin of satisfaction every time he thought about being caught, in public, having his wife outed for cheating on him. It would make him look pathetic, and all the fussy middle-aged scolds who spent their afternoons wishing they could castrate all the high school boys, so no teenagers would masturbate or get pregnant, would then take pity on him, and offer to let him suck on their weathered old nipples until rancid milk began dribbling out. Which would be all the more humiliating, but, since he was a very secretive man, the Supervisor was much more content to keep this fantasy between himself, his wife, and the clueless, soon-to-be-appointed-by-the-Board-of-Supervisors Judge) so that he might appoint the Judge through his official capacity as Chairman of the County Board of Supervisors, once a vacancy had arisen, on an interim basis until the next (rigged) election could be held.

The court clerk, sensing the impending crisis, rushed over to the Judge's side, splashed a glass of water in his face, slapped him, and in an angry whisper, told him to take a recess. "The– EGH!– Court is, uh– ERGH!– taking a– HEH-HUH! Thirty minute recess." He then quickly waddled to his chambers, and called his dad, who knew all there was to know about everything.

"Daddy, what is it to be restrunchtable again?"

His father sighed, annoyedly. "Son, do we really have to bring this up all over again?" But, of course, they did, and the Judge's father would never miss an opportunity to spend a few hours mansplaining something over the telephone. He was, after all, retired.

The legal doctrine of Restrunchtability was an arcane concept, and only most sparingly used in modern judicial proceedings. But, since Rob's lawyer had been ballsy and reckless enough to ask for it, it went something like this:

The process begins with a troglodyte named Mortimer, who is called that because he has the personality of decaying flesh. He also fancies himself a storyteller, and he will, on occasion and only when plied with copious amounts of alcohol, regale any unfortunate audience members who may be present with the following story:

The fable was first told to Mortimer by one D'leik Witter, an afrikaner scribe and part-time pedophile who would often invent fanciful tales in order to evade legal trouble. The girls, he figured, had been more than adequately compensated with MDA-laced candy (he was too cheap to spring for legitimate MDMA) and "PINK"-branded apparel. Mortimer had been on Safari, trying to prove that he was a real man with an actual penis by shooting a docile, large mammal, when he came across D'leik in a small watering hole on the Namibian border.

D'leik immediately recognized Mortimer for the fellow scoundrel that he was, and made him sit down and buy multiple rounds of warm beer, that was not actually very good, in spite of the longtime Anglo-Dutch influence of the area, that, one would expect, would have resulted in at least a decent lager being able to be produced domestically. Anyway, as the two degenerates proceeded to get mildly more intoxicated, D'leik started to tell Mortimer a tall tale that he'd more or less pulled directly out of his ass:

A man had recently undergone a failed fecal transplant. He'd done so at the urging of his health guru, who ran a small, unlicensed medical practice called "Shambhala" (that people who knew better would lovingly refer to as, "SCAMbhala") in some forgotten ex-logging town in Northern California. Against the advice of actual doctors, the man had gone ahead with the procedure; complications immediately arose. "It was a mess," D'leik told Mortimer, who had then told it to the Judge's dad. "Like what happens at an orgy for the morbidly obese. There was a lot of sighing, grunting, and phlegm gurgling, and big rolls of fat everywhere."

The man's colon immediately identified an incursion by foreign matter, and reported it at once to the autonomic nervous system, which proceeded to muster an army of white blood cells and stomach acid to repel the invaders. Then, after several days of retching up dark particulate matter and evacuating the entire digestive tract via explosive diarrhea, the man's body subsequently had him court-martialed and brought up on charges of fraternizing with the enemy. The prosecution was led by an angry cluster of prions, seated deep within the man's brain.

While they were waiting for the court to be called into session that morning, a few random red blood cells who were serving as legal interns for the defense attorney, a role played by the man's left ventricle, struck up a conversation with the temporal lobe. "What's your favorite work of literature?" they asked it.

"Hmm. Probably, that would have to be *Markovian Parallax Denigrate*," the Lobe responded, obscurely.

"No way!" the red blood cells responded, defiantly. "We thought they had erased all the known data files still containing the original content!"

"Freshly, I read it still when it was," the Lobe replied, haughtily. "I was begun of the first to have ever entirely recorded the transcription." Which was his way of saying that, although the Temporal Lobe was not the best with words, he could remember things better than any of them.

The Judge was late to court that morning, much to the chagrin of everyone; but, they couldn't *say* anything about the situation, since it was, of course, the Judge, and everyone knows that you don't ever question a judge, no matter what you do. The Judge was also a gob of snot. He was stuck inside of the man's nose, waiting to be whisked away to his chambers by a thorough sneeze, or emphatic blowing into a Kleenex. The Judge came from a proud lineage of boogers; his older cousin had auditioned for the leading role in the classic film, *The Blob*.

The various organs and cells were floating around in the man's sputum while the Judge was descending to the bench. Someone spotted Solorgnum, the car that had touched some children improperly, in the defendant's box, waiting to be sentenced after the matter of the illicit fecal transplant had been concluded.

There was another reason the Judge was late that morning, though. He'd heard a rumor that one of the attorneys present was going to proclaim something about "Restrunchtability," a concept with which he was wholly unfamiliar. He proceeded to harden his exterior into a thick crust, the sort of which can only be dislodged by a long, dirty fingernail inserted deep into the nasal cavity. He felt pretty smart about himself, having bonded forcefully with a thick clump of sturdy, black nosehairs. There was little chance that the man was going to do one of his signature *pick-n-flick* maneuvers without an audience present (which he would invariably plot strategically, positioning himself next to a school bus stop for children, and waiting until a bunch of prepubescents gathered in a throng, which was in and of itself a completely horrifying thing for any reasonable person to behold, but he did it in an entirely incognito manner, so that, as the children were distracted and gossiping amongst themselves, he would discretely launch his quiver of boogies at the unsuspecting youngsters. Leading psychologists had no firm theories to present as to why the man would see fit to do such a petty and unhygienic thing, except for that maybe he was holding onto a long-standing childhood grudge against some fellow urchins who were upheld as being more disgusting and impoverished and overall pathetic than the man, who was then a kid, was), so the Judge figured he'd have a long delay before being compelled to open the court for business for the day.

He picked up a phone, made sure to dial *Starmitchlication-69, and then tried to get the operator to find Regis Philbin to help him call a friend.

"But sir, Mr. Philbin has been dead for several years," the operator told the Judge, impatiently.

"It doesn't matter. Just call someone at random," the Judge ordered her. The operator, being a conventional woman from the 1960s, sighed, took a quaalude, and proceeded to patch through a random person's telephone.

"Hello?" The person on the other end of the phone line asked, confusedly.

"Yes," the Judge began, "I am calling to inquire about 'Restrunchtability.'"

"I don't know!" the man on the other end of the telephone line wailed inconsolably. "I'm sorry!" He sounded rather elderly and senile. The Judge was disgusted.

"You know, they keep looping back on themselves," the old man said, experiencing a stunning moment of clarity. But the Judge was wholly disinterested by this otherwise intriguing turn of events. He wanted to get to the bottom of the situation, which just so happened to be a child's fat ass.

Which reminded him: someone had once drank out of the Judge's sippy cup when he was little, and it continued to bother him to this very day. Some might argue that he was suffering from a repressed bout of obsessive-compulsive disorder. He would repeatedly run his fingers through his thinning hair for hours on end in the midst of some particularly challenging cases (the fact he had hair was a feat accomplished by his aforementioned theft of nosehairs, being as he was a booger, after all), and tune out counter-arguments from the defense, so he could vainly attempt to count to 250,000.

So, unable to reach his favorite TV talk and gameshow host, who was by now deceased, the Judge took matters into his own hands, or should it be said, *tendrils*, and tried vainly to attach himself to a remote control that would change the television screen that was constantly blaring in front of the man's eyes.

It didn't work, to the surprise of no one. The Judge was frustrated, and thought to himself, *someone should have added footnotes about this kind of a thing.* Nobody cared enough to, though, and now the Judge had no other alternative but to dig deep within the recesses of his own mind in order to avail himself of the true meaning of "Restrunchtability."

That would be impossible, however, so instead, the Judge made up a story on the spot in order to attempt to justify this thing that someone told him he was probably going to have to learn about, in order to make a good impression on the criminals that were presented before his court:

Some person (who was not *somebody* or *someone*, mind your manners), had been intercepted while they were playing with their own poop.

It was runny, messy poop, the kind that should be better left in a sickly child's diaper and discarded in a public park's waste receptacle, in some lower-mid-tier American city, like Toledo or Tulsa. Embarrassed, this person tried to shift blame onto Soupy Litchten.

Soupy was the person that the Judge *would* have called, if he had been able to get onto *Millionaire* (and if Soupy had in fact been an actual real-life person), in order to use that particular lifeline to aid in answering the question, "What is Restrunchtability?" Soupy was anything if not *not* respectable. He spent his time collecting dirty pennies and whining about stampedes of Hondurans amassing at the southern border, thinking, mistakenly, that they possessed vast natural supplies of commas that were being imported to the United States, cheaply, and thereby corrupting the otherwise unimpeachable perfection of American Literature. Soupy was too stupid to know whether or not they even use commas in Spanish (they do, just not obnoxiously), and instead, went onto an internet forum where he could attempt to articulate his very inarticulate argument against immigration, and try vainly to incite an uprising against the nation's leadership.

Well, it just so happened that the President at this time was one Joseph Robinette Biden. *Junior*. This was very interesting to Soupy, because he'd heard a rumor, somewhere in the background processes running behind the front-facing application layer of the website he was attempting to utilize in order to spread his half-truths and other mumblings, that there was a trial being held somewhere, where a *Robin* Biden was being held to answer for a certain poopy scandal. Was there a connection?

"I'm sorry I pooped!" Joe Biden cried, obliviously. He thought that he'd been caught pooping in other peoples' pants, when in fact it was his *own* pants that he'd defecated into. An aide attempted to explain this to him, gently, but Joe merely shooed the boy away, because he was black and was probably going to steal Joe's pocket change. That happened once, when he was little, in Delaware.

Joe Biden had a terrible time keeping track of things. His wife was a doctor, but she wasn't *that* kind of a doctor, you know, the kind who can actually fix people and do cool things. No, his wife was the sort of doctor that was just called a doctor, for reasons that normal people can't comprehend, but it was something to do with being good at teaching. She could not, however, fix her husband's impending senility. She could help him relearn the alphabet, however.

There was a problem, though. By the time they got to the letter "O," there was an agreement that Mrs. Dr. Biden would give her husband, the President of the United States of America, a blowjob. He did deserve a reward for making it that far, after all. His brain was so damaged, that it was amazing that he could even count past 20, since that's how many you have to count using the fingers-and-toes approach.

Anyway, while the President would get prepared to get sucked off (this time by his own wife, for a change, which, it turns out, is far more wholesome than getting a blowjob from a lady that is *not* your wife, like President Clinton did; or cutting the beating heart out of a nine-year-old Mexican child and sucking the blood out of it, like President Bush did; or smoking a cigarette, like President Obama did; or the stuff that happened after, which isn't fitting to talk about in the presence of good company), Dr. Mrs. The Biden wouldn't be properly prepared, by which it is meant, she would be wearing a horribly coarse lipstick that would act as an abrasive on the head of her husband's official penis, like sandpaper.

It wouldn't work. It didn't take the Judge to figure this out, either. No; instead, there should have been a party for Joe Biden not having pooped in someone else's pants, a party with balloons and cake and a clown. But, since he *had* pooped, but he did *not* poop in pants that were not his own, the costs and the benefits balanced out; and, since he didn't like getting sucked off by his old lady anymore, he just gave up and went back to the telephone, like any responsible borderline-senile fool would. He picked up the handset, and breathed heavily.

None of this did anything to further advance the plot. A twelve-year-old stealing dirty sausages at a discount state fair in New England could do a better job, in fact. There were complaints coming in left and right, and forwards and backwards, and from the top-down, and from the bottom-up. The only thing that anyone could agree on that *was* helpful, was the fact that Dr. Jill

Biden was supposed to give her husband, President Biden, some good ol' sloppy head if he was able to count up to the letter "O." That, consensus held, was *hilarious*.

What was not hilarious was Hillary Clinton, but that sort of goes without saying, doesn't it? Well, no, obviously, because it was just said. Things like this sometimes can't be formally acknowledged, for legal reasons, but it *can* be mentioned as a side-note. Since this particular narrative doesn't believe in notes, however, things of this nature will continue to be stated in the main body of the text.

So, the Judge was still stuck on this whole drama with trying to explain to someone, from a position of authority, about what "Restrunchtability" was all about. He was still struggling with the enormity of the situation. He was a component of some dude's body that might be put to death if it was conclusively proven that he had violated multiple international treaties by attempting to inject foreign fecal matter into his own bowels. Of course, if it came back that the man was, in fact, guilty of having committed this heinous crime, all of the parties present for the trial would themselves be wiped out of existence, as they were all part and parcel of the same criminal organization, that being this particular man's body. It made the Judge mad that someone would've put him in this position in the first place. It wasn't fair that some selfish prig would shove some alien poop up inside of his butt.

"Does Restrunchtability mean something that I've just invented as a hail-Mary copout in order to avoid the inevitable consequences of someone else's reckless disregard of law and order? Do I have the fortitude to will something completely absurd into existence, merely in order to evacuate myself from an impossible paradox?" the Judge asked, unconvincingly.

Well, no. It doesn't work like that, not even for the best of us. You can't simply make up some stupid shit and expect it to fly. Not here, and *certainly* not in a court of law.

But, they kept going, regardless. Now, there was a commotion and the Judge and his non-existent friends started a small fire to keep warm and stroked themselves while the next critical thing happened:

A cat door opened up into someone's house, and a furry head popped through. It looked around, first left, and then quickly to the right, before it fixated on its intended target, smack dab in the center of its vision, directly in front of it: a bowl of some kind of animal kibble. It was about 25 feet from the door, deep in the depths of an unclean kitchen that the animal was particularly wary of, since the animal apparently had higher standards of hygiene than the owner of the grotesque room.

The animal was the sort that walked, most of the time, on four legs. It had a combination of black, white, and a small amount of orange fur. It was not a cat, and it was not a skunk. It was something from out of a Dr. Seuss book, most likely, although one that was never deemed fit for publication, since the animal was also a flaming racist against Japanese people. Japan, as you may well be aware, popularized sushi after they lost the war, and all was therefore forgiven, by contractural agreement.

The animal, then, was cast aside by the history books and took up a stalking presence around a minor neighborhood where its comings and goings would likely be unnoticed; or, at least, they were unlikely to be reported in a manner that anyone in a position to do anything would take seriously. The animal, therefore, embarked upon a little crime spree. It stole winter gloves from children's cubbies and pinned the blame for it on a particularly dumb black cat owned by one of the neighbors. It fidgeted in front of an autistic girl and caused her to have a full-fledged meltdown that her mother had to deal with for the first couple of hours of the day, until she remembered that her daughter would immediately calm down as soon as she had a Happy Meal to rip apart and devour. McDonald's didn't do the Happy Meal anymore at this point in history (at least, not the memorable, original Happy Meal, with the gelatinous meat product and the whimsical toy that served to teach children the meaning of fast food, which was, of course, to eat as quickly as possible and then demand more, on a regular basis); but fortunately, the mother had hoarded a big supply of them during the nineties, when she was younger, and everything was cheaper, and strategically stockpiled boxes upon crates of Happy Meals with their cheap, horrible burgers and fries, and little plastic toys that are now worth a small fortune for some dumb, unknown reason. Now, later in life, she counted herself as the most fortunate woman on the planet for having some cheap, old crap with which she could distract her spastic kid. So, she did.

It almost worked perfectly, until the day came that the mother had her daughter in the same room as the mother's mother, who was quite old and frail at that point, and used a walker. Just because the daughter was autistic, didn't mean she was a *nice* person, and indeed, as soon as her mother's back was turned, she immediately dove in and stole her granny's walker.

"No, thank you!" her grandmother wailed, plaintively. She had had a stroke several years before, which left her unable to say anything other than, "No, thank you!" The granddaughter knew this, and took full advantage by pretending that she was too retarded to understand that her grandmother was in great pain and anguished by the theft of her walker, which was the only way the elderly woman had any semblance of mobility.

Naturally, the mother, who was supposed to be caring for her at-risk family members, was nowhere to be found. Too poor and stupid to qualify for a driver's license, she had instead taken the bus to the discount grocery store, and then lost track of the bus schedule (actually, the bus driver had intentionally fucked off on the job that day, in order to smoke cheap marijuana laced with dish detergent at the dirty park down the street with his loser friends from high school), and she'd also forgotten to fetch a batch of Happy Meals from out of the basement to distract her retarded kid.

Granny was at a loss for words as her granddaughter began dueling with imaginary pirates, smashing the walker into windows and antique wine bottles and stained glass and other worthless trinkets that the mother had scattered around the house; well, other than being able to scream, "NO, THANK YOU!" at the top of her lungs, like it would really mean something.

The only person who heard the commotion was Mailman Tom. But, since all Mailman Tom heard was, "NO, THANK YOU!," he figured it was just an otherwise polite and innocuous conversation transpiring between some people who happened to be hard of hearing. He chuckled, and thanked blood Jesus that he was able to still hear normally, and continued on his mail-route.

Meanwhile, Grandma was on the verge of another stroke. "No, thank you," she muttered in defeat, as her granddaughter started yelling triumphantly and high-fiveing all the broken glass she'd just created, which led to some bleeding, and then some cussing and further outbursts, and meanwhile, there was a bowl of mayonnaise jello sitting out on the counter, melting away into muck. It was supposed to accompany, as a side dish, the rotisserie chicken that the mother was supposed to be bringing home from the store, which was never going to happen in time, due to the bus situation.

The mother, reluctantly, realized this. She sat down on the curb in front of the dirty grocery store, and she did drugs. And while she was doing those drugs, she reflected on some of the choices she had made, and thought to herself that if she hadn't been so fucked off, that maybe she could have been a successful lawyer, or, at least, have played a convincing one on a cheap daytime TV drama.

If she had been a lawyer, or at least pretended to be one, the mother figured, she'd get a few things straightened out around here, that was for *damned sure*. Firstly, she would mandate that there was a mediator to referee any disputes between a disabled elderly person and a mentally challenged kid. No more throwing spaghetti-O's at the TV and forcing a morbidly obese 85-year-old heart disease victim to clean it up. There should be someone, a certified host at *Friendly's* (or similarly family-friendly themed restaurant chain) to volunteer their efforts in the off hours, to bring about a greater understanding between

Uncle Mr. McFatticus
(Incorporated, I Presume)

A Novel

Chapter I

ALDREN CLETUS SPENCER HAD WRITTEN THAT BOOK, "Uniform of a Maniac," and there is that line in it that everybody knows, when he's describing how unspeakably happy he his about landing his most recent kill, where he cut some guy's head off and is doing a happy-dance around the still-standing corpse spewing blood out of the jagged hole which used to be its neck, and he goes off about how he saw angels, and actually, it's a really beautiful passage of literature.

Well, the official Literary Review Book Club of Plain Meadows did not agree. Comprised of a bunch of stern-faced, vaguely masculine women, they eschewed any and all overtures to violence through writing. They much preferred softly-lit straightforward romances about female winos struggling to earn enough tips from the dumpy diner at which they were currently working to buy a seasonal greeting card to cheer up their crippled half-child, who was of course severely intellectually challenged, for Christmas, along with maybe a used gift card to the Plain Meadows Country Club's Pro Shop that had been drunkenly discarded by someone's uncle who was getting all stupid and sloppy because *he* wasn't invited to the family Christmas-cheer-ritualistically-conformed-celebration event, because he was *nobody's* favorite uncle; and indeed, he sucked, being a true asshole who made his mother cry at her own funeral. And that gift card would probably have very little, if any, balance left, maybe just enough to buy a single used golf ball.

The woman in the cheap novel wouldn't be deterred by this. Her half-child was easily amused and would happily wait out most of the rest of the upcoming year before finally having a big, exciting outing by taking the bus to Plain Meadows Country Club, so he (or she) could spend the small amount of remaining gift card balance on that single, used golf ball, that the half-child could then chuck at an elderly man chomping a cigar and being warned by his wife to not let his lighter get too close to the supplemental oxygen tank he was obliged to carry in the back of his cart, lest he start having fits of COPD. Or, the woman's half-child could find a common bird, like a pigeon, or a crow, or maybe even one of those viscous feral cockatiels that they'd mentioned on the news were flying around loose and attacking people, and chuck the precious golf ball at that instead.

So, she works up the courage to ask her boss at Dumpy's Diner and Finest Shortcake Roadside Food Stand to get a forty-cent-an-hour raise. The boss sneezes a contemptuous torrent of snot in her direction to make clear his disdain for workers requesting more money out of him. He had a serious drinking and blowjob habit; he had to pay the greasy haircutting lady next door to come suck him off behind the flattop after shift, *and* he was spending about thirty bucks a day on cheap whiskey, *and* he had to share half of it with what's her face, the hair-whore.

So the darling little strumpet has to start working her own hair, and her tits and ass, and getting right in the face of any male-bodied (or male-identifying, or suspected to be as such; she didn't care, she was *desperate*) patron walking into her designated territory of what was really a sorry excuse for a restaurant. She was hungry, for tips, and sometimes, on special occasions with the right person, anal sex. She really did have a butt that wouldn't quit, and people say this in an offhanded manner lots of times, but in her case, it was completely true; sometimes, her sphincter would keep her up at night, whispering strange and conspiratorial things, like it had just smoked a whole bunch of meth.

Sticking her rack in the face of each middle aged man whose table she waited got her *maybe* a few extra dollars in tips. It also got her some dirty looks from these mens' wives, but our starlet couldn't be bothered. There is no honor amongst thieves, or women for that matter.

With this money, she immediately goes to the nearest Hallmark (can we say that?) gift-card shop. Actually, it was a dollar store, but she liked to pretend that she was doing well enough for herself that she could go to a brand-name greeting card supply store, and then brag about that to her Auntie Марфа. And while she's browsing the discount rack, trying to find an inventive way to repurpose a card that is designed for a dying dog's last birthday to satisfy the strange compulsion of her half-child's desire to receive the best Christmas card ever, she just so happens to find a casting call booth for the *actual* Hallmark Channel's annual slog-a-thon of appropriately cheerful holiday programming. And she wins the role!

Now, since the attention span of the ladies of the official Literary Book Review Club of Plain Meadows was starting to disintegrate, mostly because they'd now been reminded of how much they really would rather be dressing up in ugly Christmas sweaters and binge-drinking box wine while watching an *actual* Hallmark holiday-cheer-themed movie than discussing long-winded and tedious books that contain unnecessary details and odious levels of repetition, not to mention consistently inappropriate use of adverbs bordering upon some sick obsession with perverting the rules of English grammar and proper use of vocabulary, the remainder of the plot is summarized as follows:

- She gets cast in a pointless film involving a woman who drinks wine to excess and reads shitty romance novels she bought from the dollar store at night in the bathtub crammed underneath the rafters of the half-attic apartment she lives in, because she's poor

- She starts having hallucinations (said to be "flights of fancy," but no, she truly is mentally ill) involving the shirtless minotaur heroes of these cheap, terrible books coming into her boring and tragi-comic life to rescue her from tedium

- Then, it actually *does* start happening, and her half-child doesn't know how to explain to his or her special needs classmates (you know, the kids they section off into the retard part of the school, usually the basement, near the art room) that its mother is slowly losing her mind, so it's implied CPS is about to get involved

- Meanwhile, the lady goes on more incredible (but limited to PG–13 standards) romantic adventures that she is actually convinced *are* happening

- The authorities investigate, and decide that she shouldn't have custody of her half-child anymore, in a dramatic courtroom scene when she imagines she's dating a lawyer who doubles as a superhero at night– or *does* she imagine it?

- No, it turns out that she's just a drunkard experiencing alcohol-induced delusions. BUT, one of the handsome fantasy men turns out to be the friendly neighborhood UPS driver, with muscles
- He's making enough money to buy her half-kid a nice, talking, ten dollar Christmas card, and that shuts the little spaz up
- The government decides they can't afford to take care of her mentally disabled half-child, and gives him or her back to the lady, who promises to the judge, up and down, that she is *not* going to be drinking wine in the bathtub and reading cheap exploitative paperbacks any more
- Everything is happy-ever-after, except that she *does* still drink box wine in the bathtub and read shitty romance fiction, but all the roleplays involve UPS guy, representing a committed heterosexual relationship, which is what Jesus would have wanted, but just a *little* bit naughty, and it's Christmas, so the ending is appropriate for the intended audience.

Now, one thing the official Literary Book Review Club of Plain Meadows could agree on is that A.C. Spencer would never have written such a charming little story. A.C. Spencer was full of piss and anger. He was from New Hampshire, just like G.G. Allin, and that says it all. So, just because someone thinks that something is a stunning work of written genius, even a *heartbreaking* work of *staggering* genius, doesn't mean that it actually is; even if a lot of people think that it is, there will always be an official Literary Book Review Club out there, somewhere, that is going to find it repulsive and offensive and complete trash, and substitute it for something far superior, something digestible and accessible to the masses, a work of good feelings, and nothing more.

THE SHRAMLICORE CORPORATION WAS IN CHARGE of who was allowed to back up in front of Tommy Duckweiler's house. Tommy Duckweiler had gotten killed as a kid over there at Sʜɪᴛ Cᴀᴍᴘ, Iɴᴄ.; then he went on to become a successful adult who rented a house with his two children (from different mothers). He successfully scammed the government into giving him foster care benefits, because when both of his kids were born (to different mothers), he had feigned schizophrenia and refused to sign his name to either of their birth certificates; well, actually, he *did* have certain schizo-affective tendencies, which were inherited genetically from his father, and his father's father before him, but since he was never legally married to either of his kids' moms (because they did, in fact, have different mothers), when the women inevitably left him alone with his two children, due to random drug and mental illness addictions, Tommy was entitled to claim that the children were not in fact, his own biological offspring. But, he did make a convincing argument in front of a judge this one time, and it went:

TOMMY: Judge, I have these here children.

JUDGE: Go on, Tommy. You can do this. I believe in you!

TOMMY: And it's two kids, see. And I don't know rightfully whose is they belonging to. But, they did come by the ways of my house this one day, well, each kid did now come over of on their own accord, about one per particular day, it was...

JUDGE: Tommy, you're doing really well!

TOMMY: And, uh, well now I don't know the laws specifically 'bout this kind of a thing, ya know, never did occur to me in the slightest, but, uh, you reckon, Judge, that maybe the state's see fit to permit me lookin' after these here young ones, at least, 'til, maybe such a time as they should have their own natural folks come back 'round here to recollect them?

The Judge smiled at Tommy, because that's what you do when someone is simple. You smile at them and hope for the best, and prepare for the worst; but normally, you don't need to worry about the worst, unless some completely scatterbrained fool put the simpleton in charge of, like, a military ammo dump or something. Then you're going to have a whole crew of Fish & Game wardens out there picking up the corpses of thousands of dead animals, some of which are bound to be endangered, and that's enhanced charges, extra fines; "Yadda, yadda, yadda," as a guy once said.

Tommy was, however, granted custody *and* payment for the sake of caring for his own children, and he was very proud of himself, too. And the

Judge was also very proud of Tommy, for having been able to successfully pronounce the word, *custody*, during the hearing, instead of what everyone else thought Tommy was going to say, which was *custardy*.

So it came to be that, on this particular night in question, Tommy noticed a truck backing up in front of his house that he didn't know to be pre-authorized by the Shramlicore Corporation. Shramlicore Corp was very specific about their rules and policies regarding trucks backing up. That was the main reason why Tommy felt safe having rented the house in the first place. Not a lot of people were qualified to back up trucks.

"Daddy, how does shoes work again?" Tommy's oldest son, who was actually a teenager, asked him, blankly.

"Shhh. Daddy's having a think," Tommy replied, forcefully. He wasn't concerned that at the age of 16, his son still didn't know which shoe went on what foot. That child's mother in question was known to be particularly reckless when it came to recreational substance abuse while pregnant, and this obviously was the result of that.

Still, Tommy was more concerned with this strange pickup truck. There was a man inside of it, backing up in front of his house, and leaning out the driver's side window (which was facing the opposite side of the street as Tommy's house), and yelling something Tommy didn't understand at someone else, who Tommy couldn't see. They actually looked to be backing into the driveway of the apartment complex across the *other* street from Tommy's house; but Tommy wasn't placated at all by that observation. The man could be yelling curse-words out of his window, for all Tommy knew.

Tommy was getting so worked up about the backing-up-truck, that his breath became quick, and quite moist; and, being a rather cool night outside, it caused condensation to quickly accumulate on the inside of the glass. Tommy became more agitated as he could see even less, never having learned how to properly de-condensate a window. He knew that it would get "drippy," from time to time, and when he asked the Shramlicore Corporation to do something about it, they would smile and pat Tommy on the back (because that's what you do with simple folk like Tommy).

Tommy had a machine gun, though, hidden away in his closet. He'd been given it by his older brother, who was a Marine, before he defected to the Muslim side during the Iraq War. Tommy's brother had actually been recruited into Al Qaeda months before he hatched his plan of putting military hardware into his simpleton brother's hands; the *Mufti* who approved the mission saw there to be great wisdom in providing highly destructive weaponry to a mentally marginal man.

DONNY DICHTON'S MOM HAD TOLD HIM to sit tight and wait for her outside the store, and to NOT poop while he was waiting for her. His friend Davey, however, had other ideas.

"Donny, you gotta poop," Davey said, helpfully. Donny wasn't sure he could remember how without his mommy there. She would normally lead him by the hand to the local women's restroom and help him sit down on the toilet once they'd entered the stall. It always smelled sweet, and nice, to Donny, who was the sensitive type. Donny's mom would smile at him, encouragingly, and stroke his palms to try and relax his sphincter so that he could do #2. She'd coo at him, make baby noises and even give his little weenie a tug every now and again, just so he could calm down and make BM.

"Comeon, Donny," Davey said, sinisterly. Davey was not the smartest kid, but he wasn't a complete and utter retard like Donny was, either, so he could giggle and rub his hands together excitedly while tacitly encouraging his "friend" to commit a gruesome act of public humiliation.

All Donny's mom had explicitly told him not to do while he was waiting for her, was to poop. Now, any reasonable person would be asking at this point: why didn't Donny's mom take him into the store with her, rather than leaving her special needs child tethered to a bus stop bench? Well, probably because his mother was a whore, and not of the wholesome, goody-two-shoes-that-a-rich-man-paid-for-in-exchange-for-booty-call variety, either. She was blowing a crackhead in the changing stall at a Ross Dress-for-Less.

"Hey, Cranchlaford!" someone yelled in the distance.

Donny looked up for a minute. "Don't look up, Donny!" Davey yelled, distractingly. "Just poop!"

Donny wasn't sure. Maybe he should pull his pants down and do his duty on the sidewalk, directly; or, maybe he shouldn't even wait that long, and instead, just take a big ol' dump in his trousers, and then see what happened.

Davey was hoping for the latter. He knew that if Donny shat himself, he'd then start bawling and screaming about how much he wanted his mommy to come and wipe up his dirty butt. Davey was grinning with anticipation, and hopeful that he could find a nice, warm slice of pizza to munch on while he was enjoying the spectacle, that being of a grown man named Donny Dichton, with the mentality of an immature five-year-old, pooping in his underpants and then hollering about it for all passersby to behold. For Davey, it was the best day ever. And also, when he got home, after he talked Donny into soiling himself in public, he was going to get to watch the whole series of Lunch-A-Leashtions! Little Lunchaleashtions! Yeah!

THERE WAS A PROBLEM, THOUGH. It was called Sciclopan (pronounced PSYCH-lo-pan) Sharneshta. It claimed to be its own thing; however, everyone who knew better realized that it was just a cheap imitation of Micropan Marneshta, a terrible and cheesy knockoff that imperiled the entire economic empire surrounding the legend of Marneshta.

You see, Micropan Marneshta was by far and away the most successful of the entire bunch of Micropans. What started as a lousy wannabe kids show on early morning terrestrial television had morphed into a nostalgic cash cow that preyed upon the fond, yet inaccurate memories most millennials had of their miserable childhoods. Micropans were there to play, and not even in a particularly inappropriate way (save for Marneshta, who really was never suitable for children, since it would spend most of its time on the small screen licking its genitalia). But as they got older, these children of the nineties became more ensconced in cynicism, and grew infatuated with the discount schlock they were spoon-fed many a cold morning before school.

Marneshta was intrinsically nasty. It had a matted coat of fur, probably slicked down from rolling around in random piles of shit. The adult millennial loved that sort of thing, and when it was found out there was a limited release of Micropan toys from that era that had long since been forgotten, suddenly every remaining example of Marneshta was snapped up. The fucking stupid things were going for in excess of $9,000 on Etsy one week. That's how Sciclopan Sharneshta got started.

Some greedy moron wanted to make money, and here we go:

It began with Mohammed Fisher-Price, the token toy muslim. In the interests of promoting racial inclusiveness, the toy company decided they were going to offer a limited-edition styling of an Arab man, complete in ceremonial headdress, with a scraggly beard and dark, sunken eyes. They didn't officially issue weapons, such as a cutlass, an AK-47, or a "suicide" belt lined with plastic explosives; however, they also didn't *disallow* such third-party additions. However, they felt like they'd done their due diligence in making the character look as menacing as possible, so that children may think twice before picking up the toy and going to play with the Islamist kids down the street, and becoming radicalized jihadists as a result.

Mohammed was getting pretty tired of this treatment, actually. He merely wanted to possess one or two child brides, for him to sequester away and do with as he pleased (sexually), maybe show them off/trade them to his friends from time to time; but otherwise, he just wanted to be left the hell alone. That wasn't good enough for the likes of the fearmongers and social-justice-warriors of cable news. The pundits insisted upon making Mohammed a pawn in their never-ending quest for ratings control, so the toy ended up being continuously pulled into one news cycle after the next, a scapegoat for cultural phobias, and a martyr for civil rights.

Another thing that should be known about Mohammed was that he was friends with Fred X, who operated in the shipping & logistics industry (some were even known to say that he was an "EXpert" in these things) and therefore was able to hook Mohammed up with some truly dirt-cheap rates for transporting goods overseas. Mohammed realized that anything he was about to do was going to have to be coming from China, first of all, because all of those little oriental people with the tiny hands were so good at making stuff at exceptionally low cost, thereby delivering value to customers, managers, supply-chain folk, the Chinese Communist Party, and pretty much everyone who wasn't working in these factories, cranking out cheap shit.

Also, Mohammed knew how easy it was to circumvent US copyright law by making knock-off products elsewhere, then importing them and selling them at a discount to the authentic item being imitated. So it was obvious that, if he were to get his full enactment of revenge as promised through the Quran (and, before that, as it was told to the Prophet by Ragnar, the Instigator), Mohammed Fisher-Price would be targeting that most asinine of momentary-fad collectibles, the Micropans.

Before they did anything else though, Mohammed and Fred would need to seek the approval of Solorgnum, the child rapist (who, incidentally, was also a racist, in that he refused to fuck Mexican or black children). He lived in a magical cabin in the middle of a hippie commune compound, out in the woods near an old gravel quarry. Everyone who wanted to be anyone had to first gain the respect of Solorgnum.

And Solorgnum, being a child rapist, was particularly intrigued by the prospect of being able to lure his underage prey with the false promise of a genuine Micropan toy, when in reality, he was too cheap to spend the kind of loot one required in order to possess a *real* Micropan. But Solorgnum knew that the children loved Micropans, and that would be the easiest way to entice them back to his bedroom without making a scene.

When you go to visit Solorgnum, you must bring with you a box of assorted glues. Solorgnum will then sniff around with his ever-so-delicate nose and select the prime candidate from the selection presented, so that he may imbibe through his hand-crafted paper bag set aside specifically for this purpose, that being, huffing.

And this was what caused a little bit of a problem. "I don't think we got the right kind of glue," Fred X moaned. He'd heard that Solorgnum had a preference for industrial adhesives, not hobbyist grade model glues like what Mohammed had purchased from the toy store that he was secretly plotting to blow up as a "Plan B" should this most likely ill-fated meeting with Solorgnum not work out, or amount to much of anything.

"I heard it said that, if you do not at once give him something he very much likes, Solorgnum will then do a butt-fuck of a child right there in front of you," Mohammed said, confidently. His English was improving, although he still had a habit of including unnecessary modifiers in his delicately thought-out sentences, verging on the point committing of tedious run-ons with obstreperous detail and meaningless words incorporated for good measure, so that someone who didn't know him any better would suspect that Mohammed Fischer-Price possessed an education far superior to that of their own, and would then cede the high ground of authoritative status, accordingly.

They needn't have worried, though. Solorgnum had sworn off his signature habit of inhalant abuse, after being told that he'd appreciate the experience much more if he saved his few remaining brain cells for obliteration later on in life. It's not as if he were capable of fully understanding, or even partially comprehending this; the decision had been arbitrarily enforced by his capable crew of enablers, members of his personality cult who entrusted themselves with the power to enforce Solorgnum's wishes, as they very well may have been, had he still been capable of coherent speech.

When Mohammed and Fred walked in, his assistants were quickly scrubbing down Solorgnum's private parts with wet wipes, after he'd just successfully ejaculated inside of an 11-year-old's ruptured rectum. The jism had dribbled down and out of the child's rectum and soiled the improvised "throne" upon which Solorgnum sat (his followers being of the mind that having belief in Solorgnum's divine status was enhanced by such a contrivance), and it was determined that the next child that Solorgnum had nonconsensual sex with may be weirded out by coming into contact with old, cold cum that was intended for a *different* child, and not the one that was, at that moment, currently being fucked. Solorgnum actually believed he was doing God's work by sticking his wilted, weathered pecker inside of a virgin's bodily cavity, and that the child should be grateful to be on the receiving end of this sex act, and therefore feel special and privileged, and having direct knowledge of God's eternal love. Hence, the aides and the baby wipes, continuously keeping the area somewhat sanitized (it was, after all, a derelict shack in the woods, decorated with license plates scavenged from rotted-out cars and the summer hides of various Raccoons and Skunks that had been caught in the act of stealing trash from the open, festering piles strategically located throughout the compound, as there was no garbage service available to this particular neighborhood, nor would the garbage company be willing to risk sending a truck and driver to their location even if it was on a regular route for refuse collection; so the cult members, being the enterprising folk that they were, set about carefully placing heaping mounds of waste around the property that had been so appropriated by the original actions of Solorgnum, while he was still known as Jerry Strichtmann, a disillusioned environmental engineer who actually *hadn't* been addicted to inhaling paint thinner before he got carried away with the weight of celebrity that was conveyed upon him when he began allowing transients to camp out on some old-growth Redwood forest tract that he'd kinda bought from a lumber company, but never quite held clear and unambiguous title to, so even if the garbage company was willing to provide necessary services, there was no legally-named person for them to send a bill to each month, as the theoretical account would become due), because it was generally assumed that this was an act of holy consecration, and the anointed one must be maintained in as close to collectible condition as was possible, given the all-around circumstances.

It was going to be a short meeting. Solorgnum's assistants were cuing up a showing of *Ernest Rump*, a heartwarming film about a man with severe cognitive deficiencies who nonetheless managed to find himself at the center of a number of historically noteworthy events, while assuming the identities of multiple personalities in order to circumvent the spies he was sure were following him around from one famous situation to the next, all the while attempting to track down his dad, who was said to have fucked his mother in the ass in order to conceive the shit-baby that was, Ernest Rump. It was Solorgnum's favorite movie, but due to his recreational chemical abuse, he was unable to remember the plot even though he'd already watched it 157 times. So, they needed to show it to him again.

The meeting went like this: Mohammed and Fred told Solorgnum they wanted his permission to start producing a line of toys called "Sciclopans" to compete with the authentic, but they felt, entirely overpriced Micropans. They furthermore wanted to make the lead Sciclopan be called "Sharneshta," because the Micropans had Marneshta, and the partners felt that would be a close enough approximation to fool most people. Mohammed framed a Chinese factory owner for espionage on behalf of the CIA, and extorted the man accordingly in order to make his slave-laborers crank out these toys that he'd designed, based off of publicly available patent designs for the Micropan line. Fred already had devised a strategy to fly the shoddy merchandise on cargo airliners directly to a small airport in the Mojave Desert, where nobody would notice what they were up to. Then it was just a matter of enlisting the help of some fat, whiny RV-warrior types who were otherwise engaged in serial arbitrage to start selling the Sciclopans on Amazon under assumed identities.

The plan was fool-proof. Solorgnum looked up at them for a moment, cocked his eyes in opposite directions, and made a half-grunt, half-nose-blow noise/gesture that resulted in mucous being spread around the immediate vicinity, then allowed his neck to go limp like a wet noodle and brought his head to rest on his chest. The aides nodded their approval for Mohammed and Fred's plot to proceed.

Solorgnum, however, wasn't entirely helpless. Inside his head, he still was capable of engaging in vibrant thought-conversations with himself. For instance, all the while these peons were rambling on about their stupid little plot to counterfeit some toys and associated merchandise, Solorgnum was reminiscing of how *easy* it used to be to sexually abuse children. Long ago, in the eighties and nineties, nobody was paying so much attention to what their kids were doing, and the media wasn't so hyper-vigilant about predation. Also, the taxes on child rape were far lower. Ronnie Reagan saw to that, dag-gummit, and Bill Clinton kept it that way. It wasn't until the liberals started getting all antsy about how to pay for art films about fancy pedigreed dogs urinating on everything that they decided to hone in on Solorgnum's main pastime and occupation. He'd gone to jail over the tax debt he'd incurred, and to this day, he wasn't sure how much he still owed for the last kid he'd fucked up the ass.

Mohammed was thinking, too, as they were all standing there in the same room, awkwardly not saying anything aloud to one another (although one or more of those assembled presently were maybe drooling a bit, from here to there) about how Mullah Omar, his mentor and main source of inspiration, would rather obliterate the Micropans than try to orchestrate a cheap knockoff run financed by some shady Taiwanese businessman. Mullah Omar destroyed idols, like those Buddha statues, in the name of furthering a pure islamic understanding of the world. Mohammed wished that he had that level of determination, but he didn't want to come across as a copycat. He would, however, kill both Solorgnum and Fred as soon as the opportunity presented itself, because he was just a vile, evil muslim toy.

Fred X, meanwhile, was trying desperately to avoid the fate of his uncle, Malcom X. He didn't trust Mohammed, because he was a muslim, and not a black muslim either, but a *muslim* muslim, and there were still some unspecified, unresolved issues surrounding the schism in the domestic islamist movement opened and perpetuated by his uncle's assassination. So, Fred was instead planning to get Mohammed, or whatever wealthy moron was bankrolling his operation, to charter a freight plane, which he could then hijack and demand a cash ransom for the lives of the flight crew and the value of all the counterfeit merchandise, then parachute to freedom with enough cash to buy a small plantation on some nondescript small island in the South Pacific, and spend the rest of his life having sex with coconuts decorated with the feathers of exotic birds.

There was another complication, however: the person who they thought was Solorgnum, minor cult deity and definite sex offender, was in fact not a man at all, but a 1997 Honda Accord station wagon. Not only that, but the incognito automobile was also working as an active informant for the CIA, FBI, NSA, ATF, FCC, FTB, NRA, and several autoworkers' local unions (naturally). The jig was most definitely up. Mohammed quickly ducked into a bin of compressed, recycled plastic pellets destined for remanufacturing into cheap, useless do-dads that lowly paid office workers are compelled to gift one another over the holiday season, quickly returning to the waste stream as unsalvageable refuse destined for the landfill. However, as he did so, Mohammed Fischer-Price was consumed by the polyethylene fumes and found himself being transformed into a *real* toy, one that a child could pick up, hold, and possibly, for reasons completely unknown, to *love*. Obviously, this would have to be some third-world wretch, a grubby Afghan preteen who's good with a kalashnikov and not much else; a student of the Taliban, as it were.

Fred also took flight; he literally commandeered a cargo jetliner and deliberately crashed it into the ocean near Polynesia, because he'd always been curious about what that would be like, to intentionally wreck an aircraft and then be stranded at sea. He quickly perished and was consumed by cartilaginous fish. But, as he was dying, a thought happened to cross Fred's confused mind: why would someone convert what appeared to be an actual elderly man with dementia into a shoddy used car?

Why, indeed? It wasn't particularly fair, to Mohammed, or Fred, or indeed, to the audience witnessing this entirely inexplicable turn of events. Sometimes, though, people just turn into piece of shit cars. It's not because you did anything wrong, it's just life.

Someone else was going to have to pick up the pieces of the Sciclopan Sharneshta scheme. Probably, it was going to be Monstreeshen, who was said to be (allegedly) someone's (ex) boyfriend, and possibly a low-ranking royal or other manner of European nobility. It didn't really matter, though, because Monstreeshen was a committed do-nothing, and would never care to invest one small flick of a pinky finger's worth of effort to do anything with the marvelous act of massive fraud that had been set into motion. It was a shame, too, because some of those kids were really getting tired of Marneshta and the Micropans, and wanted to play with something different, more accessible, less exclusive and out-of-touch. Sciclopan Sharneshta could have been that thing. It's a shame, really. Just a sad and useless waste of time and energy. So tragic.

"MOMMY, I HEARD SOMEONE WAS GOING TO say something bad about MICHAELPAN," the child wailed, obtusely. Nobody cared at all what some fat, immature little turd had gotten his feelings hurt about. The prevailing opinion was that he should go up to one of the obese women in the ice-cream aisle at the grocery store, who had no earthly business being there, and complain to one of them. Then, maybe, just maybe, he could gain their sympathy long enough to earn a flavored ice-cream popsicle.

That wasn't the most interesting thing, though. What was far more intriguing was, rather, the story of the poop popsicle.

"Micropan Marneshta and Rushugula Stevens Present: A Poop Popsicle," the advertisement read. It was posted outside of that store, *Hot*

Butts! that sold booty shorts and stubby cigarettes. Nobody thought that whatever it was that was, in fact, being advertised (some kind of show, it would appear) would ever be a good idea coming from the twisted minds of those two as producers. Rushugula in particular was a nasty example of street urchin, the worst kind of off-beat poet, a giant woman with dreadlocks and angst who bestowed upon anyone around her an unique brand of existential misery; so whatever kind of song-and-dance routine she'd crapped up along with the most wretched of all the Micropans, Marneshta, was going to be the utmost of disasters to have ever disgraced a public theater.

But Mega Sex Wrestle was just then walking home to Koreatown, and was about to collide with the whole situation. Check it out:

Mega Sex Wrestle, or "The Abominable Asian," as he was professionally known by nickname, was a minor gargantuan of approximately 400 pounds, with the girth to prove it. He had long since been discredited by Edward Said's theory of Orientalism, though, so he'd spent most of his career pursuing small one-off gigs that capitalized on his willingness to be exploited. He wasn't actually a wrestler, although he would fight if that's what the job entailed.

He did pretend to be Japanese, however, which was a grotesque act of cultural appropriation, if you asked just about anyone. Mega Sex Wrestle did *not* ask anyone's opinion about this, which is unfortunate, because anyone would have told him that this was a silly thing to be doing, playing games with his ethnicity and whatnot. He was embarrassed about being Korean, and secretly fantasized about having been born into a *Meiji* period family, to become the ultimate Sumo-Samurai warrior who would vanquish his enemies by sitting on their faces.

And also, it was Edward Said's fault that Mega Sex Wrestle couldn't just be open and honest about his cross-cultural identity, because Said was the grandfather of cancel culture, after all. So this just left a fat, confused asian to wander around coastal California in search of a purpose, and for more work as a freak-for-hire, as well.

He *did*, for some strange reason, have two friends: Styro and Toilet Lips. Styro was not actually a friend of anyone, but moreover, a generic sociopath of mixed-breed heritage. He managed to get Mega Sex Wrestle an invite to a party in Oakland one time, that was supposed to be hosted by Dave Eggers (who really should have been criminally charged as part of that pirate ship fire affair, because Eggers knew that scene, he passively encouraged that whole hipster crowd of the East Bay at the time, selling them dress-up kits and writing exploratory "journalism" type articles exploring the subculture there, probably; or, at least in a broader sense, legitimizing the entire movement, which was really more of the fabric of a loose-fit sweater from a thrift store that sold its wares by the pound, another mainstay of the Hipster lifestyle, and even though Eggers moved to New York or some shit, he still bore a lot of the responsibility for the rise in boorish buffoons and talentless hacks who donned nonsensical costumes and bragged about drinking cheap beer as if it were fine wine, when in reality, they could well afford something of greater quality to intoxicate themselves with, but they would rather spend their money given to them by their parents, and maybe sometimes earned in part by slinging coffee at some overpriced cafe that specialized in burnt sewer water, on reclaimed furnishings and obsolete Eastern Bloc propaganda posters, and definitely *not* on fire extinguishers and smoke detectors, and so the entire sordid affair could have been prevented had Dave Eggers just been a little bit less of a piece of shit), but he didn't want his name on it, for obvious reasons, so Styro told Toilet Lips he was going to have to MC it, and Toilet Lips agreed only on the condition that Mega Sex Wrestle could come and put on his act.

So, there was this party, and Dave Eggers was producing it, but he wasn't going to be there in actuality, since he was too embarrassed. He led innocent people to believe that, since they imagined themselves to be pirates, somehow the water spirits would protect them from fire and just general, all-around recklessness. It doesn't work like that, skipper. You need to put in your sweat-and-vomit-time on the high seas before the water spirits will ever *think* about defending you, even in a mundane social conflict. Like the one that Dave Eggers now found himself in, even though this was a lot bigger than a small disagreement over dinner about the genetic basis of intelligence.

The band that was going to be playing at the party, a hardcore act from New Hampshire, called The Local Dirtbags (named after a particularly quippy line said by the father of this girl who went missing, and probably died under mysterious circumstances, some years back, in New Hampshire, and after awhile everyone stopped caring except for her dad, who was convinced that she was abducted, raped and murdered, possibly not in that order, by a quote-unquote "local dirtbag"), and they *did* have a song they wrote, peripherally, about Dave Eggers, called "Nigger/Faggot/Eggers," which was actually well-intentioned, with the live performance of the song often accompanied by a bag of big, fat, black dildos that would then be handed out to the members of the audience with the goal of getting them to slap one another across the face as hard as possible with these dildos, to the point of causing serious bodily harm, which was the main objective of the Hardcore Punk scene (and not that other thing, called "Happy Hardcore" which was some monstrosity of electronica and a source of continual infatuation by dirty, drugged-up European nouveau-hippy trash, the difference in which was found out the hard way once upon a time, when a group of people went to a music festival in the foothills of the Sierra Nevadas that advertised it as having "Hardcore" music and was the set-up for a momentous occasion of great disappointment, but that's another story entirely), and then slid up some peoples' butts as a form of apology in the aftermath, since sodomy was also something greatly enjoyed by denizens of the Hardcore set, in general.

Before they were able to set up and "get down to business," so to speak, there was a much more prescient matter to which everyone's attention would first need to be paid: Mega Sex Wrestle's butt was itching. *Hard.*

Probably, what had happened was, he missed a spot when he was wiping, and it lingered for a few weeks, as the residual stomach acid slowly burned its way through the soft tissue of his anus and let some of the poop get past the epidermal barrier. Now, it was festering and infected, and Mega Sex Wrestle just knew this was not a problem to be easily resolved. Toilet Lips, of course, realized immediately what was up with his friend (why do you think he was called, "Toilet Lips," after all?), but Styro definitely *did not* have any idea of what was happening, and Mega Sex Wrestle and Toilet Lips needed to desperately keep the situation under wraps, so that Styro didn't end up finding out and then making fun of Mega Sex Wrestle in front of a bunch of nominally attractive people, as he liked to do.

"Yes, YOU DID! I saw it with my own eyes!" she screamed with great delight. "It was a chicken man! With a purse! Carrying a purse! I did see it, all of it! With my eyes," she continued, matter-of-factly.

And sometimes, like this time, people do and say things that don't bear much relevance to the situation at hand. For instance, Smiles Gumption used to walk through downtown, every Sunday, to buy a few lottery tickets from the local pharmaceutical chain. The lottery tickets generally always lost, or only paid out a few dollars, which was a few dollars less than what Smiles had spent on them. But, since Smiles was a simple fellow, and that was the cohort that was most preyed upon by the machinations of state-sponsored gambling, it was allowed. Not that Smiles should've been content with the situation; if he was of anywhere close to normal intelligence, he wouldn't be, but since he wasn't, he was, so he didn't complain very much, if at all.

People were starting to get worried about Mega Sex Wrestle, though. For one thing, he seemed like the most interesting character they'd been introduced to since... oh, golly, that senile old man in the seedy motel. Mega Sex Wrestle, while being more or less completely inappropriate for children, still had a charmingly immature presence about himself. He was, after all, just a big, fat, Korean boy inside a big, fat, fantasized Japanese man's ego. That was *something*, and everyone was dying to meet him.

And they were about to, at the party, except for the fact that Mega Sex Wrestle was about to be in BIG trouble. Like, the kind of trouble that meant they'd have to call over Firefighter Bob, which was never a good sign. It wasn't as if he was *intending* to commit a small act of arson against yet another make-believe pirate ship warehouse; he just had a tendency to get up to no-goodness. And sometimes, people lost their lives to an inferno.

It was a mistake, at the end of the day, for Dave Eggers to have invited Mega Sex Wrestle and his crew. They needed to go to jail, all four of them.

THERE WAS ANOTHER ANGLE TO all of this: another person happened to see the "Poop Popsicle" poster and thought something of it.

This person, however, was distracted by what he saw in front of him, lying on the sidewalk and completely disregarded by everyone else who had stepped over them: a crusty pair of underwear.

The person immediately became aroused. Either they were going to be girls' underwear, which was pretty neat, because the girl might have farted and even, most likely, peed a little bit into them. This could, in turn, increase the monetary value of the underwear exponentially.

If they were a guy's underwear, then that would also be something, since the person who was considering this life-altering purchase of zero dollars for found underwear off the ground also had a deeply-repressed homosexual desire to fondle another man's soiled drawers.

Just kidding. The person was still Mega Sex Wrestle! Yeah, he was a total pervert! Exciting, right? Yay! Real interesting. The story was almost starting to go somewhere, now.

"There were some shitty little morons over there," someone said, defiantly, well after the fact. "So, we had to get rid of them." And that was more or less what happened: a few people got arrested for facilitating underaged prostitution, a clown was taken in for questioning regarding possible indecent acts committed against a camel, and Mega Sex Wrestle just *had* to be put away for the sake of the community.

This neighborhood was an up-and-comer. For the longest time a refuge for fishmongers and black people with no assets, now it was descended upon by trendsters and hippity-types. Cheap beer was fashionable again, and the local Arab shop owners couldn't keep up with demand. They were assaulted and harassed by the black muslims, naturally, but continued doing what they did in defiance of the Prophet and everything that he stood for, because it made money, and they were in America now, after all, and money was what mattered, almost as much as taking advantage of idiots did.

Mega Sex Wrestle was not compatible with the new, highly tolerant image that the neighborhood association was trying to cultivate. And if he was going to be scooping up dirty underwear off the streets, and *not* properly disposing of it by placing it inside of an upcycled plastic organic produce bag, and delivering it by scooter to the local Goodwill affiliate so that they could mark the price up 2,000% and advertise it as being "vintage," then he just wouldn't ever fit in.

Smiles was supposed to meet up with the Committee to Free Mega Sex Wrestle at the John Danforth Museum of Snot; but, he was late. Smiles couldn't be counted on for much of anything these days, so it didn't matter, in his view, whether or not he was tardy to any given event, or indeed, if he even attended at all. The Committee did not realize this about Smiles, and thought that he was being rude. They left in a huff to go drink their bruised-ego-woes away at a craft distillery.

It wasn't looking good for Mega Sex Wrestle. He was beginning to sweat profusely in his holding cell. The detectives stared, and pointed, and laughed at him, and they jangled keys in front of Mega Sex Wrestle in a mocking gesture of offering him access to the *real* bathroom, the one that actual Police Officers were allowed to use, if he would only just give up some information about his co-conspirators. That way, he could sweat, and poop, in peace, and imagine like he was some sacred Samurai perched on top of a Volcano about to let all hell break loose from his bowels.

Smiles got distracted, again, by a Tarot card vending machine while he was walking to the Jail. Smiles didn't understand how Tarot worked. He thought it was like a more complex version of Solitaire, a game that he'd need to pay someone to teach him how to play. So, when he saw that he could have a vending machine dispense a card to him seemingly at random (but at the same time keeping in the spirit of the scam and presenting him with a plausible sign of his impending demise), he was confused, and also felt obliged to insert a five dollar bill into the money slot.

The machine slowly whirred to life, and shuffled through the deck and ejected a single card at Smiles: Death. Smiles panicked, and ran out into oncoming traffic, and was hit and killed by an industrial-food-product delivery truck. Which was ironic, because the Death card actually meant that Smiles was going to win the lottery the following night, signifying the demise of his being broke all the time, and had he not freaked out like a retard and gotten himself killed, he would have been rich. And then everyone would have liked him, and helped him spend all of that money, on things that they liked and wanted. And when the money was gone, Smiles would be ostracized again. *But at least he would have had a more interesting story to tell than the one that he did end up with that he maybe could have told someone, if he hadn't been killed, about how he died by being stupid and getting run over by a big truck.*

ANYWAY, SOMEONE WAS GOING TO ATTEMPT a certain strategy in order to rescue Mega Sex Wrestle, once and for all. This approach was contingent upon the *Get Out of Jail Free — Fat* card, which was something that the R&D department at Hasbro had been developing for some time. It was a very specific revision that applied only to very special, very *fat* people, just like Mega Sex Wrestle was. It was NOT intended for use by the girls in the ice cream aisle, mind you. They would end up taking advantage of it too often, and then end up *not* going to jail for the crime of being obese in public, which would be a darned shame for all of society. Hasbro's engineers intended for the card to be used only very sparingly, if indeed it ever needed to be used at all.

Mega Sex Wrestle was facing some serious charges. Firefighter Bob accused him of burning down a pirate ship themed amusement park. Really, Firefighter Bob was the one who set the actual fire that roasted several dozen people alive on that particular night, but because he was very tall, and a firefighter, everybody took his side when he instead blamed it all on Mega Sex Wrestle. Ours is a patently unfair civilization, after all.

The technicians they sent out from Hasbro weren't sure that the *Get Out of Jail Free — Fat* card would even work. They snuck around, like the first guys who blew up an atomic bomb in the desert tried to avoid the native Rattlesnakes who knew what they were up to and tried to crawl inside of their boots and inject them with as much venom as they could muster before the miserable Humans could press the button and destroy the snakes' natural habitat, carefully and delicately disguising themselves with dollar-store paste-on novelty mustaches in order to gain entrance to the local detention center wherein Mega Sex Wrestle was being housed.

One of the Hasbro agents was about to throw the card down on the counter that the receptionist-officer equivalent was sat behind, and scream and laugh and declare Mega Sex Wrestle's impending freedom, when the other agent recognized someone very distinguishable sitting on one of the securely-anchored and horribly ugly, barely-upholstered chairs that were somehow uncomfortably wide and inappropriately ass-hugging at the same time: it was Alden Cletus Spencer.

"Hey, you're A.C. Spencer!" the agent shouted, joyously.

"Hey, you're dead!" Spencer responded, jovially. He then drew a sawed-off double-barreled 12-gauge from underneath his trenchcoat, pointed it right between the agent's eyes, and pulled both triggers simultaneously. The man's brain matter sprayed in the most fine mist you could ever imagine, atomized, leaving a consistently sticky coating of meat residue over every object in a 25-foot radius.

The other agent cried out in horror and anguish. His plot to free a man who, by all accounts, fully deserved his impending incarceration, if only because he was so fat, and such a fake Asian man, with a silly made-up name that suggested that parents should not allow him around their pets or children, that he should have been put away years ago before any of this nonsense started, was now in jeopardy of being completely and utterly blown up by this random asshole's abrupt appearance.

"Did you like the part about Solorgnum, and how he was just a shitty car in disguise?" Spencer asked, quizzically, as he was calmly and carefully reloading.

"No, you didn't write that part!" the agent yelled, defiantly.

"No, I didn't write that part," Spencer replied, giddily. "My Jewish friend did. He's a vegan. He cuts up carrots in small, little pieces, and feeds them to people who have undergone involuntary brain surgery."

"But wasn't that what he wanted for Bar Mitzvah?"

"*Unnecessary* brain surgery."

"What's that got to do with anything, anyhow?" The receptionist-officer asked, disgustedly. This had become one digression too far. She was about to demand answers.

"He was the one who inspired all of this," Spencer declared, confidently, sweeping his arms in grandiose fashion to indicate an all-encompassing expression. "He thought it would be delightful to find some mutant freak like the man who you have detained under false accusation, and march him through these neighborhoods."

"But, what about Monopoly?"

"It was merely a distraction. A ploy to gain your trust and confidence, so that I wouldn't be recognized until–" Spencer paused dramatically, and then, when he didn't get the response he was looking for, raised an eyebrow quizzically and swatted away an imaginary mosquito.

"Until what?"

"Until it was too late." Spencer leveled his weapon at the agent's head.

"There will be more of us!" the agent shouted, uncertainly. The receptionist-officer laughed. Everyone knew how Hasbro operated; if one of their operatives were compromised, the company would deny any and all affiliation. This man was fucked.

"You're fucked," Spencer said, connivingly. He fired again, this time a pair of slugs that ripped the back half of the poor man's skull asunder, and left just the most amazing, steaming head cavity you've ever set eyes upon. Spencer nodded at the receptionist-officer, who grabbed her keys, and merrily they skipped down the hall, to where an overjoyed Mega Sex Wrestle was about to be freed, to pursue more low-level antics and crimes in order to entertain some worthless hipsters, all up and down the coast of the State of California.

"IT WAS OKAY, BUT IT WASN'T as good as a Jonny Johnson story," the book club member sighed, discontentedly. Johnny Johnson was a better author than that darned A.C. Spencer.

Johnny had written a series of books about innocent young girls who inadvertently stumbled into their parents' raunchy internet sex lives. This was in the dialup era, so most of the action had to be left up to the imagination, but there would always be some oblique references made to BDSM, coprophagia, and child prostitution. The middle-aged white woman demographic loved it.

"I wish I were little Cristobel," said Patty Lichten, one of Jonny's regular readers. "If someone paid that much attention to my twat when I was eight years old, I wouldn't be the shriveled up old hag I am now."

Johnny took this as a compliment, even though he was gay. But he wasn't *that* kind of a gay, if you know what we mean. No, *that* kind of a gay is the sort that becomes a total worrywart that he might possibly get identified for having a live-in-boyfriend, when his body of work was the kind that appealed to insecure heterosexual white men.

You know the person we're talking about. Let's hall him Chad Pukeonadick. He would write things that were vaguely offensive in an otherwise socially acceptable way, in a "let's laugh at these freaks" sort of well-intentioned spirit. He would gently poke fun at society and let people feel like their own sense of disillusionment was being acknowledged for once, while actually not accomplishing any sort of societal change, even at the smallest level. But his audience would *believe* that they were doing something subversive and revolutionary by reading his drivel.

The publishing houses loved it, the Hollywood morons optioned all of his stories to make into big-budget major motion pictures starring the studs and starlets of the month, and the money was just flowing in from all directions.

The problem was that little Chad had a secret penis addiction, which really in and of itself wasn't a problem, or it wouldn't have been for most people; but Chad had struck his reputation as being an alienated average white dude who, it was widely believed, *loved* the pussy. That's why he was upheld as the literary genius of his time, while poor Johnny was stuck being pigeonholed as a 50-cent paperback writer whose targeted clientele were borderline illiterate, trailer-dwelling, frumpy single mothers.

It didn't go on like that for forever. You see, some upstart journalist had gotten a tip that Chad liked to shack up with other men, *in a sexual way*. The reporter confronted Chad about this in a brief interview. "Well, I don't see how it's any of your business," Chad said, brusquely. But (and this is the most important thing for any tabloid news story), *he didn't deny anything*.

Sure enough, the story broke, and Chad had to begrudgingly admit that he sucked cock for fun when he wasn't writing stupid garbage that appealed to degenerates who wanted to feel some sense of validation for existing in the first place. It was a big, fat scandal, and even though at this point (the late 90s-early 00s) nobody *really* cared about being gay anymore, it also didn't appeal as much to the intended audience, so the movie industry's interest in Chad's material waned, and he slowly emerged as a has-been author, irrelevant to the modern era.

A.C. Spencer didn't have that problem, though. He was merely a homicidal maniac and part-time wordsmith. A.C. Spencer had actually *lived* the brutality of his writing. He would never be exposed as anything other than what he was. And that was just fine.

Uncle Munchlucus

A Novel

Chapter 1

"MR. ROBIN BASKINS?" the loudspeaker asked.

"What?!?" Rob exclaimed, startled.

"We have a survey for you to take."

"What do you mean?" He was very nervous, for a man who had nothing to admit.

"Just a brief questionnaire," said the voice, soothing yet hollow.

Rob didn't feel like he had a choice. OF COURSE he was here voluntarily, had done nothing demonstrably wrong, didn't even have the slightest tinge of guilty conscience stabbing his gut, not now, not ever. But maybe one time. That one time, though, was certainly not now. Now is now-time. Now is the time that is on the clock. That is the only time that matters, for now and ever and ever, in all times. Time is right just this second now. RIGHT now, not just now, like a small while ago, and certainly not a little bit later on.

"Mr. Robin Baskins," the voice stated, again, gently admonishing. "We need for you to just quickly answer a few questions, if you could." It was phrased to sound like a simple request; there may have been something slightly more sinister about it, however.

Rob used to skateboard, so he wasn't particularly impressed. There was a defiant streak in him during his younger years, a period of minor rebellion by cutting class at the end of the day, pounding energy drinks with his dopey friends, going five days in a row without bathing. His father was not a proud man. His mother would have loved him anyway.

"Mr. Robin Baskins, the form, if you please." He looked down at the plain ol' desk with the plain ol' pencil staring out of its plain ol' pencil-holder-cup-thing, and actually, come to think of it, everything in the room was just very, very plain. Normal as normal gets. The clock was there on the wall humming slightly like the 110 volt hard-wired programmable school wall clocks always were. There was a second hand that rotated smoothly, and a minute hand that jerked abruptly, and an hour hand that seemed to never move its stumpy little self.

The document the voice had so urgently but politely asked him repeatedly to fill out, *to the best of his ability*, was a multiple choice style survey. The first question was looking for a simple, yes or no response. It read:

1. I FEEL PROUD OF MYSELF WHEN I HAVE A SUCCESSFUL BOWEL MOVEMENT.

Rob had to admit that, yes, in fact he was quite pleased whenever he was able to bridge that impossible divide between diarrhea and constipation and land a good burrito-sized turd into the bowl in one shot. He knew they were watching, and they'd know if he was lying, and actually it was kind of like seeing a doctor or a lawyer; it wouldn't help his cause to deny the truth. He circled, "YES."

The next question made him jump out of his seat and yell. "Oh no, no no no, what are you trying to do to me?"

"Mr. Robin Baskins?" The voice didn't say anything, but it didn't really need to, because it did a little upward inflection on his alleged last name.

2. I AM RELATED TO CAROLE BASKINS.

"I can't say anything about that!" Rob cried. "What do you want, me to get sued? What's wrong with you people?"

"Mr. Robin Baskins, it is just a simple test. There are no right or wrong answers except the truth. And you know what the truth is, don't you, Mr. Robin Baskins?" It was a really, *really* bad idea for Rob to act like he didn't know the truth. Because he did. Once in the third grade, he bit another kid's kneecap off, and when his mom was summoned to Principal White's office that fateful day, she tried to act like he didn't.

"Robin really doesn't know the difference between right and wrong, Mr. White," his mom said, lyingly.

"But what if he does?" interjected Mr. Wong, the vice principal.

"Well then, you probably wouldn't have issues with kids shitting in the urinals, now, wouldya?" the mother spat back, accusingly.

"We called you to this conference to try to civilize your son," Mr. White continued. "Unfortunately, I don't think that's possible."

"My husband doesn't love me anyway. He's going to leave me for one of the girls who was mean to me when I was little. They think they're so pretty, all 'ooh' and 'ohh.' I hate their guts!" Mother became very agitated in this moment, forgetting why little Robin wanted her to lie about his biting the other kid's kneecap clean off his leg in the first place. She lunged across the desk and started throttling Mr. White with his own necktie.

Mr. Wong picked up the electronic flyswatter he had modified by removing the plastic safety guard and pressed the button to charge the wire grid, landing a smack square on mom's ass as he did so. Nobody knew it at the time, but Mr. Wong was typically using that heinous device on children, and he actually had been a little bit nervous about deploying it on a fully grown adult.

Well, but it did calm the lady down some.

"Mr. Robin Baskins?" The voice was persistent.

"I'm not that kind of a Baskin. That's not even my legal last name," Rob pleaded with the voice. He could just tell that either way he answered the question, he was going to get into trouble, big time.

A NEW MUSICAL PROJECT, THIS BAND called, SHITLER, wanted you to check out this track listing from their first album, *Lunch*:

1. A BIGGER BIRD
2. THE SLOBBERY
3. PUSSY CONTROL
4. WHAT IF DEAD ANIMAL?
5. MR. GIGSBY
6. CHARLIEGENIE
7. OLD CHINESEY LADY
8. MUNICIPAL WASTE DISASTER
9. I ONCE DID A BAD THING
10. DONALD'S DUCK

We begin with "A Bigger Bird," which is an homage of sorts to Big Bird, our dad's high school acquaintance's character, and someone we grew up around, for which purposes Shitler would be highly inappropriate. Our Mom would never have allowed us to listen to this band, even if it had a legitimate connection to Sesame Street. Which it did not, as it was a knock-off, and not really much of a song at all if you think about it: it starts with some low-fi chord progressions, indeterminable noises in the background, then a sudden flurry of bird squawks and backwards chanting, and then a sixties-detective-show-sounding-guy comes on and says, "We're gonna need a bigger bird."

"The Slobbery" is a sound collage of samples of dogs slobbering and some quiet discussion of a violent, armed robbery of a cannabis farm. "Pussy Control" is really just a shot at Donald Trump. It does contain the catchy hook, "We now have Pussy Control," which is said in the same manner as if you were a commander on a submarine, or an automotive mechanic fiddling with channels of engine computer data in order to diagnose a sloppy running condition (only there it is known as "Lambda Control," which is when the car is adjusting the air-fuel mixture ratio according to information being sent from the oxygen sensors that are positioned both before and after the three-way selectively reducing catalyst).

"What If Dead Animal" is a story about going to the San Francisco Zoo with a vulnerable foster child and having said kid completely traumatized by watching a baby elephant get beaten to death by a gorilla. It may have gotten started with a bad review on Google, but it ended up in a bloody mess!

"Mr. Gigsby" is a salute to all of the alcoholics of America and their collective psychoses. It is also a cautionary tale of a local cable company's saturation advertising featuring a very racist white unicorn lecturing to black people on why their laziness was resulting in subpar broadband internet speeds. Of course, the black family in the ad completely ignores the unicorn, who is called "Mr. Gigsby" by an animated Issac Newton.

"CharlieGenie" sounded pretty funny to say repetitively, in a higher-pitched voice, and also to present a message directed at a mentally disabled individual named Charlie who keeps saying how he wishes he had not done so many terribly stupid things in past moments of his life.

"Old Chinesey Lady" is a political tract criticizing immigration policy that allows elderly asian women to hold tenured faculty positions at public universities. "Municipal Waste Disaster" is based on true events, when a meth lab next door burned a hole through the local sewer line and left sludge backing up through the streets for a couple of days.

"I Once Did A Bad Thing" is the keynote track, where we list a series of terrible things we may or may not have done, including, ripping our girlfriend's nosering out during a dinner date because we were just too curious to know what would happen, opening a car door at a decisive moment in traffic when a bicyclist would ride right into it, and ejaculating on the face of a twelve year old taiwanese boy. "Donald's Duck" is a followup to "Pussy Control" except it incorporates another guy named Donald who had a heroin addiction he was trying to kick, so he opened up a duck farm to help himself work through his issues. It wasn't effective.

What about the tracks at didn't make it, for one reason or the other? We had suggested a piece by the name of "Shoot that Nigger!" which was rejected by the label. We even had a video for it:

We, Shitler, and our hip-hop DJ backup act are laying down a sick beat in the tradition of early 90s Rap. Then we cut to a random white guy in a collared shirt and tie eating his whole-grain-cereal breakfast with some 2% milk. As we're singing through the first verse (the song is just an advice column to police, reminding them that if they want to commit violence against black people, they need to strike quickly and decisively, by executing their victims before anyone realizes what's happening; then, they will be much more likely to get away with it), suddenly our troupe breaks through the *third* wall, and starts pursuing this otherwise innocent looking dude through the rest of his daily routine: at work, at his divorce attorney's office, at his kid's soccer game, at the chain restaurant bar where he tries and fails to hit on the servers, etc. Each transition, he thinks he's evaded us; we're following him around with guns, mind you, real thug shit and all, and we even get one of those Reggae/ Dancehall guys to do a little guest star solo act in their patois gibberish crooning, to give it that edge you know, and at the end of it the white guy is surrounded by police, so he decides to suicide by cop, then they start shooting but it's all confetti silly string guns and it's all a big joke, and he's pissed off because HE WANTS TO DIE!

Then, there was Micropan Marneshta. The studio, or label or whatever they want to call themselves, felt like it was too risky having a transvestite style character around actual children. They wanted us to shoot the video using dwarves instead, but we refused. You cannot substitute true art. The idea was, there's some kids hanging around playing some augmented-reality game with their smartphones, or maybe they're playing with actual playing cards or jacks or some shit, whatever the little boogers are into these days; but then walks up this, uh, person, obviously doing a really horrible job of crossdressing, a big tall lanky motherfucker wearing a dress and all done up so much you can't even make out a hint of his real face, pretty much a mask of solid makeup, and big, bushy over-the-top wig, and he comes up to these kids and starts asking them about Micropans. "Do you guys play with Micropans?" he asks, and the kids, being kids, are obviously offended by this patent weirdo. They reject our tranny character, *decisively*. If these dumbass kids knew anything about Robert's Rules of Order, they would have blocked him with a supermajority vote.

Our dejected character is sulking for a bit, but then cheers up when he's reminded of his favorite Micropan, Marneshta! The song then begins like a gameshow being played out: he dances, very poorly, in his platforms, but manages not to trip up too much and there's all these oddball gremlin-esque characters on the sidelines, cheering him on. Meanwhile, there is a analog-style number-meter in the upper right corner of the screen keeping count of his score, and it keeps increasing with stars and sparkle effects for the rest of the video. Then he's stirring a big vat that looks like it has witches' potion brewing inside of it; each time some creature says the name Micropan Marneshta (it goes, "I want to know about / Micropan Marneshta"), you get a closeup of the mouth that's saying it, then some new gameshow act, and so on and so forth, until at the very end, there's snakes and five arms extending from our Tranny friend, who it turns out isn't so human after all, and is much, much better than the kids at playing whatever stupid game they have going on, so they all run away screaming in fast-motion, and our dude wins! Yay!

WE ARE SURE THAT YOU experienced some sort of ostracization when you went public with your support for MICHAELPAN. It was a very difficult election cycle; friendships were shattered, families were lost, small dogs and annoying children may have been mildly physically violated in contravention of state and local ordinances. We know that it wasn't easy for you to come to terms with your support for MICHAELPAN.

You were so embarrassed, in fact, that you couldn't even bring yourself to write in MICHAELPAN's name on the ballot, on the line right where it said "Write-In." And you weren't alone. Several famous Michaels were remiss to actually take the small but important step of formalizing their support for MICHAELPAN, their legally designated next-of-kin:

- Michael Keaton wasn't sure that he was actually registered to vote. He may have had some traffic citations from out of LA County some years ago; and wherever he was living now, he didn't know, first of all, if his local DMV was, in fact, participating in the "motor voter" regime. "Motor voter" was a way to get stupid people who were still, for some reasons unbeknownst to the certified geniuses® who founded this great country, allowed to drive even though they were too dumb to be bothered to join the rolls of registered voters. The work was done for these lazy, sloppy bastards as a joint effort of their state department of motor vehicles, along with either the secretary of state's office, or perhaps a local town or city hall that maintained the right to grant permission to citizens to have the privilege of casting a ballot. So, Michael Keaton didn't know if he even *was* registered in whichever of the 50 United States (and Puerto Rico, and minor outlying islands, and maybe even the rest of the world, vis-a-vis an absentee ballot scheme probably arranged through an exchange program with foreign countries, like high school students spending the year immersing in an alien culture and language), if indeed he even *knew* which state he could legally declare as his residence, and even then, those goddamned traffic tickets not having ever been paid may have effectively prohibited him from the prestige of engaging in participatory democracy, unless he paid cash. So, as much as he felt like he *wanted* to vote for MICHAELPAN, on a strictly Michael-to-Michael basis, he didn't think it would be plausible.

- Michael Jackson was dead, or else he totally *would* have voted for MICHAELPAN. Michael Jackson was never criminally convicted of molesting underaged boys, so in theory, he *could* have voted, had he not died. And he probably most definitely would write in the name MICHAELPAN on his secret ballot (Michael Jackson LOVED secrets), not just because of the "Michael" connection, but also because there was a small rumor floating around that MICHAELPAN was actually Peter Pan's less-magical bastard half-brother.

- Michael Myers meant to go vote, but he also was a closeted cocaine addict, and he was too high and paranoid on that fateful November day to actually take the initiative to go and find a voter assistance center where they would give him the ballot that he already should have received by default, several weeks ago, in the mail, had he not pissed off his mail carrier for not having paid his cocaine tab (the mailman was also a part-time drug dealer, for supplemental income, since the Post Office was cutting back overtime due to concerns about election security).

- Michael Jordan actually *did* vote for MICHAELPAN. He liked it because MICHAELPAN reminded him of the nineties. The nineties were good to Michael Jordan. But, because he was black, his ballot got thrown away instead of getting counted.

- Michael Tyson was outraged and offended that anyone would call him "Michael." He was more of a "Mike," and proved it by biting off the ear of anyone who dared to call him, "Michael." Also, he threatened to jump into the boxing ring with MICHAELPAN and beat him bloody unconscious, and then go off and have sex with MICHAELPAN's girlfriend (that he didn't have).

MICHAELPAN was a real boondoggle otherwise. He rode around in an old limousine with his campaign team and spent most of the election season screaming drunkenly out the window at hapless citizens. They deserved it, no doubt, but it was later determined to not have been the most effective strategy. That's why MICHAELPAN didn't get that many votes; actually, he got less votes than that Mormon weirdo who kidnapped that teenage girl and tried to make her his third wife, and he was in prison at the time. So, MICHAELPAN really wasn't that cool, or effective, or even really that relevant.

A STRANGER WALKED UP TO THEM. "So, I need to know about Sumpy Lumption," the stranger said, matter-of-factly. "I need to know about shmarmlicants, I need to know about pschilcofords, and I need to know about getting grunchy." The stranger had plunked down a half-drank fifth of vodka on the counter, and it wasn't some pussywillow's flavor of stiff drink; this was some custom-distilled, 162 proof shit made from grapes that had been discarded from a discount vineyard in California's wine country. He wasn't fucking around, they could tell that much.

Going back a bit, they were struck by the last thing the stranger had said, about getting "grunchy." Someone had defined the term, as a matter of fact, rising to the occasion by offering an explanation and actually accomplishing something for a change, contrary to assumption.

"Grunchy" was what would happen whenever a group of people would congregate in an urban setting, with a brick-walled background. Midgets and victims of the Down's Syndrome then emerge from the cracks, riding tricycles. Nobody in their right mind could differentiate them from trolls. A low-fi hip-hop beat would drop as a wood-paneled station wagon rounded the corner down the block, with a Wheelchair Kid® stuffed into the very back of it. Elaborately attired transvestites *and* transexuals would begin dancing, a tall black person would start swaying back-and-forth with a boom box perched atop his gangly shoulders, his younger siblings dribbling, passing and shooting a basketball behind him. The color purple featured prominently. It was getting to be late evening.

The sign on the door read:

Meghan McCain's

STUPID MEATBALL BITCH

Pasta Emporium

And behind the door, there was an author, hard at work, trying to make sense of the poorly-written novel that was sitting right before him. "You can't let your characters interact *too* much," he said, to nobody in particular at all. "It's not safe. The more people get to know each other, the more they'll want to kill one another." It was true. The leading cause of homicide was, indeed, the victim being acquainted with the perpetrator. *Well* acquainted. And the author wanted to avoid this kind of conflict in his story.

This author, you see, secretly despised violence, and actually, *any* matter of serious disagreement or social discord. He figured that if he could just write about silliness, about stupid but otherwise well-meaning people (who would have been full of good intentions, had they been any smarter, but since they weren't, they really didn't have any socially redeeming value in of themselves, so therefore it could not truly be said that these were *decent* folk, but at the same time, they didn't do anything too absolutely terrible, at least, not most of them; they mainly ate, drank, pooped, and played with make-believe friends, and were not, by definition, even capable of having any clear intentions whatsoever), that he could distract his audience from the seething desire to exact revenge upon those with whom they may have once been familiar, and even cordial, but from whom they had suffered some catastrophic betrayal, either imaginary or perceived, and now could consider nothing short of cold, hard murder as being an adequate remedy.

The author disputed this readily-accepted interpretation of human nature. So, he fixated upon the other uniting factor, common to all of mankind: an unhealthy obsession with bathroom habits and crude sexual fixations. Surely, some of the content he wrote was problematic; there were depictions of sex with children (even non-consensual acts of sex with children), and things said about black people and the mentally challenged. But he had to write this sort of thing out, because it was the truth. It was the "big T" T-R-U-T-H.

Every time the author had ever had a psychedelic revelation, there was always a big, heaping, stinking pile of garbage nearby, or he was stuck in a porta-potty (which, on some occasions, he was convinced the government was going to quickly acquisition and remove him and his shit-filled tomb to places unknown where they stored questionable creatives in order to remove them from being able to influence society, even in the smallest of ways).

People sucked. But not in any exceptional capacity. It was just a ho-hum, middle of the road suck. So, the author didn't see the need to bring any specific or lasting harm to any of his characters, which is why he was so goddamned determined not to let them cross very rigid boundaries with one another, unless it was to in the service of furthering some plot device involving an uninvited act of defecation.

But why was there a sign suggesting something about a spaghetti dinner that also served as a "dis" of Meghan McCain?

SHUPPEL UPTION AND HIS DIPSHIT FRIENDS were cruising around one Friday night. They all thought they were so smart, wearing their varsity jackets from PFU (nobody had ever explained to them that there was no *varsity* at a collegiate level; they were entitled, after all, and it was easier to just let them have their stupid sense of self-worth, so that they might not bother the other students, who may actually accomplish something with their lives), and they thought they were really cool, too. Shuppel was wearing sunglasses, and had his hair all slicked back, styled like the caricature of the *WallStreetBets* forum on that otherwise worthless website, Reddit, even though he didn't know anything about finance and had never invested his own money in anything save some counterfeit cocaine that a scummy scam-artist high school friend of his had once retrieved from out of his own rectum; but, Shuppel knew that this was a popular subject in the social media circles he affiliated himself with, and as such, he felt compelled to emulate the style of the forum's avatar as much as was possible in a real-life scenario. He wanted to make some quick money by being dumb, and even though his parents were rich, which meant that he didn't even need to bother with pretending to know anything about stock options, he still wanted to attain a certain level of respect, elevated to the ranks of first amongst simpletons, a true trophy of American boy-manhood, having failed in all the particular ways that belonged him to high society.

These cretins were tromping about in their brand new Corvette convertible, that had been custom-modified to put in a backseat, and decided they would take a pleasure trip to the local discount grocer. They fancied themselves as clever and brave, daring to come into direct contact with the ranks of the great unwashed. But they had a plan. Well, more of a plot, really.

The setup was as follows: all of Shuppel's spoiled, uninspired friends had, on a whim, decided to visit the local dollar store (where all the merchandise was priced at no more than $1.25), instead of attending philosophy class like they were supposed to be doing, being a bunch of humanities majors (yuck); and within the disheveled, unorganized shelves of the dumpy, dismal, florescent-lit discount outlet, they did locate several off-brand squirt pistols and assault rifles, along with generic-labeled ketchup, mayonnaise, and mustard (the one misfit of the crew, Limpy Demption, also grabbed a bottle of no-name steak sauce, just to be weird; accordingly, he was mocked and ridiculed and completely ostracized by the rest of the group, and continued to weather such abuse, until the time came that he snapped, grabbed two Glock-22's with extended-round magazines, and proceeded to massacre every attractive woman he saw until the school police department's SWAT team executed him on sight), and a few birthday balloons as well. They loaded this all up into Shuppel's brand new, customized Corvette, and then headed to the local skid row.

There, at the Grocery Outlet, they found the perfect target: a group of unkempt, but not yet ruined-by-street-life twenty-somethings who were obviously living on the streets. Shuppel approached the group:

"Hey." They nodded in recognition, beginning to congregate around the sports car in anticipation of donation.

"I heard you like to play with your lunch," Shuppel continued, impishly.

"Gurk-a-doo?" One of them, named Fubblard, who was intellectually challenged and not a native English speaker (he'd been brought up speaking Middle Gibberish), asked hopefully, with an upward inflection.

"But Marneshta, I don't want your arts and crafts," a person then said, mournfully.

That was the signal for Shuppel and his friends to open fire upon the entire hoard of dumpster children, coating them in all the cheap condiments from the discount store.

Then, all hell broke loose. The following things happened, more or less simultaneously:

- Two or three of the miscreants that were targeted by Shuppel and his friends, and their cheap condiment shopping-spree, counter-attacked with a series of snot rockets shot out through Loogie Launchers ® (that they had actually made by hand, using various dumpster-pickings and ill-begotten proceeds from vehicular vandalism), splattering the friend group and giving at least three of them Hepatitis-C.

- One of the hoodlums thought that the bedlam would be a perfectly fitting opportunity to grab a can of spray paint and scrawl out his signature tag, "A$$." It was intended to be a sublime critique of late-stage capitalism, poignantly highlighting the various blights visited upon society by this outmoded and outdated economic system. Structural inequality, after all, was first and foremost the making of many a fat, greedy businessman sitting at a desk somewhere and pitting the working class of this country against the indentured laborers toiling away at sweatshops in lesser Asia; this was the "ass" being sat upon by the very fat person who was making these very poor choices on behalf of a corporation. Then, there was the aspect of sluttiness implied by the dollar signs, like this was a strip club wherein those being exploited were grinding and groping and gyrating around in abject desperation, scrambling over one another in order to be rewarded by a few dollar bills stuffed into a sweaty thong or "G-string." Also, it might occur to someone to call such a scum-sucking opportunist (the sort of which would run a disreputable company that under-compensated its employees and sold substandard products to its customers, leaving them without any reasonable means of recourse) a "pompous ass." There was a lot going on with this simple, yet eloquent act of outsider art. It was a real shame that it ended up being used as evidence by the fascist local cops that responded and broke up the melee.

- Fubblard started striding to and fro like a rooster. While doing so, he invented a song on the spot, that went something like,

"Butt-chug-ula!
Butt, butt, butt, chug-ooo-lah!
Buttchug, butt-chug-ala!
Buttchugger, buttchug,
Butt-chug-gug-ula!
Buschugula! Buttch! Buttch! Buttch!"

- Several bystanders, who were native rednecks (by which, it is meant, that they are Indians, of the "Cowboys and Indians" sort, but they were also borderline-uncivilized hill-dwellers who would get into gunfights over junk cars left abandoned for the past twenty years on their cousin's forty acres) picked up Fubblard's chant and made it their war cry. They proceeded to overturn shopping carts and run into the store to steal shopping bags to set on fire.

- Someone's dog farted. But this wasn't *any* dog; it was the runner-up dog for the award for overall fluffiness at the Westminster Kennel Club Dog Show, four years ago. When the dog farted, it actually *sharted*, and sprayed a fine mist of fecal matter all over itself, which was really apparent since the dog had a pearl-white coloration. "Heavens to Mergatroid!" sighed the dog's owner, who was overcome with a combination of fear, guilt, and heatstroke, and proceeded to collapse in the parking lot, blocking traffic for a solid fifteen minutes while the store manager ran out and attempted to resuscitate this person (who he thought was a woman at first, so he pressed his lips hopefully to hers while trying to inflate her lungs, which is something you should *not* do to a heatstroke victim, and actually, it wasn't a real woman after all, but a rather hideous 56-year-old man wearing a dress and lipstick, because he never felt close to his mother when he was younger, and she would always talk exasperatedly about how she wished she'd had a daughter instead, because the father had run off with some beer tramp he met at the bowling alley anyhow, so the mother should've had a female offspring with whom to conspire; the store manager was completely disgusted when he found this out, and even gave the dog's owner a coupon to the Grocery Outlet two towns over, so that he wouldn't ever have to see the cross-dressing man at his particular store, ever again, hopefully), which undoubtedly led to the police building a wrongfully prejudiced case against the street trolls, when actually, it was the douchey hipster college kid crowd that instigated these shenanigans.

And so on, and so forth, this nonsense continued, until Sleppy Division emerged and put a stop to everything. Sleppy was the archnemesis that Shuppel never knew he had, until now.

THERE WAS A STORY THAT NEEDED to be told. Smorvald, the Gremlach, is now going to present it:

Stifled by garbage, Smorvald pretended that he was the alien prince of Sweden, and was on the prowl for a woman suitable for dating. Yet Smorvald was also a compulsive hoarder. He had barricaded himself inside of his hovel, so stuffed full of trash he could only be offered small mealtime items by the concerned townfolk who would walk past, sullenly, shaking their heads in despair that such an otherwise interesting fellow could be so mentally deficient. There was something incontrovertibly *wrong* with hoarders, and so Smorvald was shunned accordingly. Shunned, but still fed.

And that was a problem, since he would hoard little bits and bites of the morsels that would get handed through the strategically positioned slots tunneling through the mess by random strangers passing. Slowly but surely, the pile grew ever more enormous and despairingly out of control.

So it was, while he was forcibly imprisoned inside of his humungous trash heap, that Smorvald sat, and stewed, and thought about things. And, he was reminded of a kid that he once knew, by the name of Lichtsht.

Lichtsht didn't have any other names besides just that one, which was alienating and difficult for ordinary people to pronounce. He was about twelve years old, as Smorvald could best recollect. He was angry and suffered from repetitive migraines. He was also missing half his head.

It was said that this particular condition was the result of a botched childbirth, wherein medical professionals suddenly lost their professionalism, and did something recklessly stupid. It's not as if doctors could be trusted in the first place; they were greedy and egotistical by nature, and thought that they could just invent certain procedures that would harm and maim their patients, and that nobody would ever question them about it, because they were doctors and everyone else was stupid.

[Keep in mind that doctors made the Nazi regime semi-successful. They, at the very least, were able to perform freak experiments on Jews. Ironically, many modern Jews actually force their children to become doctors, who then perpetuate the legacy of tormenting unsuspecting human beings who were foolish enough to trust the doctors in the first place, just like these Jews' grandparents trusted the Nazi regime doctors who told them that Zyklon-B was an effective pesticide, and that it was indeed a form of apology for the Nazis having corralled the Jews into the ghettos in the first place, since they wouldn't have had as many parasites infesting their hair and their skin if it weren't for the fact they were forced from their ordinary homes into squalor, instead. Jews aren't designed to be living in such conditions, which is made abundantly clear by their old leader who told them not to eat pig meat, because it can carry some nasty diseases that upset your stomach and make you poop irregularly. Other people just ate the pigs and got sick, and got over it, and built up immunity to the pig-germs; but Jews were more sensitive. They should have all been vegans. The Nazis were vegetarians, which was close to, but not the same thing as, being vegan. So, it wasn't okay after the war was over for a Jew to *not* eat meat, so long as it was beef or chicken, or maybe lamb on a rare occasion when they were willing to pay for it, because lamb meat is more expensive since they are cute and people feel bad about stealing them away from their mothers, and slaughtering them and eating them with mint jelly and crumpets. So, the butchers charge more, because they feel guilty, and money makes guilt feel less bad. Which is also why the Jews love money so much, because they're guilty as well. Not of killing Jesus, exactly, but they did set him up, which was particularly mean because *Jesus was one of them*. And lots of other stuff the Jews did, like they killed off the actual Jews and assumed their identity, for instance. But still, it was bad that the Nazi doctors did things to their Jewish prisoner-patients, and then it's even worse that Jews become doctors a lot these days, because doctors are terrible and should be outlawed. They can't be trusted, they suck, and they are actually mutants who want to spread disease and misfortune across the land.]

Lichtsht was one of the many unfortunate victims who were generally mutilated from birth by doctors. He was an outcast from the very first day of preschool. Even the adults would put their hands over their mouths and try not to vomit and scream in terror when he approached them. He seemed like the kind of thing that should have its own creepy theme music precluding its entrance into any scene. The truly bizarre thing was that Lichtsht had both his eyes, and actually a complete face, but had a very menacing glare, and the missing part of his head was the back half.

Later on, when he tried to ride the school bus home, the driver took one look at Lichtsht through the closed glass doors, shook his head and mouthed the word, "No," and drove off. Lichtsht walked home, frowning intensely. He stopped at a pizza parlor because he was hungry, and asked for a slice of pepperoni. The inept Greek man who owned and ran the kitchen literally threw the piece of pizza at Lichtsht and told him to get the hell out. It slapped Lichtsht's face fiercely and then fell down to the gutter, where three starving stray dogs started a fight over it.

In Lichtsht's world, everything was right angles, like a bad abstract painting from the eighties. A girl with big tits who everybody liked confronted him. "Your name is weird and stupid. You're ugly," she shouted hoarsely, and spat into Lichtsht's face. All the other kids screamed and laughed in encouraging agreement.

"I feel like I need to wear a helmet, just to be in the same room as you," one particularly chubby bully said, smearing a rancid hamburger he'd been saving in his backpack for the past three months across Lichtsht's distorted head. Lichtsht ran, sobbing, to the nearest bathroom so he could dunk his head into the toilet and wash the rotten meat off his brow. Finding out that he was doing this made the other children laugh even harder at Lichtsht's expense, but it wasn't his fault; his mother had told him that was the only manner of bathing of which he was worthy. She'd drank herself into early liver failure over her despondency about having never won the lottery. When she was a little girl, her father always went to the corner store to buy beer, cigarettes, and instant scratch-off tickets, so that he might escape the soul-crushing existence that was his lower-middle-class, hourly-waged existence. Lichtsht's mom looked up to her daddy, and, when he died, felt it was her personal obligation to pick up where the old man had left off, trying vainly to match all the numbers and walk away from this miserable shit, with a hefty jackpot in her hands.

Since this win never happened (yet, and probably never will), she became increasingly enraged every time her son came home asking for help in getting whatever random dogshit or fermented-juice-box-residue was stuck to Lichtsht that particular afternoon, and decided that he should learn to clean himself up, even though he was missing almost half his brain.

So, it was with all of this confusion and hatred as the backdrop that Lichtsht was walking home one afternoon, since he wasn't allowed to take the bus on account of his disfigurement, that he came across some helpful slime floating in the gutter.

"Hey kid, what's your bother?" the slime asked, disinterestedly.

"Everyone hates me because I'm ugly. I hate myself. I kicked a dog," Lichtsht said, unconvincingly.

"I hate dogs, too," the slime said, in total agreement. Lichtsht didn't know it, but the slime was actually a strain of toxic blue-green algae, the kind that stupid mutts love to lap up out of stagnant pools of water lurking around the desiccated river banks in the high summer heat of Northern California. The dogs would roll around in it, and then go bounding off, tongues and tails wagging in unison, until 12-24 hours later, when the moronic canine would have to be taken to the vet to get put down, because it was suffering from massive organ failure.

The slime had a plan, and that was to convince a miscreant like Lichtsht to help it propagate itself into the municipal water supply, so it could start killing babies, and immunocompromised people, as well. After presenting itself as his only friend, the slime coerced Lichtsht into putting some of its retched self into Lichtsht's water bottle, and then taking a stroll up to the town's water supply, clambering up to the top of the tank, and dumping the whole load into the clean, pristine water.

Then, Lichtsht used some of his knowledge of chemistry (which he'd picked up with the intentions of creating undetectable poisons with which to murder this tormentors, silently) to sabotage the chlorination system so that the slime wouldn't get killed through the sterilization process, which was mandated by a bevy of state, local and federal regulations. This was a white community, after all. The fluoride was fine.

Fortunately, a local Michael intervened and destroyed both Lichtsht and his new slime friend with a flamethrower that he happened to have been practicing with nearby the water tank that fateful afternoon. The Michael could just tell that this deformed loser was up to no good, and wasted no time in obliterating the little scoundrel. The dented part of Lichtsht's skull was still visible for awhile, as the rest of his flesh roasted and turned into a fine, crumbly ash. Really, what more did you expect?

ONE THING THAT WASN'T FULLY DISCLOSED previously was the fact that Lichtsht had some very powerful financial backing for his ill-fated bioterrorist operation. The Fürstwarfer Bank and Trust had been secretly funding this attempted contamination of the city's water supply. They were heavily invested in a bottled water company, and their analysts projected that the local demand for this product would soar by at least 76% once people started getting sick, dying, and panicking.

So now that Lichtsht and his slimy buddy were reduced to a smoldering heap of ash, *someone* was going to have to pay for all funds that the bank had forfeited. The Fürstwarfer's crack team of attorneys quickly filed a lien on the Michael who had ostensibly saved the day from Lichtsht and his trashy plans. They were led by Ugly Dachenfulya, who had a reputation as one of the fiercest, scummiest litigators ever to disgrace the district courtroom.

He had, in fact, single-handedly engineered that famous lawsuit against Mother Shutckler's Daycare Center and Roadside Zoo. She had this guy working for her, named Limp Dickless, who was a small-time criminal with a heart of gold. He was very pleasant and friendly and funny for the children, but he also may have worshipped at a satanic temple, although strictly on a part-time basis.

Well, one of the mothers of the children that went to Mother Shutckler's got wind that her best friend's sister's girlfriend ran into Limp at the grocery store, while she was buying condoms, and he was buying several gallons of beet juice, to use as a substitute for blood in one of his silly little satanic rituals (because he was a vegan), and he might have mentioned something to this effect, although that wasn't what had bothered the best friend's sister's girlfriend. No, what *really* stuck in her craw was the fact that she had heard, somewhere, that Limp had been hanging out with Paul Reubens at an adult film theater, and, as a matter of fact, they had been out together that entire night, fapping around the town.

Was a serial fapper the sort of person who could be trusted around small children? Ugly didn't think so. Even though, that same weekend, the township was playing host to the fourteenth annual Excellence in Child Pornography Awards ceremony, and Limp and Paul came nowhere *near* the run-down motel on the edge of the town limits where the event was being held, Ugly still thought that, for the purposes of an impromptu moral crusade, these piddling masturbators made a far juicier target.

So, Mother Shutckler's got shut down, and investigated, and prosecuted, and served with a massive class-action civil lawsuit. Ugly crowed and bragged about how he was single-handedly responsible for depriving the community of low-cost, dependable childcare services. In reality, he just hated children.

It was alright, though, since Mother Shutckler was allowed to go on and open up her own bakery, which had vegan options on the menu, so the Bean Kid was allowed to come. The Donut Master, however, was *not* welcome there, because he only made disgusting things that were rancid and smelly and swarming with harmful microorganisms, which were typically egg-based, which is *not* vegan-friendly and therefore, wouldn't be any good for the Bean Kid to consume.

What about Limp and Paul, though? Paul was trying out a new character called PeePee Heroin, where he would whip out his dick and inject various forms of opiates into the tip of it. Which never really impressed anyone, because opiates were out of style, and also, Paul's pecker would remain shriveled and flaccid, which absolutely *nobody* wanted to see.

Limp, on the other hand, or should it be said, on the other *penis*, had previously entered the World's Smallest Dick® competition, which was a joke, since he possessed an average endowment and provoked great outrage in the micropenis community by even attempting to participate in the contest. They simmered and stewed, and retreated hastily to their mothers' basements in order to post long tirades in their "Incel" internet forums, decrying Limp and how much of a "Chad" he really was, and determining that the best course of action would be acts of mass violence against random women.

Anyway, the legal team representing the Michael that was implicated in the whole Lichtsht debacle was headed up by the crack firm Fraudburger and Associates. And literally, they made most of their income by selling crack cocaine to black people. On the streets. In broad daylight.

"You know, you really shouldn't call people niggers," one of their low-level hustlers said to another one fateful afternoon.

"Why? Are they black?"

"Well, yes."

"Then it doesn't matter. Nothing that a black person thinks or cares to complain about has any relevance or bearing on the rest of society," the associate said, sardonically. Of course, he was right, because he was talking about *white* society, which was the only one that really matters, at least, in the eyes of high finance.

Actually, the Fraudburgers *had* represented the Fürstwarfer Bank and Trust previously, on a gentrification matter. They wanted to tear down some desolate and hideous low-income housing, in order to construct fanciful single-family dwellings that might appeal to recent Chinese immigrants. They had lily ponds and Buddha statues strategically positioned, both around the design plans for the landscaping of what would otherwise be known as "cookie-cutter" style homes, and prominently displayed on the literature advertising this development, which was translated, poorly, into both Mandarin and Cantonese.

The Fraudburgers had one job in that particular assignment, which was to covertly generate friction and feelings of general animosity between the black and Chinese communities. In one corner, they had Chiny Chinko, the bucktoothed, slant-eyed mascot of the impending oriental invasion, and in the other, there was Ozeubuko Standafter, a six-foot-eight sub-saharan behemoth who was descended from a mixed lineage of African witch doctors and pedophile British explorers.

"But, Grandpa, why did they only let grown men rape children in Africa? What if some white children wanted to rape the other kids?"

"Well, now, little Bethany, you have to understand, things were different back then," Grandpa said, dubiously. Bethany wasn't sure, about the veracity of this long-winded story, or about Grandpa's continence, either.

The children had been warned before being dropped off, or abandoned, at their derelict grandparents' house for the weekend by their alcoholic, gambling-addicted mother who'd just cashed her child support check and was hopping on the next bus to Atlantic City. "Grandpa might have some trouble pooping," their useless mother had informed her offspring, belatedly.

Actually, the nurse who was paid by the county government to look after Grandpa and his myriad health issues said that this week, he earned a 92 (out of 100) in the bowel movement category of his health report card. He'd been getting up from his chair and using his walker to hobble over to the toilet at least five minutes before he thought he was going to need to poop, and as a result, he was succeeding in getting just about all of the fecal matter properly deposited into the municipal sewer system. His wife, who was advancing through the later stages of senility, had forgotten to change his adult diaper on a few occasions, which led to a bit of leakage making onto the carpet in the hallway outside the bathroom (although Grandpa had remained diligent in at least *attempting* to deal with the situation on his own), so that was why he did not get a perfect score on his bathroom grading that week.

"Why don't you stick your head up your *own* ass?" Grandpa exclaimed suddenly, to nobody at all. He was also starting to get a bit feeble minded.

"Grandpa, you bore us," Bertrand, the grandson, said, contemptuously.

"Well, how about *you* try thinking you need to pee and have some poop come out instead," Grandpa retorted, disparagingly. But what exactly was Ozeubuko Standafter up to, anyhow?

"You know, knowing things, is not the best," Ozeubuko said, maliciously. "A person who knows things, he is not worthy of being trusted. What he knows, he will lie about. A simple man will not tell you those things he knows are untrue."

The other people in the room just stared at Ozeubuko. The Fraudburgers were definitely people who knew *a lot* of stuff, and they were generously compensated to lie, repeatedly, on a daily basis. They weren't sure who this African thought he was; a sage? A prophet of some bizarre hybridization of christian and nativist beliefs? And weren't the Fraudburgers just a bunch of Jews in the first place? Was this really relevant?

"Confucius say, knowledge good," Chiny huffed, coincidentally. He didn't know enough English to be too sure about where the conversation was headed, but he did understand the word *know*, even though he couldn't differentiate it from the word, *no*.

The Fraudburgers had brought Chiny on board since they got told by someone that he could predict the future, because he was Chinese and they are good at math. Unfortunately, that was not the case; or, at the very least, with Chiny in particular, they'd been sold a defective model. It really all went back to the production of *My Pretty Penis*, a musical number that the Fraudburgers were talked into producing after Chiny came to them chattering on in his native language and gallivanting around with some spreadsheets. It was implied by all the commotion that this would be the best investment of the year, and the Fraudburgers could all have a *very* happy Hanukkah after the opening night.

It bombed, however, because, as it turns out, people weren't too eager to go and see a play about an overweight adult man whose passion in life is running up to and flashing random 10-year-old girls in public places. In fact, most people were *pretty* upset about the whole thing. The Fraudburgers even got sued, which was anathema to their very existences, which were collectively spent instigating litigation, not being on the receiving end.

So, they would've been better off listening to Ozeubuko. And also, there was that problem with the lunch that Chiny had attempted to serve them.

The Fraudburgers were petty people, okay? They saw an ad that had gotten hung on the exterior door handle to their office complex, and it advertised a full-course Chinese lunch for a very reasonable $8.95. Having spent all morning furiously ruining the lives of unassuming small businesspeople, the Fraudburgers had built up *quite* an appetite, and an affordably-priced luncheon (that wasn't even served buffet-style, which was a nonstarter for the Fraudburgers, as they were complete germaphobes) sounded just right for that early afternoon in question. So, they closed up the offices and headed down to Chiny Chinko's Cafe, not thinking for a second that the name sounded suspicious.

Well, maybe they should have. As soon as they sat down, they knew something was off. The tea tasted stale, and old, and somewhat like a used tampon. Junior Fraudburger twisted the cap off the soy sauce bottle, and, yep, there were bugs floating around in it, chunks of hideous carpenter ants and derelict corpses of fruit flies; and *then*, once the first course was brought out, egg rolls, Daddy Fraudburger bit into one and discovered that it was still half-frozen.

In fact, the egg rolls had been purchased in bulk, on discount, from the expired freezer section at Sam's Club. And it only got worse from there. One of the main ingredients of the fried rice was, apparently, shards of steel can. And, worse of all, there were no little pieces of pineapple with toothpicks stuck in them for desert!

The Fraudburgers swore revenge, and, when they found out that the giant known as Ozeubuko Standafter had just arrived off the boat from Africa and was looking for a job, they decided that they would offer him a copy-room position, so long as he first fought Chiny.

The two immigrants looked over one another, unassumingly. Ozeubuko had never had Chinese food in his life. Chiny thought that he was a scruffy upstart prizefighter, about to step into the ring for the first time, and, he assumed, wagering would be available. [Like all good Chinese folk, Chiny was a compulsive gambler, albeit an unsuccessful one, obviously, because he ran a dingy restaurant with his wife and assorted nieces and nephews, several of which were below the legal age of employment. What, did you think that people who are doing well in life spend their time plastering the doors of shady law firms with promises of food that they can't deliver?]

"There, that it is, again. Thinking that you are knowing something," Ozeubuko said, sincerely.

"Confucius say, wisdom good," Chiny muttered, confusedly. Actually, Confucius the philosopher hadn't said anything so banal. Chiny was referring to Confucius, his Pekinese dog, with whom he often attempted to have conversations while drunk. Confucius said a lot of things, *deceptive* things, and Chiny would go along with it, unquestioningly. In fact, it was Confucius' failed advice that led to this whole situation with the Fraudburgers, which was, in fact, unravelling quickly, since neither Chiny nor Ozeubuko knew what they were supposed to be doing there, and the Fraudburgers, huddled together to strategize, decided it was too much of a liability risk to actually come out and say that they wanted the two men to engage in physical combat.

Alas, there was still the looming trial over the Lichtsht case. Ugly Dachenfulya had some serious dirt on the Michael, the Fraudburgers were relatively certain, and that could be a real problem, since none of them were actual lawyers, and Ugly Dachenfulya was a vampire. He'd sucked the blood out of a sixteen year old bimbo the night before, while the Fraudburgers hadn't had a decent meal in weeks (no thanks to Chiny).

"Heey urgh, uh-wah, hiiiiiii!" said Paul Rubens, in disguise as PeePee Heroin, who was loitering out front and decided to staggeringly stick his head in the door. His presence wasn't acknowledged, and he lived for attention, so he quickly made his exit, which was temporarily interrupted by his flaccid penis, still fully exposed and now ridden with injection-site sores, getting caught in a fake potted plant that was strategically located, and long since forgotten about, in the corner of the entryway.

The one thing everyone could agree on was that Lichtsht sucked, and deserved what he got. All the mutants and other degenerate types who try and mess around with public utilities should be condemned, as consensus held. The Fraudburgers were not very good at being defense attorneys, or litigators, or whatever the hell role they were supposed to be playing in the whole mess. They weren't even sure who'd hired them, and how much they stood to get paid, should their side emerge victorious. It was a failure on multiple levels; but, if they'd hired an expert in Lean-Six-Sigma, they could have had all the weak spots in their value chain identified and remedied.

"And that is why Grandpa went into consulting!" Grandpa shouted, incessantly. It was all he could ever talk about these days, how he'd spent the first half of his career selling extended warranties on used cars, and then going out, in the middle of the night, and sabotaging his clients' vehicles, so they would have to go and have repairs done, which were reimbursed at half cost by the warranty company. It wasn't a very good scam; it *could've* been, if Grandpa had been in cahoots with any of the mechanics shops that begrudgingly agreed to accept the heavily discounted rate offered by the warranty plan. But, he wasn't, so he ended up losing his money, and his license, and his eyesight, and went to jail for a brief stint.

Bertrand wasn't listening anymore. He'd gone out to try and find PeePee Heroin so he could cop a fix and feel like what it felt to *truly* be high. Bethany was on instagram, attempting to solicit a black guy to rape her. This is why children shouldn't be told stories like the ones Grandpa liked to tell, because they were suggestible, and often tried to recreate the bizarre and inappropriate situations that adults liked to drone on and on about, because they still were possessed of sufficient youthful vigor to go out and *live* these experiences, unlike those old farts who just sat around and talked.

Grandpa stood up and looked about, confusedly. He felt like fixing himself a snack, but he wasn't sure what he liked to eat, anymore. There had been some Poopwells® brand digestive biscuits in the cupboard above the hot plate that someone used to cook crystal meth, but the kids had devoured them all earlier in the day, so they could get into a shit-throwing-fight with the delinquents next door.

It was around this time that Grandpa wondered how long it had been since somebody changed his adult diaper. He felt like there was some extra mass sloshing and writhing around down there. He couldn't remember the last time he'd had a regular bowel movement, but suspected that it might have happened just a short time ago. He didn't know where his wife was, either, which left him at a terrible disadvantage, since these were the sorts of things that wives were always supposed to know about.

Grandpa had never followed Ozeubuko's advice about knowing things; or actually, maybe he followed it *too* well. Grandpa wasn't too certain about anything these days. Which was what Ozeubuko and all of his followers claimed was the proper mental state for one to possess in order to claim a moral high ground; if Grandpa *did* know when he'd taken a shit, in all likelihood, given the many failings and shortcomings of the human condition, he would just lie about it.

UNCLE SMALL LUCAS

A NOVEL

CHAPTER I

"I AM OBSESSED WITH SPRESSEL-KOLICHE-tadation!" said Rambart, not convincingly. He would've known. He was the one who got Rushugula Stevens on the street, and brainwashed Maruula into staying there.

"But Rushugula," Pwippy Deluption would say.

"But Marneshta," would be the appropriate call-and-response to round out the pantomime.

Rushugula's art was dying. She would spend many hours, during the best part of each day, screaming and crying and carrying on so much to anyone who would listen. In San Francisco, that was too many people. They tried vainly to comprehend what she was getting at with her admonitions.

[A side note: OK, first of all, this isn't like your friend "Lunch" Alieeshten or some shit like that. You can't make this kind of thing up. One cannot lie about the ways of the street, and the people that live alongside and upon them. No, for then there wouldn't be half as much a story to tell, if morons went around making this kind of trash up: "I know a kid named 'Dirty'!" they shout.

"I didn't know I couldn't poop here, man!" Dirty hollers as he plants a load right in the middle of Mrs. Miles Jessupsen's petunia garden. Petunias, always like pink sweet little panties; naughty little no-nos! Anyway, after sneaking a sniff of her drawers, Spongebob Squaredick (or whatever he wanted his street-person name to be this particular week) took a whack at Mrs. Jessupsen's cherry pie, if you know what we mean. Well, Sponge-dick *didn't* know what we meant, and went way too far over the top by removing Mrs. Jessupsen's front door and leaving a real mess for the police to find later. The police, in fact, were the same arresting officers who initially responded to a public health nuisance compliant regarding what appeared to be human fecal matter, placed strategically within a sad plot of pathetic flowers. The flowers drooped even worse due to the presence of poop; do you know how bad shit is for flowers? Real bad, if the dietary habits of our beloved local bums are any indication. They scavenge through public refuse containers, looking for any sort of organic residue to fuel their metabolisms long enough to locate the actual source of their strength and powers: drugs. So, Lunch can make up his own story and try to entice you with his pop-psychology insights, but reluctantly we must press on with this (unfortunately) mostly-truthful account.]

"DID ANYBODY EVER TALK TO YOU ABOUT the 'Sharnatooshta Two-Step?'"

"No. What?"

He cleared his throat, handsomely. "It goes a little something like this:"

1. The guy gets home from work, he's frustrated and excited simultaneously. Not in a dirty way, like that dickwad Robin Bentlee or whoever his name was, the guy who was all over the news about a year ago from that court case about the sexual harassment where some quippy witness came up with the term "Stupid Blowjob Game," and the press went insane for the next two weeks, the national media picked up on the story and started repeating it endlessly on a loop, the nighttime talk show goons would be slobbering over how funny the concept was, like how would you even think of such a thing, normal person? So, no, it WAS NOT that level of excitement that the man felt; it was more mundane. The workday was done, he was at home in the state of California and ready to play the lottery! Yeah! He started yelling, parading around the house, calling out Sharnatooshta by name—

"Shutup!"

Okay. So, he's going to go down to the liquor store, the gas mart down the street, the place closest nearby where he can pick up some lotto tix and this is it, this IS going to be the night he hits the big one, the high jackpot, all thanks and praises!

2. Then everybody has a parade for him. There's a customized instrumental song composed by some ostentatiously modern musician that strikes firm chords with no slop, no warm fuzz, just a crisp little tune that

reverberates so sharp in the skull it had been known to cause headaches; unlike anything anyone had ever quite heard before, the orchestra was playing *inside* the thick skull of our nefarious "friend" here who wanted to fancy himself a winner for once in his life. And then, the audience starts shouting, "Somebody give this man some children!" And sure enough, the government does, they start *flinging* kids at him, abused and neglected little nothings that nobody would ever love ever again, being retarded with trauma and singled out for shame due to soiling themselves whenever someone scared them, the little dipshits, so of course the government collects these kids, and,

"And they give them to people like our Hero, who think children are funny and also make good hostages, so nobody can fuck with him."

"Wow. Smart."

"But what if somebody poops? Well, they did think of that." And it seemed like they did: there were disposable diaper dispensers strategically positioned at every intersection along the parade route. They had diapers of all sizes and for all ages, both mens' and women's, and although the diaper-dispensers were only placed there out of an abundance of caution, to protect the sanctity of our Hero's celebration, there *was* some misuse going on. Like, some people, the very young, the very old, and the very retarded, can't help their bowel movements, or don't know when to predict the ol' turtle-head-popping-out, so they *do* need diapers. But then, there was a group of *other* people who were far more normal (at least, that's how they would have you think of themselves), and these folks wear the diaper and shit themselves *for pleasure!* This was completely inappropriate, and ran entirely contrary to the civic spirit of the occasion. The diaper-wearers, then, were subject to intense scrutiny. A team of inspectors were sent out into the field to anonymously survey and accuse those who didn't actually need to be wearing the diapers of taking advantage of the situation and the extreme generosity bestowed upon the masses by the municipal government. These diapers were not to be taken for granted. Plus, every decent person was already offended on an intimate level by the goings-on of diaper-wearing around them, and tried to look away and not barf, but it was becoming increasingly difficult as the day wore on and MORE PEOPLE WERE WEARING DIAPERS WHO REALLY DIDN'T

NEED TO BE.

So, they would be executed.

"But what about the kids?"

Well, the kids were alright, even if they were being used as body shields against liability implications that our Hero may or may not have brought upon himself through previous business dealings. He didn't love them, but nobody possibly could; these are *used* children we're talking about. They were nasty and mentally deficient. He was just sparing them, for a few more years, from an inevitable life on the streets. They were ungrateful, as any young creature rejected by its birth parents necessarily would be.

But that's it, the second step. It is the Sharnatooshta TWO-step, not more. To summarize:

1. Yell a bunch of gibberish, invoking the name "Sharnatooshta" somewhere in there.

2. Buy lottery tickets, have parade. Get given children by the government.

The diapers don't really need to be a part of it, unless that's your thing, because you think it's funny because you're a dimwit who is easily amused, *or* you are into disgusting and smelly pastimes like diaper-soiling. It's just a token offering from those high-minded folk who really just want to make the world a better place, but end up getting taken advantage of for it.

SHUPPEL UPTION WAS MAKING SOME NOISES. Not threatening ones; more like some nasty sort of regurgitation.

Shuppel had been taking classes at Pathetic Flower University, first of all. Not on a matriculated basis; he was instead auditing a few courses, because he was too cheap and stupid to be able to use the federal financial aid system in order to make money off the government by taking out loans that he would never repay, for classes he was bound to fail in pursuit of a degree that wouldn't ever get him a job.

It was a beautiful act of futility. In fact, the only passing grade he received that semester was in postmodern philosophy. Shuppel slept during most of the classes, except when he would groan and/or take a mug of coffee with him. Then, he would timidly raise his hand, and no matter what the lecture was about, he would start going on about this time he was hungry and got a chicken salad sandwich at a gas station. Then he'd get into an argument with his fellow classmates about whether an egg-salad sandwich would be just as good (the vegetarians, after all, thought he was being discriminatory). He asked them which one came first, chicken or egg, and then didn't allow anyone time to answer by quickly proclaiming that the story was about a *chicken* salad sandwich, not an egg salad sandwich, and who the hell did they think they were for interrupting him and trying to convince him otherwise? The professor, one Dr. John Wesley Powell, loved it. He laughed and clapped and carried on with great glee, and mocked all the other students for *not* being so stupid and reckless with their assignments. He gave Shuppel an "A" in the course.

Shuppel was the sort of character who could afford a two bedroom rental to himself quite comfortably, yet still wasn't inclined to bathe more than once a week. He stank mostly of hair-grease aroma; he never bothered exerting himself to the point of breaking a sweat. Education to him wasn't a race, nor was it a journey; it was an excuse. So, in that regard, he was actually smarter than most of the people around him, who actually *did* believe that their college-educated lives were going to be meaningful.

Then someone tried to kill Shuppel with a crab salad sandwich, to which he was badly allergic. He spent three weeks struggling to breathe, but then fought his way back into the lecture hall, spitting out the contents of his mucous-filled lungs along the way. People tried not to breathe around him, but then he invited himself into a Native American film studies class, where they would sit in front of a box-style television for two hours at a blow, watching diligently and taking notes as Indians and Cowboys masqueraded across the screen, whooping and hollering and shooting, stealing squaws and deflowering white broads, until Shuppel would let out a tremendous hacking cough, and all the girls in the room would wince and squirm and wrap their hoodies tight around their heads, pulling their shirts up to cover their mouths, hoping this wasn't one of those nights when Shuppel had been souring his gut with cheap beer that had been rejected from the local brewery and sold by the case for a few nickels (just enough to cover the cost of the glass in the bottles). Because if it *had* been one of those nights, he could start barfing at any time.

Which was ironic, because the one friend that Shuppel had met at PFU went by the name, "Barfee." Like *Slurpee*, but with Barf. He was a hippie kid who smelled as bad as, if not worse then, Shuppel Uption.

"ARE YOU ENJOYING YOUR NICE, WARM SLICE of pizza?" Davey's mom asked him. Davey nodded, and smiled, and a bit of pizza sauce and chewed up cheese, and crust soggy with slobber, dribbled down his chin. Davey's friend gave him that pizza, but he wasn't going to tell his momma that.

The contempt and sarcasm implied by the tone of her voice was lost on little Davey. She realized she hadn't bought him that pizza; but he didn't know that she knew that she didn't buy it for him. His friend had bought the pizza, and offered Davey a slice. Otherwise, it would have gone to waste. Probably. Maybe a hungry dog would've eaten it.

Davey loved his nice, warm pizza, though. He ate it with a vociferous CHOMP-CHOMP-CHOMP noise, because his teeth weren't too good, and he didn't have a firm grasp on manners. He was what they categorize as "special needs," being 57, a spoiled brat, and a sneak who wouldn't ever fess up to his own mother that he realized she hadn't supplied him with the pizza; his friend, after all, had given it to him.

Davey didn't mean for it to be such a big secret, but he did know that his momma didn't like the idea of other people giving him things. She wanted to be the only one to give him anything, ever. Davey also knew, furthermore, that his mother wasn't the smartest person in the room. Like, this one time, she had gotten scammed by a man on the telephone. She read all her credit card numbers out to the man, who spoke with a thick, dirty foreign accent, and then had to repeat the numbers three more times. Then, she gave out phone numbers and email address for twenty of their neighbors and relatives.

Two weeks later, she received the bill. Immediately, Davey's mom started screaming her head off, yelling about Nigerians trying to kidnap her, and the like. Davey sucked on his lolly-pop and watched amusedly as his mother started tearing down the curtains and smashing all their dishes on the cement slab behind their trailer, because she was convinced there were tracking devices implanted in their ceramics. She then grabbed Davey by the ear, and he started hollering out of confusion and fear, and she then proceeded to shave off all his hair. Hair was where they could hide things, little things that nobody would *ever* think to look for, little gadgets the size of fleas, putting bad ideas into the minds of everyone she cared about.

Davey's mother then sent him out to fetch up all the chickens, so she could slaughter them, slicing their heads off one by one over the garbage disposal in the kitchen sink, because they were obviously compromised by this point. Davey was stupid enough to think that the chickens were his friends, and he pleaded and sobbed as his mother set about to butchering them. What Davey didn't realize is that chickens are indiscriminate foragers, and they would peck the flesh off his rotting dead body if they had the chance. Chickens make terrible friends. They're highly manipulative, they don't care about sharing, and they have sex in public places.

That was a big no-no as far as Davey's mom was concerned, as well. She dreaded the thought of her one and only son, the special needs boy that she'd brought into this world and raised single-handedly, of ever getting the notion in his head that he should go and make the same, terrible mistake that she had, that being the commencement of sexual intercourse with a member of the opposite sex for the purposes of procreation. She absolutely hated it whenever Davey would look at a girl, no matter how haphazard his efforts at expressing interest (or "flirting" if you want to be so cruel to call it that) might come across, and how often his ineffectual overtures were met with derisive laughter from mean, pretty girls who sprayed fruit-loops scented perfume upon their labias just to mock and frustrate Davey.

IT WAS A GAME, AND THE GAME WAS CALLED, "Poop-watching."

Basically, what would happen was, a bunch of retards would get together in their jammie-jams after the short bus dropped them off from their special needs class for the day, and they would fart, and curse, and make special needs faces like only the *truly* mentally handicapped can; then, swigging on some two liter knockoff cola bottles (even though the janitor at the special school, a short Italian man with a mustache, would lecture the retards repeatedly about how drinking such filth would stunt their growth, and they didn't listen, because the janitor was the sort of person everyone universally despised, with beady eyes and shuffling around with his cart in the hallways, like he was shouldering the burden of carrying every negative stereotype imagined about Italian-Americans since the first edition of *Super Mario Bros*), and they would start poking around in the alleyways and shrubbery of their local neighborhood, peering and leering in the hopes of stumbling upon that lucky bathroom window that would nicely frame an unsuspecting citizen having a poo.

The retards' favorite target was girls. They thought it was *hilarious* when a woman would take a shit, because it was dirty, and also, somewhat of a turn-on, that is, at least insofar as a retard could be aroused as such. [And these weren't absolute caveman-specimen-style knuckle-draggers; we've merely been dealing with garden variety retardation in reference to this lot, so it's not like they'd be getting all rapey about it. They just struggled when it came to processing feelings and emotions, and the fact that more than half of them reported having spontaneous erections when actively defecating.]

Being retards, the whole concept of the poop-watching game wasn't original; they'd stolen the idea from a snarky, off-handed comment someone had once made on a reddit forum, regarding spying on an amateur stock-market trader who had to take a dump every morning promptly at 9:30 AM, right when the stock market was open for business.

"I hope you don't have to poop too bad," the stranger said. He was wearing a tee-shirt that read, "Shirtler" (which was probably a nod to that band, Shitler), and nobody could tell if he meant that remark in a menacing way, or not. The retards wouldn't have taken the warning seriously, even if it was a indeed a message advising them of their impending doom, because they were far too preoccupied by sneaking into the next public women's restroom they could find.

And that was a challenge because, for whatever strange reason, nobody had ever thought to put together a map showing all the ladies' rooms in the area. Even though that was the most frequent and popular destination for anyone of a female persuasion, there hadn't been a concerted effort made to pinpoint and advertise the nearest location of a common loo. Now, these particular retards couldn't probably even read a map, let alone fold one up neatly and tuck it into their purses; but the idea that they could at least take one and go grab the attention of an adult by tugging on the tail of a stranger's shirt until someone paid them enough mind to explain *how* they could find their way to their intended destination, give them some straightforward directions that even a, uh-um, *retard* could understand, wasn't so outlandish after all. But, since no such service existed in the first place, and because these particular people who were about to embark upon the ill-fated poop-watching expedition were, in fact, retarded, nothing would ever get done about it. It was an unmet need that nobody was comfortable enough in identifying so that the necessary steps could be taken in order to hire some expert in cartography to create and publish such a guide.

A psychologist who happened to be walking by stopped, and immediately he could tell what the retards were up to. He selected one for an impromptu field survey:

"How does watching a girl use the bathroom make you feel?"

"It makes my poop go wet!" replied this particular retard, name of Dumpy Stilsken. He made sure to pinch his face up tight, like a good example of his species, flicking his left wrist around spastically for added dramatic effect.

"What do you mean by that?"

Dumpy frowned, remorseful about his confusion. "I dunno, it's like... when a girl goes all wet!" Dumpy had gotten his poop confused with his penis again. It happens a lot when you're dealing with retards, but the psychologist didn't know, or care enough, about the mentally handicapped to factor this into his calculations of how successful the retards were going to be in executing their plot. Anyway, what Dumpy meant to say was that he would get an erection, and most likely, ejaculate prematurely as he was crouched down, lurking in the shadows, fists clenched tight, watching the girl take a nice, long dump.

"I see. And have you ever been clinically evaluated for perversion, or any other manner of sexual dysfunction?"

"I got my poop to go wet once," Dumpy reiterated, more confidently this time around.

The psychologist had heard enough. Reaching his arms far up into the air, he snapped both sets of fingers and whistled simultaneously. A crew of four burly men wearing clean, white collared shirts swept in to grab Dumpy and shove him quickly into the back of a panel van. The crew departed hastily, before any of the other retards had noticed (which was a good thing, because once they got triggered, they'd start screaming and yelling and spazzing out, hitting themselves and inanimate objects, blocking traffic, urinating and defecating helplessly while normal people would stand by, repulsed yet engrossed by the drama unfolding before them, and since there was precious little government funding available to deal with these kinds of situations anymore, most of the time it would be up to the discretion of local law enforcement as to whether to permit vehicular operators to merely drive through the crowd, allowing bodies to accumulate along the gutters and sidewalks), so it looked like they would just have to continue on their way, hoping they could find the nearest girls' room, and proceed to poop-watch without Dumpy accompanying them.

"Purple Jesus truck!" one of them shouted, pointing towards the special-needs van that had just escorted their colleague away. Nobody was sure what he meant.

"Actually, I wasn't paying attention at all, if that's alright," someone suggested, unhelpfully.

SOMEBODY AND SOMEONE WERE ARGUING OVER WHO was the more aggrieved party at the present time.

"They used my name to invoke shameful sorrow," moaned Somebody, wistfully.

"They used *my* name to cover up for vague uncertainties," groaned Someone, inconsolably.

In fact, the two of them were both wronged in the most hideous manner possible; but, only one of them had any proof to back it up.

Somebody had just returned from a visit to the doctor's office, having complained about his poop smelling like cat food. "I don't see what the problem is," the doctor stated, unevenly.

"It's not a problem that one can *see*," said Somebody, impatiently. "It must be *smelled*."

"I don't have a sense of smell," the doctor countered. It was an entirely unappreciated fact that most doctors do not possess the capacity to smell.

"Well, I don't eat the cat's food, unless, of course, the cat isn't watching; so that way, it doesn't make it real," Somebody explained, earnestly. And indeed, since the cat wasn't bearing witness to Somebody's misbehavior, there was no other living thing of record present in Somebody's kitchen, where the cat's food and water bowls were conveniently located, that would be able to testify about this crime against good taste, in a manner that would be admissible in a court of law.

"I don't think that's how logic works," countered Someone. He knew a thing or two about logic, and what Somebody had just said did not hold up to his strict understanding of the rules. Just because nobody had seen Somebody eat the cat's food, didn't make it true that the cat's food had not been eaten by something that was not the cat. In fact, Somebody had already *admitted* that he had eaten the cat's food, and was ostensibly suffering the symptoms of having done so.

"Wait, I never *said* specifically that I was eating my cat's food," retorted Somebody. Since no one had been present to argue the fact, Somebody was under no obligation to either confirm nor deny that he had eaten any of the cat's food. For all intents and purposes, he had not actually confessed to eating *any* cat food, except, of course, for the vague suggestion he'd made to his doctor that he'd done so, which was covered under the covenants of patient confidentiality.

"But you said that your poop smelled like cat food!" shouted Someone, indignantly. Also, Someone was good friends with No One, who had been present, along with Nobody, when Somebody may have eaten his cat's food. Someone had the inside scoop on what had really taken place at Somebody's house, when he didn't think No One was watching, but he *did* know that Nobody was watching; but Somebody didn't realize that No One and

Nobody are, after all, the same entity, and swap all of the industry secrets between themselves so that they may better corner the market. Someone, though, *did* realize this, and that made him far, far smarter than Somebody could ever possibly be. Somebody ate cat food, for fuck's ever-loving sake.

"Will you please get out of my office?" The doctor asked both of them (or all four of them, if you count No One and Nobody, and consider them to be legally distinct, if functionally the same being), frustratedly.

"BUT I WANTED TO HAVE SHMUGGY DUMPKINS over," the small child wailed to its mother.

"But I didn't want you to have Shmuggy Dumpkins over," the mother replied, discordantly. Shmuggy Dumpkins wasn't the kind of thing that any self-respecting woman of mothersome quality would ever permit to associate with her youngling. First of all, he was half black, half Puerto Rican, and a quarter indigenoid (because there were those people who came to prominence in the late aughts, *hipsters* you might call them, that deemed "indigenous" to be the absolutely most authentic adjective anywhere, in all the history of time; so, in response to this completely dimensionless attribute being bandied about as if it had any true significance, it was proposed that the term "indigenoid" should thus be coined, in order to reference this peculiar label in the most disparaging way possible, that educated people could still understand and relate to, because they were the ones with the money here, and certainly *not* simpletons like Shmuggy Dumpkins), and even though little kids thought that his name, which he had given himself against his own parents' wishes, was a laughing riot, the rest of him was of entirely untrustworthy composition.

"That's okay, honey, dear," the mother told her wretched offspring, sarcastically. It wasn't okay, really; but in order to maintain some semblance of peace and order, that was the line that many a mother has toed, a lie which must be told in order to avoid scolding the toddler and inevitably escalating the outburst. Instead, she told him a story:

"Have you ever heard the story of Elliver?" she asked the child, menacingly. He grunted, as they do, and shook his head furiously.

"Well, Elliver was a Hollywood Celebrity," the mother continued. "It first became well known as an actress, which means that everybody thought that it had girl parts. And actually, it was famous because it was in a movie where it played a real girl that got pregnant! Being pregnant is the number one girl problem that any girl could ever possibly have.

"Back then, Elliver was known as 'Ellen.' It was the name that her parents had given her, probably. It might have been made up in order to make her more famous, but probably not.

"Everything was pretty much okay, until one day, someone compared Ellen to Ellen Degeneres, the talkshow television hostess. Ellen, who was not the same person as this other person, who was actually a *terrible* person, got so offended that she started to think about changing her name!

"Ellen liked other girls, just like the other Ellen did, except, she wasn't as obnoxious about it. And, she was upset sometimes that other girls didn't like her back, in that way, which is the sexy way, because she *was also* a girl. Does that make sense?"

"NO!" screamed the child.

"Well, that's just because you don't have an open mind. So Ellen the actress didn't want to be thought of like Ellen, the TV bitch, so she changed her name."

"What did she change her name to?"

"Pearl."

"That's STUPID! I HATE IT!"

"I know! That's the same thing that Pearl thought. Everyone hated her new name, so she decided that, besides changing her name, she should also change her gender! Because being a girl is pretty lame, after all. But Pearl still liked girls, and she figured, she could get girls to like her back *even more* if she became a boy!"

"But, but, but, she can't be a *real* boy," the child stated, obliviously.

"That didn't stop her from trying. So, Pearl became 'Elliot,' which was closer to 'Ellen,' and people thought it was nicer. Because it was like a name that his parents probably gave him, and everybody likes it when you respect your parents."

"I HATE MY PARENTS!"

"Yes, I know you do, sweetums! So Elliot was all set, and even had his breasts surgically removed and then posed for pictures of it, because it was then okay to see his bare chest while he didn't have clothes covering it, because those nasty, naughty girl parts were gone!

"And everybody thought he was really brave, and cool, and wanted to be his friend."

"So why's he Elliver?"

"Ah-hah! You see, the name thieves got to him."

"What's the name thieves?"

"They are shadow people who come in the middle of the night and steal the names of small children and leave them with only unpronounceable gibberish for names."

"But Elliot wasn't a little boy!"

"Oh, yes he was!" the mother shouted, defiantly. "When you change your sex, you automatically lose your seniority in age. It's just like when a Democrat becomes a Republican in Congress."

"WHAT?!?"

"Oh, I'm sorry sweetie, I didn't mean to get politics involved! But Elliot got his name stolen, because the name thieves said he was legally a child again, which means it's easy to steal his name and get away with it. Poor Elliot."

"But, what happened next?"

"Well, since Elliot hadn't yet achieved majority status, he became an 'it.' And it was stuck with the next available non-name, which happened to be, 'Elliver'!" the mother concluded, triumphantly.

"Was it white?" the child asked, sinisterly. Its mother nodded. "White people problems," the child sighed, resignedly.

Now, it's fine to tell children stories. But there was nothing funny about Elliver. Elliver was an imaginary schizophrenic friend that liked to steal livers and eat them. It didn't matter what sort of livers they were, or if the things that the livers were taken out of actually needed them to live; Elliver didn't care. Elliver was completely psychotic, certifiably so. It wasn't a run-of-the-mill, harmless garden-variety sociopathy either. It really did consume livers compulsively, sometimes from people. That was what happened to Shmuggy Dumpkins. But the child's mother couldn't bring herself to actually just come out and say so, so she made up some bullshit instead.

And how did her precious child repay her for all her hard work and dedication in crafting a tall tale in order to satisfy his bizarre obsessions? He waited, strategically, until the next time his mom took him into a public location. Then he ran up behind a stranger and tugged at the man's sleeve.

"Um, my, uh, mommy, said, that you, um, eat your own poop?" the child asked, uncertainly.

The man grunted and shoved the kid to the floor, violently. He wasn't Shmuggy Dumpkins, after all.

THEY HAD TO MAKE A SEGMENT TO PUT on daytime television. "My best friend is a Micropan," the tagline stated. It was hosted by Morris Motts. It was followed up by a hourlong, heart-felt discussion entitled, "I wanted to see if somebody wanted to go pooping with me."

And that had made Morris a little bit uncomfortable, for, you see, Morris Motts had a little problem. He'd been in to see his doctor about it, earlier that week. "I sometimes poop a little bit, while I'm walking," he explained to his gastroenterologist, patiently.

"Well, Morris, that's perfectly normal," his doctor replied, shaking his head. "Is it painful when the poop comes out?"

"No, it's just..." Morris trailed off, unsure of how much he was allowed to open up to a specialist. He had a psychotherapist, as well, and the television studio company paid for that, so he would have a place to speak ill about network management in a safe and quiet space where none of his incoherent rantings would bother the public, and depress ratings. But this was not a talk therapy appointment; this was something else.

"What is it, Morris? You can tell me, I'm a doctor," the gastroenterologist said, encouragingly.

"There's some, uh, poop juice that gets on the insides of my buttcheeks."

"I see. Is it possible you know the correct terminology for these things, and are just choosing to speak like a simpleton?"

"I'm sorry. I have to dumb down most of my words, you know, for the news." Morris was being completely disingenuous about that. He knew full well that what he did on television could not in any conceivable way be construed as newsworthy. He merely facilitated pointless dramatic outbursts by low-quality people for the amusement of bored, useless, and frumpy women stuck at home while their champion superhero husbands were holding down six-figure jobs, or running crack on the street.

"Does the 'poop-juice' as you call it (it's technically known as *anal leakage*, or sometimes, *anal seepage*) cause a rash?"

"No, but there is some chafing. It hurts to walk after awhile."

"I don't believe you, Morris. I don't see how it's at all possible that it would actually *hurt* you to be walking in that condition. In fact, I don't think you could be any worse than *slightly uncomfortable* should such a thing take up residence in your drawers."

"Okay, but I still think people look at me because it smells funny." Morris was correct about this. Just about every single person who came within fifty feet of him at work, and certainly the majority of people on the subway, would wrinkle their noses and furrow their brows whenever he'd approach them. Most people were too polite to say anything, though, except for a mentally challenged eight-year-old who tugged at his stepfather's sleeve and screamed,

"Fake daddy, fake daddy! The Man smells like bum!" Morris grew beet-red in the facial region and withdrew from the situation quickly. In fact, this was the incident that led him to seek medical help in the first place.

"You need mental help, not medical," the gastroenterologist sighed, animatedly.

"Oh, but butt-doctor, isn't there something that can help me?" Well, there *was* a product for this particular complication, and it was called Butt-Huggies. Butt-Huggies was an undergarment specifically designed for professional men whose assholes weren't tight enough, because they played games with their butts when they were outside of work, which wasn't good for the health of their sphincters. The patented technology employed by Butt-

Huggies meant that the ass-cheeks would be firmly squeezed together, so tightly that the liquid stool dribbling down from the anal cavity would be stopped up like a dam, high and fortified to such an extent that it would take a once-in-a-century flood to breech. And, since only a minute fraction of men ever lived more than a hundred years, that meant that Butt-Huggies could legally advertise their product as being 99.9997% effective.

The man who developed Butt-Huggies, Richard T. "Dick" Doobler, never had thought to take out a patent on the product, so even though many men with bowel issues benefitted greatly from his miraculous invention, Doobler never received proper credit, except for being an abject failure as a businessman, which he was, for having neglected to reserve rights to his creation. It was taught in business school as an example of an exceptionally boneheaded blunder, and field trips were taken to the cheap highwayside motel where Doobler had blown his brains out in the late eighties, so the students could laugh at and mock him, mercilessly.

There is also the problem of what to do when Smorgis Demption shows up, which was happening right now, at this very juncture in the story. Smorgis was a friend of Morris's, except that he failed on pretty much every level to satisfy the expectations of what would normally be considered friendship. He snored, loudly and openly, and in public and at inconsiderate times. He told long-winded stories that lacked any real significance or relevance to anyone or anything. He would spontaneously stick his left hand down the front of his pants and fondle himself for minutes at a time, in the presence of others. He would feed rancid lunch meat to sick dogs and then follow them around with a camera, waiting for them to barf and die.

THE COURT, HAVING ALREADY HEARD, DELIBERATED and ruled on the matter of one Howard "the Duck" Gimpson being accused of lewd behavior, disorderly conduct involving animal waste, breach of contract for hiring of a sex worker without making payment, and overall scumfuckery, will now continue all other matters for a later date. For there is the far more pressing issue of the racist white unicorn, Mr. Gigsby.

Mr. Gigsby, star of an internet-over-cable-television provider's series of interrupting streaming content advertisements, erupted into controversy today when a sharp-eyed viewer happened to notice that Gigsby, who is white with some multicolored fringes, comments disparagingly about a black woman sitting lazily on a couch watching a movie on a tablet computer while her daughter, or stepdaughter or niece or whatever, is busy baking cookies for their grandmother's birthday. The woman who is the target of Gigsby's scorn happens to be using the same internet service that is being promoted by the company that hired Gigsby as a spokesperson in the first place, adding to the overall sense of ironic injustice.

The cable company enticed this woman to sit around and watch the drivel being pushed by their corporate content sponsors. They made it easy for her to just binge this unending stream of nonsense, inviting her to become an unwilling foil for some stupid Unicorn's deriding remarks.

That was when Skranjax, the Infiltrator appeared to give testimony, claiming that what Mr. Gigsby was up to was, in fact, all part of an elaborate plot orchestrated by the British Monarchy to convince children to stop cleaning their teeth.

"Shluck," said the Infiltrator, confidently. And that was all he really needed to say; the jurors could twist and distort enough meaning out of that one nonsense phrase to hand down a whole slew of convictions. A few people might even face capital punishment over this. The Judge was on hiatus, doing legal research trying to track down the meaning of what someone told him was an "arcane legal concept" known as *restrunchtability* (which was really just meant as a humorous distraction, so sufficient evidence could be compiled to get that judge fired, and replaced with somebody competent). Also, the Infiltrator didn't know English, and hiring a translator to interpret whatever he was saying in freakenese would cost money, which the Court was certainly not willing to spend on a lark. Once the suspects were all lined up on death row (to be shot, stabbed, or poisoned, as was their preference), then perhaps the Court's administrator would consider paying someone to go through and rewrite the official transcript so that it might actually make sense to someone who wasn't there.

Mr. Gigsby wasn't eligible to be charged with a crime, though, because he was a Unicorn, and Unicorns are exempt from most common law proceedings.

"Can Shunkaleena be part of the equation?" asked a small, irrelevant person. The Judge, who wasn't actually there, shook his head, flabbergasted.

"Don't ever suggest such a ridiculous thing ever again," he didn't say. He felt that, even though he wasn't physically present, he still needed to enforce the rules of the Court. And there were many of those; and, he couldn't possibly keep track of them all. So, sometimes he just made shit up.

"Hey," the meaningless character whispered hoarsely to a random person sitting next to him. "I think I kinda hate Fumpy Gupkins."

"What makes you say that?"

"I dunno. Just a feeling, I guess."

"Did Rushugula Stevens tell you to hate him?"

"I don't think so. What is that?"

"Just a thing my mind made up to occupy myself with so I don't get bored." In reality, though, the stranger was *extremely* bored, constantly. That was why he was here, in this courtroom, trying to make sense of the alleged case against the perpetrators. Of which crime, he was unsure. And that was scintillating for his attention span, since he wasn't otherwise capable of following even the simplest of off-Broadway musicals.

"Do we have Mr. Gigsby present to provide testimony?" The Judge asked, abjectly. He wasn't actually there, though, so it didn't matter.

"I don't see him, your honor!" squeaked the defense counsel, who was a rodent of indeterminable species, sized halfway between a mouse and a rat. It had been eating cheese that was left out for Mitt Romney, when suddenly, it was accosted by a flood of overhead, florescent lights and a stampede of shouting and bustling as the Court was called into session to consider these highly disturbing (and quite ludicrous) claims against Mr. Gigsby.

"Objection," said the prosecutor, morosely. He was a tall, thin character often mistaken for a pencil. Ironically, he was dyslexic, and therefore incapable of reading or writing.

The rodent *could* read, at least, on about a sixth-grade level. Still, this gave him the advantage, and he was able to summarize *A Child's Garden of*

Legal Theory in order to gain some sympathy from the Judge. The argument was quite rudimentary and mundane; yet it couldn't be dismissed outright, either. Since Mr. Gigsby wasn't actually there, and was in fact most likely to be found to be a make-believe character stemming from a drunken person's wrongful interpretation of a cable TV company advertisement, and therefore absolved forever of any wrongdoing, past, present or future, the rodent felt confident that he could actually win this case against the pencil-man.

"But, pencil rhymes with penis!" shouted a random retard. And yet, this retard *also* had a valid point. The pencil-man's dick had been criticized for being spaghetti-like, for sure, and never once did anyone who had a close encounter with it claim to be even so much as *partially* satisfied.

It was at this particular juncture that the Judge had a rare moment of mental clarity. "Someone needs to tell Micropan Marneshta to either shit, or get off the pot," he proclaimed, triumphantly, to nobody at all, since he wasn't in the courtroom, and indeed, was himself sitting on a toilet in the questionably-maintained public restroom of the law library.

The point was a valid one. What, exactly, even *was* Micropan Marneshta? There had never been a definitive explanation for it.

"Would you please stop fucking around?" one reader asked, discouragedly. "You're never going to tell us anything. If there was some deeper meaning or purpose behind 'Micropan Marneshta,' it should've been revealed already. Why are you wasting everyone's time with this nonsense? And what do you have against cockatiels, anyway?"

The Judge sighed. This was not the life he expected when he had first graduated from law school. He thought the justice system was going to be a world of juicy intrigue, of high-powered life-and-death decisions being negotiated on a regular basis. Now, late in his career, he was reduced to essentially having to babysit a bunch of morons who wasted the Court's time with frivolous lawsuits and hearsay evidence.

It was for this reason that he'd taken a leave of absence; yet nobody had even noticed he wasn't sitting at the bench. The People, whose interests were ostensibly served and protected by the judiciary, were destitute and unaware, so wrapped up in their phobias and petty grievances that they failed to follow even the most basic tenets of legal decorum.

And in the absence of seriousness, miscarriages of justice were afoot. A young man was sentenced to spend the rest of his life in prison for having used a handicapped-designated restroom at a gas station. A serial-killing park ranger was let off, scot-free, on a technicality. Pigeons were roosting and nesting, and shitting, in the dilapidated ceiling tiles.

All of this notwithstanding, as it turned out, Micropan Marneshta *was* up to something. It was going around, rooting in random citizens' garbage cans, looking for discarded hotdogs to consume. And this actually *did* intersect with the other goings-on of late, as the Judge, it turns out, was a particularly strange fellow. While he was sequestered away at his home, which was in just as bad of shape as the courtroom he was so loath to set foot inside of, he had been eating nothing but wiener sausages. Cheap ones. Like, from the dollar store kind of cheap. And, on top of that, he would only take one weenie out of the package, eat it, and then throw the rest away.

After a few days of sniffing around the neighborhood, with intermittent success, Micropan Marneshta caught wind of this. It began snooping around the Judge's curbside waste bins, timing its visits opportunistically around sunset and daybreak, expecting to mine hotdog gold from out of the assorted rubbish.

The Judge, paranoid as he was, had been preemptively affixing secret seals to the lids of his trash cans, out of suspicion that opposing counsel might send some n'er-do-wells over to rummage around and try to find some incriminating evidence that could force grounds for recusal from whichever piddling thing they were so hot and bothered by (and likely, a direct function of how much these scum-sucking attorneys were getting paid to represent whatever deplorable client was angling for an acquittal, or at least, a favorable verdict), and thereby jeopardize what had been a very lucrative and incorruptible career. Something like an abundance of used hotdog packages, for instance, could spell doom for the Judge's continued ability to preside over such cases of high public interest, like the thing where Oscar Meyer was allegedly feeding people shit.

Micropan Marneshta, however, didn't care if it *was* frankfurter-shaped feces that it was so desperately scarfing down at every opportunity. In fact, Micropan Marneshta often reveled in shit, taking every opportunity that presented itself to roll around frantically in whatever decaying, forgotten turds of indeterminable heritage may be at hand. [There was no obvious downside to avoiding such filth; if Micropan Marneshta were capable of rational thought, it may have made some hokey argument about the immune-boosting properties of repeated and intensive exposure to poop.]

So it was that the Judge became greatly agitated one evening when he heard his garbage containers being fucked with. There was nothing subtle about it; it was a crashing and banging commotion on par with that which may be caused by a strung-out teenager coming down off multiple highs, desperately clambering over countertops in order to sequester any naturally or artificially sweetened foodstuffs he may encounter, proceeding to cook said products poorly and using at least a dozen different pots and utensils (which any reasonable person could tell you was *far* too many), and then leaving a giant mess for some responsible adult, inevitably sleep-deprived from being awoken repeatedly by the high-decibel explosions of sound, to clean up the following morning. The Judge knew at once that something was badly amiss, and grabbed his flashlight, his glasses, and his shoes, and lumbered out his back door to confront the evildoer.

What was staring back at him was nothing like he'd seen in all of his sixty-eight years. It was a dog, a mixed-breed with some apparent Australian Shepherd lineage, with one blue and one brown eye. It bared its teeth and growled unsympathetically. The Judge had interrupted its nightly feed; it being a solitary creature by habit, this was an inexcusable intrusion upon its sovereignty, and no amount of rancid hotdog remnants could possibly cure this injustice.

Micropan Marneshta set upon the Judge with great fury. It tore his face to absolute shreds and broke his left arm in multiple places. Then, as the Judge lay cowering and helpless on the concrete slab of his own driveway, it proceeded to *urinate* all over the poor man, head-to-toe, completely covering him in piss, and only then did it calm down enough to continue feasting upon the byproducts of the Judge's questionable eating habits.

Now, one may ask: was this fair? Did the Judge invite disaster by being so reckless with his dining rituals? Was he being punished by an emissary from the natural world for living a life of excess? Did he not deserve to be taught a lesson about the calamity of waste? Or was he merely an innocent bystander, trying as best he could to cope with the struggles of modern life by indulging in a bizarre, but otherwise largely harmless routine, just to be caught flat-footed in the face of a monstrous being, the presence of which couldn't have been predicted or divined by even the wisest of sages? And how many dollar store hotdogs really *need* to be eaten in the first place?

As the Judge lay there sobbing, brown, overripe piss dripping from his eyes (Micropan Marneshta was prone to serious bouts of kidney and bladder infections), he thought of a poem,

STICKY FINGER DICKLICANT

Was it a penis
Or a pair of fine sandals that got grifted?
Surely a thing only a true culprit
Would know.
Things got taken, certainly:
A valuable fashion accessory
A virgin's pure eyesight
The overall innocence of the moment.
Kneeling before the altar
Of lust and money, there is
A kind man whose intentions are pure
But whose actions are misguided.

And it just goes on like that, for awhile. The poem was said to have been written by Joey Longnoodle, a third-generation Italian-American, even though it was *actually* the work of Pretty Polly Poopsicle-Megantic. Regardless, the Judge never failed to feel inspired by these words. If a public masturbator and petty thief could find redemption (as the central character of the poem eventually does, even though it is a long-winded and very boring parable) though acts of self-introspection, the Judge felt he could rise to any pathetic challenge that may present itself in the course of his otherwise noble existence.

Slowly, delicately, and with great trepidation, the Judge picked his smashed-up face off the driveway, and shakily stood up to confront this complete and utter abomination that was still digging desperately through his refuse containers. "Huh... hegh... umm... HEY!" the Judge shouted, decisively.

Micropan Marneshta looked up for a brief moment, one ear semi-aroused, incredulous that its human victim would be so daring to challenge its dominion over the trash scene. It grunted, dismissively, and went back to gnawing on a wadded-up mixture of rotten hotdog meat, plastic packaging, blood-and-shit soaked paper towels (the Judge had other medical issues), and a few bootleg VHS tapes featuring underground Malaysian torture-pornography that the Judge had stolen from an exhibition of evidence presented at a previous trial for some numb-nuts wannabe child sex trafficker.

Turning over, and shifting all of his weight to his one remaining good arm, the Judge's confidence slowly grew. "You! Gettaway from my trash!" He was reminded of another inspiring tale from popular media, one particularly bizarre and unappreciated film, he couldn't recall the title of it, but there was a famous line (famous, at least, to the types of morons who paid attention to this crap, of which there were thankfully few; and those that did were completely unremarkable in life, and unlikely to bother anyone or anything with their wasted pastimes and corrupt misunderstandings of the ways in which higher society functions), where the main character says:

I'm gonna set this pile of shit on fire, because I'm Shempis Gomblit!

It just so happened that the Judge was three weeks removed from a nasty and self-destructive smoking habit, and although he'd been doubly cautious in avoiding any hint of nicotine-related vapors, he did still carry a lighter in his pocket, as do many ex-smokers, conditioned to be terrified of getting caught without one when in need. And, as it turned out, he also knew something that Micropan Marneshta did not: those toxic, fecal-contaminated wieners in the trash bins were also *highly flammable.*

As the Judge leaned forward, he was suddenly filled with a sense of determination. This was *his* pile of crap that had been so diligently organized and placed in the proper location for one of those fine starch-pressed-shirt-wearing young garbagemen to come and collect in a neat and tidy fashion the following morning, before ordinary people had even had their coffee and had the first clue of what was going on. Micropan Marneshta had no explicit nor implied rights to the mess.

The Judge locked his bleary eyes onto the horrid monster that was still engorging itself on the spoils of its ill-begotten victory. Flailing around with his still-intact arm, he grabbed a chunk of brick from out the decorative masonry enclosing a small garden of wilted, neglected flowers adjacent to the walkway leading up to his front door. Squinting mightily, the Judge lined up his shot, aimed, and launched the projectile directly at Micropan Marneshta's rear end. The creature shuddered as the brick made impact, stood upright, began choking on a half-chewed hotdog, dislodged it in a forceful fit of coughing, spat the nasty crud out, swung its head around, and locked its dichromatic eyes with those of the Judge. Pure hatred seethed from its glare. It began emitting a rapturous growl, baring its yellow, crooked teeth as infectious discharge dripped from the corners of its mouth and down its stained, matted facial fur. The Judge leered back, ready for battle. And in an instant, it was on, a fight to the death for the pride of the trash that was still sitting, half-strewn around the Judge's yard, for a waste management professional to remove.

In the tussle, they tumbled into an old eighties-style boombox radio/cassette player combination battery-powered portable listening device. The Judge had left it out on the curb, thinking it was a useless piece of trash; but this piece of trash had one hit left in it. It came to life and began playing that song, "Oh, Baby, Do You Have Back?" by The Retarded Paperboys.

Well, Micropan Marneshta didn't know any of the words to the song, but the discordant melody and off-key ramblings by the vocalists were too much for its sensitive ears to tolerate. In a flash, it retreated, galloping down the street, quickly forgetting about the treasure trove of rotten hotdog meat it had relinquished. It was going to take its business elsewhere.

Once again, and probably for the last time in what remained of his life, the Judge was victorious.

"THE STORYTELLER IS THE ONE THAT IS IN CONTROL," the man said, cunningly. "It is that person's job to not only document the scum floating atop the many surfaces of reality, but to also scrape it back and explore the terrible things lurking underneath."

Your boyfriend, Monstreeshen, wasn't too sure. It seemed unnecessarily off-topic, what the man had been braying about like a lost donkey, and didn't quite fit in with the rest of the overall premise. But, then again, neither did Monstreeshen, who was only a minor monster and didn't contribute much by the way of action or excitement to any story in which he may find himself a participant, willing or otherwise.

"Yes, but what was this business about a zipper, anyway?" somebody else asked, tangentially.

"Well, you see, it was a zipper *malfunction*," the first man replied, dryly.

"Oh, I have a hoodie that does that!" the somebody remarked, irrelevantly.

"It wasn't that kind of a zipper. What happened was, this guy was in an accident, and–" the man looked around at the other diners, carefully, and continued, "I'm not going into details, because it seems like some of these people may be trying to enjoy their lunch, or something. But he got all fucked up, and they had to operate, and there wasn't enough skin left to graft together the terribly mangled torso, so, in a pinch, they added a zipper."

"Oh. How distasteful."

"And it wasn't a good zipper, either! It leaked. It got all rusty, they didn't even tell the poor guy how to properly care for it in the shower, and after a few months, the teeth started to tear off, got all out of alignment, like, and after a brief struggle, it was no longer functional." At this point, Monstreeshen *lost* his lunch, and had to be escorted out of the dining facility.

"Was it a..." the somebody gulped, fearfully, "A... *Micropan*?"

"Yes. You see, gentlemen, Micropan Marneshta is still at large," an expert said, butting into the conversation, obnoxiously. "It must be stopped, yet all efforts to contain it have been futile."

"What would you suggest, sir?" The first man's curiosity had been piqued, enough to stifle his otherwise understandable outrage over the uninvited interruption into what had been an engrossing private conversation.

"Perhaps it would be advisable to get a Michael involved." Those presently assembled looked to one another, confusedly. Nobody had seen a Michael in quite some time. In fact, there was some genuine doubt as to whether or not Michaels even still *existed*, or if they had been rendered obsolete.

There weren't even any phone books available to look and see if they might have a Michael listed somewhere within the local dialing area. They weren't even too sure if telephones still operated in that manner, or if the advent of cellular technology had displaced any and all rationale behind the assignment of numbers.

"All I know is that one of my coworkers had an encounter with Micropan Marneshta, and hardly lived to even tell about it," offered up another eavesdropper, a dumpy woman who had obviously spent far too much of her meager paycheck on cheap cosmetic products. "If you catch it, let me know. I want its disheveled fur to make a fine coat," she continued, drooling with anticipation.

Just then, a telephone began ringing. Nobody knew what to do at first, until a befuddled waiter noticed there was a small cupboard, tucked away in a nook at the corner of the restaurant, forgotten for decades. He reached in and pulled it out, a dusty beige contraption that still possessed a corded handset.

He lifted the receiver, just like he'd seen done in old movies, and pressed it to his ear. Silence at first, then,

"This is Michael," it said.

Uncle Shmarmlucus

A Novel

Chapter I

THEY CALL ME THE CHAINSAW MASSACRE Motherfucka. Time to introduce me, the I. I have a plan, to kill Jeff Bezos.

Jeffrey Bezos is a liar and a charlatan. There can be nothing worse than a man who, as the richest son of a confirmed bitch on Earth, is throughly *boring* to boot. He was some schmuck with a business degree who wanted to kill small bookstores for sport. He is ugly, he isn't even that tall, he's not very smart and his rocketship company sucks, too. He bought a newspaper to make himself feel important. I hate his guts.

So, here's what I propose to do, and I *am* going to do it: wait until it's time for the Nobel prize awards in Norway. He's going to show up there; it's something worthless rich people sacrifice themselves on the altar for, that recognition. And so, too, will I. I will shoot him dead on the spot, and then make an appeal to the European High Commission on Human Rights to be tried and sentenced in Norway, the scene of the crime, rather than being deported back to the USA for torture and execution. Norway, from the little bit that I know, has a real progressive approach to rehabilitating defective people who do things like murder wannabes at national awards ceremonies: they put them up for a couple of years on a pleasant island commune in some Scandinavian lake, offer some personal enrichment courses, feed them a well-balanced diet and have them care for livestock, then, after like five years, *max*, allow them to reenter society.

Now, I'm not telling HOW I will be smuggling the gun into Norway. Let's just say, when I leave the US I won't have one, and when I get to Oslo— I will!

WAIT, THOUGH. WAIT, WAIT. We need to revisit a few core assumptions before we go much further. The first and foremost, and indeed probably the only relevant thing deserving discussion, is where in the hell did "Uncle

Shtunklucus" come from? The history is unclear, how the term evolved, when it came to be accepted by the masses as a euphemism for whatever ails them, and such; it's not really relevant at this point. What we need is an origin story that may, for some small subset of the population, make a bit of sense.

Uncle Shtunklucus was only ever intended as a gibberish nickname for a cat. He was a fat, healthy, orange-and-white creamsicle tomcat nominally named "Ginger Balls." To his alcoholic owner, that name was far too straightforward. It contained an easily definable euphemism (testicles), was somewhat lewd but hilarious, and also ironic, since the cat had been neutered by the time he was a year old. On occasion, the world "Bawls" would be substituted for "Balls."

There needed to be a second act in the lives of both cat and owner. It came in the form of an enthusiastic upstart filmmaker, a scraggly college dropout with wispy, disgusting strands of facial hair contributing to an overall unkempt and highly unprofessional appearance. Crashing on the couch owned the the same person who named the cat, this listless bum came to fantasize about making a short film based around the cat and his made-up adventures.

The cat's owner felt like the whole thing was silly. Just downright silly. He was more content singing made-up songs by his imaginary band to himself in the shower every morning, than he was preparing diligently for a busy day of doing nothing but getting drunk later.

The film kid was insistent. The cat's owner grudgingly began to daydream instead about what, if anything, could form the basis of a compelling narrative to highlight the foibles of an overweight and lazy housecat. "Garfield" already existed; cats were otherwise accepted, but only as just an internet joke, something to be bandied about on a case-by-case basis whenever one of the feline persuasion should be caught in the act of being ridiculous.

So it was that, one morning, after dolloping a liberal splash of Irish cream into his morning coffee, the cat's owner started making random noises towards his pet. After about twenty minutes, he came across the combination of syllables that is approximated by this string of letters: SHTUNKLUCUS.

The film kid wasn't convinced. Sure, it was a silly made-up name, but it was lacking some uncanny context. There needed to be an introductory honorific, a launch point of reasonable, grownup prose that would subsequently be derailed by the following gibberish term.

"Well, I don't know about the cat's background," his owner said. "He's a mister. I don't think he's smart enough to be a doctor or anything. Nobody would buy that."

"What about his family?" The film kid pressed. "Doesn't he have some relative role to the other cats in his family? Like, daddy?"

"No, he ain't nobody's daddy but his own. His mom kicked him out when he got too big and she wouldn't let him suck on her teat anymore. All the other kittens had been adopted, stolen or eaten. He was left to fend for himself one sunny morning when his mama went out to have some loud, hot crazy cat group sex and get knocked up again and start the whole process all over again. He didn't know what to do. He was big enough to use his claws and probably catch a young mouse or something, but otherwise, he had no direction. He found the railroad tracks in front of the house and— Hi-CUAWP!"

The film kid got knocked over in his chair, the reverberations of the massive hiccup sending a seismic-grade shockwave through the living room floor. "Are you ok?"

"No, I'm not, but let me get more liquor in me, and maybe it'll settle down some. So the cat just came strutting down the railroad tracks this one morning. We— me, White Jimmy, and Sauron, who you didn't ever meet I don't think, he was clean at that time, or just banging xans, it wasn't until later on he got back into cooking meth in sprite bottles in his room and I had to kick him out before we got into a fight and I got his blood on me and caught the hep-C, hick-HAWWW, but that morning everything was alright, more or less. It was a sunny, warm morning in October. I'd just scarfed down a plate of leftover apple crisp with a rum-and-coffee to wash it back, then stepped out on the stoop for my first smoke of the day, and goddamnit, there's this random fucking cat walking down the railroad tracks! They never run trains on those tracks since, oh, like the eighties, long before I ever lived here, so there was no danger unless one of the bums came bumming along with their pitbulls and their smelly backpacks, then the little guy might've gotten eaten.

"The cat was walking down the track, and he makes eye contact, the little sonofabitch does, he sees us looking over there at him, being all like 'who the hell is this?' And then he comes strutting down the path, down the embankment, starts beelining at us right across the front yard, and then—"

"Then?" The film kid sat transfixed, wide-eyed, red-eyed from the marathon bong-ripping sessions he'd recently undertaken to cultivate some inspiration, long disgusting fingernails digging into the cheap wooden dining chair part of the table set seat on which he was sat, eagerly waiting with saliva dripping down his chin for the next juicy detail of the fateful meeting between animal and man.

"Then he stops, he just abruptly and completely stops, dead in his tracks, and he stares at us, and slowly and strategically, he hunches his back up, bringing his hindlegs up to meet his forearms, tail shot straight up in the air, and we're trying to figure out what does any of this actually *mean*, right? It was so obvious after a few seconds, though: the little bugger was taking a shit! Right there in the front lawn next to the opium poppy patch!"

"Ha! HAhahahahHAHA! Poop!" the film kid was shaking so hard, the cat's owner became momentarily concerned he may have adopted a wayward epileptic, which would mean the kid would have to DIE, probably with a shovel blow to the back of the head, because that was how his old man taught him to deal with the spastics.

Fortunately for him, the young wannabe stopped guffawing as abruptly as he'd started, and settled into an awkward and uncomfortable stare, off into space, focused upon a point somewhere far removed from the back of the cat's owner's head.

"Hmm. So he took a shit right there in front of everyone, proud he had an audience or something. Normally that's the kind of thing that makes you want to curl up and puke and cry and call out for your mama, right? Cat shit is so unspeakably nasty. Yet here he was, having laid out his morning turds on my fucking front yard, which was really just a strip of grass and gravel next to the industrial park, then he delicately scratches up some dirt underneath him, and, real quick, kicks it all back over the shit, like nothing ever happened!"

"What a smart kitty!"

"Well, nah, but at least he let us know he was housebroken. That's how I interpreted it anyway and he's mostly proven me right."

"But what about his family?"

"It was a year or two later, when I was bored and wanted something new, some novel invective to hurl his way that wouldn't make a lick of sense to anyone besides me, and him. Shtunklucus."

"It needed something more, though?"

"It needed something more. All of a sudden, thinking about my own useless family, I had it: he was somebody's uncle! He must have had siblings, cats always have as many kittens as they can pump out their snatches, usually from multiple dads too, betcha didn't know that, but I'm pretty sure not all of his littermates were sterilized before they had a chance to have their own little tit-biters. So, he's somebody's uncle, and he's Uncle Shtunklucus."

It stuck. Right there on the spot, these two questionable characters had struck a deal to have Ginger Balls star in the filmmaking kid's directorial debut, and it would be called, "Uncle SHTUNKLUCUS." The movie would be rated F, for being completely fucked.

ALSO, THE PEOPLE DEMAND TO KNOW: Who is "SAGAMORE?"

Sagamore is my made-up Indian name. I might want to write a real book someday, and when it does, I want no connection between my given name and this absolute mess of a smoldering trash-heap. So Sagamore it is, and that is how you shall refer to me.

Glavamore is my half-brother, if you'd care to know. We are both members of a made-up Indian tribal band, the *134A Rancheria Boys*. We made this so during the grand old days of the Todd Court Experience®, a pact borne from many months of alcohol, drugs and insanity.

Our false Native American heritage notwithstanding, Glavamore is a dirty Italian who pretends to be Irish. He's got the Irish flag tattooed on his gut, he pretends like he can speak Gaelic, and he has a split personality disorder of some variety. One time, when Ginger Balls was passed out between his legs, Glavamore woke up in his own mess and disappeared for three days. Upon return, he swore up and down he'd been asleep the entire time, which nobody for a second believed.

"Glavamore, my dude, you were eating honey grahams and drooling all over my bearskin throw rug in the living room having arguments with the sniper character on Tom Clancy for about eight hours while you were frying balls in my house last night," said Sandwich, the neighbor.

"Bullshit! I was asleep in my own bed."

"Shutttuuuupppp!" I roared. "Sandwich. Please, continue."

"Uh-huh, I saw the whole thing," Sandwich said, with growing confidence. "I saw you steal Trigger's keys and take off in his truck all day yesterday. When you got back, there were 200 blackberry bushes hanging off the side mirrors and a whole family of Mexicans crouched down in the bed!"

"Well Glavamore, what do you have to say for yourself?"

"Dude. I was asleep the entire, fucking, time!"

"You need to apologize to Trigger for stealing his truck. And to the United States Government for being complicit in smuggling dirty, illegal people into our great country. And I don't know what you planned on doing with five gallons of piss, but they spilled all over his front seat and his grandpa's blanket—"

"Five gallons of piss?" I stared Glavamore down with cruel hatred in my eyes. "You were going to sell clean piss samples you harvested off the Mexicans to some drug-addled, high-school thug-wannabe juvenile reprobates?"

"No, I. Was. Asleep."

"Fuck you. Pay me," I grabbed him by the lapels of his knock-off eBay Chinese leather jacket. "I want my cut you fuck! I let you into my house like the stray dog you are, let you pay me in your silly phony SSI check government money, in lieu of rent, and, and, and, you FUCK!" I was getting so mad, my heart started skipping beats, my beta blocker scrip had just run out and I was on the verge of a massive coronary.

Coughing up, then swallowing blood, I let Glavamore spring free from my grasp for the moment, collected myself and tried to finish what at this time was a very belabored, but I felt, highly valid point of vital importance: "You try and undercut me with the youth clean piss market? My own idea, my own brainchild, I called the cops on half those delinquents and got them busted just so I can run this scam, and now you try to own it? You try to take responsibility for my wondrous creation, this genius project I hatched in a moment of spontaneous brilliance, probably the only good, original idea I've ever had in my entire life, and you, you, you, *appropriate* it?"

"Dude." Glavamore looked remorseful; but he often did that when he was caught dead-to-rights fucking someone over. He wanted you to know that he was sorry, he didn't actually mean it, he wasn't capable of knowing any better, so even though it might very well happen again, you couldn't feel mad at him about it.

That was Glavamore. We couldn't live together, even though we were false blood half-brothers, both enrolled in the same fake Indian reservation that was a tongue-in-cheek cultural joke about my house. That was a dishonor to the memory of Todd, the namesake of Todd Court. And for that, I might have been sorry, if it weren't for what happened next.

BEZOS IS GOING TO DIE. But I'd lied. I didn't actually have a plan to sneak a gun into Norway. Next best thing: a shovel. A *tactical* shovel.

Hardware stores exist in Norway, right? I don't know anything about the country, but figure the Norweeg's would dig a good shovel. Bezos is not a large man anyhow, he's not tough and he certainly doesn't have a strong, refined Neanderthal skull like yours truly. A whack, maybe two, then done, wouldn't matter at that point what kind of purebred German security goons were following him around. I can swing the business end of a trowel or spade faster than a dirty kid can spit.

The caller didn't quite grasp my context, while I was thinking this over, so I helped guide him in a useful direction: "I am a penguin. I live at the South Pole," I told him, angry about being distracted. They were committing frog on the other end of that telephone line, I swear it.

Committing frog is way worse than even just plain old fraud. They find these dirty little people from third-world hellhole countries (the French I believe are the primary culprits responsible), they teach them bad English and then give them a phone and a list of numbers to dial. It's like talking to a frog, because they're fairly unintelligible (sorry, Kermit) and they have a singular focus that doesn't make sense to myself or any other reasonable member of the Human species. I don't even know what they want, or how the scam works; they just keep asking if I am myself, and, if so, how much money can they lend me today? Just like flies on shit, these frogs are hunting the fly *eating* the shit, so that then *they* can devour the shit-flies, and I don't know anything about it, NOR can I stand it any longer. The commission of frog occurs over three acts:

1. I'm compromised by an incoming phone call.

2. I have to wait a few seconds before I hear my voice echoing back on the other end of the line until I hear them ask timidly, "Hi sir, are you the business owner?"

3. I see how far I can get in trying to ascertain what the frog wants. I'm coy about it at times.

"I am not very myself today. The business owner will be referred to in the third person. I'm sorry!"

"Uh-huh, do you need funding capital for your business?"

"Yes, actually, I need one million Indian rupees to build my factory in Bangalore."

"But sir, don't you realize the exchange rate between New Zealand dollar is superior to rupee?"

"I don't actually live in Northern California. I just impersonate a human being who is an American citizen. Like I said, I'm a penguin, and I'm looking for funds for my factory in India. We're building Micropans!" Then usually I ask them to sing a song with me, about Marneshta or something, and if I'm really feeling generous, then I let them have "American Idol Rules" where they can sing any song they'd like, and if I'm impressed enough, then we have a deal. One guy tried crooning some Whitney Houston at me, "Ah-nd I, I will al-wayze, I love to you-oh-oooh!" I said he got a 7 out of 10, which wasn't passing, since it was the lightning round. And just like that, he was terminated.

I don't make a deal ever, though, because we're talking about frogs here. Goofy, goddamned green fucking frogs. They live in slime and swallow bugs for a living. The French put them up to it, I know they did; I can't prove it yet, but once I have enough evidence, it's on.

That's another reason Bezos must die! He's hired the French frogulent call centers to hock his wares with the Amazon. I'm going to buy my weapon on his omnipresent selling-platform, to be poetically just about this assassination. It's still happening in Norway, however, since I just couldn't bring myself to actually go to France. I'll get sidetracked and end up getting the guillotine for slaughtering a whole office complex full of frogs with their robocalling systems. I'll set the place on fire and go out for a baguette. I'll pull a beret down over my eyes and light an unfiltered cigarette.

No. It just won't work out that way. I'd much rather go to a nice little cottage on an island in some Norwegian lake and think about how smart I am for pulling off the world's perfect crime, get in shape, breathe in that nice fresh Scandinavian air, and finally feel whole and content in my manhood, with chest hair and homemade whiskey.

SO SOMETIMES, WHEN THE SHMARLGALASHES get too much and become obnoxious, trying to press upon your being with all of their offensive overtures about why everything is YOUR fault, when it *very obviously* is not, how do you not want to blow your brains out when you no longer feel capable of successfully hiding? You regress into an infantile state, is the answer. You start thinking about how nice it was when your mom padded your butt with a diaper, going back to that place of blurred memories that contain occasional moments of clarity, like that time your best friend cast a fishing hook through your eye when you were eight years old, that sting and the terrible fear of worm-infection becomes your best friend in this lonely night of suicidal contemplation–

But, what here are these Shmarlgalashes? Puttering middle aged women who wax poetic about their imminent demises? An ugly tweaker demanding nonsense be paid in consideration of an outlandish idea? Some smarmy grifter trying to sell imaginary roses by the streetside? Is it a puddle that used to contain a rational thought? Did you try to force it out of a steering column assembly, the magic code to solve the problem of starting the car when you were not in possession of the key? Huh? Did you really waste your entire life listening to your mother?

It's not important. Nothing is important, just getting rid of this nasty smell-feeling, a clingy stench of the worst variety, a lingering odor comprised of expired fish sauce and inescapable mechanical grease that crests the edges of your fingernails on a routine basis. You can't scrub it off to save your life; women aren't impressed when you boast about what a working man you are, showing it off in a pretentiously cheap lounge on a first date. You should know better, and where is MOM? Why can't she save me from these terrible, horrible, no good very menacing people from whom I can't escape, or maybe I just don't want to? On a subconscious level, of course.

No, your mother wasn't here for the play. She wandered off to go smoke some heroin with a 77-year-old Jewish retired contractor. They lost his car, and yet still you have to pay the taxi driver for carting their asses across the city, drunk, high and being listless from shooting up the most recent container of subpar tar while totally insisting that the fucking car is parked *somewhere* around here, just give them another minute or two and they will have the very spot pinpointed on some stupid map.

The Shmarlgalashes— they are foreigners. They don't belong amongst us freedom-loving folk. They test boundaries and resent us when we can't remember why they were bothering us in the first place. But bother us they still do! With their cardigans, and their sorry stories that always end up being your fault, someway, somehow. Feel sorry for yourself on your own doorstep, Shmarlgalash! My mom didn't remember to change my diaper! I'm confused, and messy. I yell.

"You squirt-headed shit-node, why are you bothering me right now? Can't you see, I just want to be left ALONE?"

"Yeah, brother, I get it," junkie Johnnie said.

"You wouldn't." And he nodded. Not off, not entirely, but in some primordial sense of agreement. He was my best friend, and he never put up a fight. Not one competitive bone in his body.

"I get everything you just said."

"I didn't say anything, I just thought it."

"Same difference. I would have killed myself. I just hate the idea of those assholes winning."

"Johnnie, is that you?"

"No, it's me." That was a lie, but Johnnie was clever like that. Who was talking? Fucking smartass.

"I know it can't be me, because if it wasn't you, then I'm just inventing this conversation inside my head, exclusively."

"Yeah, right on, man!"

"Shutup. I'm in control of this show."

"Nobody said you weren't." And nobody ever would. They have to respect the King, the be-er of all beings, the mother of all fuckers– the vanquisher of all Shmarlgalashes. They would pay for what they did. A holocaust will befall them. It's just a matter of time. No remorse, no forgiveness, no admitting culpability anymore.

NOW, I WANT THE PUBLIC TO UNDERSTAND what it means when it is said that "I will destroy my enemies, because Ragnar the Instigator commands it!" Because it will really help put things into context once my plans are revealed to the world.

Ragnar the Instigator came about as a manifestation of drunken despair. There was a mormon, a moron, and a couple of cockatiels, and between the lot of them, I became aware of Ragnar, in my periphery, for the first time, ever. [When we were younger, the Virus and I had derived an entity known as "Asen'hôyah" after what we *thought* we overheard in the background of a Jerky Boys-brand prank telephone call. And it offered what we desired, an original sense of identity, came about from a mutual belief in some abstract being that may or may not wield actual powers, but which we could *pretend* as such, and, for a game of make-believe, for a couple of kids freezing to death in the harsh winter of New Hampshire, it could've gone much worse.]

Ragnar was a repeat offender. It became obvious (after many rounds of trial and error to actually get *clean*) in the shower, over many mornings, that never would the shameful stench of all the drinking and all the batshit crazy ideas truly be washed away; but, plans that got hatched on too many a hazy night, so therefore we had to create Ragnar, to enable our poor behaviors.

Ragnar was a perfect excuse to act like an invincible imbecile. Ragnar only cares that you go about your life first and foremost in service of the divine idea that only YOU are correct, and everybody else is wrong; YOU call the shots, YOU are the beginning and the end of all that is relevant, and everything in-between. YOU is really the I, and what Ragnar cares about most is satisfying the prime condition that "I", *me*, will be the responsible party in the lawsuit about to be commenced against all who have done us wrong. And there is where "YOU" and "I" reach a merger deal, a marriage of convenience, so we can mutually identify and exterminate any and all who threaten our continued existence. Don't read too much into it; we just do this out of sheer necessity.

Jackie Bopper, the Shit Camp, Inc. counselor was quick to intercede. "I think it would be a great idea if we sang all hail and praises to Ragnar, the Instigator, every morning! Yeah!" Her enthusiasm was completely inappropriate, as usual, but still, it stuck a chord. If a degenerate cocaine addict like Jackie Bopper could get behind this questionable ideal, *anyone* could.

Was I not being the vengeful, petty person I believe that I could have been if I had just tried a little bit harder? Jackie said that it was so. "Just *believe* in Ragnar, yeah! And Ragnar will fill us full of hate, and it is. So. Much. Fun! It's completely great to destroy our enemies!" I should have listened to her long-ass time ago. I would have been so much more successful, or at the very least, I would have ended so many other peoples' efforts to parasitize the labors of those who did nothing wrong, except attempt to exist. Hearing random people shout incoherently about Ragnar, the Instigator, many years back would have saved me quite a bit of time, stomach ulcer blood, and having to scavenge for tobacco.

Scavenging for tobacco is the worst thing you can possibly ever end up doing with your time. You and me both know what it's like, to be in that position where you only have $7.87 in change to your name, but the turbaned Indian man at the gas station down the street, the one with the cheapest price on the brand of cigarettes you smoke (American Spirit, Turquoise) will sell them for $10.60, and goddamned California and the sales and sin taxes we somehow put up with from the liberal glitterati have to be paid, but still you can't quite bring yourself to commit armed robbery over something so trivial as a pack of smokes, so you instead spend most of your morning (a sunny, otherwise nice morning when there's no wildfire smoke lingering in the air, and having not even yet heard the madcap dash of an ambulance wailing its sirens through traffic to get past the first stoplight of many en route to the hospital that never fails to invoke a sense of complete foreboding and absolute dread, every time it rushes past you when you're out in the main parking lot of your business trying to vacuum up heroin syringes, and you're struck with that ultimate feeling of despair, thinking, *when will that be me? That corpse riding on its way to an early grave lined with massive amounts of pain and suffering at the hands of incompetent medical technicians? When will I be the one drowning in the drivel of those self-righteous morons who think they can do something to save me, but actually can't, because they are a fast sequence of grade-school dropouts whose rapist daddies talked them into nominal certification as medical professionals so they can support his cocaine and pre-pubescent child molestation habit?* You don't get a satisfactory answer, or indeed, any other sort of resolution to that line of inquiry; but rest assured, once you land that sweet state-subsidized hourly labor gig, everything will be gravy and smokes!) puttering around for about ninety minutes, trying to piece together a cigarette from the discarded butts and residual resin stuck to detached filters lingering about the parking lot, hoping that you can source enough valid by-products from which to reconstitute a single, solitary cigarette. So long as you can at least make some kind of a positive identification that leads you to believe that the source of the tobacco product was at least within a half-day's drive of the plantations that produce your preferred leaf, you will have something to smoke, in shame.

That is the level of frustration by which we must then consider invoking the name of Ragnar, the Instigator. He doesn't take any shit, for one. Someone thought that he might, and that person is now dead. From natural causes, maybe, if you want to believe the "official" record. Those of us who know better, do not. We realize that there is divine intervention at hand. That hand is probably owned by none other than our beloved Ragnar, the Instigator.

"And I will destroy my enemies, because Ragnar, the Instigator, commands it!" says Jackie Bopper, confidently. She knows what she's talking about, for once. "She" is starting to look like a former "he" that wore a bunch of makeup and lipstick and girls' clothes to appear more like a "she," but if you already accepted Ragnar, the Instigator, into your heart, then you are not the kind of narrow-minded troglodyte that cares about these kinds of things. Hatred as much he may espouse, still rest assured that Ragnar's heart is a small one; literally, like he was incarnated as a cockatiel that one time before he got eaten by a falcon. That, more than anything else, should serve as everlasting proof that he will return and encourage us only to destroy our enemies; nothing more, nothing less.

"I AM GOING TO BINGE EAT, AND BINGE drink, all this week, because it's Thanksgiving!" Elon Musk said to me, boastfully. "Thanksgiving day. Yeah, and I'm gonna get fat, and I'm gonna get drunk, because I am an AMERICAN!" He should've had a cowboy hat on, goddamnit.

And as I nodded in passive agreement, acknowledging his moral turpitude and his omnipresence as a billionaire in all of our lives, the cat darted past my bookshelf, stealthily. It might have been important, later.

What did I want with such an egotistical buffoon? Elon Musk wasn't even an *actual* American; he was a South African, and last I checked, they were a borderline enemy. They had nukes, dontchaknow. Yup, they were even thinking about using them against their own black people. They and the Israelis, the dirty Jewish bastards, probably colluded on an illegal nuclear test in the South Indian Ocean, in like 1979. Fucking Jews, leave it to those penny-pinching shysters to not want to foot the entire bill, or ethical responsibility, for blowing up an atomic weapon in the atmosphere even after all the die-hard capitalists and communists of the times had come to a mutual understanding that radioactive fallout was a threat to all life, everywhere, and the better option was, if they weren't going to use the goddamned things (and they never were, it was just for show, just an excuse to waste the People's money), at the very least they could dig a deep hole or trough somewhere out in the desert, away from any haphazard shepherds or diddly-whacking folk of the forgotten corners of the world, and leave it to the computers and robots to determine how destructive and deadly their little toy bombs *might* be if they ever got into a big-boy shooting war. So Elon Musk hired me to be a consultant to all of his business interests, because he was at that time the second richest man on this whole entire green Earth, but I had an ulterior motive; I wanted him to finance my plot to kill Bezos, who was the richest person alive[*], and very much the object of my homicidal affections.

The thing you should know about Elon, is that he is a small man with very withered-pecker style desires. He doesn't want anything more than to *feel* important, even if he really isn't. I understood this kind of mentality since the age of 18, taking a Psych-101 class at Pathetic Flower Community College. These sorts are pretty easy to manipulate, you just goad them until you get what you want, and have a few bases covered by way of credentialing theory; then you're pretty much a made man.

"I like doughnuts," Elon said, about a half a bottle of Wild Turkey into the evening. I offered to let him into my house for several reasons:

1. I was about to be evicted. My landlord didn't want to fix the defective electrical panel outside the house that powered everything in the kitchen from the microwave to the refrigerator. I asked him to fix them, and he told me to find a new place to live.

2. I was living in a fairly small house, not even quite 1,000 square feet I don't think, and Elon *loved* decrepit hellholes like this, especially when he was drinking to the point of getting drunk. He didn't ask twice when I invited him back, because he knew I was nothing, that I came from nothing, and that my bank account and my credit report would satisfactorily answer any legal argument over whether I was, indeed, nothing.

3. I was playing David Bowie, and Musk *hated* Bowie, unless he'd been drinking; then, he'd get sloppy, and start grooving and dancing along with all the songs on *Diamond Dogs*.

4. He was a useful alibi, not that I thought I'd get off entirely for clobbering Bezos point-blank with a tack hammer; but I could argue that I was just a hapless pawn in some kind of elaborate brainwashing program of that dastardly Musk and his neural-net experimentation. Everybody suspected that he was some kind of evil mad scientist, but I knew the truth: he was nothing

---

[*] not anymore

more than a closeted drunk, and a slob, and an all-around completely *uninspired* excuse of a man. He got lucky, once, made a couple of dollars on some stupid online classifieds ad service in the nineties, and then had a couple of financial fuck-boys work his capital into a big, fat mess of dollar bills. Being the weird little man that he was, he started hanging out at Comic-Con, drinking whiskey from a *Wonder Woman* water bottle and trying to talk some of the chubby, cosplaying high-school girls into taking a ride with his "magic wand" in the ladies' restroom (he was actually afraid of going into the mens' room, because he was operating under the constant fear that he'd get beat up, or raped, or made fun of for his penis size).

While he was passed out on the couch, I took his shoes off, and gently asked, "Does AI have to tell you if it's a computer, if you ask?" I didn't think he would have an answer, but I needed to know, for future reference.

"WHAT'S UP, DOC?"

"Just trying to figure out how to kill this fucker," I told the Doctor. Good old Dr. Dirty David, automotive mechanic. 40+ years experience in trade. And here I am, obsessed with this foolish, cartoonishly-violent plot to assassinate the world's richest man.

"Do you only care about violence?" No, but then again, neither did the Looney Tunes, and they were perfectly violent! I just take one step forward, and two step backwards, looking in the floor-length mirror this entire time, asking, *who's that chicken in the mirror?* And if I could get closer to him, it's going to be a cockfight, to the death. That male chicken in the mirror will die, if it was up to me. But, it's not; it's up to the Universe, and, as I cluck and preen, I am forced to go backwards *two steps* for each step I take, in return, forward.

That is the plight of the working man, and that is what I wound up as, because that's what the odds bore. I'm not a vicious person by nature, but there's only so much that any reasonable man can stand still for until it gets to the point you just want to shoot, or stab, or clobber someone over the head with a comically inappropriate blunt object.

I keep doing my two-one dance with the guy in the mirror whose head

I want to rip off, ruffling feathers, and soon enough I disappear over the horizon, going backward, never to see that awful man's reflection ever again.

And I am reminded of how this got started, my closeted desire to fight; and sometimes, just to assault people, unprovoked. But most of the time, it *is* provoked. For example:

I was minding my own business one afternoon, headed into Safeway in order to procure a half-gallon of vodka, or maybe whiskey if there was anything along the lines of a decent American Bourbon on sale. [It was ironic, because I'd heard and understood Safeway's parent corporation to be owned by Mormons, who don't condone drinking; but, they profited off of it. And I hate Safeway with a passion, because I also understood that they sponsored legislation against the gays, and I have an affinity for the gays, because they *can* be white and male, like me, when that is not equally true of females, blacks, reptilians, etc., or anyone else the Democrat party wants to promote the interests of ahead of my own. It wasn't ever the gays' fault that they were born defective, and craved penis. It was just another form of disability at that point; and yes, maybe sometimes we laugh at that cripple hobbling down the street and trying desperately to not trip and spill and fall all over the gaps between the concrete slabs on the sidewalk. Knowing that it is a battle the lame-legged individual is about to lose, we get all giddy in anticipation that *they are about to fall down*, and, better yet, maybe not even able to get back up on their own! As amazing as that is, when it happens, we don't guffaw extravagantly, but instead, we just chuckle a bit, lowly, happy that isn't us all toppled over helpless in a public right-of-way. And then we even extend a hand to aid Mr. Gimpy in his return to the upright-world, as long as he is one of those grateful handicapped types, and doesn't have some kind of *attitude* about it.]

So there I was, minding my own business, about to get drunk in the middle of a workday, singularly focused on how to get the most booze I could for twenty bucks; and my peripheral vision wasn't accounting for all of the comings and goings of the plebeians in the parking lot, so, stupid me, I could have just beelined it straight for the automatic doors and made my way inside to the liquor aisle, without being harassed, when suddenly,

"Hey, would you like to sign my petition to prevent Las Vegas style casinos from opening up in California?" I wasn't sure how to respond. I never in my most wretched nightmares imagined a scenario where I'd be propositioned like this. How do I respond? Unlike Michael Keaton, I *do* know that I'm registered to vote, and I even know at which address and in what state. That is an awfully huge amount of power to confer upon anyone, and I take my role in the democratic process very seriously. Which means, I am never about to just go ahead and sign my name onto some cause out there, where every ninny and toothless panhandler can see, and possibly hear, what's about to happen.

Plus, I happen to enjoy casinos.

"Nah, I happen to enjoy casinos," I told the lad. Dimwitted and wide-eyed as he was, he believed the shit he was shoveling to be worth its weight in gold. I felt sorry for him, almost. I would have felt sorry for him, if it weren't for the fact that he was most likely a practicing Mormon trying to earn merit points with his church by taking away other people's fun.

The kid stopped dead in his tracks. He seemed momentarily taken aback by my response. Nobody had ever told him "nah" before, I guess. In Mormon culture, they probably say something ostentatious, like, "Thank you, but I have a prior commitment to serve the spirit of the lord Jesus Christ, in the form of some savage Indian spirits who swore revenge on the Jews for killing him, so I am going to politely go and do that, but I respect your feedback and hope you have a wonderful and awe-inspiring time of it today!"

And in fact, the kid *could* have said these things to me, and I would've accepted it and moved along with my plot of daytime drunkenness. Everything could have been resolved peacefully. You let me continue walking into the store so I can purchase some mildly-priced alcohol in quantity, and leave me the hell alone, and everything will be fine. But, no.

Once he regained his composure (probably reassuring himself, on a truly bestial level, that he wasn't, in fact, about to vomit all over his pretty shoes from the feeling, borne from the sheer horror and absolute dread inculcated in his gut at my negative response), he pulled his wits together, and then made the biggest mistake of his life:

"Hey, would you like to sign my petition to legalize meth?" Now, there are few things that rile me like it being suggested that I am a habitual amphetamine abuser. I don't care much for being called a child molester. I hate it when people whistle around me. And I can't stand realtors. But, of all of these things, probably the most statistically significant amount of vitriol and hate I have reserved is for those who try and label me as some kind of a goddamned drug abuser.

Now, it was *my* turn to seize up for a second, paralyzed by this sense of uncertainty about what I should do next. I should live several lifetimes and never again encounter such a blatant assault on my sense of personal dignity. I like drinking, and I love gambling, but I HATE meth. Why, then, did this young man feel morally entitled to condemn me as being such a triple-conjunctive of deviancy? My fun never hurt anyone, and if some morons lose all their money at the Casino and want to cry home about how unfair it is, knowing full well that the odds were against them that entire time, so what? If they really wanted to "win" on an intellectual basis they would have hired an investing professional to manage their assets with a stable rate of return of about 7%, and spent the rest of their lives clipping coupons and going out golfing during free, or heavily discounted, recruitment weekends of the local country club. OR, they would have gambled away maybe five bucks in the nickel slots, earned enough to convince the bartender to spin them up a quick libation from the well selection, and then "win" a free cruise on Norwegian Cruise Lines, inside stateroom with no view, no meals or drinks included, still justifying that as a noteworthy discount, bring the wife and call it a vacation, and spend *more* than they otherwise would have on a *real* vacation to an *actual* place.

So I don't excuse that sort of rationalization, not for a second. They knew they were going to lose when they set foot on the gaming floor, unless Luck was on their side. Luck will show up, but spontaneously, and you very much can't count on it if you want to be a professional gambler. Unless you're going to cheat, or just play poker and hope your skills really are all that and can outlast a thousand other bros who think their card-playing shit don't stink, you have to enter the casino environment with an open mind and a willingness to lose money.

I couldn't explain any of this to Kid King-Dipshit, of course. I hadn't had a drink yet that day, which makes me terse and unable to articulate such evolved thoughts. Also, it wasn't *my* job to educate the lad. His Mormon schooling should've taken care of that, since I'm sure his parents thought he was too good for regular ol' public school.

So, I was pinched into a spot; I couldn't let the slight go unacknowledged; but, I felt, justifiably, that we were at a critical juncture in local history. This impasse was not going to get resolved through dialogue.

I then did what any rational-minded citizen would do in such a predicament: I decked him. And I'm not talking about a little love-tap. I broke his fucking jaw; I imploded the bottom left quadrant of his face with a strong right hook. He never saw it coming. I felt the bone shatter beneath my knuckles. I knew that my drinking habit would cause my hand to become partially degloved, from the loss of quality in my skin; and sure enough, a big bad red patch of exposed soft tissues went streaking down the back of my fist, almost all the way to the wrist. But it was worth it.

The Mormon moron was screaming and hollering and had blood and snot drizzling down what was left of his chin within seconds. He was struggling to use his words; a combination of shock and sheer physical damage to his mouth got in the way of his telling me how much a bad, bad person I was.

Everyone around us, all the little old ladies doing their weekly shopping, all the drunk losers trying to trade food stamps for beer, all the uptight middle class dads buying birthday cakes for their kids' soccer team captain's dog's birthdays, and indeed, every other person who observed what had just transpired (who wasn't even there for Safeway, but one of the minor outlying businesses of the shopping plaza instead), all stopped and squinted and furrowed their brows for half a second, interpreting the beautiful event that had just transpired. And then, they all simultaneously broke out into applause.

The parking lot was wired with loudspeakers, apparently, because just then the theme song from *Star Trek: The New Generation* began playing. And as it did so, the applause grew louder; more townsfolk gathered around me, cheering the incredible thing I'd just accomplished, embracing me as the hero they never before knew they needed.

The employees of Safeway then emerged from the store entrance. The manager led the crew, followed by two stockboys, each carrying a case of craft beer. The citizens of the parking lot beckoned me, *come, let us lift you onto our shoulders!* And before I knew it, I was riding highest amongst all those gathered. The manager had a look of sheer delight; under his thick glasses and mustache, he smiled, and gave me a big THUMBS UP. The assistant manager presented me with a ribbon, and a trophy, and a certificate of honor, also promising me all the booze I could drink for a year. Eager volunteers quickly loaded the beer into my car.

Apparently, the Mormon kid was some local asswipe who had been harassing their customers for many, many months before I confronted him. Nobody before had been that brave, that daring, that willing to risk the possibility of being charged with felony assault. But the kid had fled, along with his stupid petitions and poor attitude; for the moment, for that one afternoon, before I finally accomplished what I had set out to do and obtained my reasonably-priced Vodka and headed home to drink irresponsibly in a controlled setting, and forget all about it, for that one fleeting second I was a. Genuine. Fucking. Hero.

SO, AGAINST ALL ODDS, I HAD FINALLY made my way to Oslo. The Norwegians really weren't any help. The whole time, getting through their border controls, they were all like, "Wampa lampa der lipa lupa?" And I was all like, "Oompa Loompa?" back to them, because Roald Dahl was Norwegian, after all; or, at least, he was of Norwegian breed, even though he lived in Wales. And that's all I knew. It's not like they didn't know English; I know they did, the bastards, trying to pretend like they were all superior because they're some pointless country in Europe that rich people like to be seen in one week a year to prove they're significant.

By the time I got to Norway, I was almost broke. I had been sleeping in my car before I left. I'd sold my drumset, my birds, and some VIP passes to the virgin asshole of my youngest foster child. I wasn't planning on coming back to America anytime soon, but even then, it was an impossibly expensive project. I didn't even know Norway *had* an airport.

So I had like five bucks left, or *kroner*, and that wasn't enough for much of a weapon. I ended up buying a cheap hand pump for inflating bike tires from a second hand shop. It was about sixty years old and made of solid tin. It would have to work; at the very least, I figured, I could impale Bezos with it and declare my victory, just like that guy who wrote the book *Uniform of a Maniac*, that had a very quotable passage where he had just committed the perfect kill, and spoke of being baptized in blood, in some kind of pagan tradition. So, it was appropriate.

I had spent most of my money, to be honest, bribing a photographer for TMZ to give me Bezos' hotel and room number. I pretended that I was a covert journalist, a hack for freedom who was reporting from ground zero about the hypocritical acts of the rich and famous when they're trying to pretend like they want to make the world a better place. He agreed, on the basis that:

- I wouldn't have a camera on me, not even a smartphone. Mercenary-with-a-DSLR dude made me promise I wouldn't blow up his spot as an exclusive. The guy had to blow one of Bezos' executive VPs in order to get the information. He wasn't gay, but he was willing to take a load in the mouth for his passion, his profession. The guy whose dick he had sucked had AIDS.
- I wouldn't scare Bezos away. I had to be real low-key, pretend to be a local, a troll-hunter or something. Don't make eye contact, don't go in for an interview, etc.
- I wouldn't disclose anything about anyone who may have told me about Bezos' whereabouts, even if Amazon's top tier security interrogation team got ahold of me. They could tape my eyes open and force me to read pop-Christian self-help books on Kindle for 40 hours and I still swore not to tell.
- I wouldn't use mustard anywhere close to Bezos' room, because he hated it, and he'd immediately know about the entire plot.

So, with all of these conditions in mind, I made my approach. I had also bought an *Inspector Gadget* style trenchcoat, and fedora, and a blonde mustache. Why was I trying to conceal my identity when I fully intended on being apprehended? It just seemed *right*. A clandestine mission to rectify all the wrongs in this fucked-up world. A way to proclaim the seriousness of my intent through the lying, scheming, wagging tongues of the international media. *I* was a player now.

The Norwegians didn't bother me on my way up to the twenty-seventh floor. But one of them, a little man in an elf-costume, gestured frantically at a light-fixture overhanging the hallway, from which there was a chorus of the most awful screeching you'd never want to hear again so long as you still have ears. I knew the sound, all right. It was cockatiels. The Norwegian elf looked horrified, and managed to say with a stutter,

"Bird... masturbation." And wouldn't you know it, but he was right. The horny little bastard bird was grinding away on the exposed metal plate of the high-efficiency lightbulb's base, squawking its head off. Disgusting.

Not to be distracted, I went to Bezos' room door. I figured I was going to have to wait for him to emerge, anxious and hungry no doubt, probably wanting a peanut butter and banana sandwich with bacon (but on the side) like all these wannabe rockstar rich assholes do; but out of boredom, I just tried the door handle, and it wasn't even locked. *Smug bastard, thinking he would be safe in Norway, of all places.* So, I just walked right in.

Nothing could have prepared me for the sight before me. I had to shut the door behind me because *I* was embarrassed by what was taking place, right in front of my poor, blurry eyes: it was Jeffrey Bezos. In a diaper, and a baby bonnet. Nothing else. He had a pacifier stuck firmly between his lips. One of those over-the-top novelty style suckers that E-tards of the mid-to-late 2000s used to nibble on while rolling around at raves. He was sitting, cross-legged, in the enormous regal canopy bed, no doubt constructed of some old-growth, extinct variant of Norwegian Spruce. Sitting, and holding a baby rattle. There was a bib and a bottle lying on the bed next to him.

Bezos looked up at me, concernedly. I stood there, frozen, the bike pump going limp in my hands. There was a rustling in the other room of the suite. A woman emerged, wearing a housedress, apron, and knee-length vinyl boots.

Bezos looked over from me, to her, and then back to me. The pacifier suddenly dropped from his mouth. He sat there with his mouth wide open, and then started to cry.

"Baby made a mess for mommy!" Bezos declared, sobbingly. I had my serious doubts that he was at *all* sorry, though. This was some adult-baby roleplaying shit; I'd heard about these people but never before encountered them in their natural state.

"Naughty!" The mommy hollered back at her small child. Bezos was an ugly man, but he made for a downright *hideous* baby. This woman couldn't be getting paid enough.

Still, I believed that he *had* actually pissed and/or shat into his diaper, and that he now fully expected this woman to clean it all up, probably wipe his ass down with wet-naps and sprinkle some powder all over his balls while she was at it, too. Such are the lifestyles of the rich. They always count on being able to pay someone to straighten everything up for them, even when the mess in question was a result of their own poor behavior.

The woman brushed right past me. "What have you done now? Do you not realize how much mommy has to deal with in her life without having to clean baby?" And with that, she pounced on Bezos, laid him out on his belly with great haste, ripped the ass off the diaper and sent it flying across the room (just a small stream of piss flowing out from it, thankfully), and proceeded to spank him, bare-handed.

"Baby's sorry! Baby's sorry!" Bezos yelled. It wasn't saving him from his punishment; but then, that's what he must have *wanted*. As the woman continued to slap his bare, pimpled ass-cheeks, she casually looked over at me. "And what are you wanting here?"

"I– uh..." I looked down at the bike pump. "Bicycle mechanic?" I tried. "I was sent by the Nobel Prize Committee to help Mr. Bezos get his bicycle ready for the awards ceremony."

"Nobel?" The woman guffawed. [And here's where everything falls apart. You see, I had planned, in a really haphazard, having this idea-of-a-just-dessert-ending within the last 48 hours sort of conceptualization, where "I," the me, the Id, the Ego, all of it, caught Bezos in the act of something unspeakably humiliating and hilarious, just to get lectured by his Norwegian hired-dominatrix-mommy-roleplay-acolyte that I had fucked up, and confused the Nobel Peace Prize Ceremony (conducted in Oslo) with the rest of the Nobel Prizes (awarded in Stockholm), not to mention the fact that Alfred Nobel himself was a Swede, so what the fuck would he be doing commemorating some asshole in Norway? But at the last minute, as I was about to wrap this all up so nicely, with a perfect ending to what may somehow approximate a story arc, I got all caught up in thinking that these distinctly distinguished institutions of high society were being conducted *on separate days*, and that this silly woman would correct me about it and reveal me to be a small-penis-wielding, continually-limp-dicked moron who thought I had it all figured out, to tell me to come back some months later when the Oslo part of the ritual was being conducted. Then, immediately before I committed to writing this final passage of what will unfortunately remain forever the first and only chapter of the otherwise stupendous novel *Uncle Shmarmlucus*, I learnt that, although the Nobel Prize is awarded in *both* cities, it is done *on the same day*, December 10, Nobel's birthday, or death-day (I don't remember which, I am so upset), which is TODAY, the very day I am writing these words, December 10, 2020; and I didn't even realize it until I looked it up on Wikipedia. Who won? Was there even a celebration? Did people attend? Where the hell is Jeff Bezos right now, anyway? I'd love to know. I still want to kill, or at least, mildly assault him.]

Uncle Sharles Levarticus

A Novel

Chapter I

HOWARD, OR HOWARD THE DUCK, AS THE KIDS would call him, often left his wallet behind in his trailer so that, should he be intercepted by the authorities during one of his peeping tom sexcapades, he could claim his dead half-brother's identity as his own, and *maybe* get away with it. He was a sun-scarred, wrinkled, white-haired fiftysomething man who tried his best to appear intimidating, even though he stood 5'6" and was out of shape by more than a few years.

"Yes, hi. I know, my eyes are itching again," Howard explained to the expert on the call center hotline. "It doesn't matter if they're open or closed."

"Did you recently peer closely through some kind of a looking device?"

"Uh, yeah, I did. I got these binoculars that I use once a week, at least —"

"Do you clean your optical looking devices?" Howard wasn't going to admit that, one time, a few weeks ago, a bird had taken a shit right on top of his binoculars-case as he was opening it up while he was strategically hidden among the bushes, so the naked young women at the naughty beach wouldn't notice him; but, he'd almost slipped up and told the bird to GO FUCK YOUR FEATHERED SELF. He didn't, but what he *did* do (which he was absolutely not going to admit to this random stranger on the other end of the hotline, who was, in all likelihood, not even an American citizen), was something completely inappropriate, but fully in character: immediately following the birdshit incident, he whipped his pecker out (not like he wasn't going to do that already) and took a quick little piss on the outer lenses of his binocs, wiped them down, and then proceeded to leer through the still-streaky mixture of birdshit and urine.

"Sir? Your optical looking devices?"

"No, I mean, my friend does, and once he let me use them to look at a butt— a butterfly."

"Oooh, I love butterflies!" the Indian man on the other end of the hotline said. "So pretty, with so many colors, I just want to oooh, ahhhh, *catch* them all and pin them to my collective wall!"

"Do you think I have a butterfly allergy?" Howard asked, alarmed.

"No sir, I do not think you can have an allergy to a butterfly."

Howard wasn't sure. He'd met an entomologist once who wanted to hike through the forest where Howard and his wife, Meredith, would spend their summers hosting ungrateful campers, lousy urban types who didn't belong in this lovely, white, small-town village in western Massachusetts. The bug doctor wanted to have a looky-loo around to see if he could spot any unusual specimens.

Howard noticed something strange as soon as he started driving the man along one of the abandoned logging roads that snaked through the dense mixed forest. Hundreds of little critters, moths and butterflies, started swarming the golf cart. Howard grew panicked, as he had felt uncomfortable in general around these kinds of insects ever since he learned there was a type of moth that liked to suck on birds' eye juices while they were asleep. He began frantically swatting around his head, trying to clear a line of sight enough to not drive off the path and kill them both.

The bug doc chuckled. "You probably wonder why they're following us around so?"

"No, I just— can't— uhhh, see—"

"I'll let you in on a little secret. They're here to fuck me! I started playing around with pheromones in the lab some years back. We'd milk the little buggers dry of their jizz, and then my wife and I would take turns painting one another's faces with it, cooing and calling each other our beautiful butterflies, and then ripping our pants off so I could mount her like a stallion, right there on top of the bug display case. We were horny pretty much constantly, as well as being completely ripped on acid in those days, right? But turns out it's actually really stupid to play with insect semen like that, because it never washes off! And for the rest of my natural life, everywhere I go, Monarchs and Swallowtails and Luna Moths will be swarming me, trying to make sweet love to my face! Ha ha!"

Howard froze in fear. He didn't want this little Indian man on the telephone hotline to know *any* of this. But he had a bad feeling that the little Indian man already knew.

"Howard, my friend. I already know about the butterflies," the voice said, coyly.

"ONE TIME HE MADE A GIANT PICKLE for Thanksgiving, instead of a turkey," she explained triumphantly. "Nobody knew what to say. It was about three feet long, it was grayish-brown, it had spots and it was served piping hot."

"Yeah, and, and I heard that he writes bad poetry, too." And he *did* write poetry, terrible poetry, like the kind that can't even rhyme even though it's piled upon with gibberish words. For instance:

> *The Dysentopes were extravagant*
> *As they smiled in the parking lot, strangers*
> *Arrived a lot. Stranded stragglers,*
> *And I ask myself, is this a vapid terpitation?*
> *Or just some kind of mild frustration?*
> *It's a sharmlication, but really*
> *It's just a small location.*

Shit like this really rankled the poor slobs who happened to be exposed to it, day in, day out. Running around without any makeup on, she continued, breathlessly:

"He *would* do a stupid thing like that. I wonder, sometimes, if he knows how much we all hate him." He probably didn't, and that was the reason he would do foolish things like attempting to serve a pickle for Thanksgiving dinner. It just didn't work that way, not even for a poor Lithuanian Jew immigrant whose normal meal would consist of shoelaces, served with a fine reduction of glue sauce, reclaimed from cardboard boxes. He drank away his own concerns, and those of the others around him, as well.

"I don't think I'll ever go to his house again," she sighed. Of course, she was wrong; she knew full well that once that month's welfare check had run out, three days after the first, several gallons of cheap whiskey, a carton of cigarettes and being chased out of a trashed hotel room by some angry Indians later, she'd be back groveling for a place to stay. And he would allow it; he would not mind the company as he spent all night delicately repotting succulent cuttings stolen from the neighbors' yard waste piles, refrigerating leftover dirt, filling up the drinking glasses in every cabinet in the kitchen with various samples drawn from different iterations of compost tea, or excess runoff from overwatering the wretched weeds.

"How do you cut a pickle?" she asked.

"Just grit your teeth and bear it, I guess. It was a giant, awful thing. About eighteen inches thick. Disgusting, the way it glistened so sickeningly. Ruined the whole day. Thank god we were all drunk."

"I heard he threw Cammie into the recycling."

"Shhhh. That's just gossip." But everybody knew that he did, and what was more, that she belonged there, because it was his house, he was drunk, and he'd fuck whoever he wanted.

THEY WERE DOING THE ANNUAL Gibberish Movie Festival. Some of the features that were playing this year:

- *Deshengu Latch-a-lacha*: Some mereglicant named "Deshengu" goes on a shulacka for duck shoes. It's scripted in its native language (pure Gibberish), and stars Galacky Monfrelu in his triumphant return to the big screen for the fist time in eight years.

- *Shlop*. This modified-Gibberish picture depicts one Shkleky Bershuda on his quest to find recheglicanation. Billed as an "alt-comedy," there is also a dramatic story arc wherein Gregladew, the love interest, is stricken with nipple cancer and must undergo an experimental treatment where live shorluphages are applied to the lacerated nipple wounds, in order to troplicate Gregladew's microtumors.

- *Snorvelastions*. A few snorvy Mutilatoids end up lingering around a small town after their transporter crashes. A song-and-dance number mostly delivered expressively (with a minor reliance upon minimal Gibberish), this sci-fi romp is both family fun (the little Mutilatoid is a show-stealing cutester), and slightly horrifying (the adult Mutilatoids feed upon dog viscera, regurgitate it for their offspring, and violently murder any humans interfering with their canine-hunting routine).

- *In a Shmikes-maree!* Another musical. Shmikel, a character from some stupid cartoon, had tried to host a telethon, for Don, and has a hell of a time getting people to answer the telephone once Longmont Potion Castle gets ahold of their hotline number and proceeds to wreak havoc. Guest starring Amini Caruleearmination. It is presented in marginal-Gibberish.

- *Lochaleashtion.* This was a work of complete and utter Gibberish, where Klocky Maph was gorrelleging down Rellyahop Slit, and Berchanger D'lop came and sprashlicated a bief of pulonga galee. Everyone's certain it's going to sweep the awards this year.

- *The Unrestrunchtables.* Rated "F" for being completely fucked, this semi-Gibberish film depicts a die-hard team of top-tier trochlicants as they aspire to reach a higher plane of existence, through martial combat video game technology (with touchscreens!). The saddest part of the film is when you find out that Cloppy, one of the trochlicants on the ill-fated mission, used to be an actual person who played football in high school.

And then, there was a serious movie. Billed as *Marzuck, a Millipede Duck*, the hour-and-a-half long documentary follows a balding, pudgy, middle-aged man with a mustache who has a pet duck named Marzuck, which he is obsessing over feeding a millipede, in order for the millipede to become embedded in Marzuck's bowels, and then continue living, and feeding upon whatever may end up in the duck's digestive tract that a millipede may care to eat. Critics have called it "bold" and "*Fly Away Home* meets *The Human Centipede.*" One of the high points of the film comes when Marzuck's owner goes to a local avian biologist's office and presents his outlandish theory. The expert, a professor at the Pathetic Flower University, is stunned to hear the man rambling on about live millipedes taking up residence in a duck's intestines. He then takes a moment to compose himself, chuckles and shakes his head ever so slightly, to-and-fro, and comments snidely that, "I think all that would happen would be that Marzuck would get a tasty and healthy treat," if the man fed his pet duck the millipede.

Millipede-rights activists didn't concur. They felt like the picture was a slight against their movement, *specifically*, and threatened to boycott any movie theatre that would dare show such a piece of trash. Others took a more aggressive stance in protest; a fundamentalist cell of the group launched an attack on one particular venue, where members snuck in cartons of millipedes that they proceeded to throw at audience members, right at the climax of the movie where the bald man is losing his mind over Marzuck's refusal to allow a living millipede to enter his gut, and has already grown bloated from eating over a thousand of the small arthropods, until finally, having stooped to his knees and thrown his hands up to the sky in sheer frustration, the man looks over at Marzuck, who has assumed a sitting position with his ass pointed directly at his owner, and the man notices a millipede sticking its head out of the duck's vent, wagging back and forth and trying to make sense of its predicament.

Anyway, some brain-tumor lady was about to have a stroke over all of this. And Smiles Shinderson was calling.

SOMEONE TRIED TO MAKE A TELEPHONE CALL. "Hello, yes?"

"Hello?"

"Is this Taco Bell?"

"No, it's Burger King." Burger King had just been elected the absolute worst fast food restaurant chain that people hated, *ever*, in the history of asking people which fast food restaurant chains they hated.

"Oh. I didn't really want to talk to Burger King," the guy said, wavering between contempt and anger.

"Can I help you?"

"I wanted to know if I come in there, can I get a soda to go?"

"Yes." Really, what the hell kind of a question was that?

"But now, here's the thing," the guy who placed the questionable telephone call in the first place continued, drolly. "If I come in there, and I order a small cup of soda— how much is in the small?"

"Sixteen ounces."

"Yeah. If I ask for just a small soda to go, then you're going to laugh at me, aren't you?"

"What?"

"You sound like the kind of girl who would laugh at me for ordering a small soda."

"Are you for real?"

"Promise me you won't laugh." He was getting agitated, and sexually aroused, at the same time.

"This isn't, you, you aren't— do I know you?"

"No. You don't know me. I'm just a stranger. I'll always be just a stranger!"

"I'm calling the cops," and with that, the fantasy was over. He wasn't actually brave enough to go into a Burger King (and he knew full well, the entire time, that it was Burger King he was calling, and *not* Taco Bell, but he wanted to call a fast food restaurant that had two distinct words in its name, not one that was just someone's last name, or a place like Carl's Junior, which wasn't even franchised in the local market area; but, for reasons of plausible deniability, the caller needed to have an excuse for getting the names of two very distinct fast food chain restaurants confused, and therefore, he needed something that was a name comprised of two proper nouns, and these were the only two that somewhat matched, although, that being said, he could have just as easily dialed a Taco Bell, and pretended like he actually meant to be calling Burger King, and kept the charade going for another night, but the consumer reviewing agency he believed in had just ranked Burger King as worst, worse even than Taco Bell, so that's where he went with this whole thing) and order a small soda, or even a regular soda or a combo meal with french fries. He knew for a fact that girl and all her teenaged friends would be laughing uproariously the entire time, even if it was just a brief interaction going through the drive-through window.

He had the idea to come dressed in a trenchcoat, with nothing on underneath, and stroke himself in the parking lot for fifteen minutes *before* he tried to place an order, just to reveal his erect penis to these ungrateful girls at the last second when they were about to hand him the food. His friends, when they were younger, would stockpile bags of the cheapest shit they could order off the menu at any given fast food establishment; then, every other Friday night, they would proceed to pelt all the workers at said restaurant with the crappy, soggy, sorry excuse for cuisine they'd previously bagged up and sold. His friends would laugh, and cuss out the workers, who they felt were beneath themselves intrinsically, by merit of the fact that their parents had bought them cars in exchange for exacting small promises out of them, like promising to not flick their boogers at the television screen during dinner, and putting their poopy underwear into the laundry hamper, and not just leaving soiled drawers strewn about the hallways of the family residence.

But now that the caller was older, and wiser, he decided that a better tactic would be to wave his uncircumcised pecker around like it meant something. However, he was man constantly stricken with shame, so he did not do this. Instead, he just used euphemisms like "small soda" to ascertain whether or not a young woman would give him a hard time (no pun intended) for having a slightly below-average dick. There were freckles on it, too, even though he didn't sunbathe in the nude, and also, the veins would pop out and press themselves against his foreskin whenever he'd get excited down there.

Sometimes, the caller realized, it's better to just assume that people don't want anything to do with you, than to actually present yourself for the repulsive degenerate you actually are, to be judged publicly for it, and risk having to come to terms with your own decrepitude.

"THE SLUNCH OF LAURETIA"

Was the name of a character featured on a program, or should it be spelled, *programme*, that was cobbled together by a few undergraduate students in the hopes of impressing their professor, an aspiring independent filmmaker who was never quite able to write even so much a short script, or learn the technical details of camera operation, *or* have the capacity to direct actors in any manner (not like anyone would actually show up to the few casting calls that had been advertised, sadly, on Craigslist).

Anyway, they had the idea over lunch one afternoon, to make a parody of the workday lunch ritual. They entered into the lobby of the establishment that was making itself available for their poor imitation of the workday lunchtime ritual, past the official greeter, who was mentally handicapped, and had a fun little song to be singing:

"OHHH, SHARNESHTA! Why-do-you-do-these-things-to-me?"

[Which was of course, to be sung in the patented retard falsetto. He once had tried to make a bit more sense of things, in terms of these random outbursts, by asking a hipster girl he kind of liked if she was down with forming a noise-rock band called the "United Snakes of Pie Thieves." She promptly fled, screaming in horror at his abject retardation.]

One of those meeting for lunch, or should it be more appropriately termed, *slunch* (and why it was determined that was a more appropriate way of describing the shared meal to which these two were about to sit down, is better left unexplained for now, since, in the current company, that being you, the reader, it is neither prudent nor fair to your own limited intellectual capacity to get into the minutiae of higher-level terminology at this juncture), had taken the time to write some poetry:

These are the names of monsters
And they, the faces of the guilty
For it is simpler to be just a vague liar
And eat your regret with the milk
Of your earnings
Since nothing is now come
To save us from ourselves
Down here on the floor
Of reactor number four

Of course, poetry was something that was reserved for those who did not know how to properly play with their lunches. Some children, during the grade school years (when they weren't being taken into a broom closet to be sodomized), were too uptight to have fun during lunchtime, and actually play with their food: steal condiments from the cafeteria, make margarine sandwiches and feed them to the weird kid, and overall learn and develop the true moral fiber of a real American.

Lauretia was the title of her poem book that she was composing, after the name of one of those uncles from the "League of Lunch" series. Hardly anyone remembered about this limited run show, however, so it wasn't particularly relevant to anything. She was hoping that the person she'd be meeting for slunch would be in publishing. This book, she felt sure of, was going to be a complete game-changer for the industry. Poetry had grown dull and predictable; she wrote words that actually tried to look like they were saying *something*, without going through all the effort to actually be profound.

It was toilet-back poetry, the sort of book that boring people with too much disposable income have displayed semi-prominently in their bathrooms, along with toilet seat cozies and candles shaped like the Virgin Mary (to be light on those nasty times right after taco night when the stench of fecal matter emanates from every crevice). It might as well have been written on a long roll of TP. It would be more useful to most people to have these poems conveniently presented in a format with which they could also wipe their asses.

Anyway, the erstwhile poet wasn't ever going to actually meet up with her intended slunch-date. You see, he had been killed from being impaled by a poopsicle on the way to the retard-restaurant. [Poopsicles happen when a stream of diarrhea is suddenly ejected from a passing passenger airliner. Airline regulations strictly require that any loose stool is immediately evacuated from the aircraft, as that could be indicative of an imminent outbreak of the norovirus. So, the offending bowel movement is shunted off into an emergency poop-chute, where it is released at cruising altitude, immediately freezing solid into a shape most resembling an icicle, and then plummeting back to earth at free-fall speeds.] So he was instead being replaced by someone's friend, who would do obnoxious things like invent made-up holidays on other peoples' birthdays so that it would distract and detract from any sense of joy or celebration this guy's unfortunate friends may be expecting to experience on their most special of days. He would spout off some gibberish and make it sound somewhat legitimate, and then claim religious significance in order to coerce people into abandoning well-laid plans for the birthday bash in order to lead a solemn and incoherent procession to what he claimed to be a high holy site of consecrated tradition. Usually, it was an Indian casino.

But the man who would try and steal other peoples' birthdays with made-up nonsense wasn't the point of the scene and setting. In fact, he wasn't even so relevant as to have been given a proper name.

The poet, however, very much *did* have a name: Pretty Polly Poopsicle-Megantic (in honor of the recent tragedy involving her actual friend that she was supposed to be meeting for slunch on this fateful day). And the guy who liked to try and steal other peoples' birthdays *also* was a writer, of sorts. He had written and gotten published such books as:

Thank You, Michael Braeshtion

That's Enough, Michael Braeshtion

Stop It, Michael Braeshtion

Goodbye, Michael Braeshtion

"Don't write it too well," he would tell himself, constantly. "They might get excited if they think the story's going somewhere. They're going to feel all self-righteous and proud that they actually read something *interesting* for once, and then there goes our profits! Nobody's going to buy any of the other books!" And sure enough, some of his readers would accost him, randomly, on the sidewalk, as he was dodging out-of-control bicyclists, and in airport terminals, as he'd be trying to covertly use a payphone to make a bomb threat using a poorly imitated Arabic accent.

"Excuse me! EXCUSE ME! What do you think you're doing?" one girl had asked him, indignantly.

"What?" he asked, in utter disbelief and confusion. [Well, except it *was* all planned and orchestrated, for being otherwise an improper and highly confrontational conversation to be having with a stranger; but, he felt the need to act out the part, as he never was entirely sure what he was supposed to be, in a creative sense— a writer of mediocre books with common and relatable characters throughout the whole series, or maybe he should have been an off-broadway actor, highly trained in improvisational humor. We shall never know how he may have faired, should he have given up being a novelist and instead pursued his very queer daydream of becoming a thespian.]

"Those books, the Michael Braeshtion ones," she continued, accusatorially. "Don't you realize what kind of harm you have been causing, to the youth? Didn't you know how that might confuse them, about the true meaning of MICHAELPAN?" He hadn't thought much about it, to be honest. He was pangnostic, and didn't care about the cult of MICHAELPAN or any of its adherents. He did know that someone, at some point, tried to rally all the Michaels of the world in support of MICHAELPAN, in order to bring about the Great Michaeling, but that was mostly discussed in the pages of supermarket tabloids, and not the haute society magazines to which Mr. Birthday Thief subscribed.

"No. Do you know who I am?" he asked the disheveled young woman.

"No. Do you know who I am?" she responded, by asking the same question, which was a terrible and extraordinarily lazy thing to do to any writer. Neither one actually knew the other person, though, and she was, moreover, interrupting his fake-bomb-threat-in-the-airport time, which was a special monthly event that this guy never wanted to miss, because it was so hilariously disruptive for all the average morons to have to get bum-rushed by machine-gun wielding Homeland Security apparatchiks, and watch as they trampled over one another in a frantic stampede down all the escalators and moving walkways just to spill out into the poorly designed traffic oval heavily populated by predatory cabs and Uber drivers; and each time he would do this, at least four prepubescent children would get hit, run over, and dragged a few football fields' distance down the asphalt, going unnoticed until the panicked masses would stop and reevaluate themselves, an arbitrary distance away from what they felt to be a safe blast radius from the non-existent bomb.

It was frustrating, though, that not only did he not know the crazed girl who may or may not have a pistol concealed inside her skinny jeans (it was actually a penis), he never actually *would* get to know her, sexually or otherwise. And she hadn't even read *part* of a *Michael Braeshtion* book; she had evidently just been told by somebody, who may or may not have been a North Korean double agent, that this guy had written these books, which were problematic for so many reasons, and couldn't she just walk up to him and harass him for a bit? Please?

Pretty Polly Poopsicle-Megantic didn't know about any of this stuff that had happened to her tardy Slunch partner, at some point prior to their meeting; she probably wouldn't have cared, even if she had known about it. All that she had been told was, once her actual friend had been killed in the poopsicle incident, that this replacement companion had a nasty habit of making shit up in order to ruin peoples' birthday parties. So, even if he had tried to tell her about any of this nonsense involving screaming at airport security screeners and secretly filming stupid girls flushing their emotional support dwarf hamsters down the toilet while he was suppressing an uproarious fit of laughter, she wouldn't have believed him, first of all, and certainly *would not* have actively listened, or passively listened, either; she would have mentally disappeared into some earbuds and screamed for the PC Police to come and arrest this man for being imbecilic in front of a lady. No woman deserved to be subjected to this level of mumbling bullshit and non-sequitur marksmanship. Not in today's modern era, no way, no sir, no ma'am, no whatever-gender-ambiguous-thing-you-are-today-with-a-cherry-on-top, you're not!

"Uhm, I actually wrote a thing about how much Shlurpis Dermit sucks," she said, unconvincingly. Saying that was *so* last yesterday, anyhow.

And it wasn't Shlurpis's fault in the first place that he sucked. He had simply gone down to the Bureau of Bureaus and Departments one day in order to resolve a procedural mistake that had led them to question his legal status, and he was commanded to bring paperwork to prove that he was, in fact, a real person. There was a small misunderstanding wherein he presented a used Tastycake cream-filled cupcake wrapper instead of his social security card (which was a completely honest mistake, have you ever noticed how similar they look?), and he was immediately remanded to custody and charged with minor terrorism.

Pretty Polly had no business commenting on Shlurpis's affairs, yet she, being a cutthroat journalist with a bloodthirsty desire to climb the ladder into the upper echelons of the editorial department, dived deeply into the whole sordid affair, conducted countless hours of interviews (247 hours, to be exact), and double-checked all the cross-references and even hired a professional schizophrenic to write down all the facts on 3x5 inch index cards and stick them with thumbtacks onto a corkboard, with 24 different colors of yarn connecting the imaginary logical pathways that connected all the parts of the puzzle in order to form a solution.

And the solution was that Shlurpis Dermit sucks. That was all Pretty Polly Poopsicle-Megantic had to write for the leading story in the Summerhaven Crypto-Shopper's Sunday featurette. Some people were very disappointed that it took her nine months to reach such a basic conclusion, so she was fired for cause, and that was what led her to this particular slunch where she was supposed to interview as a personal assistant for a real writer, who had real, deeply repressed, sexual needs, that Pretty Polly was slated to satisfy with her primp lips and plump little rump, except for the complication that arose when the original writer was killed in the aforementioned airplane poop mishap.

It was all okay, though. It was about to be over. Pretty Polly was going to get arrested and charged with grand arsony, because Firefighter Bob had agreed to wear a wire and implicate her in a plot that he had actually masterminded, naturally. But, since Pretty Polly was a journalist, and the government doesn't care for journalists, she had to go.

And, she was gone.

"DID ANYBODY EVER TELL YOU ABOUT Poop Soup?" No, thankfully, nobody had– *yet*. There was a growing fear that someone was about to, though.

And sure enough, they did. Poop Soup. The original recipe was focused mainly on goose diarrhea, as it was promoted as a sort of French delicacy (actually, it was just a cheap ploy to capitalize on the very abundant byproduct caused through the production of *Foie Gras*, since the geese would shit out all the feed that was forced down their gullets, all over the place, and they had to hire a deformed man named Philippe to shovel it all up into a pile so it could be properly disposed of, in the river; well, Philippe had other plans for all the goose poop, and decided he could instead market it as a magical elixir that would be good for horses and the people who owned and rode and groomed them, and at first, it was an abject failure, since Philippe had tried to disguise it as "humus collected from the seven sacred vortices of the continental mainframe" and everybody knew that it was absolute gooseshit, so after he'd been cursed at and spit on in the local farmer's market for five Saturdays in a row, he just shrugged, crossed out the label, and replaced it with a crude drawing of a goose having an explosive bowel emergency, *then* people felt satisfied that they weren't being lied to, that this was, in fact, diarrhea collected from a flock of overfed geese, they relaxed, and were content in buying the product, which didn't work as advertised), but after several celebrity chefs found out and took it over and tried to claim ownership over the diarrhea derivatives, naturally other animal sources needed to be found for optimal exploitation of the growing fad.

Poop Soup was a catch-all solution to deliver affordable, edible fecal matter to the masses. The inventors would take random pieces of crap from any place they could, and liquefy it, which made it safe for old people and babies to consume. Then, it would be conveniently dispensed from a device that somewhat resembled a soft-serve machine, operated by a disinterested teenager at one of a multitude of locations, both franchised and company-owned.

It was created first and foremost by a pioneering entrepreneur, a man who was one half of a gay couple, and had what some would perceive as a bizarre hobby: he would collect stool samples, from various individuals and animals, often stooping down while walking along the street in order to carefully and delicately swab and document each fecal example, which would then be cataloged by card in a very large and bulbous portfolio that this guy would be carrying around with him, at all times. He had managed to accumulate a small library's worth of poop when he had the inspiration to steal Philippe's conniving scam and turn it into a hugely successful business. He had an advantage, of course, because he had a diverse research database from which to calculate precise ratios and combinations of scat in order to derive the ideal flavor profiles for each featured "Poop Soup of the Day."

The man's investors were so overjoyed and confident in the imminent success of his business model, they hired that band, *Obviously, Department* to headline the corporate launch. Their lead singer, Lunch Launderson, was extremely hungover and terribly confused. "Ay, this s'posed to be sumkinda poop place?" he drawled, incoherently. Lunch was half English, half Swedish, and fully doused in southern Americana. He was a pioneer of Scandinavian outlaw death metal punk, and completely original. Nobody had even ever come *close* to what Lunch had accomplished. That band, *Shitler,* actually named its debut album after him.

Lunch wasn't the best fit for the Poop Soup launch, however. First of all, he was a closeted vegan, which meant that he couldn't eat any of the Poop Soup offerings, because they hadn't yet found out what it is that plants poop (hint: it's sugar).

It was okay, though, because, as it turned out, Poop Soup was actually some flavor of a scam. It was contrived by the Pied Pooper of Hamsylvania, who wanted to lure children away from their homes so he could abduct and torture them, because he had dysmorphia and was insecure about his body. So, the Pooper invented a tall tale to get all the adults thinking that he was a useless piece of shit drifter with a heart of gold, by conjuring some nonsense about getting the whole community to work together and gather in a common area to enjoy a meal. He'd tell them that the Poop Soup, while being quite good by itself (meaning, it was just made out of the poop that the Pooper had made, which he did, a lot; why do you think they called him the Pooper? Only Shoop the Motherfuckin' Poop could challenge him for that title, but Shoop already had his own name and title of nobility, and didn't need to be bothered by this commoner bullshit) could be made *even better* if everyone in the town were to contribute their own fecal matter.

Sure enough, the challenge quickly turned the village into a total narcissistic jerkoff fest. Each man of every household had to outdo his neighbors, and there was a run on the local pharmacy, to grab as many fiber pills and laxatives as possible, and then they pulled down every inflatable kiddie pool from the shelves at Dollar General and Wal-Mart, and proceeded to empty their bowels, in a very loud and highly public fashion, into the pools, so that everyone else might see exactly how much poop they were contributing to the Poop Soup.

Then, once it was "ready," as all the egotistical men of the shire had shat out their guts and were at the point of severe rectal bleeding, the sludge was collected and blended together into one giant pot, and ladled out into bowls so everybody could have some. They ate carefully and suspiciously, eyeing one another aggressively as they devoured their Poop Soup. It tasted kind of nutty, and slightly tangy at first; after a few hours, everyone came down with a severe infection caused by fecal coliform bacteria, and most of them died.

While they were distracted, the Pooper stole their children. It was horrible.

DAVEY WENT OVER TO HIS FRIEND'S HOUSE to eat some pizza. His friend was Clifford, the Big Red Penis.

"Have some pizza, Davey," Clifford said, condescendingly. It was Clifford's favorite thing to feed pizza to Davey, because he was such a little sneak who would get the biggest grin on his dirty face as he munched on the pizza, and that made Clifford feel a little less dead inside.

Clifford's penis *was* badly infected, which was how he got his nickname. Some unnamed disease that he'd contracted from a blowjob given to him by a transexual prostitute in Kabul was likely to blame. Now it was 45 years later, and his doctor told him that he was about to stop being able to pee, and would then die soon, of kidney-and-bladder failure.

"Your mother was the most disturbing person I've ever met," Clifford told Davey, as Davey stuffed his face with the pizza. It had extra dipping sauce on top, so it would be all nice and messy, which would help Davey make even more a spectacle of himself, to Clifford's great delight. "Is she dead yet?"

Davey shook his head and grunted, *no*. He didn't like to have to use his real words when he was eating pizza.

Clifford didn't care too much anymore; he was grateful just to receive any attention at all. He was supposed to star in a local production called *The Junk Merchant of Venice*, about how the Jews that controlled the local zoning board were plotting and scheming to make him surrender his hoard of derelict cars and scrap metal that he'd been accumulating in and around his house the whole time he'd lived there. It took place in Venice, California. A couple of drama-theater-geeks from the local community college thought that it was a great opportunity to highlight the societal struggles of mentally atypical people.

Clifford was certain that he was going to be able to sell these things, eventually. But, they would need to be sold on his terms, and his terms alone.

An annoying advertisement came on the television. "MY BEST FRIEND IS A MICROPAN, MICRO, MICRO, MICROPAN!" some retard crooned, joylessly.

Clifford started counting on his fingers to see if he could figure out whether or not this statement was accurate. He was getting old, and he had that problem with his dick. It was making him somewhat loopy in his retirement years, the sort of mild senility that might cause a person to believe that they could derive meaning from a nonsensical advertisement by performing basic arithmetic.

The retard on the TV screen proceeded to pour goop all over himself, in order to demonstrate his supreme commitment to Micropans. He screamed and stuttered as the slop dribbled down his hairline and worked its way up underneath his eyelids.

Clifford realized he couldn't quite count all the way to twelve, so he gave up. He might have had an easier time if he'd remembered to take off his shoes, and use his toes to help add up the numbers. But, he didn't.

The TV news then resumed broadcast. The topic of the day was scrawled across the bottom of the screen: "AMERICA: IF YOU DON'T WANT TO MAKE THINGS EASY FOR ME, THEN FUCK YOU." A guy who looked like a shaved scrotum wearing a grey suit with a cute little bowtie was shouting incoherently about secret Muslims sneaking toys into the country.

Be very careful, Clifford. Davey's mom once harvested a crop of fine young penises, and cut them off to boil them to make a pot of broth. But she was drunk, and she misplaced the recipe, so she tried to wing it, and it was a total mess. The seasoning was completely off, it was far too salty, and she might have touched her butt more than a few times while she was stirring it, with her hands.

Clifford didn't necessarily buy everything the TV people were selling. Sure, they might have figured out a way to get their voices inside of his head, without their lips moving, even; they would just glare out at him through the television set, grinning manically, while their diabolical commands were transmitted directly to insides of his earlobes, telling him to go grab such-and-such from the store, or to run over so-and-so with his old pickup truck, the next time he drove into town.

Davey wasn't very satisfied with his pizza, though. It was too small, and he had finished it too quickly. It came from a place called the "Pizza Oven," which as it turned out, was a name born of a compromise between two business partners, one of whom wanted to call it the "German Oven," because he thought it was funny, because it would upset people, and that would make him laugh. His partner thought that was just the most horrific thing anyone had ever suggested, and threatened suicide if the first partner actually followed through on it. Since the original partner who wanted to call it the "German Oven" was, in fact, a pussy, he immediately backed down and agreed to compromise, because deep down inside, he was a frightened little boy whose father had blown his brains out in front of him when he was six years old and the state-run liquor store had closed an hour early because the cashier had explosive diarrhea, and the business partner who wanted to call the restaurant the "German Oven"'s father had been a seriously dedicated alcoholic, and hard booze was the only thing he found in life to be worth living for, so when he all of a sudden couldn't have that sweet relief, he had but one option, and found the snub-nosed .38 special he kept in the glove compartment, and killed himself right there in the parking lot, witnessed by his only son. The business parter who liked the name "German Oven" took suicide threats seriously, even though the other partner, who was also a pussy, had no earthly intention of actually following through on it, because he was a coward.

Their delivery drivers weren't much better. The one who had been tasked with delivering the pizza pies to Clifford's house that evening had been forty-seven minutes late, and had casually reached over and grabbed a slice out of the box and taken a few bites out of it, and then put it back like nothing had happened. Clifford didn't think to look when it finally got dropped off at his front door, because he'd been distracted by his disorganized thought processes, and left it to Davey to find out and complain. But Davey did not complain, because he too was afraid of his own mother.

"I think my mommy's looking for me," Davey said to Clifford, unironically.

"Smile like the bitch that you are!" some other jibber-jabber advertisement on the television claimed, without evidence. The ads were endless on Clifford's television; sometimes, he wondered if he actually *had* lost his mind.

The McGlurchten Group was on next, a bunch of middle-aged men congregated around a poorly-lit roundtable to complain about things that were largely irrelevant to everyone else. They would grump and grumble about, gesticulating wildly and reaching inappropriate conclusions to inquiries nobody ever wanted answers to, because if they did, *The McGlurchten Group* would be absolutely the *last* source they consulted. If you want to know why a nearly-destroyed patrol boat from World War II should be preserved (as if that were even a controversial topic), these old men could cough up five reasons, none of which would be valid.

Davey was officially done with his pizza. He stared directly at Clifford. "My mommy always told me to wash under my foreskin, real good," he said, sinisterly.

Clifford was shocked. He'd never told anybody about his badly infected pecker; at least, he didn't *think* that he ever had. It had been a long time, so he might have slipped up and accidentally informed someone else about his penis problems.

She also pickled penises, Clifford. She also pickled them.

And did you know that Micropans had actually started off as a series of micro-*penises*? That wasn't very relevant, Clifford figured, but still, it was sort of interesting.

Clifford was bothered by a small creature that suddenly appeared in the corner of his dark cupboard, in his derelict kitchen-area. It stared at him with such a menacing gaze, Clifford was about to light a match and call the fire department. The creature inhaled deeply. It was a small gargoyle-looking thing, pale and with membraneous skin. "What if Brian Cranchlaford said something about you?" it asked of Clifford, quizzically.

Clifford didn't know how to respond. Between the bad things that he was thinking about pertaining to Davey's mom and his dick, and the constant interruptions from the daytime talk-TV circuit droning on in the background, he hadn't even had time to sit down and consider how the grade-school bully who had tormented him over fifty years ago might be plotting to harass him, now.

Brian Cranchlaford, also known as "Brain," because he intimidated people into thinking that he was smart through the use of coercion and abject violence, was now living homeless on the streets of San Francisco. Clifford had visited San Francisco the previous fall, and decided that he was sick of the city. Still, it was the closest place that provided him with the free VA medical care to which he was entitled.

"Marinate your brain with the elixir of imagination!" cried out yet another commercial. Clifford thought that they were referring to his friend, Brain, who was not so much of a friend as much as he was just a codependent little jerkoff who subsisted upon Clifford's charity, and then would go and steal power tools out of the bed of Clifford's pickup truck and try to return them to the tool store for a full refund. Brain thought he was really fucking smart, but he was just another serf, in the grand scheme of things.

Actually, the thing making Clifford think about how Brain probably said this thing that was being repeated, *again*, on the television screen (but in such a way that it was successfully disguised as a commercial that blended itself subliminally into the background), was that Brain was a gimp, and Clifford felt sorry for him. In his distorted view of the world, Clifford fully believed that the disabled were put here on this Earth by a god who wants us to feel better about the fact that some of us can, indeed, still walk without difficulty, and that the thing that the television was trying to get him to buy into was this make-believe fantasy world, to which only the severely disabled needed to escape. Normal people could stay in the regular world, and everything would be fine.

Clifford was procrastinating the most important thing he was supposed to accomplish that day by thinking about Brain, instead of focusing on what was far more significant and consequential to his long-term wellbeing, and that was collecting a pile of small, wooden splinters so that he might insert them strategically underneath his gumline, in order to humiliate his dentist at the Veterans Affairs clinic. Clifford hated his dentist, and wanted to make him suffer psychologically, every bit as much as Clifford would be suffering physically, by abusing his gums in such a reckless manner. His dentist was Indian, and Clifford didn't like that, not one bit.

"I once met a very important piece of poop," Davey stated, unconvincingly.

WELL, BUT IT WAS THE SAME YEAR that Geery Grubbleston won election as the town toilet commissioner. He campaigned on a very aggressive platform of radically expanding the department to hire on at least ten new investigators, who would then be tasked with finding and punishing violators of the sewage-control ordinance. Geery was Indian, so he knew a lot about poop, the places it could be hidden, and what happens when people don't follow good solid waste disposal practices. Thus, it was a very special, very important piece of poop indeed that did evade his watchful eye for so long.

But all great things must come to an end; and this is the story of how that lone holdout assemblage of turd managed to fight the town hall and eventually be flushed down the drains, dying a true hero's death.

The account was fully documented on an independent blog, *thesimperingshemplicants.com*, which mostly relied upon gossip and paranoid rumors to drive traffic to its sponsored affiliates. Someone's butt had been touched, and this web log was the first the report the scandalous affair. At first, though, they neglected to follow the story to its next logical step, which was when the person whose butt had been touched pooped, for the first time after having been touched. The long, stringy piece of shit that emerged into the toilet on this fateful day was brought into this world by an act of violation, and the enormity of that cosmic injustice caused the poop to become sentient, and ashamed.

It immediately crowned itself as the King of Shits, posturing as some sort of prophet sent to liberate all manners of bowel movement the world over. Through its teachings, it would go on to inspire the religious movements known as the Colonic Church, the Proctologants (and all their derivative sects), the Asstafarians, the Sphincter's Witnesses, the Latter-Day Fecal Matters, and the Scientologists.

But trouble was brewing. Grubbleston invited all of his supporters down to the Kool-Aid farm, so that they might scheme and plot. "My goal is to sew every single person's butthole shut, and solve the poop problem once and for all!" Grubbleston proclaimed, promisingly. The crowd cheered him on; they were quite drunk, and didn't take Grubbleston seriously at all. They thought that he used to be some sort of a minor standup comedian with a premium-subscription cable TV talk show, that now was trying to play some sort of a morbid prank on the small community.

They didn't know Geery Grubbleston. After having grown up listening to his parents complain about *their* parents having to have been born into the slums of New Delhi, where they lived in squalor before they learned how to count to five and landed tech-support jobs, Geery was determined to eradicate the threat that had been facing his family by raw sewage and its negative health implications. So, it wasn't in an entirely joking manner that he was promising to attempt to prevent people from taking dumps.

He was about to play the role of the arch-demon to the very, *very* special piece of poop that had emerged to proclaim itself the spiritual leader of the global sewage-rights movement. They did battle, in a very metaphysical and extremely epic affair. MICHAELPAN only wishes that he was so fortunate as to take a dirt-bath in the refuse left behind by the mighty conflagration. Ultimately, the King of Shits was broken up by a toilet snake and unceremoniously flushed down the pipes to several different municipal wastewater treatment facilities, so that any attempt to resurrect the little turd would be forever thwarted.

Geery Grubbleston did get his, however. Since he was a dirty Indian, and he did bad things, like forcing people to sew their buttholes shut, he got caught and sent *back* to India, where he would resume his former life as an inglorious member of the *untouchable* caste, never to be seen or heard from again.

"DONNY, IF YOU DON'T THE BATHROOM DOOR so the bear doesn't come in and try to steal some poop, I am going to slam it on your goofy head," bellowed the Forest Ranger, morosely. They had a serious problem with bears trying to steal whatever they thought was edible, and that included poop. Human poop is an incredible natural resource for a lot of sensitive ecosystems that would otherwise be deprived of all the valuable nutrients that are expelled every time somebody makes BM. But the bears were getting spoiled, and other living things depended on the bears' diet of seeds and berries, and the occasional child, to then be shat out and devoured by the forest.

Donny Dichton didn't know or care about any of this. Donny was a simpleton, and often he ended up being manipulated by his best friend Davey into doing embarrassing things in public. For instance, one time Davey made Donny drink his own pee and then write a song about it, and *then* perform the song on a busy street corner where there were five other delinquents begging for money and trying their hand at that questionable artform known as "busking." These bums got quite upset that Donny was upstaging them by being a geek; and, since Donny was also a mental invalid, performing his show for very-little-to-no pay.

The Forest Ranger didn't realize how entirely defective a person Donny Dichton was. Donny once ran out into traffic because he thought he could catch a lollipop being dangled at the end of the string tied to this red balloon that was floating around. What Donny didn't realize was that the balloon was filled with a combination of helium, nitrogen, nitrous oxide, and hydrogen cyanide, all deliberately combined by a mad scientist in order to create the perfect equilibrium that would cause the balloon to drift aimlessly about, seven and a half feet off the ground, so it could be used to bait children and retards into disrupting the otherwise orderly flow of cars, large trucks, bicycles, and horses along the town's main thoroughfare. Also, if the balloon popped, the gas would drift at approximately mouth-level, and as people inhaled it, they would feel elated by the nitrous oxide, and then they'd feel very dead from the cyanide. It was funny.

What wasn't funny was how these fucking bears came to feeling so entitled and emboldened that they could just crassly wander up to a public restroom in the middle of the forest and go foraging for poop. Usually what would happen was, a person would be desperately needing the services of a toilet, because they just undercooked a sausage patty, and ate it with some water that was flush with fecal coliform bacteria, which means they'd already have a little trickle of poop-juice running down their backside, and they knew that if they didn't deal with this, like, *now*, everyone within a half-mile radius was about to get their evening ruined, *permanently*.

So, this desperate person is quickly approaching the bathroom in the woods, and they notice that the door is open, and they're feeling a bit relieved, and hopefully there isn't anybody in there that is already using the toilets, but they're feeling confident since there aren't the typical sighs, groans, and hoarse singing that normally accompanies a filled-to-capacity restroom in these parts, and things are actually smelling pretty good and this person having the bowel emergency is feeling more and more confident that the impending shit-disaster is going to be narrowly averted; and then a bear shows up, poking its head from out behind the toilet-building, and this person just stops dead in their tracks, and then, a total avalanche of diarrhea comes cascading out of their butthole with such force that the bottom of their polyester shorts quickly balloons, and then, as it reaches full capacity, begins to creak ominously, and the person is starting to sweat, but they can't move, and they still think there's an exit strategy to this rapidly deteriorating situation, and the bear is still staring at them with its beady little eyes, and it sticks its tongue out a bit and licks its snout, and then the person's cheap Walmart short pants can't handle the load any longer, and the dam is completely breached as all of the half-digested raw sausage and contaminated water come splattering out onto the ground, just outside the bathroom where this all could have been averted, had this person not panicked when they saw the bear.

But the bear *knew* this person's response to its presence would be one of abject terror and hatred, and that it would be a lot easier to then strut over and lick all the sloppy stool off the ground, rather than having to risk the wrath of the Forest Ranger by attempting to bodyslam the reinforced steel door to the bathroom in order to gain admission and hope that the automated flushers on the toilets were broken again.

The Forest Ranger had seen a few of these incidents, firsthand. This time, like all the others, he drove up on his golf cart, got out, walked over and comforted the person who was still standing, shivering, in complete shock at what had just happened, too far gone into their own fear and anxiety to even feel the slightest bit embarrassed by the mess that they'd made, and the Forest Ranger then pulled out his sidearm and executed the person, right there on the spot. Because when the sign tells you not to feed the bears, it doesn't make any exceptions for accidents or acts of poop.

Donny didn't know this history. Donny had no idea that this Forest Ranger was living with the trauma of having had to kill at least eight people who found themselves in similar situations. All Donny knew was that his buddy Davey said he would buy him a popsicle if he broke the hinges off the door to the bathroom and left it permanently half-ajar.

Davey's motivations herein were quite selfish and sinister. He wanted the Forest Ranger to kill off a whole bunch more people who were staying at the park, because they were supposed to be having a pizza party that night, and Davey wanted the pizza all to himself, because he was a creepy little sneak like that.

The Forest Ranger saw that Donny had no intention of stopping what he was attempting to do (which he would never be able to actually pull off, because he was retarded), so, being an honorable man of his word, he kicked Donny in the shins and forced him to the ground, and then pinned his skull against the door jam, and proceeded to use the action of the heavy door to bash Donny's head until it was just a pile of red pulp, and the Forest Ranger was crying and screaming the entire time about how Donny had the choice, he could have stopped fucking with the door and not been trying to make the Forest Ranger's life so impossibly difficult, what with these bears wandering around and trying to steal poop, and why don't people ever listen?

Donny didn't listen to anybody but Davey. It wasn't his fault, but, then again, the world wasn't any worse off for not having Donny Dichton being still alive inside of it.

NONE OF THIS MADE ANY SENSE to Howard. He was still suspicious, and a little bit afraid, of the voice on the other end of the telephone.

"Who told you?" he asked, horrifiedly.

Geery giggled. "I was there, Howard, with you there, in that forest."

"But, you're Indian! I don't know any Indians!"

Geery guffawed. "No, but you do now."

<u>Uncle Bluchlucus</u>

A Novel

Chapter I

DIANA MURLESHTEN-STYLES WAS A FANCY WOMAN; but, she was about to get *un*-fancified.

"Do you guys make a good sausage sandwich?" she asked. Her actual name was McSusan, but that's not really a name, so nobody in her life ever took her seriously. Also, she was a woman. So that was when she decided she had to become Diana Murleshten-Styles, which sounded more refined, regal almost, worthy of at least some obscure title of nobility, like "Baroness."

Almost nobody else agreed. An eight year old girl once came up to her and told her that her made-up name reminded her of the sound of a cat retching.

The girl was right. Diana Murleshten-Styles didn't work; neither did McSusan, or whatever her name actually was. She didn't work as a character. No longer needed, she was whisked away into oblivion, not to be remembered by anything or anyone inimical to the plot.

Depressed, Diana slunk off to the nearest dive bar. "What's gotcha down, sugar?" the bartender, a portly redheaded woman who was working the 10AM shift, asked disinterestedly. Well, ok. She was *kind* of interested, not so completely detached from her piss-wage job to the point that other peoples' misery wouldn't cheer her up throughout her day.

"I don't exist anymore," Diana moaned.

"Aw. honey, I know how ya feel," the bartender said, with great confidence. "Trust me, he just ain't worth it. He'll come home when he finds out what he was missing." Yet, what this nominal woman failed to realize was that HE was the author of the novel, the genius that held Diana's life together; and now that he had removed her purpose entirely, so forcefully and without notice, Diana in that moment decided to *do* something about it.

"Your honor, if this man is allowed to continue writing about me, I won't be able to continue living," she huffed to the Judge, that cunt.

"I see. And Miss, Mizz, uh— *Murleshten-Styles?* That can't be right. Is that your actual name? Clerk?" The clerk nodded, enthusiastically. He didn't say anything. He couldn't say anything. He was a mute freakazoid they'd recruited through the state's affirmative action policy, offering the retardeds a chance to perform some mundane task in exchange for being allowed inside the house.

"Look, if I don't have someone being honest with me, I'm declaring a mistrial," the Judge warned, even though this was in fact just a hearing for an emergency restraining order Diana was seeking against the author, trying to protect herself from the harm of being forced out of existence.

"I used to go by 'McSusan,'" Diana suggested, unhelpfully.

"It's okay, dear," the Bartender said, slobbering slightly. She'd always had repressed lesbian desires, and now she was trying to act on them, and not in a particularly smooth way, either. She was a closeted dyke who thought all women were intrinsically gay, and that she should therefore be able to take her pick of the bunch. It didn't work.

"I used to work in a sausage factory," Diana warned her. The bartender showed no sign of recognition. She just stood there, frozen, paralyzed by frustration, with a small dribble of urine running down the inside of her jeans.

Diana was disgusted. Didn't they have health inspectors enforcing against this kind of thing?

"Ms. Murleshten-Styles, I think you're becoming distracted," the Judge quipped. His authority was demonstrated by the capitalization of his title, while the bartender's role was relegated to lower-case capacity.

But it was okay.

"Were you named after Princess Diana?" another random little girl, about 10 years old, drinking a glass of milk at the bar, asked her. It was completely inappropriate, and the little girl should've immediately been slapped and thrown into the "time-out" corner, but for some reason, it make Diana feel, suddenly, relevant.

"First thing you should know," Diana started, was that she was born, not a she, and not a he, but indeed, an "it." When she came out of her mommy's twat, Diana Murleshten-Styles was some sort of deformed, intersex mutant. The doctors quickly diagnosed "bifurcated urethra," which was a nice way of saying that she had two pee-pees, one taking the form of a mangled little microscopic penis, and the other one, a short, stout, ugly clit. Further up inside, the plumbing on this poor creature grew infinitely worse. There were testicles completely contained inside of ovaries. The uterus was infused with the erectile muscles of a phallus, meaning that whenever this thing would get upset, startled, aroused or injected with the paralytic byproducts of infectious bacteria that form the basis of modern treatments for ED, the uterus would grow enlarged, throbbing and protruding out from the navel area, like a grotesque parasite attempting to break free of its host.

Diana's mom was beside herself with grief; but her dad found great satisfaction in the entire ordeal. He quickly jotted down "MCSUSAN" as the child's first name on the birth certificate, as he wanted to pay homage to the lady parts ("Susan") with the grittiness of a working-class Irishman's surname-prefix ("Mc"), to symbolize the struggle that every man goes through when crying into his beer at the end of a long shift, realizing he will never be taken seriously by any woman in his life, because he has a tiny dick.

Not yet satisfied, Diana's dad quickly raced back to the hovel he shared with his common-law wife and fired up the desktop publishing program he'd recently acquired on his predictably outdated personal computer. Within days, he had produced and was in the process of hawking merchandise proclaiming the existence of his freak child, enticing any passers-by to commemorate the occasion in carnival-busker fashion. Diana's dad was a devotee of Ed Wood and other such signature acts of exploitation cinema, so it was in true form that he sold an obese, chain-smoking, middle-aged woman called "Debbie" three shirts exclaiming, "I TOUCHED THE FREAK BOY-GIRL BABY!" after allowing her to grope and prod Diana for up to 10 minutes.

DIANA WAS ABOUT TO BE CONFRONTED BY someone at the bar over her support for MICHAELPAN. She first had to go over to Longe Licraposa's Lounge, for some of his famous mimosas. It was morning, and that was the most intoxicating beverage a lady of her stature would be able to elegantly consume in such context. She wasn't aware that she was not, in fact, elegant, or lovely, or even barely a lady; she also didn't exist, mind you, and she *was* aware of that, but she certainly wasn't acting like it.

So, while Diana Murleshten-Styles made her way over to Longe's, and had a few dainty lady-drinks to ease her nerves while awaiting the inevitable, the sponsors of her non-existence were gracious enough to hire the master list-maker, Helmut Nuckmiëler, to articulate the reasons for Diana's support of MICHAELPAN, so she wouldn't have to (not like she'd really be able to, anyhow, not in her condition, being an intersexual alcoholic):

REASONS THAT DIANA MURLESHTEN-STYLES SUPPORTS MICHAELPAN
FOR PRESIDENT

- MICHAELPAN does not explicitly prohibit intersex people from existing. [This was a big one for Diana.]
- MICHAELPAN does agree with guaranteed subsidies for bars, or restaurants that serve alcohol, *or* shacks in the swamp that traffic in (formerly) illicit moonshine. These are the sorts of places that are most welcoming to people like Diana (although the seedier, the better).
- MICHAELPAN is sort of a dad-figure to the country, and if they let him, the world. BUT, he is not a very *good* dad-figure, just a realistic one. MICHAELPAN probably has some questionable personal habits. Like that one time he went rabbit hunting, and he shot his best friend and hunting partner in the eye after he'd had about fifteen beers (although, this man had a birthmark covering the entirety of his left face, and couldn't see out of that eye from birth, which was the same eye that got shot out, so it really wasn't that big of a deal, he just had to have the real eye that couldn't see replaced with a glass eye that couldn't see, so it wasn't too bad, and MICHAELPAN was decent enough of a person to pay the deductible on his friend's vision plan).
- MICHAELPAN doesn't plan on bothering anyone. So, people like Diana, who, before they ceased to exist, would only want something like a small house to themselves, and their guns, and their birds, and

to otherwise be left the hell alone by everyone else, wouldn't have been harassed by MICHAELPAN.

- MICHAELPAN plays the drums, but not well. Diana wasn't sure what that *did* for her, exactly; but frantic, unrhythmic drumbeats always evoked a tingling sensation from that piece of her that was authentic lady-parts. She was never quite sure *what* to do with that feeling (which is honestly a big part of the reason why she doesn't exist), but there was an awareness, at one time, that bad drum performances could potentially have led to something that may, eventually, have represented at least a rough approximation of what an orgasm may feel like for an intersex person.

- MICHAELPAN hates doughnuts. So does Diana. Very few people felt similarly. He will move to ban them, if elected, which cost him the endorsement of the National Brotherhood of Police Officers (even though he already wasn't likely to receive their endorsement, since they would rather support a candidate for President who might *actually* have a chance at winning).

"If that thing said 68 minutes ago, I'm going to tell you to go fuck yourself," Longe proclaimed. He wasn't having a particularly easy morning, and now, amongst all else, he had to deal with the intersex trash being that was Diana Murleshten-Styles. He didn't really care about her support of MICHAELPAN, unlike some of the patrons of his high quality establishment. There was the guy who ate worms because he thought he was some kind of a bird, for instance. He did not agree with, or in any way, shape, or form endorse MICHAELPAN; in his mind, he was a bird, and birds don't do democracy. Except for penguins, but then again, they're hardly even birds.

The worm-man sat in the same cubbyhole booth each late morning and early afternoon of every weekday during the migratory season. He was on the hunt for a mate, and expected that could legitimately pass muster as a full-time occupation of sorts. Since he wasn't stupid enough to *entirely* believe he was a bird, he instead relied upon human pickup mannerisms, to find an actual woman-mate, one who would not be repelled by the small bowl of squirming grubs he'd be munching on along with his Irish coffee. If anyone could do it, it was going to be a drunk girl.

The worm-man also detested Diana, however, for she was not an actual woman. [The worm-man didn't realize that Diana's birth name was "McSusan," which implied that there was some hope of defining this "it" person/thing as a female somehow, someday, with a sufficient amount of gender-affirming surgery.] The worm-man wasn't interested in the media's self-proclaimed "pronoun wars" of the late-teens era. He was actually a closeted bigot and a borderline sociopath, one who listened to conservative talk radio with rabid passion and self-identified as a member of the *alt-right*. McSusan, or Diana as he knew her, had no earthly right to exist as an intersexual being in his worldview. It's lucky for him he didn't have anything to say about it, for Diana Murleshten-Styles most certainly *did not* exist, at least, not any longer. That was why she was here in Longe's basement, in the first place.

"I think they were afraid, because you were implying that MICHAELPAN was a figment of their imaginations," Pwippy Deluption piped up. Pwippy wasn't allowed in Longe's place, because no dogs were, but still managed to sneak in and harass the clientele on a regular basis. Diana wasn't sure what to do about it.

"They can't say something like 68 minutes," Longe growled. He was very upset with the system that would allow for such a thing. It should say one hour, and eight minutes.

Longe's place was located along Crown-Vicking Street, which used to be a fairly well-to-do promenade, featuring haberdasheries and boutiques. That was, before Diana stunk it up with her defective sex organs, which dribbled pus on a regular basis, and not even a regular, septic-infection level of pus; no, this one was weird, it was male *and* female odors of rot, simultaneously. Everyone within a sixteen block radius got sick. Soon, it was not a pleasant street anymore. Diana wouldn't leave, so just about everyone else did instead.

Longe was almost gone, himself. He was tired of being accused of making such great damned mimosas. The mimosa crowd was fickle, and cheap, and certainly boorish. They extended their pinky fingers ever-so-delicately from the champagne flute as they sipped the mind-numbingly plain and stupid concoction of Prosecco and OJ. *It was so fucking easy to make*, Longe shook his head, perplexed about becoming famous for his. Did he put a small amount more alcohol in his drinks than his competitors? Did the girls who thrived on that swill find him attractive, or mysterious?

REALLY, DIANA SHOULD HAVE CONSIDERED HERSELF fortunate. She had two names, Diana Murleshten-Styles, and McSusan; that was two more names than a lot of characters (who, unlike Diana, *did* exist) got. There were plenty of other wretched fools who got descriptors instead of actual names, like "Paul's brother" or "The cat's owner." These nameless morons accomplished very little with their existences, just sitting and spinning in place, holding circular conversations with other miscreants who somehow manifested within the confines of the narrative. Diana Murleshten-Styles had hardly ever existed at all, maybe not even in the first place; but she was in a much better place than many of those who did.

Anyhow, nobody was quite sure what Longe Licraposa was going on about with his 68 minutes tangent. Was it about Mike Wallace's signature television news-magazine program? Which network did that even air on? [It's been so long since broadcast television was relevant, one can be forgiven for not properly recalling this long-obsolete culture.]

It was almost time for Diana to move on, anyhow, after she had outstayed her welcome with discount brunch-hour fake mimosas. But everyone was waiting on maybe one or two more things to happen before Diana went along to her next stop. Some kind of minor interaction with another peripheral character, for instance. One more vulgar depiction of what all entirely was wrong with Diana's downstairs plumbing. Perhaps an appearance from a random animal or mythological creature.

Actually, it *did* remind Diana of one time when she read a book in a Waffle House. Or, rather, one time that she *didn't* read a book in the Waffle House, because, after all, she didn't exist.

It had been a rainy day, somewhere in the South. Diana had fled a termite-ridden house in which she'd formerly been squatting, in the vicinity of, let's say, Tallahassee, when the frame began to rumble and roar that morning. The goddamned bugs were 98% of the way through chewing up the entire structure, and Diana got out of there with not a minute to spare before the whole hovel imploded.

Going to the Waffle House was the only thing that made sense. Diana was driving so fast, she got pulled over; and when the cop politely asked what she thought she was doing violating the law in such a flagrant manner, Diana began mumbling something about having bit her lip. Literally, her teeth had punctured the right side of her mouth, which was now swollen with bacteria and beginning to ever so slightly leak even more pus (adding only further to the general sense of malaise and misery that would pervade any social setting in which she may find herself, given the already awful amount of discharge flowing from her mutant genitalia). And when she told the cop she was headed straight to the Waffle House, and that only, he let her off with a warning (and also, he was disgusted and concerned he may catch whatever it was that obviously made Diana so extremely fucked up). Southern cops would willingly buy "Waffle House" as an excuse from a white woman, as long as she wasn't *too* drunk.

Nobody was really paying much attention at this point, which was a major relief for Diana. She was already non-existent, though, so the hazards presented by being an actual thing no longer applied. Still, she couldn't quite shake the feeling like somehow, for some reason, things still *mattered*, at least in a minor capacity. So, once she got to the Waffle House, she pulled out a book.

"I got in trouble for reading once," her waitress said, pouring Diana a cup of coffee she hadn't asked for. The South does not understand coffee. Their version of coffee is based on instant "coffee" crystals, which is a bastardized concentration of previously brewed coffee, which was itself sourced from the direst, foulest, cheapest beans leftover on the market that day. [By "market," it is implied that the institution being referred to is the Free Market, which is as nasty a place as you'd never want to visit. It's located somewhere in New York City, and it smells like rotting fish heads. Deformed, dirty men in Victorian-era garb shout and holler scattershot prices and the names of random goods, and grab one another by the lapels, oftentimes landing body blows and grappling around on the filthy ground in order to beat a given price-point. False teeth go flying, raw sewer rats are devoured whole, and the wayward random woman who finds herself in the middle of this mess is subject to being manhandled, groped, having her well-kept attire torn from around her bosom and crotch area, until she is naked, ashamed, humiliated, violated, and gasping for aid from some kind-hearted Knight of the Order of Most Chivalrous Conduct, who she feels confident and hopeful will soon alight the wretched scene in order to whisk her away back to civilization; but this hero of the moment never materializes, so, she must suck and fuck her way to freedom, ironically, in order to gain liberation from the "Free" Market. And somehow, in the midst of all of this, a boatload of coffee beans was forgotten; and then, right as the Market was about to close for the day, it was acquired for 15% of fair value by a dastardly scoundrel with a curly mustache.] The coffee that was brewed from those terrible beans was boiled down into something that resembled a shit-colored flavor of powdered drugs. But, there was hardly any viable caffeine left over. It was just enough to break a headache caused by a long-time coffee-drinking addict experiencing a soul-crushing midmorning withdraw from caffeine consumption.

"What happened?" Diana asked, horrifiedly.

"My husband almost beat me to death," the waitress replied, nonchalantly.

"But what were you reading?"

"I don't remember, dear. It was some book-of-the-month thing." The waitress had, in the strictest of confidence, joined a clandestine circle of book-reading women that met at an undisclosed location every month, and taught one another how to read. From a starter picture book called, *Something's Wrong With You, Dick!* all the way up to whatever drivel Oprah was pumping up that week, the waitress found a new life in the world of literature. She had moved on, independent from the rest of the group (she was a fast learner), pursuing a long-running series of romance novels that had a symbiotic relationship with Hallmark TV movies. One in particular, about an alcoholic degenerate failed mother who was stumbling down the path to sheer insanity before a package-delivery man swept her off her feet, had captivated the waitress to the point of being sloppy: she was caught reading in the bathtub by her husband when he had burst in, experiencing a critical bladder emergency, having just shotgunned 15 beers back-to-back, only pausing to occasionally breathe, during a rowdy round of watching college football with his very-bestest-of-buds. What happened next cannot be described due to the severity of the physical violence the poor woman endured. Someone may get upset.

"BUT DIANA," PWIPPY DELUPTION WHINED, obnoxiously, "When are you going to tell us about the purple truck?" Yes, the purple truck, the one that says "JESUS IS THE ANSWER!"

Jesús worked at Dirty Sanchez' Muffler and Chop Shop, but that was irrelevant.

"Happy, sad! Happy, happy, happy, SAD!" A voice sung out, abrasively. Diana's and Pwippy's heads turned in unison. It was man, but not much of one. He was a failed used car dealer with bipolar disorder, most likely exacerbated by exposure to dirty automotive fluids.

"Have you seen my pet ants?" Another voice from a dark corner of Longe's lounge disturbed them, instantaneously. "They got out of their ant-farm, and, uh, they're climbing on my counters!"

Jesús was not particularly proud of his work, which was still irrelevant; but on occasion, he would meet a person who had some, let's say, *special needs*, who thought that he was GOD, and the son of GOD, and that also, this person would like to have their pickup truck painted purple.

"Happy/sad/happy, happy, happy, sad! SAD!" The bipolar man was reminiscing fondly of a time he went to Las Vegas, when he shouldn't have. He blew the company's cash drinking artisanal cocktails and playing dollar slots at the Cosmo. Nobody could accuse of him of not having class, however.

"Those ants meant *everything* to me," the other man continued, "until that bitch left. And little Jonny! He was so *amazed* by the ant colony." The man had a vaguely Dutch accent.

Pwippy Deluption's left leg started to shake, violently. It had to pee, quickly; but it didn't want anyone to notice. That movie, *The Peeing Poodle*, had just come out, and Pwippy, being a dog, was afraid of being profiled as just another canine with a lazy bladder. People were watching, maybe.

"JESUS CHRIST!" the bipolar man shouted. He slammed a whiskey glass against the bar, sending shards of glass flying in every direction. He then began sobbing, profusely.

Jesús wasn't there, fortunately; but his last name wasn't *Christ*, anyway. It was Hernandez.

"And when one little ant found a sweet crumb of sugar, all the rest would follow," the other man said, confidently. He spoke with great affect, like he actually knew what he was talking about.

"But Diana," Pwippy said, its eyes looking up pleadingly at Diana. Diana wasn't sure *whose* idea it was to tell the story of the purple truck. Had Pwippy actually asked about that, or was there someone else asking the questions? Someone *invisible*?

"HAPPY! SAD!" The bipolar man didn't like to admit that he struggled with alcoholism, but now that he was no longer employed, and had blackmailed his former employer into admitting that he'd been fired *without* cause, even thought the reason was that he stole the company's money and gambled it away on the Vegas Strip (which is actually located *outside* of Las Vegas proper, in the unincorporated place known as Paradise, Nevada), so the man could collect unemployment benefits, and spend those funds at an establishment like Longe's place, early in the morning most weekdays when decent people would be having coffee, and going to work, and *maybe* having one or two benzodiazepine-class drugs in pill form; but that was it. They wouldn't be getting drunk in a dive bar when the trading day had just begun.

Jesús hadn't aspired to work at a small, dingy garage owned and managed by a small-time criminal syndicate. In spite of his Mexican heritage, he was born in Brownsville, Texas, USA, and his parents, who *were* born in Mexico, definitely thought he could do much better than this; or at least, they *would* have thought that, had they not perished in the great Butter Contamination Catastrophe that befell South Texas in 1997. 64 people died after being fed rancid butter, on a dare, by a man who we are not legally allowed to identify, but who later went on to have a successful career as a podcaster.

The ants had actually taken over the other man's house. That was why he was hiding at Longe's; he didn't even drink *that* much, but he didn't want to go home and admit that he had an ant problem. He'd heard from some associates of his that Longe made an *amazing* Mimosa, and he figured that was as good an excuse as any to not have to go back to his house and deal with the situation there.

Pwippy Deluption was at about 115% above holding capacity for urine. It started whining, harder, until the noise was so bad that Diana began to wonder if it was not coming from *inside* her head.

"HAPPY and SAD, and HAPPY and SAD," the bipolar man continued. Longe had disappeared, and nothing was being done about the glass that was all exploded over the bar. And nobody was quite sure what the defective man would do next.

Jesús thought that purple was a hideous color for a truck, and also, he knew full well that when the truck's owner, who was white, was asked by his white friends who had painted the truck that particularly puke-worthy shade of purple, he'd tell them that it was a Mexican, and all the white people would have a good chuckle at Jesús' expense. Except, the man with the truck *wanted* it to also read, "JESUS IS #1" because he was a fundamentalist Christian, and Jesús got a chuckle out of getting to write that on there. [He was a part-time Aztec priest who would occasionally sacrifice goats with a ritual scabbard on an altar dedicated to Montezuma and drink their warm, still-flowing blood, and then bless all gathered neo-pagans with his semen.] He also surreptitiously added a license-plate frame to the truck that read, "DIRTY SANCHEZ AUTO BODY," their phone number, and "SE HABLA ESPAÑOL."

"I don't drink, at least, not that much. Not to excess, anyway," the other man continued, disingenuously. He didn't have a tolerance for liquor to speak of, so therefore, whenever he had more than two drinks, he was drunk, and he'd make a sheer fool of himself. Like, one time, he went out with his old high school chums after work at the insurance factory, for some beers. At the end of the evening, he was fumbling with his keys to get into the front door of his house that his (ex-) wife had locked up tight against fear of the creatures of the night. He was juggling a bulbous package in his arms, taking great and hilarious pains, and physical pains centered around his lower back, in order to keep from dropping everything and making himself look the drunken fool that he was, at least, in that moment. The package was marked, "Hobby Ant Farm. Ages 4+. For Entertainment Purposes ONLY."

"Di-ann-AHHHHH!" Pwippy howled. A small trickle of pee was working its way down its right rear leg, staining its calico-patterned fur a harsh, deep, dark, and highly accusatory shade of yellow.

"STOP! STOP! FUCKING STOP! LEAVE ME THE FUCK ALONE!" Diana screamed. She always wanted to be thought of as like Princess Diana, and now, she finally felt what it must have been like to actually *be* Princess Diana.

AND SO IT WAS THAT PRINCESS DIANA, Murleshten-Styles, Nonexistent, had happened to have entered into a relationship with one Monstreeshen, who was at that point reportedly someone else's boyfriend, but who similarly fancied himself royalty of some variety. Diana needed financial support, and Monstreeshen seemed like he had a sizable inheritance.

Seemed to, anyway. The reality was starkly in contrast to this mistaken assumption. Monstreeshen had just been let go from a debt-collection call center. He had been diligently dialing deadbeats' telephone numbers and haranguing them with veiled threats of having their disability payments from the government intercepted and garnished (actually, federal law prohibits debt collectors from doing this, but Monstreeshen's bosses had told him during the two-hour mandatory orientation that debt collection agents were actually like cops, insofar as they could lie to members of the unsuspecting public and get away with it). This worked, for a time, although by "worked" it is actually implied that Monstreeshen would be yelled at, cursed out, and been hung up on more times than he actually came across some sad and pathetic repentant person, who, most likely drunk, would sob and blabber on about how much they meant to pay their bills, but then a baby got cancer, someone's dog got run over, an aunt went on a killing spree with a hatchet, etc., and so forth until Monstreeshen had learnt the entirety of the *Encyclopedia of Excuses*, all 26 volumes of it, cover to cover, and practically memorized every article entered in alphabetical order. It was fine; it was a job, of sorts, at least until the day that Monstreeshen, having been violently verbally assaulted for the 134,234th time, proceeded onto the next file. He was surprised that he recognized the name. It was his own.

"When do we get to hear the rest of the story?" Howard asked, impatiently.

"Yes, I'd like to know if this is going to go anywhere," sighed Robin "Rob" Berkowski, antagonistically. "We're running out of time."

"Shut up. This is all very relevant and important," the Narrator relied, authoritatively.

"Hey, that's my favorite band! The Shut Uppians!" Some stranger just randomly had to interject themselves into the conversation, as they normally do.

"You can't use the 'they' pronoun to refer to an individual!" Howard screamed.

The stranger didn't bat an eye. "It says right on my Twitter profile, that my preferred pronouns are 'They/Theirs!'" The stranger remarked, triumphantly.

"Fuck this. I'm just going to call you 'Me!'" growled Rob, agitatedly.

"But I'm me! I'm not you, or any other person, so you can't say that! You have to call me 'They!'"

"But if you're 'They,' what do we call them?" Howard asked, gesturing to the other people in the immediate area.

"You call them 'They' as well," said the stranger, condescendingly.

"But I'm calling you 'Me.'"

"I don't know. He doesn't look like a 'Me.'"

"I'm not a 'He!' I'm a 'They!'"

"Whatever. Before we were interrupted by me, what were you saying?"

"What was I saying, or what was me saying?"

"All I remember is they said something stupid."

"Do you mean me said something stupid?"

"Shut up."

"I love that band!" The Shut Uppians were on hiatus, and nobody knew if they were ever going to get back together. There was more than one of them, so it was OK to refer to the collective members of the band as, "They."

But there was a problem, insofar as Monstreeshen had never gotten clearance from the United States INS to legally reside in the country. He wasn't black; but he wasn't white, either, if you catch the drift. So, he was illegal, AND he was already married, or at least, in a committed relationship outside of what he was trying to get started with Diana.

He wasn't trying very hard. He used his alcoholism to justify his impotence. In reality, he was a horny beast, but he really did not want to have Diana take off her, or *its*, clothes. He'd heard enough rumors to want no part of whatever it was that was going on in that particular female-identifying-person's crotch area.

He didn't speak good English; he smelled funny even on a good day when he'd bothered to try and find a bathhouse and flip a few nickels to a young boy in order that he might not be harassed by any gay men for a few minutes, and also, so he could have a dick-measuring contest with the kid, which he would normally lose. He was, as we're already aware, fired from a job that wasn't even really a job, but more of a pyramid scheme. His hair was greasy, and not in a good way.

To put it nicely, Diana could do better.

THE STUPIDS WERE A FAMILY OF PERFORMERS, well, *vaudevillians* really, who never put on that much of a show, certainly nothing award-worthy or even that credible; but Diana, for whatever reason, still felt tickled by watching them perform.

Diana remembered this, as she was gathering her things in anticipation of finally leaving Longe's Lounge for the day, setting out and about in the Big City to accost more regulars in some of her favorite haunts (dives, every single last one of them). But right now, she needed to take five and have a trip down good ol' memory lane:

Firefighter Bob's Spaghetti Fundraiser Dinner for that year was going to be featuring that cut-rate act, *The Stupids*. "Stup-ped," Bob cackled to himself, incrementally. Firefighter Bob was a big man, but not much in the brains department. In fact, he'd been described by some of his longtime friends and associates as a "mental midget." He did know how to put out fires, and he was dedicated to the cause of eating, and feeding others, spaghetti and meatballs.

After he'd been weaned, Bob's mother had given him a baby's-sized portion of canned noodles with some lumps of what might legally be allowed to be referred to as "meat" (it was the eighties, and the government was playing loose and fast with what was acceptable for food corporations to tell people they could actually eat), being both soggy and dense as a kidney stone, simultaneously. Well, that got Bob hooked, not that it actually took very much effort to play into Bob's obsessive-compulsive personality. He would eat nothing else but spaghetti and meatballs for the rest of his natural life.

Bob grew up in the same town as Diana, and they would commiserate after classes on many a warm afternoon, holding hands while Bob, giddy as a two-year-old, would run down the trails meandering through the pastoral outskirts of the village center, skipping and laughing, catching butterflies and ripping their pretty wings into shreds, kicking stray dogs in the face when they'd come up to him, tails wagging, begging for food; and, he would set trash cans on fire.

That was how Firefighter Bob come to be. The principal, and the policeman, and then the judge all told him that little boys *were not* allowed to light fires in trash cans, despite what Bob otherwise believed. They gave him an ultimatum: either he could cut the shit, and become "Firefighter Bob," putting out the fires that they believed he very likely would've caused in the first place; or, he could go down the other path, and continue being known as "Spaghetti Bob," which was his superhero alter ego that he'd transform into after having spent the better part of a day huffing paint. Then he'd try to get a job yelling at people waiting in their cars at the stop light before merging onto the freeway.

And he'd get married to Diana. Well, that stopped our old boy dead in his tracks. Nobody wanted to actually be *seen* with Diana Murleshten-Styles (then better known as McSusan), other than as a dare, or to be edgy in that way that only a nineties teenager could understand. But that certainly didn't mean Bob had any intentions of marrying her.

So, he decided to take the judge's offer and become Firefighter Bob. He could put fires out. He also could help out his *real* wife in the kitchen at the church's recreational hall when the time came to feed up to a hundred townspeople his favorite spaghetti and meatballs dish, from a recipe that he said his mother had handed down to him, which was a lie. His wife found it in *The Joy of Microwave Cooking*.

Diana was excited for this particular installment of the spaghetti-based fundraiser dinner, that being for the year 2011, because *The Stupids* would be there. Diana had heard of them, and pretended to all of her friends that she had seen them multiple times, and they were, well, just her favorite thing, *ever*. But she lied, and that was part of the reason why she no longer existed; she was just a terrible character, even being intersex and weird the way she was. It wasn't special, or important.

But *The Stupids* didn't even know who Diana Murleshten-Styles was, or even who she *wouldn't* become. They wouldn't care, even if they did. They were pretty soulless people. Mama Stupid would use her bra cups as ashtrays and then sing horrible songs until Baby Stupid started bawling its lungs out. Papa Stupid would then emerge, shirtcocking (naked from the waist down, but still wearing a top, like a true buffoon), drinking cheap beer and smoking nasty cigars. He'd start laughing, and clapping, and pointing. Then he'd squat down and take a dump, which was very difficult for him at that stage (IV) in his colorectal cancer. He'd grimace and grow red in the face as just the smallest tendril of fecal matter dangled above the stage; then, with one more mighty gulp of the swill-in-a-can that was sadly referred to as "beer," he would yell, "MERRY CHRISTMAS!" and with a heroic fart, make at least a small burrito's worth of poop plop down right underneath his butt.

Sonny Stupid wouldn't be too impressed, though, and he'd spend most of his time lugging around a spiked baseball bat and growling incoherently. Daughter Stupid thought she was the reincarnation of Harley Quinn and would leapfrog from one senile old audience member to the next, rubbing and scratching and giggling aggressively until, one after another, the old shitheads would get stiff and then die of hemorrhages and the like.

Meanwhile, Firefighter Bob was applauding profusely. Everyone else was shocked and appalled, but they went along with it, because Bob was big, and he knew how to start fires just as good as he knew how to put them out, so you don't fuck with that, period.

Diana tried to get fucked by that, for what it was; but it wasn't much, so she didn't. She didn't know what to think about *The Stupids*, either. She didn't know if she should continue putting people on like it was her favorite thing anymore. Diana didn't know much about anything in those days.

DIANA WAS FEELING STUCK IN THE MOMENT, at Longe's, before she successfully dislodged herself from that one particular bar setting, and stumbled out onto the street, at about two in the afternoon. Non-existence was actually really difficult.

But then Diana found herself picked up and spontaneously relocated. [*Poof*; it's just that simple.] She was suddenly in another nearby drinking hole, known as *The Wandering Duck*. It tried to imitate a French-Canadian laundromat, where hairy men in wifebeaters would loiter in the parking lot and munch on spruce twigs sprinkled with truffle shavings. It was somewhere else; somewhere *different*.

"Now, one thing that I find fascinating," said the first person Diana encountered upon her arrival at the Duck, "is the concept of identity." Diana immediately knew that this person wouldn't actually have anything truly interesting to say. It was going to be some dry, academic drivel from someone who had run out of enough gas to fart out, to sniff in order to feel important, and also, they'd had a few drinks, and any semblance of hesitancy that this person may otherwise experience that would prevent this atrocity of social interaction from occurring in the first place was way gone, so Diana was screwed now. *Royally* screwed. This was going to be SO boring, and pretentious, that she almost tried to slip away unnoticed. But, as she was non-existent, there was nowhere left for her to escape.

"I would like to propose, first of all, there being a class, or moreover, a *categorization* of individuals who reject the conventional constructs of gender.

They reject these defining characteristics on a complete basis, eschewing any and all attempts at ascribing dichotomic labels unto their beings.   Therefore, they assume the identity of intersex."

Diana might have had something to say about this, but since she didn't exist, she didn't matter, so she didn't try to interrupt.

"Yet there are these people who reorganize themselves around the *title* of being intersex, and those that actually *do* succeed in becoming as such."

"It's a pillow-king cat, yes, he's a pillow-king cat," another stranger in this particular drinking establishment said, intrepidly. "It's a pillow, it's a king, and he's a cat. The pillow-king cat, gets to be positioned on the pillows, every night, on the couch, he is the KING of the pillows, all the pillows get placed underneath him, the cat, because he is the king!"

"What a retched interruption," the erstwhile philosopher commented, drolly. But nobody could forget about the French Laundromat. Who even knew that Frenchers would wash their clothes in anything but a mud puddle next to the cheese shed, and then hang them out to dry into the consistency of 2x4's on a few crooked lines strung clumsily above the big wooden vat within which grapes were crushed by the beautiful feet of virgin maidens in order to make wine?

"Can we get back to the point?" asked Diana, pleadingly.

"Yes. Some people aspire to be both the masculine *and* feminine, never able to choose betwixt the two. Therefore, they become ambiguous, but in the most aggressive manner. They attempt to occupy the space of two gendered identities, simultaneously. They hate being called, 'they,' by the way. It is much preferred the honorific *Herr*, or *Hisums*. Any pronoun that incorporates extra, highly unnecessary letters will serve to satisfy these dreaded folks' perverted desires."

"HELP! Somebody just got fucked in the ass!" Some idiot had entered the sneering setting with a plaintive wail. A gross act of injustice had just transpired, and this person, who shall remain genderless, saw fit to interrupt what could have been a very engaging conversation between two lovely and interesting individuals in such a crude, rude manner that a small man sitting on a cocktail stool promptly lost his lunch. Everyone in the room was suddenly filled with the most empty, sour-stomached sense of existential dread that even the worst *New Yorker* cartoon could never hope to instill amongst its hapless readership. Snot flailed helplessly through the air as the snooty took their comeuppance, straight up the poop-chute. It was never intended to happen this way; but then again, anything was possible when following around one Diana. Murleshten-. Styles.

That was the great advantage of non-existence, after all. Nobody could stop the non-existent from doing whatever they pleased, even if what they pleased happened to invite antisocial behavior and reckless conduct ill befitting of cultured society. No one could likewise demand that the non-existent person take a shower, or guilt trip them into walking over to the Post Office to check their mailbox either. A non-existent person had all the perks of personhood with none of the responsibilities.

Suddenly, Diana spoke up: "I don't need to listen to this drivel anymore!" she announced, glibly. With a fantastical flourish, she twirled around her chiffon robe and strode confidently out the door of this boorish excuse for a bar, freed forevermore from overeducated men who felt the insatiable need to explain the politics of sex to anyone gullible enough to listen.

THERE WAS A SIGN, JUST STUCK THERE in the ground, all by itself. "THE END OF THE WILDERNESS," it stated, bluntly. It was positioned semi-strategically in a swamplike area, with half-dead marsh plants and forlorn-looking trees sticking up crookedly through the soggy ground. The sky was gray, and flat, and dull, and boring, and listless, and highly uninspiring. It was a completely random place, with no end (or beginning either, for that matter) visibly apparent.

What did it mean, though? Was it supposed to be some kind of a parable? What was the significance of all this? Had some manner of logical conclusion been finally achieved? Why would someone say that, on a sign like this, out here in the middle of nowhere?

Rode Dhal (not the author you're thinking of, of course, for legal reasons, because UK law is very strict about defamation) once wrote about

Vermicious Knids. He was drunk, and angry; and, he hated Jews. So, by writing some nonsense words contained within a book that was ostensibly designed for children, he was able to express his dismay in a roundabout, abstract manner that avoided having to confront his prejudices and existential despair head-on. People wouldn't stand for it if he were to actually have written down what he was *truly* thinking about, so he spent his time writing about silly made-up things instead.

Diana didn't know anything about that. Diana Murleshten-Styles didn't have any answers, and that was why she no longer existed. Actually, she never existed to begin with. For isn't it true that a character is only relevant if they have a clear reason for existing? And if they don't have such a reason, then they are not relevant, and therefore, they do not need to exist in the first place.

Now, some may take the view that all this nonsense got underway when Loureschten started slurching. Slurching is an abominable habit, in case you're not familiar; it is a horrific combination of slouching, lounging, and lurching, all done in the service of a futile and pointless lifestyle. Diana had tried to teach us all about the merits of *not* existing, but then we have Loureschten, who, against all odds, actually *did* exist, and didn't care to understand the very important lessons imparted by Diana's story when conducting his own sordid affairs within his nominal state of being. He was a shitty character, standing about six-foot-two, with a cleft palate and a knack for buggery. In spite of his glaring physiological deficits, he was in fact a skilled grifter, one who could charm and sneak his way into any rich girl's panties. Whenever he'd get in trouble, Loureschten would claim that he was sorry, yet those who knew him best would never for a split dirty second believe him. You would grunt, and sigh, and consign yourself to cleaning up his puke that had been violently spewed all over your bathroom and in the adjacent hallway areas, after plaintively asking him to take some goddamned responsibility for once in his life, just to be answered with a wholly pathetic argument regarding his failing eyesight and impending legal blindness, as if that were a sufficient excuse for binging on cheap spiced rum and ecstasy and then deciding it would be a grand idea to scarf down a 24-pack of generic frozen corndogs in the middle of the night while clutching his balls with his left hand and stroking the ever-melting sides of the gas range cooktop and surrounding walls with his right.

Loureschten did his best to alienate all those suckers who ever had the foolish impulse to take him seriously. Take, for instance, what he did to friendly neighbor Nazi Mark's bathroom one night. Nazi Mark had generously invited Loureschten over to drink whiskey and have a frank and thoughtful discussion about white power politics, but Loureschten just couldn't hang. He excused himself to the bathroom at one point, and proceeded to drop his drawers and shit all over everything: the bathtub, shower curtain, carpeted toilet seat cover, even one of Nazi Mark's mom's doilies left for purely aesthetic reasons on the top of the toilet tank lid. Loureschten, in other words, managed to get his poop everywhere *except* where it actually belonged, in the toilet bowl.

It was around this time that someone pointed out to Loureschten his most fatal failing:

"Didn't you realize what was happening?" He hadn't. He'd merely been reading along, blindly, just like the rest of them. "You were participating in nonsense. Sheer nonsense. Didn't it occur to you that what you just spent too many hours of your life consuming was nothing but a cavalcade of non-sequiturs? Had you no clue that your attention was being continuously misdirected by some horrible miscreant who fancied himself the ultimate literary troll?" There were plenty of warning signs along the way: gibberish names, slippery-slopes that evaded any attempts at cross-reference, and ultimately, a total breakdown of causality.

Worst of all, Diana Murleshten-Styles was about to stop non-existing, *for good.* But not quite yet. Diana was evesdropping again, like the terrible Intersexual-American that she was:

"But I don't know how to end a story," the author sighed, indecisively. "Do I just... stop?"

"Sure, whenever you're feeling tired, just go ahead and give up."

"Should I cut it out?" He wasn't sure if that would be the best way to approach the situation, and if it was, what sort of cutting should happen? Should he just cut in line, like an asshole about to be stuffed full of New York

Sewer Rat when the rest of the bus passengers find out what he's done? What about cutting excerpts from other peoples' intellectual property, plagiarizing words without proper attribution, and passing the words off as his own, just like Joseph R. Biden, the 46th President of the United States, had infamously done? Or maybe he should cut up the words that he'd already written, slice the sentences into ribbons, you know, *just cut them up like regular Chickens.*

Or, maybe he should cut it all like cheese. Cutting the cheese, obviously, was first and foremost a euphemism for flatulence, which would fit perfectly into the overall tone that had been established throughout the narrative. But there was a deeper layer to all of it, and that was the story of cut *up* cheese.

In the mid-1980s, it was understood, Mitt Romney would only eat small cubes of cheese, just like a rodent. Bain Capital, his employer at the time, referred to it as the "Rat Diet" and thought they may be able to capitalize on this novel approach. Mittens was referred for a Bain Scan, which was Bain's own proprietary mental hygiene assessment process, during which several psychological and psychiatric professionals would survey the neuro-synaptic signals generated by showing him increasingly large piles of cash.

So, Mittens' brain was scanned, and they found an interesting side effect that was most likely linked to his cheese-only diet: a complete and utter indifference towards scat. This made perfect sense to anyone who knew the story of Seamus, the Romney family dog, who Mittens had unceremoniously strapped to the roof of their station wagon in a doggie-crate for a trip to Ontario one summer day. Seamus lost control of his bowels somewhere on the New York Thruway, and Mittens very cooly pulled off to the next car wash and doused the car, and the dog, all the while the spoiled, rotten Romney kids were bitching and moaning and screaming and threatening to puke their McBreakfasts up all over the backseat of what was probably a Buick Roadmaster (since Mittens' dad was once Governor of Michigan, it wouldn't look to good for his progeny to be driving an imported automobile, even though he secretly always wanted a Porsche 911 along with a blond German man to drive off to some lookout point, and then giggle and poke each others' buttholes while being sneakily naughty, as only a truly devout Mormon can;

that was just a fantasy, and he would lose any credibility that there might be left for his family name amongst the unionized workers of America, so he just gave in and purchased a sub-par GM product that guzzled down gas and belched up motor oil), sickened as they all were by the smell of doggy-doo, and Lady Romney was turning purple and fanning herself frantically as Mittens smiled his snide smirk, totally impervious to his freakish, miscreant nature.

"Did you ever feel, like, a satisfying little smear of poop, right outside your butthole, that itched ever so slightly, but you didn't feel like going to all the trouble of dropping your trousers and dabbing at with a little square or two of TP?" someone asked Mitt Romney, but, since he wasn't here, Diana didn't know what to think. This all came across as really inappropriate, and irrelevant.

"Jerkson was a good character," someone else told her. "It's a shame he didn't make the cut." Yes, a shame indeed. But Jerkson couldn't beat out someone like Loureschten for being completely deplorable, and the narrative couldn't accommodate *both* of these friggin' fucks, so the decision was made that, since Loureschten was based on an actual, real-life, fully terrible person, and Jerkson was only conjured up at the very bitter end, there would only be room enough for the one of them.

And so on. Which would continue, ad nauseam, until someone stops and says something to you, along the lines of, "That's not very lunchlike of you." And then you break into a cold, septic sweat, anxious and confused and suffering from some completely undiagnosable ailment, spinning around in circles and talking aloud, first to yourself, and then to your cat:

"It's Uncle Shmarms! Uncle Schlumpy-Kuss! Uncle Spunzks! I wuv my big fat puddy-cat!" The cat, staring back vaguely, slightly annoyed, yawns profusely and then turns back to licking the shit off of his tail. So you wander outside, looking around for a convenient and discreet place to take a shit, and think that perhaps the cow pastures would be appropriate, since there are constantly piles of dung strewn about, the stench of which constantly blankets the town, stinking up the whole place on a regular basis, so indeed, what worse stench could come out of your sphincter that would be detectable?

But the farmer noticed what you were about to do, and he yelled at you, and you know entirely all-too-well that you can't poop while you're getting yelled at. So you reluctantly pull your pants back up, after waving your bare naked ass at the cattle, mockingly, and retreat further down the street, eyeing that half-built house on the corner that nobody has moved into yet, but for which the toilet drains have been embedded already in the concrete pad, offering just the most delightful opportunity of the month to qualify yourself as the owner of the house's first act of defecation. And as you're walking towards your destination, head of a turd starting to poke its way out through your asshole and beginning to grind itself on the insides of your bulbous butt-cheeks as you waddle to and fro, you can't help but think about the glorious history of different manners of toilets, including the most ingenious of all, that being the Chinese pig-toilet, a gaping pit filled with hogs over which an outhouse would be strategically positioned, so all the poop would fall into the pigpen and feed and fatten the swine until they could be slaughtered and barbecued and eaten, so the cycle of shit could renew itself perpetually.

You think about what a real shame it is that the same could not be done in this country, because of the Jews. They get all limp-wristed and squirmy about even the thought of eating recycled poop, and also, they had brainwashed everyone in the country into cutting off the foreskins of baby boys, and it was really just too bad that they couldn't go somewhere else and not bother anyone anymore, because it would be great fun to eat pork reared on human feces.

Your destination isn't as comfortable as you thought, as it is just a hole in some concrete, and not yet even connected to the main sewer line, so there is an absolute lack of suction, which makes you feel sad, since your favorite thing to do whenever you experience a successful bowel movement is to shout, "Suck the shit out of my asshole, bitch!" at the top of your lungs, to nobody in particular. So, you start flipping through this book you bought. It's an anthology of sorts, yet none of the stories seem to ever go anywhere, and as you flip through the pages, you come across a few marked, "THIS PAGE INTENTIONALLY LEFT VAGUE." Diana knows about this, all too well. Well, she would have known about it, if she had actually existed, which, as we all know, she did not. So, she couldn't explain it to you, even if she wanted to, and even if you actually cared.

Suddenly, Shuppel Uption burst through the door, screaming and crying and carrying on. It seems that there was a chicken salad *salad* that some discount fast-food chain had just invented, thus depriving Shuppel of his main claim to philosophical fame, and beating him at his own game of psychosomatics. He was absolutely devastated by the news, and felt like, since his Chicken Salad Sandwich concept seemed outdated and horribly childish by comparison, that the entire world was ending and it was all somewhat, kinda, but mostly not, his fault.

Diana attempted to comfort him and cup his balls; but Shuppel yelled, "Get outta here, you intersexual freak! I can fondle my own nuts!" And indeed, he reached his hand down the front of his pants and—

Someone gasped. He was hit by the realization that *that* was the very flavor of cat food that Somebody had been suspecting, but not proving, his poop to have smelled like, that one time when he went to the doctor and claimed that he maybe did *not* eat his cat's food (and then instigated an entire existential crisis as a consequence), and the flavor of the canned cat food that Somebody had been giving to his cat was Chicken. Salad. *Salad*.

Someone knew immediately that this was the most significant thing to have ever happened, anywhere. Diana wasn't so sure. Diana hadn't ever actually had anything happen to her, since she never had existed in the first place, so being sure of something and knowing anything in a definitive way was not a feeling she would ever have. Indeed, she was both blessed and cursed with a perpetual indecisiveness, not knowing the true relevance of any hard or anecdotal evidence that was presented in the course of casual conversation, but also not being expected to have any particular expertise or qualification to comment on any matter of actual or perceived significance. Diana could be lied to and still be okay. Most women wouldn't be able to handle that. But then again, Diana wasn't a woman, per se; she merely presented as one, in as much a manner as could possibly be expected from a non-existent person. In the end, Diana merely felt slightly confused most of the time, and sought distraction from any source possible.

She looked down, intrusively, upon the feet standing next to her, and said,